Praise for *Storytellers at the Columbia River*:

"Inspiring. . . This is a much larger story of what could happen anywhere, told in such a grounded, knowledgeable and appealing way that the readers' hearts are won, and perhaps their political convictions too. A real gem."

~ **Dr. Evelyn Pinkerton**, professor emeritus, Fraser Univ., B.C.

"Engrossing. . . This is an intriguing novel about a little-known episode in American history--the production of plutonium at the Hanford nuclear reservation in eastern Washington State. The author brings together a compelling cast of characters in an amazing setting--the arid Columbia River basin in the rain shadow of the Cascade Mountains. The characters are driven by their passions rather than by a historically informed understanding of what happened at Hanford, but the emotional response is an important part of the story, and the history is available elsewhere. Includes some wonderfully evocative writing about how globally significant events can affect the lives of everyday people."

~ **Steve Olson**, author of *The Apocalypse Factory:*
Plutonium and the Making of the Atomic Age

"Given the growing global threat of climate change, the Trump administration's undercutting of conservation and environmental protection laws, promotion of the fossil fuel and nuclear power industries, *Storytellers at the Columbia River* by Nancy Mendenhall is more than a simple work of entertaining and engaging fiction, it is a clarion call for the support of Native American rights with respect to the land and the waters and the wildlife and people that depend upon them. Especially and unreservedly recommended for community and college/university library collections."

~ *Midwest Book Review*

"Mendenhall has crafted a rich array of characters who explore the history of the mighty Columbia River from the views of Native tribes, colonizing settlers and those who suffered through World War II's first atomic bombs fed by the Hanford nuclear plant. Humanity's historic and current struggles provide insight into this massive source of fresh water, fish, transportation, power and nuclear destruction. The book is an easy read, expertly researched, that leaves you with indelible images of this great river and its people."

~ **Cheryl Richardson**, Alaskan urban planner and environmental activist

"*Storytellers at the Columbia River* is a strong voice for the power and importance of place...through a series of carefully constructed interlocking stories that connect the Hanford Reach's different cultures, generations, and (involved) countries. Underneath her web of stories, like the deep current of the Columbia River, is this lesson on the use of technology: do not be too quick to adopt new technology until the consequences are known and can be controlled. Mendenhall illustrates this lesson with the fate of "downwinders" who were infected with radioactive iodine from the Hanford reactors and the slow creep of radioactive waste toward the river. These problems have been with us for 75 years without adequate resolution. The river once supported large runs of wild Pacific salmon, whose habitat was traded for another technology, hatcheries, as the river was developed. The fate of the salmon is a thread that weaves its way through several of the stories. And in addition, it's a great read."

~ **Jim Lichatowich,** author of *Salmon, People, and Place:*
A Biologist's Search for Salmon Recovery

"Fascinating. . . rich with cautionary tales about the coming of the Atomic Age to the Columbia River Valley. Mendenhall tells a complicated story--in reality many cautionary stories told by the book's diverse characters about violence done to people and the environment in Washington state's Columbia River Valley in the 1900s. Participants in (this) fictionalized reunion describe how Indigenous people were dispossessed of their ancestral land and food sources, how Euro-American families were evicted from their farms and orchards in order to build the Hanford nuclear facility, and how the construction of huge Columbia River dams prevented salmon from reaching their spawning grounds. The deep emotions expressed by the book's characters bring issues of grave social and ecological concern to life."

~ **Dr. Gerald W. McFarland,** author of *The Buenaventura Trilogy* and
A Scattered People: An American Family Moves West

"A great read; would make a great film! Mendenhall has the unique ability to allow the reader to understand the environmental issues of the Columbia River history. She develops complex characters that come to life."

~ **Dawyne Sawyer**, physician assistant, England

"This book is brave, inspiring and beautiful! Given that we have now entered into this post-truth age of digital information overload it seems more and more people are disinclined to even consider (important) questions. But I find it fascinating that every single character in this novel in varying ways attempts to deal with these existential questions without—through no fault of theirs or the author's—ever mentioning the word Capitalism. They wrestle with impending environmental collapse, genocide against aboriginal peoples, the atrocity of wars, the crushing of communities and working people lives, but all too often bottle up their feelings with self-doubt and a sense of helplessness in the face of cruel fate. Yet the redeeming inspiration in the characters is when they begin to connect the dots and sense that they are not powerless and alone. And more importantly that collective solidarity and not an endless divisive struggle in conditions of artificially created scarcity is their only salvation. Mendenhall's novel is a sterling tribute to the concept of community and communitarianism. How vital it is. How fragile it is. And hopefully how eternal it is. I truly admire her grit, determination, and courage in writing it."

~ **Dennis Brown**, author of *Salmon Wars: The Battle for the West Coast Salmon Fishery*

"Gripping...Tragic... (with) a cast of characters who tell their personal stories, bringing alive the tremendous losses suffered because of nuclear weapons, thermonuclear war, the internment in concentration camps of Japanese immigrants, most of them U.S. citizens during WWII, the oppression of the Wanapum Indians, who lived on the east bank of the Columbia, the construction of dams on the river that has destroyed the salmon runs that provided food for the Wanapums and other residents along the river and for millions of people across the U.S. Mendenhall's book weaves all these critical issues together. She is a wonderful writer (and) writes with much wit so there are also plenty of laughs."

~ **Tim Wheeler**, journalist, author of *News from Rain Shadow Country*

"An engaging novel of people dealing with a difficult and challenging situation rather than being a didactic book using characters to illustrate a viewpoint, and the author achieved it well. The importance of the river, its history, and its challenges all came through, but the author's take on it all was not clear, which is what a novelist wants. (Mendenhall) showed the complexity, because each of the characters had his or her attractive aspects, but none was perfect. (They) grappled with the issues. . .

and didn't solve any problems and that was realistic and helped make the book literature."

~ **Laird Hastay**, Oregon college educator

"Rich, questioning, funny . . . *Storytellers at the Columbia River* has the social flavor of a traditional novel but with a multicultural cast of characters who struggle with their unique histories while bombarded with today's challenges to the river and its people. The challenges are global, while the Columbia, a river I love myself, can use this attention, and the lively plot holds us tight to its banks."

~ **Dr. William Keep,** past resident of Yakima, WA.

"*Storytellers at the Columbia River* is beautifully written and about important things: life and love--especially love for the Columbia and the people along it."

~ **Gretchen A. Davis**, activist, author of *Blacklisted: A Family Targeted by McCarthy*

"Essentially an argument against the furtherance of nuclear power."

~ **J.W. Smith**

"Mendenhall tells it like it is in an easy-to-read novel (asking) some truly hard-to-answer questions about what can be done to help preserve the natural beauty of the Columbia. Character-driven drama with a blend of history and humor."

~ **Robin C. Thomas**, fisherman, entrepreneur

Praise for *Orchards of Eden:*

"*[Orchards of Eden]* gives us important insights...a well-documented story."

~ *Journal of Rural and Community Development*

"A richly woven human story...a history that reads like a novel. Mendenhall has brought to life in vivid detail the birth, maturation, and death of a tiny desert town."

~ **Dr. William Keep**, retired English professor

"Vivid and authentic! The life of an isolated river community before the Hanford Project ushered in the firestorm of the atomic age."

~ **Helen Hastay**, raised in White Bluffs, WA

"Mendenhall's excellent and exhaustive research shines a spotlight on the distant, hidden influences that were at work while the early farmers toiled in the dry sandy soil to bring their dreams of Eden to life."

~ **Margaret Wood**, retired director, University of Alaska; descendent of
Ea. Washington farmers

Praise for *Rough Waters*:

"In this impassioned and broadly researched book, [Mendenhall] plumbs today's fraught seascape from the west coast's state-managed fisheries to federal policy to plights in other regions."

~ ***Boston Globe*** (Katharine Whittemore)

"A *tour de force* so far as exposing the insidious threat to small boat fish harvesters and coastal communities posed by a worldwide governmental obsession with privatizing fish resources... [Mendenhall's] firsthand experience with the fisheries elevates her voice to a unique and compelling stature."

~ **Dennis Brown,** author of *Salmon Wars:*
The Battle for the West Coast Salmon Fishery

"As long as writers like Mendenhall exist, the voices of the underdogs will be heard. (Her) meticulous research shows how corporate interests have taken over the pollock and crab fisheries, and how quota management has shrunk the state's black cod and halibut fleets with little or no conservation benefit, especially in western Alaska."

~ **Paul Molyneaux** (in *Fishermen's Voice*); author of *The Doryman's Reflection*

"Mendenhall covers the terrain in an amazingly comprehensive way...an insider's view of what it means to be a small-scale fisherperson."

~ **Dr. Evelyn Pinkerton**, researcher and author on fisheries, B.C.

"Not until I read Mendenhall's book did the dry statistics become real people who work hard...and who have to contend with policies that seem to care little for both the fishermen and the fish."

~ **Dr. James Lichatowich,**
author of *Salmon Without Rivers* and *Salmon, People, and Place*

Storytellers at the Columbia River

Also by Nancy Danielson Mendenhall:

Beachlines: A Pocket History of Nome
Orchards of Eden: White Bluffs on the Columbia, 1907-1943
Rough Waters: Our North Pacific Small Fishermen's Battle
--A Fishing Family's Perspective

Storytellers at the Columbia River

Nancy Danielson Mendenhall

Far Eastern Press, Seattle

Storytellers at the Columbia River

All rights reserved under International and Pan-American Copy Conventions. For information on permission for reprints and excerpts, contact Far Eastern Press, Seattle

Front cover photos: White Bluffs, and the slough at White Bluffs, by Marion Burns
Back cover photo: Hanford Reach, by Rich Steele

ISBN: 0-9678842-4-1
ISBN 13: 978-0-9678842-4-0

Far Eastern Press, Seattle, WA

This story is dedicated to the people whose lives and communities were made, those that were lost, and those that are still being made through the spirit and power of the great Columbia River and through one of the river's great gifts, its salmon runs.

A cavern below the Columbia was the bomb's cradle, born not that men might live, but that men might be killed.

~ Dorothy Day, 1945

So powerful are the ties between humans and salmon that even in rivers and streams where salmon are still running—but in numbers severely diminished—the ghosts of salmon are rising. Salmon resides in the hearts of humans.

~ Freeman House in "Totem Salmon"

If stories come to you, care for them and learn to give them away where they are needed. Sometimes a person needs a story more than food to stay alive.

~ Barry Lopez

CONTENTS

INTRODUCTION

THIS IS A story of fiction, but based on actual communities, events, and issues on the middle section of the Columbia River from 1906 until the late 1990s. Almost all of the locations mentioned actually exist, and many events in the story are based loosely on historic events. But though some historic personages are briefly mentioned, the characters in the story, and the plot, are fictional. The main characters include three mid-Columbia settler families, their Native American tour bus driver, several members of his family, and a small group of first-time attendees who converge at a fictional 1998 annual Settlers Reunion at Richland, on the banks of the Columbia. The newcomers arrive with agendas of their own: a wounded Middle East wars veteran who brings an elder's memoir of early times on the Columbia to get the settlers' reactions; his partner, a graduate in anthropology, who is struggling to choose a dissertation topic and is soon captivated by the settlers' stories; an older anthropology professor, her friend and mentor, who has tagged along mainly for fun, but ends up asking universal questions; a Japanese American college student who needs to fulfill a promise to her mother and grandmother; an Indigenous shaman—a river healer from Siberia; and two young kayakers with a protest agenda.

The Columbia's troubles have two main sources: the defunct Hanford Nuclear Plant and whatever is causing the disappearance of the river's famous salmon runs. These issues are also a big concern to a small group of Wanapum Indians who live thirty miles up the river, who created a rich culture thousands of years ago, and still place high importance on the natural river and the disappearing salmon. The tour bus driver takes the reunion guests into the closed area near the Plant and becomes involved in their related issues that circle around the river. He entices them with more of the valley's history, including that of his people. The Siberian invites everyone to do a blessing of the river but runs into resistance. All of the newcomers soon become entwined in risky projects of their own.

The settlers at the reunion are mainly orchardists who were evicted from the Hanford-White Bluffs area to make room for the government's creation of the Hanford Plant in 1943. Their happy recollections of small-farming life are interrupted by the emotional bus trip into the fifty-year-old site of the former farms. After the bus trip the newcomers have less time for listening to storytelling as they are submerged in clouds of misinformation, bitterness, argument, plotting, and uncompleted promises, all interspersed with clearing skies of insight, agreement, new friendships, and even people falling in love. All of this is in some way connected to the unsolved problems of the Plant's radioactive waste disposal. And then there is the huge issue of the Columbia's missing salmon. To accomplish anything, they all must learn how to understand and trust each other.

The actual history behind this story is a rich but troubling one. The reunions did take place in the area from about 1968 until 2005, and were mainly nostalgic social events. Most of those attending were three generations of original white settlers who were part of a private experimental irrigation project to start orchards on the banks of the Columbia. Mainly they were city folk caught up in a "back to the country" movement who had bought sagebrush-covered tracts along the river. For about thirty years these settlers strived to learned how to green a desert and make a living from their orchards, herds, and gardens. Then they were evicted to make room for the Hanford project and the production of plutonium, which was the key ingredient of one of the atomic bombs the U.S. dropped on Japan. Not many of those evicted settlers are still alive; they would be in their nineties now, and the reunions have ended, the descendants scattered across the country.

The theme of "eviction" actually covers several historical groups living along the mid-Columbia. The Wanapum Indians were among those who refused to go to the Yakama Reservation in 1855, choosing to stay at their remote riverbank sites. Japanese and Japanese American families, mainly

American citizens, who were farming on the west side of the river, were among those sent away to internment camps for the duration of World War II. Then, in 1943, all white settlers and Indians were evicted by the federal government from the area around White Bluffs and Hanford to make way for the secret WWII project, the bomb dropped on Nagasaki in August, 1945. It was not until sometime later that any of these groups knew what their land had been used for.

The Hanford Plant—over the decades it has had several names—is now closed permanently, but there is still much work of demolition. Most difficult to solve has been how to safely and permanently store the largest stockpile of radioactive waste in the country. Another interesting piece of history: In 1998, the year this story takes place, a group of Athabascan people of Northwest Territories, Canada, did send a delegation to Japan to offer a formal apology for their unknowing role in producing uranium ore at Port Radium that was most likely some of that converted to plutonium at the Hanford Plant.

After the Hanford Plant was permanently closed for domestic uses in 1987, the mid-section of the Columbia continued to get much federal attention. A new commercial nuclear plant to provide domestic energy, Columbia Generating Station, was already operating by the 1980s and accumulating radioactive waste in tanks. Waste in similar tanks from submarines and ships was also being shipped to Hanford for storage.

Other important development has taken place in the mid-Columbia region. Hanford Reach and Saddle Mt. became a U.S. National Monument in 2000. The Hanford Reach Interpretive Center at Richland tells the story of the area: its unique flora, fauna, and human groups. Hanford Plant's B Reactor, the plutonium producer, became another interpretive center, and then a part of the Manhattan Project National Historic Park in 2015. The history and culture of the Indigenous people on the river is preserved at the Wanapum Heritage Center, just up river a few miles at Beverly.

For those readers interested in more background history, in 2013, fifteen years after the story takes place, it became public that the Hanford area contained over 100 radioactive waste tanks that were leaking, eventually over sixty of them. In 2015 the State of Washington entered a lawsuit against the federal government demanding a solution to the radioactive hazards at the site. The federal government had been searching for years for a permanent underground waste storage site somewhere in the country, but arrangements had always fallen through when regional residents objected, and the problem remains. In 2016 the federal government settled out of court a long, massive lawsuit by "down winders", compensating them for their high incidence of thyroid cancer and other illnesses that they charged were due to intentional atmospheric releases of radioactive iodine at the Plant. Cases are still being processed.

A recent strategy to address Hanford's safety concerns was for the radioactive waste to be stored in glass containers that would not corrode, then sent somewhere to deep underground storage. But the cost of enclosing all of the waste in glass and shipping it is very expensive, and so there was a new proposal to downgrade most waste to a level where it could be legally stored underground at Hanford. The remaining high-level waste would be of small enough quantity for the glass containers and shipping to be an affordable solution. But the downgrading of the "lower level waste" for local storage raised a new outcry from residents of the Hanford Reach and others: "Not in our backyard!" Thus, in 2019, Hanford's radioactive waste was still looking for a permanent solution. Meanwhile the federal government cut the budget for nuclear waste storage.

Every nuclear plant in the world has similar problems. Nature itself imposes serious threats and accidents, such as that at the Fukushima nuclear plant in 2011. But although the initial cause there was from nature, an earthquake, the estimated deaths of 1,600 were almost all due to evacuation problems that some experts see as avoidable. In 2018 Japan's State Prosecutors stated they would seek five-year prison terms for Fukushima executives who, they say, failed to provide adequate tsunami protection for the plant even though there had been several years warning of possible tsunamis.

One message from this history is that we should be focusing more on other forms of alternative energy where inevitable human errors won't have such catastrophic potential. Yet many countries, including Japan and ours, feel dependent on their nuclear plants for energy despite the recognized dangers.

Germany, an exception, is closing down all of its nuclear reactor plants—half of them are already closed—and is moving rapidly to wind power.

2018 was a year of other legal as well as moral insights. The U.S. finally officially recognized in the "Korematsu" lawsuit something long unofficially accepted—that the sending of Japanese Americans to internment camps was a judicial and ethical error, an error it recognizes was based on racism.

--->==⊙ ⊙==<---

Another important background history often referred to in this story is the huge problem the Columbia River endures with its salmon run losses. Treaty tribes that traditionally fished the Columbia/Snake system won a federal case awarding them fifty percent of the harvest in 1974. The rapid growth of high dams seemed to be a main cause of the run declines, and hatcheries, including some later run by treaty tribes, were the simplest solution. Gradually wild salmon were replaced by human-raised. The Hanford Reach was for years, and probably still is, the only significant wild Chinook salmon spawning area left. In 2012 the federal government settled with the tribes over the loss of fishing sites.

Short-budgeted state and federal agencies and tribes continue to rebuild decimated salmon runs where they can, but recent years of drought have meant fewer and fewer spawning salmon, including hatchery salmon, make it to their traditional grounds, in some cases as few as five percent of forecasts. The survival of juvenile salmon has also been poor for drought-plagued warming rivers along the entire coast. So far, the only important dam breaching or removal to be completed in the West has been at the Elwha River in Washington, where a return of a great wild Chinook run is rebuilding. A removal of dams on the Klamath River in California was federally authorized but as of 2017 was not funded.

In 2018 the State of Washington finally demanded that the federal dams in the state do what the other dams (private, municipal, etc.) had done some time ago: control the temperature in the dam reservoirs to no more than 68 F. in order to reduce the mortality of salmon. The temperature in recent years had gone into the 70s in many locations, in part an effect of dammed, slowed currents, then encouraged much more by warming through drought brought on by climate change.

As of this writing, however, the warming condition of the Pacific (The Blob) is seen by many scientists as a major influence behind the diminishing runs, especially of Chinook salmon all along the coast to Northwest Alaska. In 2018 the return of salmon in Washington was about half the forecast, which was already very low. Many species along the coast are on the Endangered list. What we can do about The Blob is worth another story. Fisheries management never gets easier.

Also, as revealed in this story, northern regions' Indigenous shamans do continue to try to bring healing to lands and waters poisoned by human misuse. And in recent years, many cultural and private organizations have offered formal apologies to groups, especially Indigenous groups that have been harmed by wars, colonization, and toxins. We also see frequent media stories regarding the need to protect the Columbia's endangered flora and fauna in this last large stretch of natural "shrub steppe" in the country.

The issues brought out in this fictional story of a 1998 White Bluffs-Hanford settlers' reunion and its aftermath are all real and continuing.

CHAPTER 1

A DESERT REUNION

THREE PEOPLE SAT in a circle in the heat of an August desert afternoon, surrounded by sagebrush that spread for miles. Their camouflaged bug jackets were tied around their waists—it was too hot for bugs to be active—but they wore long-sleeved shirts and jeans, and their camo hats were important shade. Many species of birds were all around them but they were in hiding now. The man and two women were all young and in good physical condition, yet the heat was wearing on Marta, and if the other two were even noticing it they didn't admit it. Mental images of the cooling waters of the Columbia River, not far away but invisible and unreachable, didn't help her.

Two days before, they had crossed the Cascades from Puget Sound into Eastern Washington by bus and saw a world such a contrast to the west side that it was like passing into a new country: miles of green vineyards, orchards, and alfalfa fields. Where is the desert, they'd wondered, until they realized that what they were seeing was, of course, the irrigated section. Today they were in the natural world of the Columbia River, a dry shrub steppe, what most people did call desert, all in muted colors except for the green border along the river. Sitting in the sand here, they were surrounded by sagebrush, but they barely noticed its refreshing odor, as all three were totally consumed by the scouting task they were committed to. The day was hotter than they normally dealt with, but Bruce knew the extreme heat of other deserts, and barely noticed it; his thoughts were on other problems facing them, while Suki had too much at stake to let the heat bother her, and Marta had steeled herself not to be a whiner. They all waited silently.

Why did I agree to this insane project, Marta wondered, as she watched Bruce chew on dried fruit and stare off into the brush. It was a stare she recognized; her partner caught up in a new challenge. She fanned her damp face and paged through her bird identification book while she covertly watched Bruce and Suki for some kind of signal between them. She saw that Suki, though also sweating, seemed to be calm as she looked through her own bird book.

"Isn't it hot for you?" Marta frowned, sure she had not been told the whole story. Bruce's adventures were always a little scary—an important part for him—but this was different, this was approaching suffering.

Suki smiled a little, "Yes, but I'll survive."

Marta knew she could have stayed back at the hotel of course; she wasn't part of Suki's—now also Bruce's—project. *So why did I insist on going?* Then she admitted to herself that she didn't want Bruce trekking around in the desert with an attractive woman, one whom they had known little more than two days. *But how ridiculous a scenario: lust under the broiling sun?* She swatted a praying mantis off her jeans leg. And birdwatching was a laugh. They had seen very few birds driving out; it was already so hot that they were hiding. Marta thought they should have brought insect I.D. books instead.

Suki peered at the mantis, saw it wave its arms and giggled.

"It's funny to you, all this?" Marta wondered.

"Come-on, eat something and drink a little," said Bruce in a stage-whisper voice. "We don't want to be thinking about food later. But don't drink too much water. We don't know when we'll get more." He rose and started a bent-down creep into the brush. "I'm going to look around and see if I can find more elevation."

Then he saw the person standing just at the fringe of their clearing, looking at them. He stared back in amazement at this man who'd popped from nowhere in the thigh-high brush. *Have I lost that much of my senses? I just saw him out on the road.* But he took a breath, smiled, then spoke softly, "Hello, Uncle, you want to join us?"

Uncle? Marta peered at the man as he came to them and pulled off his backpack, and she saw that he was an older Indian man. It was like Bruce, she realized, to use "uncle" as term of respect.

"Thank you." The elder looked around in the brush, then squatted down by them, pulled off his aged bill cap, and wiped his face with his neckerchief. "I'm Esau," he said.

"Well, glad to meet you, I'm Bruce. And Marta, and Suki." He motioned to them.

Esau smoothed his white hair as he gazed a moment at Suki. "I thought maybe you're from around here, or had relatives here."

"Well, I did, yes. My cousins down by Ringold—their name was Hayashi."

"Ah yes…down by Ringold, your people! They were right on the line then—1942 wasn't it? I was always sorry."

Suki nodded, "It's okay. They weren't the only ones driven out of here."

Esau nodded and smiled. He gazed around again and gave the three a sharper look.

"And none of us should be here now."

Marta swallowed. She agreed they shouldn't be where they were, but now this elder was muddying the water more. Suki too, was already nervous to start with, though she had been determined not to show it. Who, or what, had sent this person to complicate things? She tried to catch Bruce's eye, but his attention was on the encroacher.

"Have something to eat, Uncle?"

"Thank you… and I have some elk jerky here. Want to try some?" Esau dug in his pack, pulled out a small sugar bag of dried meat. "Here, try it. I got it last fall."

Everyone reached for a piece. "It's very good!" said Bruce after a moment of chewing and trying to think of what to do. He looked at the elder and thought him handsome despite some missing teeth and wrinkles showing his age. He thought that the comment "None of us should be here" must be a reference to the nuclear plant. Walking into the brush, they had seen, just a few miles off, what looked like smoke rising. *So then why are you here, Esau?* He decided not to ask it. After another long minute of everyone's silent chewing, Esau said in a quiet voice,

"I come down in this area once in a while. Today I'm looking for my grandson. He's trying to be a man, but he's been gone long enough now. So, what are you folks looking for? Or maybe I shouldn't ask, here in no-man's land?"

⇢▗▄◗ ◖▄▖◠

Two days before, three travelers had joined scores of others to cross Eastern Washington from all directions to arrive at Richland on the bank of the Columbia River. Their destination was the White Bluffs-Hanford Settlers' Reunion, an annual event popular enough to have survived over fifty years. They climbed out of pick-ups, cars, and Greyhounds at the entrance to the Riverside Motel, and August's desert breeze hit their faces. For most it carried a nostalgic, even loved scent of sagebrush; for a few it was totally new. Though the travelers had all been warned, for those few 90 degrees was a shock after their air-conditioned rides.

Most of the travelers were coming to visit with old friends and neighbors from the early 1940s, but some had special interests. Marta, a graduate student, was hoping to find fresh information for her dissertation's topic, Smohalla, the region's famous Indian religious leader of the 1800s. Some descendants of his followers, she understood, might live just up the river. She had also come to keep Bruce, her partner, company. A veteran, he was uncomfortable in large noisy crowds, and they expected this one could be just that. Bruce had known of these settler reunions for years, but had avoided them. He had agreed to attend for the sake of his favorite great-uncle Harold, one of the settlers, who had just completed the draft of a memoir about his early days. Harold declared he was too stiff with arthritis to travel but was eager for reactions to the draft from his old friends and neighbors on the mid-Columbia. Bruce's job was to get those reactions.

He and Marta, both in their thirties, well-tanned and lean, were used to an active outdoor life hiking and kayaking around Puget Sound, but had never crossed the Cascades, so the trip was an unusual one for both of them. Marta's mentor, Leon, had never been in Eastern Washington either, and had tagged along, partly to support her in her research. Partly it was for himself, for the nostalgic experience of a desert, as he had spent many of his early research years in Australia. A slim, gray-bearded man in his mid-sixties, he wore deeply tinted sunglasses due to cataracts, but hoped to do a little hiking in the shrub steppe regardless. The three had come by Greyhound because Bruce and Marta's car had needed a sudden repair.

Another stranger to the area climbed off the bus behind them. Not yet thirty, Suki was glad to see other youthful faces among all the elders entering the hotel. She, like Bruce, had come only because of a promise to someone dear to her, but in her case one made years ago. Guilt, as well as curiosity, had forced her finally to make the trip.

Stepping down from the bus and taking her first breath of Richland air, Marta thought it was like landing in Mexico. "Whoof!" she half-laughed, but was determined to manage it for three days. For Bruce the heat was *déjà vu*. He had learned to easily handle other deserts' heat, but still had reasons to feel anxious. Now he patted Marta's shoulder.

"Don't worry, the hotel is air-conditioned—and the tour bus tomorrow."

Marta was reading the banner spread across the front of the hotel: WELCOME WHITE BLUFFS-HANFORD SETTLERS 1907-1943. She had vowed to be a good sport but wondered aloud why these farmers always scheduled their annual reunions in sweltering August? Was it to help them remember their actual lives here, that they didn't want a cooled-down version of their history? She would have to ask. She had other questions that Bruce hadn't been able to answer; he was depending on his uncle Harold's memoir. Harold had admitted to him there was still much missing, and that some of his life he was never going to be able to write about.

They all got in line with the rest to grab their luggage from the bus cargo bin, then heard the comment of a teenaged girl in shorts and t-shirt ahead of them.

"Wow! So hot! But Grandma, this is a pretty town, not like I thought. Not like a place where they made bombs."

"Not right here, up the river more," said the stout older woman with her.

"They didn't make the whole bomb," said her husband, "just the plutonium."

"Just the plutonium," mumbled Bruce to Marta, "yeah."

"What's plutonium, Grandpa?" the girl asked, and Bruce wanted to tell her, but it would lead to a long story. Not now.

As the bus riders all found their bags and moved on into the hotel, the girl persisted,

"I still don't see why they put a bomb factory right on a lovely river."

Bruce looked at Leon, "Why put it anyplace?"

The girl's grandfather, dressed just as Bruce thought his uncle Harold would for a meeting—bill cap, clean suspendered overalls, and white shirt— turned to gaze at Bruce.

"Your first time, I think. Go to the lecture the plant always puts on for us, and you'll find out why they built it here, just a few miles upriver. Right where we were living."

"Come on, Orville," said the elder woman in capris pants and tee-shirt with him, "let's get registered. You can talk your head off later." She gave Bruce a nod and smile and pushed her spouse forward.

"The girl's right, it's a pretty town," Marta commented. "Look at the park with all the shade trees over there, right along the river."

"What water can do for deserts," grinned Leon as he followed her into the hotel. But he wanted to see not watered parks but indigenous desert flora. On the ride across the desert he'd marveled at the radical change from his rainy Puget Sound home. It was as if the Cascades had created two separate worlds. Yet he knew the Native Americans that he and Marta studied went back and forth in their subsistence life. The essential thing both sides shared was the long Columbia River.

Bruce scooted their luggage along the line to the registration desk and grinned at Marta, as she breathed in relief in the air-conditioning. He looked around, hoping to recognize settlers from the descriptions he had been given by his great uncle. Coming without Harold had been a disappointment; as far as Bruce knew, he had never missed the reunion since the 1950s.

"Hello everyone!" came a call. A tall, white-haired woman in a royal blue pantsuit strode toward the crowd at the registration desk. "For those who don't know me, I'm Louise, your reunion coordinator." And she gave them all a smile of welcome.

"Hi, Louise," called the grandfather ahead of Bruce, "You're as good-looking as ever!"

"You too, Orville. Now if you all can get registered, and find your rooms, we'll start in one hour in the conference room. I've got great new activities this year I know you'll like."

"A bar?" called someone. She waved them off, "Back behind the café is the bar. But I'll see you soon."

An hour later Marta, Bruce, and Leon walked into the conference room to find it packed with people, some standing, some sitting at the small tables scattered about. Bruce saw that most were in their sixties or over, some surely eighty and more. The crowd looked the three newcomers over. After all these years, it was unusual to see new faces unless a familiar elder was by their side introducing them around. Muttered comments floated, "Who are they?"

"Darned if I know. Unless it's reporters."

"Or lost birdwatchers. But they usually come earlier."

Bruce gazed around the room, already nervous, but determined to carry out his duty. He was searching for particular name tags. Harold especially wanted a memoir critique from families his folks had known well. Marta saw Bruce had removed his cap he liked to keep on. He wanted to agree with the old farmers, and they had all, through custom for indoor events, removed theirs.

"Do you want to find a table?" she asked, relieved that their jeans and t-shirts were just what the younger people were wearing. She saw that the older women were mainly in cotton long-sleeved shirts and capri pants or cotton slacks while the older men, all in suspendered overalls, all had their shirtsleeves rolled to their elbows. It was a style to accommodate heat, she saw.

Bruce shook his head. "Let's walk around a bit. I need to find some people."

Louise, with social coordinator energy, began to speak up front.

"Welcome, welcome all of you, to the many of you returning and to you new faces too! We'll have you introduce yourselves later, but right now I want to tell you what's on the agenda—I didn't get it copied yet. First, we have a great slide show we'll run in about an hour. And there are more of the old photos over on the side tables. You can have fun identifying people. As usual there are sheets of paper next to them for you to write on if you see someone you recognize. And I'll bet you will.

"Then on the back wall this year we have a message board and tacks, and stacks of note cards and pens on the table by it. We thought you could use it to help you to track down people you might want to share some history with. So the board is divided into sections for you to tack your notes. Like there's work, and community, and recreation. And one for miscellaneous."

"Like sex?" came an elder's voice from back. Orville's granddaughter choked back a whoop of laughter. Bruce's eyebrows shot up. This could be more informal than he'd pictured.

"Okay, if you say so," Louise called back with a smile. "You get the idea. If you want, put your room number on your notes—up to you to get together. And tomorrow at 3:00 in the smaller room will be the man from the Hanford Plant with the lecture."

"You mean like about the evictions?" came a different voice.

"That too, probably. And you can ask questions, you know."

Bruce heard Orville again, but in a stern voice this time: "All I want to know about that place is when they're going to get their mess cleaned up."

"Shush!" came his wife's voice.

"Well, it's the big issue still, ain't it?"

Bruce grinned. "I like these old folks."

Leon and Marta were both glad to hear that, as the success of the trip largely depended on Bruce.

Louise shook her head, "What on earth did you people have in your coffee anyway this morning? Now about tomorrow. For those of you who don't have passes to get into the closed area, or don't want to go, don't get on the bus. We will have a great program for you here. For those of you who do have passes, I want to introduce your bus driver for tomorrow. This is Ike Jackson. He's from just up the river, so he can answer most of your questions."

"Not mine," muttered Orville. "I don't know why I keep coming to these reunions."

A man probably two decades younger than Orville but dressed the same, answered, "You come here because you don't have the sense to go where real action might be."

"So why are you here then, Walt?"

"To bug you." Walt's smile had a touch of sneer in it.

Ike, the driver, had come forward. A very tanned man in his mid-thirties, he was dressed in the common white shirt and jeans, but sported black braids. Marta saw the bone pendant on his chest. *Oh, good.* She hoped he was from the Wanapum tribe, the one she hoped to contact.

"Hi folks," Ike greeted the crowd. "I'm looking forward to this. I'll try to answer your questions, but to answer one of you, I don't know much detail about the Plant's waste problems. I know a little about your own history, a little more about mine. We'll be leaving here right at 8:30 to beat the heat. We'll be out there about three hours, leave some of you off at Hanford and park with the rest at White Bluffs, and you need to be back at the bus at noon. Please bring a hat with a brim, sunglasses, maybe sun-block, and about two quarts of water for each of you. Can't drink from the river you know."

"Will you tell us why not?" said Orville.

Ike said, "I think you know."

"Yes indeed! Not giardia!" called someone from the back. This time Bruce, Marta, and Leon all couldn't help laughing along with several others.

"Anyway," Ike went on, "I've been asked to pass on a message that will interest some of you that are here for your first time, or just to remind the others. There are two other points of interest north of here, right up the highway. There's the Priest Rapids Dam, and right below that on the river is my home, the Wolf Rapids Indian community. I can give you directions later. We're building a Wanapum Heritage Center, eventually welcoming tourists. It will tell the history and culture of my people. And we're going to have authentic Indian crafts, and some are available now—nice crafts made right here on the river, not Pakistan. So not far away are two interesting things for you to see. But back to the bus ride, unless there's questions, I'll see you tomorrow out front at 8:15 AM. Don't forget—sunglasses, bug dope, hats, and plenty of water."

"You think we don't know that, when we take that ride every summer?" said one woman, but she said it in a joking voice.

Ike nodded, smiled and moved to the side as Louise came back with a pile of papers.

"The agendas are here, please pass them around. And then we'll do some introductions."

Bruce looked over the agenda. Good, the bus ride was in the morning. The afternoon's activities to choose from: a lecture on the history of the Hanford Plant and the role it played in the 1945 bombing of Nagasaki. *Skip that!* Or a lecture by a fish biologist on regional salmon problems. *Skip that! Hear it every day at work.* Another one: historical photo viewing. He thought that would be a good one for talking to old settlers.

"Okay, the newcomers. How about these young people up front?"

Marta tapped Bruce. He hesitated, took a breath, and stepped forward.

"I'm Bruce Wilder, and I'm a descendant from MacPhersons that came in 1907 and their daughter, married into the Wilders—up at White Bluffs. I'm sure happy to be here after all these years. Harold Wilder, my great-uncle, many of you know. He couldn't come, not well this week, and he asked that I bring the draft of his memoir he's been working on all year. He wants you to comment on it. And this is Marta Stenoff, my partner."

Marta nodded at the crowd. Someone called, "Glad to have you!" Clapping broke out about the hall.

But then "Another Wilder? No kidding?" came in a growly tone from the crowd. Bruce scanned and saw other faces turned toward a man who seemed to be glaring at him. He wondered what that was about, as Leon introduced himself simply as a friend of Bruce and Marta that had tagged along and that he was interested in desert plants. About ten others followed, a mix of young and old. Then the young woman who had gotten off the bus with them stepped forward.

"Hello. I'm Suki Matsuda. This is my first time here. I had cousins living at Ringold, the Hayashis. They had an orchard and vegetable farm. I would like to meet some people that knew them in the 1930s or early 1940s."

Again people clapped. Then Orville stood up slowly. "I'm Orville, here again, as you see, to try to find out from the cotton-pickin' government when I'm going to get decent compensation for my folks' lost orchard!"

"Orville, sit down," an elder called, "you know you're never going to get it."

"Where's your patriotism," came the growly voice. "Where's your pride."

"I am proud, Walt. I'm proud of what we had here before they took it away."

"We came here to have some fun, you know," called another.

"Okay," said Louise, still smiling, "It's over fifty years in the past. Now let's enjoy ourselves for a couple days. There's iced water, tea, and lemonade over there on the side table. Help yourself, please."

A hubbub rose as the crowd headed to claim empty tables with chairs. Marta went to pick up note cards. Bruce looked around for the name tag "Roger". Harold had explained to him that before he let his memoir "out to the world" he wanted Roger to read it or at least hear key parts of it for accuracy, and what he might have left out, or what he might need to leave out. Of the regulars at the annual reunions, Roger and his wife Thelma were the ones Harold trusted the most to recall events the way he did, so Bruce kept looking for them while all around the big room the older people, and a few younger ones, were greeting each other, shaking hands, giving hugs, voices each minute louder, most of them in happy tones, but with an occasional exclamation breaking in, *Oh, I'm so sorry, we'll miss him (or her)*.

"Kennewick Man country!" Marta caught a younger voice's comment in passing.

"Hey, Leon, hear that?" she nudged him. "Kennewick Man?"

She was teasing Leon in a way he was used to. She knew that after thirty years he was sick of his profession's internecine war over piles of bones, the latest find at Kennewick just down the road. He was weary of his colleagues forever trying to outshine each other with their research to prove the origin of the Native Americans. Recently he had walked out of his last conference on the topic and transferred his research to the Indigenous peoples' use of native plants. Something less political, he'd assumed, than the challenge of ancient bones. He gave Marta a snort, and she returned him a grin and a light punch to the shoulder.

Bruce, gazing around the room, straining his eyes at name tags, didn't see the browned faces he would have seen on almost all the older men and many of the women if life had gone on normally from fifty years ago. But these were retired people now, not people taking a day off from their orchards. He saw a few exceptions in very tanned younger men who were still following their ancestors' occupation. But he knew from Harold's comments that there wasn't much of a living to be made in small farming these days, and those who still tried probably had another job to support it.

It occurred to Bruce that perhaps Harold wasn't so ill, that maybe he had thought his old neighbors might be more honest in their reactions to the memoir if the author wasn't there. After all, his uncle was certainly no polished writer, and he had his own viewpoints. Roger, an old neighbor of his family, was one of his generation who had spent time at college and might have some punctuation pointers. He kept looking for him, but the hubbub was growing and he soon whispered to Marta,

"This is getting pretty noisy, I need to get out of here a bit."

Marta was used to this from him. "Well… let's go out in the café and get some iced tea."

"I'll join you," said Leon, "but first I want to ask the bus driver something."

Marta nodded. Perhaps Ike, the driver, could provide some information today about the Dreamer religion and Smohalla. As they left the room Marta saw the growly man giving Bruce another unmistakable glare. She was glad Bruce didn't catch it.

⋅→▐═◉ ◉═▌←⋅

Two months earlier, in frustration over slow progress on her dissertation topic, Marta had complained to Bruce, her partner of three years, about its sterile feeling. "I need to get interviews from living people. Some stories at least. But I don't even know if there are any living Washani believers, some primary sources—you know what I mean."

Of course Bruce did; she was always pursuing them. And she was always saying that he should be the one writing a dissertation, not that he was tempted to write anything. But he was interested in her topic, and he had asked her where the Washani religious leader, Smohalla, had been located.

"You know—east of the mountains, on the Columbia River, mainly the middle section."

That was when he'd been inspired for this trip. "Well then, go with me to the White Bluffs-Hanford reunion in August!"

And he explained to her that his Uncle Harold's arthritis had flared up, and he wanted Bruce to take the memoir and get the older settlers' reactions.

"I need to go for him. You know I've never been to a reunion. I do owe it to him, and I could sure use a day away from the job. You go too! But I need to know soon because I have to apply for passes to get into the closed area around that damn plant. You can't just go waltzing in!"

Marta had often listened when Harold talked with Bruce about the big annual reunions for the Hanford and White Bluffs people, his family among them, who had all been evicted for a secret military project in 1943. Everyone in Washington over age seventy probably knew something about the Hanford Plant and its war history. They possibly knew something of its current problems, as the *Seattle Times* regularly reported them. But the whole story of the eviction for the Plant and its production was one topic Harold didn't write about. He'd been drafted and was in the Pacific. His memoir covered his years growing up in White Bluffs, and much more that he'd gleaned from the saved boxes of family letters—three generations of life there.

Bruce had felt no interest in the family history when he was younger. Now he couldn't understand how he'd passed by the stories and letters. But he'd been a very different person then. Marta, fretting over her stalled dissertation, now saw how the trip would be good for Bruce, but could be a jump-start for her. Today's Wanapum must have elders that recalled passed-down stories of the famous Smohalla.

Bruce had waded through the federal application process in no time, received the passes to get into the closed White Bluffs area, took leave from his job at a salmon hatchery, and picked up the memoir to start reading it. As for Marta, she was already on leave from everything until she finished the dissertation.

Leon, when he heard about the excursion, was glad to join them. He'd read that Central Washington was home to the largest area of natural shrub-steppe desert left in the entire country, and for some reason he'd never been there. He'd been away from deserts for years and was curious to see this one. But when he had stepped off the bus his nostalgia for his time in Australia was filled with as much pain as pleasure, swept back to that time when he had been so young, so full of energy for research and for life. In Richland he would have no real assignment, nothing on his plate but to sit back and enjoy the settler's stories. He suspected that was what he needed.

Chapter 2

WHY THEY CAME THERE

BRUCE, MARTA, AND Leon carried their iced tea back into the crowded conference room, hoping to find a likely place for three to sit. Leon had found out from Ike, the bus driver, that a main encampment of Smohalla's Dreamers had been north about 35 miles, at Priest Rapids, and that it was still an active Wanapum community. Ike was from Wolf Rapids, just a few miles downriver from there and smaller. Marta knew she wanted to talk more with him for sure, and Leon, with his indigenous plant specialty, could provide a *segue* for her. He often reminded her that Native Americans were weary of being researched. They would say so in a joking way, sometimes not so joking. Bruce's object was to take the reunion's tour bus and find his family's place, and he doubted he'd have much trouble locating it. Harold had assured him that in the 1940s everyone knew everyone in the long, irrigated strip along the river, and any one of those here from White Bluffs could help him. The older people in the room did seem to know each other. But with people two generations younger among them, Bruce was relieved to see that he and Marta didn't stand out that much.

Marta had written a question on a note card to post: "Any information to share on Wanapum Indian-settler contacts? Marta, room 266." She showed it to Bruce.

"Why don't you go put it up?"

Leon said, "I'll put one up too—were any of the Native plants used by the settlers?"

Bruce showed his note: "Recall the boys who had to crawl through the irrigation pipes to clean them?" and another, "Encounters with rattlesnakes?" He was teasing Marta with the snake note, knowing that was her other hesitation, aside from heat, regarding walks in deserts.

"Hey, you'd think I was some kind of a wimp!"

Leon laughed, "We know you're not by any means a wimp, Marta. Everyone has their pet phobia. Did I tell you mine is spiders? Not so good for a wild plant specialist, eh? And one with cataracts at that. What's yours, Bruce?"

"Mines," he muttered.

"Uh, yeah.... should have guessed that." Leon stopped himself from glancing at the deep scar on Bruce's forehead. He'd seriously tried to overcome the reputation some anthropologists had earned, but even he could put his foot in it.

Bruce nodded and went to post the notes, glancing around again at name tags. In addition to Roger, he was trying to find names he recognized from Harold's writings and anecdotes. They were the ones that went to the Grange meetings, or Presbyterian Church, or Ladies Aid, he assumed, as these were groups mentioned most by Harold. Leon had observed that in a small town such alliances were so important—a typical Leon remark. The three found a table in a corner.

Aside from getting reactions to the memoir and looking over his family's place, Bruce wanted to know what the settlers thought about the Hanford Plant now, fifty-five years after their eviction for its creation. But that wasn't what Harold had advised as a starting topic. Just two years after the settlers' eviction, he had been with the Marines landing in blown-up Nagasaki. He told Bruce that when he'd first gone to the reunions, yes, he had tried to talk about the Plant.

"Some of them sided with me, lots said nothing, and there were some furious with me. The coordinator said I'd better drop it; it was being too disruptive. Most the folks just wanted to talk about the good old days of their orchards and their youth. That's what the reunions are about— socializing over memories. So I decided to shut up. They'd been hurt themselves, and that's they were thinking about—losing their own homes, evicted. The Japanese were the enemy then; their suffering was way across the ocean."

Bruce took heed and planned to be cautious on the topic. But not to bury it.

Leon came back from talking again with their bus driver. "Well, I had some luck. I don't know if wild plants and their uses will get many takers on the note cards, but Ike says they're in the process of building a facsimile of a traditional meeting house of tule reeds up at Wolf Rapids. How about that? A real tule reed house, like they used to build. I have to see that!"

Marta smiled, having no idea what tule was. "You're lucky, hope I am. Is Ike easy to talk to?"

"Oh yes, that's part of his job as bus driver, I'm sure."

Marta certainly hoped so. She decided to skip posting more cards, but Bruce wrote out several more, hoping to entice people to come to him. Bruce's included "Bringing drift logs downriver for firewood", "Catching lost lambs", "Sailing on the river", "The Fruit Market".

"I wonder if they have any photos of the eviction," Bruce mused. "Like one Harold has of my great-grandpa riding out of White Bluffs on the back of the pick-up, on top of their household goods. You know, like the *Grapes of Wrath* movie."

"You're kidding." said Leon.

"Nope. There was only room for my great-grandma in the truck cab. Each household was granted one truck and driver for all their stuff."

"I doubt the Plant would show any of that scene," said someone next to him.

Bruce looked over and saw it was Suki, the young woman who'd had relatives at Ringold.

"I suppose not. You say you had family living near here?"

"Yes, just up the river and across. Cousins."

"So it's your first time to a reunion. Me too." He reached to shake her hand, and wondered why she, like him, had decided to come here, after so long. Marta watched and was glad he was being social, something hard for him, a guy who, he'd admitted to her, had been voted "most friendly" in his high school yearbook.

Bruce had gone on, "Uh, were your relatives some of those sent off to, uh… internment camps?"

Suki gave him a surprised look. Most people were too embarrassed to ask that question.

"Yes, some of my family were."

"I'm sorry. Must have been tough."

"Yes, for sure."

What else could he say? She made it easier for him, "You had family here too."

"Lots. Three generations."

He was trying to think of more to say when an older settler strode up.

"Well, here you are, Bruce Wilder! I've been looking for you; your uncle Harold called me, told me be sure to visit with you. Is this your group? Please come and sit our table."

Bruce read his name tag and grinned hugely, "Roger! So glad to meet you! These are my friends Marta and Leon, and this is Suki…"

"Matsuda…cousin of the Hayashis."

"Can she sit with us too?"

Roger gave Suki a nod, "Oh, of course, Hayashis. Ringold people, I remember."

They saw, to Bruce's amusement, that Orville, his wife, and their teenage granddaughter were already at Roger's table, and the men pulled another table over to make them one of the larger groups in the room, and introductions went around.

"Did you bring Harold's writing?" Roger got right to the point.

"I did." And Bruce pulled the memoir from his daypack.

Thelma, Roger's wife, said, "We're dying to hear from it. You know his family was in that first group that came when they put the irrigation systems in. Harold has memories passed down that others don't."

Leon asked, "Do some of these people come here every year?"

Dorothy, Orville's wife, laughed, "Oh yes, we just come to see each other and tell stories about our lives. Harold will have great stuff for us I bet."

The newcomers listened a few minutes to a story Orville had been telling from his youth. Then Marta said, "So it was fun growing up here? I don't know much about farming, but I've always heard farm kids work so hard they leave for the city as soon as they can."

Orville snorted, "Work hard? Darn right we did. But we didn't leave, we got driven out!"

Roger said, "True. But we had plenty of fun as kids, always had time for it except at harvests. You were swimming in the river, same as the rest of us, every time they gave us a break."

He set the women to laughing at Orville in a friendly way. Bruce was amused when they continued with more anecdotes about fun on the river, swimming, rafting, rowing, ice-skating, even sailing, and fishing for carp no one knew how to cook right. Orville told about tough, scary work that was also fun: capturing their only firewood from the river each spring at high water.

After more such recollections, Leon decided to ask about something that puzzled him.

"I'm from Puget Sound, so I have to wonder, why did your people want to start orchards in the desert? It's pretty hot here today, just to stand outside, let alone pick fruit. Why not start farms where it's more pleasant in the summer?"

Roger sat up straighter, "Harold probably writes about that, but I'll tell you. In 1906 the land was cheap, and lots of it along the river where they could get all the water they needed...they thought. Only a few of those first settlers were people with money. And not many were farmers either; they were city folk looking for a way to get out of the cities. Full of coal smoke and TB, my folks told us. Many of them came to the desert for their kids' health—the doctors sent them. Some had already lost kids."

Thelma said, "I saw one of the ads put out by the land companies—very attractive. Everyone would get rich! Not so, but it really was a healthy place— that part was true. The river water was pure then."

Leon went on, hoping that his question wouldn't offend anyone. "That's really interesting, an early back-to-the-country movement? But I wonder, why orchards, not potatoes? Surely more difficult, and it would take longer to get a return."

Roger nodded, "Yup, it took at least three years before an apple tree would begin to bear. But they would plant some other things while they were waiting—spuds, asparagus, berries, alfalfa. A neighbor had cows and sent sour cream down the river by boat to some buyer."

Dorothy said, "The big thing was the fruit they were counting on. They'd seen the orchards in bloom over on the Yakima River, so they knew they could do it."

"There's nothing more beautiful." Thelma nodded. "We still look forward to the orchards blossoming every spring. We live over at Prosser now—I'm so glad there's orchards there too."

Bruce could hardly keep up and wondered how he would fit in actually reading from the memoir and getting comments from them.

"That must be a sight. And they thought in a few years they'd have an orchard and it would all pay off?"

Roger smiled, "It turned a lot more complicated than that. Well, farming always is but…"

Louise's voice broke in, "Okay folks, we are set up now and the slide show will start in five minutes. You might want to get a drink of water or something."

Several men got up, some to head for the bar. Bruce asked Roger, "Is the slide show interesting?"

"I suppose mainly to folks that lived here, seeing their old places, old friends, family."

"My uncle really wants your opinion especially, with your sharp memory. But, also, I'm really looking forward to the drive up to White Bluffs, and seeing my family's places."

Roger gave him a thoughtful look. "Well, don't…don't hope to see too much. I mean, what you'll see is what was left by the bulldozers—hasn't changed much in fifty years. But the river and the bluffs are the same marvelous sight. Try to imagine what it was like full of orchards, and from what Harold writes."

"Are you going on the tour?"

"Always do, I'm not sure why. I know why we come to the reunion, Bruce, but why do we go on that tour? Well, you'll see."

Volunteers had put the slide show together from old photos contributed from family archives. For the next two hours the room was filled with calls such as "That's Billy Brown, cute little guy!", and "That's old man Lester's horse, isn't it?", and "Look at those awful bathing suits!" All accompanied by hoots and laughs. Bruce, Marta, and Leon watched some of the slides, read the often-funny notes on the bulletin board, and after the temperature dropped a bit, they walked out through the nearby green grassy park with its welcome shade trees bordering the Columbia. Bruce and Marta were happy that they'd connected so soon with Roger and Thelma. Leon had found the session entertaining even though there was little to compare with the hunter-gatherer groups he had spent his career studying. He, too, looked forward to hearing more in the next two days, whether or not he found out anything about the area's traditional use of native plants.

Suki had been interested but quiet during the storytelling, but she had not stayed long at the slide show, as there were no photos from Ringold. She told the others she would see them in the morning on the tour bus. She, too, headed for the river, but to be alone to think, anxious about her task. It was pure fantasy, she thought one minute, and the next minute she was fully committed. She had been on the Columbia before, but down near the mouth. Here in the mid-section the river was much narrower, clear, with ripples moving slowly, ducks drifting, herons posed along the banks, and wild geese grazing past them. Above, great flocks of pelicans circled, dipping their wings in unison—black, white, black, white, so beautiful, and no hint of danger. She stood motionless on the edge of the bordering reeds and watched the current until her grandmother's voice came to her in Japanese: *"Do this for me, Suki, do it for all of us." "I am not sure I am the right person, Grandmother." "Who is, then? We are all the right person when we are called on." "I want to help, but I need help myself." "Your help will be there in the nature around you... you call on it." "I won't know what to do, what to say..." "You put yourself in touch with nature. Open your heart, it will tell you what to do and say." "All right...when I feel ready."*

She didn't feel ready. How could she ever, raised so differently from her grandmother? But she was here.

At the buffet dinner Bruce moved around and introduced himself to several groups. He found all welcoming except the one glaring man. Many of them knew his uncle Harold and were sorry he hadn't come. The settlers from the even smaller town of Hanford, eight miles away, had not known Harold well earlier, but had visited with him at the annual reunions, and several said they, too, wanted to hear what he had written. Just as at Roger's table, most people were talking about their lives as kids, growing up on the river.

At 6 p.m. a late-arriving woman checked into the hotel, unnoticed by Louise. She went on upstairs, but not before Bruce, out on the sidewalk stretching his legs, observed her. She was wearing an outfit that looked counter-culture—a long fringed skirt, beaded blouse, and headband, and fringed and beaded boots. Was she an Indian? Did people really dress like that around here now? As she passed by, a man, about fifty but dressed like other older settlers, came out of the hotel and walked over to Bruce.

"Did you see that?"

"Yeah, gorgeous, huh?" Bruce smiled, but recognized him as the man who kept frowning at him in the conference room.

"If you like the dark ones. Maybe you do—you're a vet, maybe? Been over there?"

Bruce didn't answer. He tried to ignore this kind of remark; it was too easy to get into topics he didn't want to talk about.

"Sorry, if that bothered you," said the man. "I respect vets. But her? Better not be coming into our reunion."

"Why not? Maybe she's from here. Maybe that's her ethnic dress."

"No Indians around here dress like that unless they're trying to make money off tourists. She's probably from Seattle. Here to disrupt things."

"Why is that?"

"Or she's most likely a whore."

What the...? "Hey, how do you know that?"

The man smirked, "Or maybe she's a hippy and it's for free."

Bruce looked to see the man's smug expression and felt acid seep into his gut. He knew he'd punch the guy if he got started, so he walked away. *Do I look that strange that I attract this sort of asshole?* He searched around for Marta, and found her right behind him with a look of disgust on her face. *Harold never said a word about the reunion attracting this kind of character.*

But back in the meeting room their mood rose again when, after buffet supper of sturgeon chowder, corn bread, and apple pie, a bluegrass band arrived and provided the rest of the night's program, including sing-alongs. After everyone had said goodnight and climbed the stairs to their rooms, there was time for him to reflect.

"Is it boring to you—the conversations, Mart?"

"What? No, not at all. I love listening to these old folks! It seems it was a unique experiment in getting out of the city—like the flower children in the 1960s."

They agreed that the first day had been entertaining, educational, and friendly except for the one nasty man. What was his problem anyway? But the real adventure would begin the next morning. They crawled into bed, and wrapped their arms around each other, floating into love, pleased so far with the reunion and with themselves.

Suki had skipped the dinner and evening entertainment and walked again along the river. Crickets filled the air with chirping that was truly racket. The pelicans were gone, but even more drama swooped in the air around her, and she didn't know what these dark birds could be until a person walking near her called out, *Oh these damn fruit bats—scary!* So strange this country! She had expected to be calmed watching the slow-moving current; instead she was just more agitated. As she went back to her room she passed the woman Bruce had felt outraged over and turned to look at her. *But that outfit, where's she from?*

Walt Croaker, the cranky man, sat at the hotel bar with a buddy. It was 10 p.m. and he had switched from beer to bourbon. His friend broke into his thoughts,

"A bunch of new people showed up this year, eh? I wonder, is it just a coincidence or is something being planned?"

Croaker snorted. "There's no coincidences."

CHAPTER 3

NO MAN'S LAND

THE BUS FULL of settlers and their descendants, along with a scattering of academics and newcomers, sped north on the highway. The noisy, mainly happy crowd of yesterday was quiet now. The desert was not at its best, the hot and driest part of the year, but the bus was cool. Muted colors dotted the landscape in all directions, the same colors you'd see in any desert, mused Bruce. *So familiar, too familiar.* He saw that the terrain was often gently rolling, with raised hillocks crowned with basalt, and frequent draws with enough moisture to nurture cottonwood stands. He identified Saddle Mountain, visible to the northeast, from Harold's memoir and a road map. He saw few birds—a hawk, a quail, a grouse of some kind. *Not even nine and it's already too hot for birds?*

Marta thought the scene rather monotonous, so dull compared to Puget Sound when you got away from the river. She spoke to the driver, just in front of them as they had hurried to board first.

"What are those dead bushy things piled on all the fences?"

Ike smiled, "You're not from around here. It's tumbleweed, mainly Russian thistle, and a bunch of other stuff that gets caught up in it."

Leon, in the seat across, joined in, "Tumbleweed. It's an immigrant, right?"

"Yeah. It's not pretty but it's smart. It rolls along and scatters its seeds as it goes."

Leon chuckled—a metaphor the others probably didn't get. A moment later he was surprised again that, living so close at Puget Sound, he'd never driven across the Cascades before. But then he knew why; he had been avoiding what he saw now from the bus window—a landscape too familiar, too full of memories. He shook them away; he needed to immerse himself in the day.

"I picked up a plant book last night in the gift shop. You've got lots of immigrants, exotics. What about those yellow-flowered bushes over there?"

Ike wasn't used to such questions. Usually the riders were from the area originally. "It's rabbit brush. Another immigrant, first came in with the cattle herds. They're taking over all the time more, and they aren't good forage, the introduced plants. Most aren't good for anything much."

But Leon thought they were pretty—and smart, like tumbleweed—just useless to those trying to be ranchers or orchardists. He wondered if the Indians had thought the same way about the immigrants to their country. *Well, why wouldn't they? Maybe they still do.*

Marta asked Bruce, "Why is almost everything so pale?"

"All deserts are like this—I don't know why."

Ike answered; it was part of his job on these tours. "In the spring this country's full of brilliant flowers, but they dry up soon. Only the irrigated acres stay green."

"Oh, I see. When it gets too hot and dry, no energy to be colorful. Was it tough for your people living here?"

Ike laughed. "No way, well, not usually. The river makes all the difference."

Leon moved up closer. "That is the difference. The Australian desert, same thing. Ike, is that bunch grass out there, that yellowed grass?"

"Yup, bunch grass is one of the native plants—and very good forage, or it was. It's been overtaken by that other grass you see, the cheat grass. A poor trade."

"How's that?"

"It's not as nutritious and too hardy."

Bruce remembered Harold telling of how farmers had tried to stop the takeover of the cheat grass and failed. "So, just one of the problems here."

Ike nodded. "Of many."

Marta was glad that Ike had done his homework for any newcomers. She'd have ample questions for him. Then she saw the shapes of buildings a few miles in the distance. They were too tall to be houses.

"Ike, is that the Hanford Plant?"

"No, that's another nuclear plant that started operating in 1984 and still is. See the steam? Not for bombs, though. It's purely for regional power."

Bruce made a face. "So has it got the problems solved, like the radioactive waste?"

Ike glanced at him. "Not as far as I know. Hey, Roger," he called back toward the other passengers, "Did that new power plant get the radioactive waste problem fixed?"

"I doubt it," Roger came forward. "If it did, the *Seattle Times* would sure have a story on it, and I haven't seen one."

Bruce nodded. "I didn't think so. Those plants all have the same problem and they just keep putting it off to the future."

"That's right I'm afraid," Roger sighed. "Harold's probably said something about it? It makes people pretty nervous, that we're just doing the same thing, storing the waste again."

"My uncle doesn't like to talk about it, gets too upset I think. You ever read about Chernobyl?"

"I sure have. Mostly because of this place here."

"Yeah. Not too hard to make some connections, eh?"

Roger nodded and went to sit back down after a moment. Ike hadn't said more, since there were no more questions, but he thought it was an interesting conversation on a topic most settlers didn't usually bring up. Bruce's thoughts went back to White Bluffs and his family's old place, which Harold had told him was so near one of the original reactors.

In another few minutes, the road turned east toward the river to arrive at the first stop, ghost town Hanford, right on the riverbank. The travelers were struck with the sight of the blue Columbia and the great tan bluffs looming up just across the water. Small cries of awe filled the bus from the newcomers.

Ike parked and called to his passengers, "Never gets old does it?"

"I come every time just for the bluffs," called back one elderly woman.

Marta said, "Well, I can see why. They're magnificent."

A familiar voice came up the aisle: Orville. "Of course everything else is destroyed."

Suki, just behind Marta, heard him and muttered, "Destroyed, yes. So beautiful, and so much destroyed."

Marta glanced at her but decided not to respond.

Ike turned to begin his tour guide role, "Well, our first stop. For the newcomers on board, here's what used to be the little farming town of Hanford that they named the Hanford Plant after. You're right, no sign of a town here now except for that one building over there, the brick high school. But back in 1906 Hanford was the first big steamer stop above Kennewick, and it was a busy place. These settlements had no train until 1913, so the paddle-wheelers were their lifeline, but it worked. They'd just run them up to the bank and throw down the ramp. Off came a new bunch of settlers."

"Who'd they get the land from?" asked someone new to the tour.

"A land company, which bought it from the railroad, which got it from the government cheap, which got it from the Indians super-cheap." After a pause he went on, "Anyway, when the land company opened up the tracts the settlers came flocking up the river, pitched their tents, unpacked their sup-plies, and started digging out sagebrush. Maybe you've seen photos—that all along the bank here was white with tents. Some of the settlers stayed in those tents summer and winter for years while they were tending their fruit trees, waiting for them to bear."

Bruce nodded, "Yup, like my family."

Ike continued, "Yes…my family knew yours. I wonder if some were maybe shocked at what they'd bought, but anyway they ordered their baby trees, tore out the sagebrush, dug ditches, got the water flowing, and some had little orchards going all in one season."

Bruce was pleased with the history lesson. He broke in again, "My uncle Harold says they got just about everything from the river. Their water, ice, a few of them fished, and their wood fuel came down the river. Got every-thing, just about, and of course the water for the orchards and gardens, and pastures, then it floated their produce to market. Everything from the Columbia."

Ike nodded. "And for my people too, you know, almost everything from the river."

"Yup. But, my god, I had no idea of the bluffs. They are really, really something! So high! You don't get this from old black-and-white photos. Harold couldn't really describe them." *What my grandparents saw every morning, looking right across, as they rushed through their oatmeal and coffee. Wow.*

"Maybe what kept them going at first was the sight of those incredible bluffs," said a younger passenger.

"Well," said a middle-aged woman, obviously one of the settler descendants, "it wasn't based on pretty views let me tell you. Like he says, all based on the river and hard work."

"Same with desert farming anywhere," said Leon, wanting to get off the bus.

Marta tried a feeler for Ike: "I'll bet those early settlers learned a lot from the Indians."

He laughed a little. "I'll bet they did." He liked a crowd like this that had something to say; it made the job so much more interesting. He called out to them,

"Okay, for you folks getting off here at Hanford, be sure you've got your water bottles, sunglasses, everything. Be careful of too much sun. There's an awning set up over there, see it? Thank Louise for that. We'll go on up the road and be back in three hours. I've got a radio if this bus breaks down, don't worry. You folks new to this, listen to the old-timers. They know what not to do."

The Hanford group debarked, some of them rather creakily.

Bruce frowned, "It's going to be 90, Ike, are these folks going to be okay for three hours? I know what that's like."

"They'll be okay if they listen—and they will."

Bruce shrugged. *If he isn't worried why should I be? No one's shooting at them either.*

"Okay, next stop, White Bluffs," and Ike started up the bus. They traveled away from the river and then north again through a few more miles of small rises and flats of sagebrush. But approaching the turn-off to the White

Bluff site, they began to see something new: acres of rows of small black posts sticking up among the sagebrush.

"What's that?" Leon asked. This time Ike didn't answer, and behind them they heard a woman start to sob.

"Ohhh, ohhh, I didn't...I didn't think to see this sight," she choked.

"Jesus, it's the stumps of their fruit trees, isn't it?" called a young man's voice.

"You're right," said an elder after a moment. "What was our families' orchards, terrible the first time you see it. Made me cry too. Can you imagine, watching them cut down?"

"What did you expect to see?" grumbled someone. The sobs had squelched further comments.

"I wish I could see better," said Leon finally. "These cataracts will be gone next month."

"You don't want to see it," sighed the tearful woman.

Ike nodded to himself. There was always at least one crying on every tour he'd driven. He slowed and stopped again, and gave another short history lesson.

"Okay, another little ghost town, White Bluffs. The second site for White Bluffs actually. Over there is a concrete foundation of a warehouse. Over there is the bank building, as you see, also made of concrete, and too much for the bulldozers, so it stayed. And a couple concrete pump houses. It was called New Town White Bluffs, all by itself out in the desert. But there's also Old Town where we'll park, right down at the river, a pretty place where the town should have stayed—another story."

A young woman spoke from the rear, "A bank? So these folks made enough money on their crops to actually have a bank?"

"Well, a few made money, I'm told."

Bruce said, "My family didn't stay for the money, I'm positive."

Murmurs of agreement came from other listeners.

Suki asked, "Can you see any of the reactors up close where we're going?"

Ike looked around to see who had asked that and caught Suki's eyes. *Another one interested in the Plant.*

"Well, no, not the buildings. But maybe you will see signs of one soon."

He started the engine. "Next stop, the real White Bluffs, Old Town. They were only a mile-and-a-half apart, but that meant a hot walk in summer, a cold one in winter, to get to the store or any business. Or you hitched up a horse. So why did the town leave the river? Can you guess?"

Bruce had a fast answer. "My great-uncle Harold writes it was the railroad. It laid its tracks out here and bypassed the original town so it could create a new town site and make money selling that land for business lots. He says it happened all over the West."

"It's true," said the talkative older woman in the back. "Harold got it right. And it created an angry split in the town."

"Why is that?" asked someone.

"They took all the services with them except the traveling library."

"Knowledgeable man, your uncle," said Ike. "Why didn't he come this year? I wanted to talk to him again."

"He said he wasn't feeling well enough."

"Oh, I'm sorry."

"This place is full of stories, isn't it," said Marta. "I'll bet your Wolf Rapids community is, too, Ike."

He glanced over and answered her in a low voice, "You're right. Come and hear them."

Then once more he brought the bus to a stop. "Okay, folks, here we are, and here's the bluffs again. I have no words for them," and he stared across with the rest, where just as at Hanford the bluffs rose up steeply, as much as to six hundred feet above the river. But here they were even more arresting: a gleaming chalky white with occasional shadowed streaks. The response of the new passengers was a cry of even greater awe.

"I had no idea," said Suki. "Nor I," Bruce sighed.

After a moment Ike said, "Okay, is everybody ready to climb out? We'll be here about three hours, folks. Don't forget your water bottles, bug dope.

You can see there's shade under those cottonwoods. Watch your step out in the brush—scorpions, snakes maybe."

Bruce was probably the most excited person on the bus. His plan for the day was to immerse himself in the scene, to color the nostalgic words from his uncle Harold with what stretched out before him. Even so, he noticed the other Asian-looking woman come from the back of the bus and climb off and walk down to the river. Dressed in tee-shirt and slacks like the younger women, she didn't seem so unusual today, but still captivating.

Ike stood by Marta and Suki, looking across. "Magnificent, yes. But if you come from the other side, the public side, you're under the bluffs and then, looking this way, you can't see them; you're just looking at the river and the desert. But if you're living here, back then, looking across every day like this, do you get used to it, kind of take it for granted?"

Marta shook her head, "I don't think so."

Suki said, "The reactors are all up along the river on this side, right?"

Ike nodded. *She sure has something besides the view on her mind.* "All nine of them."

"Can you tell me where B reactor is from here?"

What? He studied Suki through the dark glasses they both wore.

"It's way up around the bend, the last one. Up near the bridge."

"The Vernita Bridge."

"Uh-huh." *She's not just a tourist.*

"What is that smoke?" She pointed toward the closest bend upriver.

"It's steam. One of the defunct reactors. Why is it still steaming? I don't know. They're doing cleanup on all of them. What a…contrast to the rest of the scene, eh? But, you know, better to forget all that today and spend your time enjoying the bluffs and the river."

Ike waited to see if she had more to say but she was quiet, staring at the rising steam. He looked around at his charges. He saw Bruce listening to Roger and smiled. He reminded them all again to keep track of their water bottles, wear their hats, look out for snakes and scorpions.

"Any more questions?"

"Yes," said Marta, "What do you do when you're not driving this bus?"

He gave a short laugh. "Well...mostly seems like I go to fishery management meetings. But I'm also on the team for the heritage project I told you about, up at Wolf Rapids. Okay, folks, enjoy yourselves. You've got till eleven-thirty."

Marta persisted. "What are you going to do, while you wait for us?"

"I'm going to stay here, go for a swim, and maybe take a nap."

But in truth he would be keeping an eye on the older people as they dispersed along the riverbank path, though some headed right for the shade trees.

"Hear that, Leon?" said Marta, "about snakes? Watch your step."

"You are my eyes, my dear. You lead, I follow."

Bruce was already headed down to the shore. Suki followed him.

"Do you mind if I tag along? I'd like to hear your memories you've got from your family. You said their place was right up there?" She pointed upriver.

"Not more than a quarter mile. We're going to walk up there. Sure, come along."

"Thanks. I'd like to get a look at the Plant, too, if I can."

Bruce looked at her, "Ike's right. We should forget it for the day and enjoy."

"I have to see the whole thing."

He thought of how to answer that, "Yeah? You're like me, too young to have been through it here. And you want to take in the whole thing, but we can't in three hours."

Suki stared over at the bluffs. "But I feel like part of me has been here."

Marta, walking next to her, nodded. *Believable, if she's talked to her Ringold family.*

Bruce, shaking loose from thoughts of the Plant, turned to Roger and Thelma.

"What are those dark streaks on the bluffs?"

"It's irrigation runoff—huge farms up there now. When my parents came, there was nobody there, nothing but abandoned homesteads."

"Oh yes, my great-uncle Harold tells about hiking up there and wondering what those people thought they were doing, up where there was no river and almost no rain."

Roger had his own interest in local history. "Bruce, there was no possible way to make a living on 160 acres up there except in the wetter years. They had to be down here where they could irrigate. It was free homestead land up there, but it's desert, and they didn't know what that meant."

Bruce remembered from his uncle that Roger was a retired county extension agent.

"Didn't the government understand that?"

Roger shrugged, "Makes you wonder, eh? We knew, us county agents, I mean. But we didn't make the laws. Say, aren't you the one who posted the question about the boys and the irrigation ditches? Well," he gave Bruce a bright smile, "I was one of those boys! Us smaller ones had to crawl through a section of them every spring. Because— see these fine old poplars—I wonder how it was they escaped the government bulldozers? Anyway, these trees would put their roots down into the wooden pipes to get at the water, and they tore the staves of the pipes apart, so smaller boys had to—"

"I know! You had to crawl through the pipes and cut off the roots!" said Bruce.

"Yup, that's what we got drafted for till we got too big. A good reason to eat a lot!" Roger swept his arm toward the river. "I can show you a lot that Harold probably talks about. See that old cement ramp over there? That was the ferry landing. Lots of traffic."

Roger motioned at Bruce to follow, and he willingly went along with him and Thelma for whatever was left to see of the old days. Marta started to follow, but stopped, "What makes these tracks everywhere?"

She pointed to a design covering the sands.

Ike laughed. "Dung beetles!"

"Ah…they eat dung? What dung?"

"Any dung. They're the desert's…I guess you'd say, cleaners. They clean up any kind of waste, maybe been cleaning up after us humans for 20,000 years here…there's one over there." He pointed to a black beetle that was rolling along a round clump.

"See, that's some kind of dung he's going to store away. Dung beetles are interesting; picture all the work they have to do…. Hey, watch out, see that scorpion?"

"Ugh," shuddered Leon, stepping back. "I'll stick with the plants. How about those pretty little trees over there? They're not willows or cottonwoods."

"You're right. More immigrants, Russian olives, all over the place now. Yeah, pretty, but full of spikes. Lots of spiky stuff around here, so watch out where you walk."

"I will! Ah-h, the woman who went on up the river, do you know her?"

"No. Well, I know of her; she's been here before. Elena."

"Interesting."

"She's not an Indian from around here, if that's what you're wondering. She's actually not any kind of Indian…from somewhere in Asia, I think."

Leon decided to follow his own advice and quit asking questions. Roger, meanwhile, having captured Bruce with his recall of local landmarks and history, said he was going to go sit in the shade with some other old-timers for a while. "Join me?" But Bruce was too eager to walk up to the site of his family's place. It would be easy to find with the sketched map Harold had provided. He set off with Marta, Leon, and Suki following.

At first the riverbank was easy to walk along. But where the island and its slough gave protection from the current, they faced a tangle of willow, reeds, and wild roses with bees and dragon flies buzzing through them, sheltered by more poplar and locust trees. Dangling on every tree were several hanging nests Ike said belonged to orioles. Leon fell behind, studying the flora close-up. He would be enthralled for hours, thought Marta. It would be impossible for her to keep an eye on his footsteps in the tangle of shrubbery. She decided to leave him to his fate and instead keep up with Bruce and Suki. The three plunged on through the brush flushing two mule deer that sprang up in their path and eased off into the willows.

"They're certainly not very shy," laughed Bruce.

Suki said, "This whole area is soon going to be a National Monument and all the flora and fauna will be permanently protected."

"Is that so?"

"Yes, the Hanford Reach they call it. Forty-three species here, I've read, and 40 mammals, and about 250 birds, to say nothing the reptiles and insects—really a special place. But at the same time, they're also trying to figure out how to detoxify it. Ironic, eh?"

Marta observed that Suki had read quite a bit about the place. *Maybe she's a reporter, or a writer.* She said, "I've read it's a favorite sport-fishing place now on the other public side. The water can't be too polluted."

"But the spirit is polluted."

Marta waited. After a moment she said, "Polluted...you mean from the reactors?"

"Yes. I guess you know."

"Not much, really."

"They say the radioactive waste is soon going to be leaking from the old corroded tanks and seeping toward the river. They've got to dig it all up and move it somewhere."

Bruce turned back to them, "So I'm told, but move it where? Who'd take it?"

Suki smiled. "So far, no takers."

Marta succumbed to her curiosity. "Your relatives were just down the river?"

"Yes."

"They never came back after the war?"

Suki, her eyes on the path, kept walking. "I think you're talking about returning from the internment camps? No, they never came back. They were not actually evicted on that side of the river, but they left anyway and didn't come back after one look at what was left of their place. When the irrigation stopped, you know, everything they'd planted died."

She began to say more, but stopped. Marta waited, then felt she had to say something.

"Are you a writer, Suki?"

"Yes. I write sometimes for Northwest magazines."

So, that's why she's here. "Ah. This place certainly has plenty to write about doesn't it?"

CHAPTER 4

A MAP AND A MEMOIR

"This is it, has to be—look!" Bruce pointed to an ancient loop of rope embedded far above them in one of the poplars, having moved up as the tree grew. But aside from the line of tall poplars along the river and the willows and reeds at their base, around him were only large piles of sand and dead brush. That was all. An image of other sand piles and craters burst in on him, and he had a rush of horror he struggled to fight off.

Marta saw his expression and took his hand, "That rope up there is an artifact from your ancestors, isn't it? But what are all these jumbled piles of sand?"

Bruce shook his head, took a deep breath, "Oh…what the bulldozers left. They bulldozed everything of the farms except the shade trees planted along the river."

Marta took a drag from her water bottle and was glad she had a backup. "Yes, ugly. The scene must have been so beautiful with irrigation."

Bruce was carrying Harold's hand-drawn map. He studied it and then gazed across the piles as if he could see into the green past. "Well, it was hot, like now, but Harold says that all along the river, especially on this side, were miles of orchards, gardens, and alfalfa. Ah, here…the house must have been here," and he waved at a hummock of sand and dead brush. For a while he said nothing, then began again, "And my great-great grandparents' house, would have been up that way a few hundred feet. Somewhere near there was a barn and a pasture where their six cows, probably a few sheep, would be grazing."

Suki sighed, "Did they have to see it being all torn up or had they left?"

"They saw, yes; they saw the first bulldozer come across their place tearing down the fences."

"So what did they do then?"

"Well, the feds loaned them one truck and driver to help them move one load, for everything they owned. A meat packer took all the settlers' animals for a song, unless they had relatives to send them to. They went to stay with family for a while. I try to imagine how they felt...I don't think I can."

Bruce was silent then, his mouth tight as he stared around at the desolation. Marta had heard the story before. She fanned herself, determined to manage, but starting to feel weak from the heat. *This must be so depressing for him, worse than he expected. Like a bombed-out war zone.*

He changed topics and tried to keep talking. "Harold's grandmother was the only one in my family with any previous farming experience. Before, most of those settlers had probably kept only a cow and some chickens and raised a kitchen garden, if anything."

"From rainy Puget Sound to a desert!"

"And created an oasis." He stared at the map, then at the sand piles. "After about a decade my family had to admit their small orchard couldn't support them. My great-grandfather was still working out. They had to borrow money for more acreage." He pointed at the map, "It was the new section right on the river where we are—ten more acres already in fruit, and a small house. Until then they were still in tents winter and summer. Below zero sometimes in winter. Above 100 often in summer. How about that? All for getting out of the city."

Suki nodded, "It was probably the same with my own family at Ringold, a couple generations later. Though they already knew how to farm."

Bruce moved on, Marta followed, each minute hotter. She thought they'd wasted their money on bug dope, as it was too hot for mosquitoes, no wind at all, and she remembered there had been breeze down by the river. But Bruce was entranced.

"Harold's grandpa decided orchards weren't his thing; he went into dairy. He found out his cows could actually find quite a bit to eat from the wild bunch grass. It's hard to imagine, just looking at it now. But he still had to have irrigation for his alfalfa for their winter feed."

He paged through Harold's memoir. "Here's what my uncle says:

'My grandfather milked his six cows, by hand of course, and at first sold sour cream down the river by steamer. It got transferred to the railroad at Pasco to go on down to Portland. That's how all the settlers' produce went. Then in 1913, the railroad branch finally came down the river, the New Town began, and everything came and went by rail.'

"I wish we could have seen it then," said Marta.

"You've seen Harold's photos. But you're right, black and white doesn't tell the story. He says this strip of green along the river was ... 'wide and long miles of blossoming orchards, vegetable rows, berries, alfalfa, and flower gardens.' But no colored photos, too bad."

Marta glanced at Suki; her face was wet too. "Aren't you hot?"

"Oh, yes, but it's so interesting." She had promised herself she'd put up with anything.

Marta shook her head, then wiped her face and whispered a curse. Bruce plucked a branch of sage and held it to his nose, then stuck it in his pocket.

"Here's more from Harold, about the orchard:

'I remember how my father loved his trees like people love their animals. He'd order samples of every new variety of apple, and cherries, peaches, cots, pears. My mother would get exasperated trying to figure out how to pack such a hodgepodge for commercial sale. But that was one of her jobs—working in the packing shed for money, and she got very good at it. My father didn't want her to, but she did it anyway.'

Marta pictured picking fruit on a day like this, then cooking on a wood stove, and felt barely able to breathe.

Suki said, "Why didn't he like it, her packing fruit?"

"Harold told me it maybe implied he couldn't properly support them himself."

Suki looked at Marta, saw she was turning pink, and frowned.

"Marta, you…maybe you should go back down by the river. I want to listen to him—for me it's a once-in a-lifetime, maybe, being here."

"It sure is—once if I live. I never can take heat." *Bruce knows.*

Bruce, oblivious, bent down to pick up a small piece of wood.

"Look at this! It's a piece of shingle. Must be from one of their buildings."

He smoothed it, turned it over, and handed it to her. She looked at the scrap. *Too sad.* She shook her head, handed it back. Bruce ambled on.

Marta said a little louder, "I want to hear more from Harold when we get back to the hotel. But can we go closer to the river now?"

Bruce half-heard her. "Okay. Oh…Harold tells about how his mother handled the heat."

'My mother knew how to survive. She'd tell the older girls to cook the noon meal while she went to the packing shed where it was cooler. I wonder now how much the women truly loved farming. But I think she and her mom were ashamed to complain. At least I never heard any of them say they hated farming.'

Bruce said, "They were Scots-Presbyterian, probably something to do with it."

Marta groaned, "Well, I can't compete with heroic Scots women. I'm going back down under the trees." She turned toward the river.

Suki looked after her, then kept following Bruce.

"What else did you hear from your family about their eviction?"

He stopped, thought for a moment. "My grandmother, and Harold's wife too, refuse to even go to these reunions. They seem to think it would honor the eviction or something. Or maybe it hurts too much. But Harold always went till this year, just had a different way of reacting. And the younger ones like me that never lived here, the eviction wasn't a big tragedy to us. Now, today, seeing this sight, I understand the ones that don't come."

Suki had rarely talked to anyone outside her family about the World War II internment camps for her people. Now with this stranger she felt an urge to open up about it.

"My family—the ones that got sent to the internment camp—some would talk about it, but most seemed to want to forget it."

Bruce looked at her. "You know, I never thought of that…a sort of a similar situation."

"Evictions…internment camps? Yes…in a way. People totally unable to refuse to go."

Marta, heading for the shade, realized how Harold had been priming Bruce for weeks for this visit. Now all these rich handed down memories were flooding out. She had never seen Bruce like this; the ugly bulldozed piles had such a powerful draw for him. For Suki too, apparently.

Bruce, tramping off again with his map, said, "I sure look forward to hearing more from the settlers."

Suki said, "Uh, Marta went down by the river."

"Oh, okay. Yeah, she's tough, but I should have been watching more. We'll go down in the shade a while."

Back under the old locust trees, he apologized, "Marta, sorry. I got carried away."

"It's okay. I know when it's too much for me." *But I don't like Suki outdoing me, and you ignoring me. You know I normally can keep up with you.*

The three waded through the brush to the river and dipped their kerchiefs in, wrung them out, and bathed their faces while watching cormorant ducks and dark water birds Suki thought were called mud hens. Now it was too hot for the blackbirds and orioles. Then they looked up to see Ike striding along the path their way looking fresh and cool.

"How was swimming?"

"Great. Cold, but just right. So, is there anything you folks especially want to see now? We've got time." He waited. "Oh yes, your friend Leon is sitting in the shade. He tripped on a root and wrenched his ankle. He says to tell you he's okay, to just keep doing whatever you're doing."

"I knew it," groaned Marta. "I needed to stay. He can't see well enough to be out in the brush."

Ike looked at their sweaty faces, "Too bad there was no real breeze this morning. Are you folks all through for now? We can go back a little early, the others say."

Bruce said. "Actually, I'd like to see the Wanapum camp that was just up river from here. Harold mentions your families quite a bit, and that they got booted out too."

"We did, yes. Well, just this stretch. There's really nothing at that camp-site to see now, but we can walk there in a few minutes. Well, it's half a mile."

"I want to see where Harold used to watch the boys spearing fish."

Marta, relieved to have an excuse, shook her head, "I'm going back to be with Leon."

Suki said, "I'll go with you guys if it's okay? And get a closer look at that reactor?"

Ike studied her. *What is her purpose anyway? Some kind of reporter? I didn't think they let them come in.*

"Well, no, you can't get a close view. But we'll be walking that way, come along."

Marta sighed, *she's going.* She watched them turn away from the shade trees, heading upriver, and hurried to catch up. The path got brushier as they went, the wild roses and Russian olives stabbing at her. *A half-mile of this.* She paused and almost turned back when she heard a shriek and a chorus of hol-lers from those ahead. *What?* She scrambled through the brush to hear Ike laughing wildly and she spotted the cause. A long, heavy-bodied, striped and spotted snake was coiled in the path, thrusting its head at him.

"Oh my god, move away!" she yelled.

Ike hooted back with delight, "Hey, it's just a bullsnake. Harmless!"

"Harmless?" Her knees were about to go.

"Yeah, don't worry, they just try to fake like they're rattlers. Hear him try-ing to make a rattling sound? You want me to catch him?"

"No, no!" Marta fought panic.

"No," Suki said after a breath, "leave him alone."

They stared at the creature as it feinted at them until it turned and slith-ered off into the brush.

"So beautiful, so full of power...wow," Suki sighed.

Marta shuddered.

"Well, here's another bit of history," laughed Bruce. "My uncle says there were never any rattlers around the orchards because the bullsnakes kept them away."

Ike nodded, "Rattlers are real poisonous, of course, so watch out where you step. What's that, Suki?"

She muttered, "Poisonous, yes. And now there's poison all around. Not just snakes."

They stared at her until she pointed toward the steam. "Nine leaking or potentially leaking reactors, right, Ike?"

Ike stared at her and nodded, "That's what they say."

Bruce said, "That's all that's here now, you think, Suki? Just poison? Yeah, but how about the river, the bluffs?"

"No...no...of course not." Suki frowned, "This river's what made it all possible wasn't it? For everyone. First good, then evil."

Ike nodded, *wow.* "I guess you could say that."

Suki walked over to the brushy slough bank, now dry. "Lots of salmon came up here, Ike?"

"Yes, and still do, in the fall, a king run. We used to catch enough to feed us all winter. And we still catch whatever we're allowed—odd isn't it? Right by the reactors is the only place left on the whole river where there's a lot of spring Chinook spawning. The runs dropped down long ago, and fishing here was illegal, even for Indians for a while. Then a white man with some feelings went to the Legislature, said for godssake let the thirty-six Wanapum left here have some salmon for their personal use. And they did."

Bruce nodded. "That was in the 1930s, Harold writes. I was surprised to read the runs were in such bad shape already by then. Almost all we can do now is raise them in hatcheries."

"Why such bad shape?" asked Marta.

"Well, almost a hundred canneries down by the mouth might have something to do with it."

They started walking again, and Marta, finally feeling calmed down, said, "So, Suki, you're going to write about all this, bullsnake and all? What you read in the news doesn't really capture this place does it?"

"No, it sure doesn't."

Ike mused that this year's reunion had surely brought in a different sort of crowd, even more interesting than usual.

CHAPTER 5

PROTESTERS IN NO MAN'S LAND

JASON SAT SHIELDED by some willow brush on an island by the west bank of the Columbia in the closed area. He had come down the river by kayak from his home just above Wolf Rapids two days before, portaging past the rapids, then slipping down the public east side to pass most of the reactors, then crossing over to the west side. Portaging was harder than he expected, though the kayak was light, as the old trail was little used and rough in places. He had decided not to run the rapids; this wasn't a trip for thrills. He had set up camp on this off-limit brushy island, near where his people used to camp every fall and spear for king salmon. It was also right near one of the defunct Hanford reactors. His idea was to be alone and think, and to decide if he was right about some things—or his grandfather was. But that train of thought kept being swept aside by thoughts of the young man, Arni, and what had happened to him just a few miles from where he sat. And that led to thinking about the Hanford Plant itself.

Esau, Jason's grandfather, had scolded him. "Let Arni be. Let his spirit rest. You can't change what happened. You had a good scholarship; go back to college."

He was angry with Jason for dropping out when only a sophomore. The boy thought his grandfather should go himself then, if it was so important. Which was a silly thought considering that Esau was over seventy. But if he could just sit a few days in Jason's bonehead pre-algebra class, the remedial English comp, and the U.S. history taught from the whites' point of view from Columbus on down, and see how he liked his days. And years of the same, all the general courses you had to take before you could think about putting your foot in the door of Fisheries Management or any specialty you really wanted. And all that time salmon runs getting worse.

"Grandpa, the fisheries are being ruined, and Ike says more restrictions are coming down. Now they say the plant waste stored near the river is going to start leaking toward it, or already is. No one likes any of it, but what are they doing about it? Talk, talk, talk."

Esau knew it was true. "Talking is what they do, so go back to college; learn to talk to them."

Jason could see the steam drifting up from the reactor, but he doubted anyone would be along to bother him if he was careful. Any legal sport fishermen were across the river. He had carried his kayak up into the willows, stowed his camping outfit in a little opening further in, peeled down to his shorts, and gone back to sit on the bank and stare at the looming bluffs. From habit he also watched for king salmon moving upstream. Right here was one place on the Columbia where there could be kings to see now. Not like the lower river where he'd been a few times as a kid, everybody arguing, whites accusing Indians of selling a catch and seizing their nets. They'd needed to go find another net to borrow. What improvement was there since? Not much according to Ike and Esau.

"It's the dams," Esau told him. "They cause most of the trouble, and hatcheries don't cure it, they're not natural, can't cure anything,"

But right here in the Hanford Reach you could still see spawning wild kings. Esau said this stretch was what the whole river was like once, and that was why Jason liked to come down here to think—the natural river. Yet, so weird, radioactive waste might be only a few hundred feet away, and doom to the salmon if that waste made it to the river. Which was only a matter of time, though they said they were storing it a few miles further back.

The river was where his questions floated, and the answers too, he hoped. But now after two days on the island Jason didn't have the answers he wanted. One more day and he would need to leave, as he would run out of drinking water. *Don't drink from the river below the reactors, Jason!* In the old days everyone would know where the springs were, but he didn't; he hadn't listened, didn't care then. Now, trying to get his mind quiet, to get some spiritual guidance, he kept having angry thoughts: college bullshit, the steaming reactor nearby, what happened to Arni, why he'd dropped out. Maybe he couldn't think well because he was too close to one of the reactors. He might have to move his camp.

He thought about the salmon managers. Finally, a while back, they had quit blaming the Indians and admitted that they needed a new strategy. And then, amazing, they'd invited the tribes to the planning table. A little late, the invitation, but his uncle Ike and Esau had gone. Now the managers were finally blaming their own policies for much of the loss, but Ike said that though so many groups cared about salmon for their own reasons, few of them agreed on how to restore them. So talk, argue, go home.

Jason was well aware that Ike, as well as Esau, was disgusted with him for dropping out of college. *But I've learned a lot from them, not much from the Pilgrim Fathers.* When they could have just listened to his grandparents, or any Wanapum over twelve. Yet, Esau always sang the same song. *"Jason, go get those degrees and come back and help your people. Help the salmon."* Like put it all on him to solve. Great.

He finished the remaining supply of his grandmother's jerky, chucked the stale crackers, scratched last night's mosquito bites, and crept over to where there was a cutbank and less brush, and he could lie and look down into a deep clear channel and wait to see a king. Stretched out there, close to the clear moving water, it was hard to believe the evil just behind him, across the dried slough. But it was too hot already, too hot even for bugs, and although he saw a few white fish and carp slipping by, any salmon weren't moving. *Later then.* He undid his braid, swished his head in the water, redid the braid, and went back up to his camp. He found a little shade under the willows, pulled on his clothes, and went to sleep.

Jason woke when he heard voices. He sat up carefully. No one should be here in no man's land. They must have come across the river from the east side. He crept down close to the shore. Sure enough, downstream up on the bank was a kayak, much longer than his, and a two-holer. He'd never seen one before. Nice. Well, it wasn't plant security on his ass; these people were as illegal as he was. But he'd come here to think, and their voices were disturbing. Now he saw a man and woman come down and carry the kayak up into the brush. *But they can't camp here, they're going to bring the guards down on us!*

He thought he might as well leave tonight before there was trouble. His whole plan was obviously not meant to be. He would have to slip on down the river to the road at Ringold and use someone's phone to call home. Somebody would agree to drive down and pick him and Ike's kayak up; even if they were mad they would. For now, he should sneak over and see what the two kayakers were up to. He crept along near the willows to where he could watch them through the brush as they set up a tiny camp stove. It occurred to him that they might bring down security before he could pack up and slip away. But maybe they didn't know it was a closed area. He decided the best thing to do was to go explain to them that they should paddle back over to the east side—or get arrested. Either they left, and quietly, or he would. He shook off his nervousness and started strolling toward their camp, singing some notes to alert them. He flushed a pheasant that flew up squawking and alerted the woman fiddling with the stove. She stood up and saw Jason. She was a young, light-haired white woman, tanned and muscular.

"Hello!" She didn't act scared, but not welcoming either.

"Hello, I was just up the shore a ways, and I saw you come in."

"Jeff," she called, but softly, "we've got company! Uh...we didn't see you!"

"No, my kayak's back in the brush. You know, you're not supposed to be here...we're not. You know that, right?"

She stared at him. "So if we're not supposed to be here, why are you?"

"I was thinking of leaving...you aren't staying long?"

The man appeared. He was Jason's size, about his age, and just as tanned. He didn't say anything.

Jason tried again, "I've been traveling down the river, same as you I guess. But maybe you better go back over to the other side, the public side.... I think I'll leave soon."

He walked up the bank to where their kayak was half-hidden. Both of them immediately walked up there with him.

"I was just going to look at your kayak, never seen that kind before."

The man answered. "It's a traditional Aluutiq design. From the Aleutian Islands, you know, up by Alaska."

Jason forgot his irritation. "Wow, Aluutiq. Can I look at how it's made?"

"Ahhh, no, it's not on exhibit, sorry. So when are you leaving did you say?"

Their suspicions annoyed him. *They should leave, not me.* "Oh, this evening maybe."

The two looked at each other.

Jason tried one more time, "Are you doing a little fishing? There's some nice kings on the other side."

"Yeah, we just wanted to see this side, you know."

"Well, you could get us all arrested. You should leave, or bring the guards down."

No answer.

"Well…I guess I'll go back up to my camp. See you later."

"Yeah, okay."

Jason felt them watching him as he walked back up the shore. *Real friendly white people.* But he didn't feel like being friendly either, not here, not now. They seemed nervous, like they were up to something; no peaceful time for him for sure. Later he crept back down through the brush to where he could hear them having an intense conversation, but couldn't catch whole sentences. Nothing about fishing, or traveling. He heard more than once "plant" and "fence", their tones those of trying to work out an irritating problem. He waited a while, but he didn't hear sounds of packing up, rather, sounds of getting ready to stay. *Great.* Sure enough, soon all was quiet, and it was dark enough for him to start on down the river as he'd planned. But he was too curious; he wanted to know what they had in mind, so he went back to his own camp to sleep. Once more the island was quiet, the way he'd expected. Just coyotes singing on the bluffs.

In the early morning Jason woke to hear the kayakers were still there. How long would it be before a plant employee taking a morning stroll crossed over to the island and noticed them? Disgusted, he sneaked to their camp to listen again. The same conversation was going on, not about kayaking or fishing, but arguing. *"How do you know it will work?"* and *"What if we can't get away down the river fast enough?"*

Not good, not good. I'll wait them out.

◦─▣ ▣─◦

Ike stopped his clients at the upper end of the slough. They were quite near one of the reactors but only steam was visible because of a rise and a bend in the channel. One of the campsites had been here, but he saw what he had expected—a lot of brush, grass, and gravel. He'd never seen the camp in the days when it was full of people, horses, wagons, tents, children, dogs, racks of fish drying, canoeists out in the river balancing to spear a king. *There's nothing here now to show these folks, just a peaceful scene—if you ignore the damn reactor steam.*

Bruce gazed around, then pointed, "My great-uncle Harold says there should be some pits along here where your people stored their supplies when they wanted to travel farther downriver."

"Probably right over there."

They pushed through the brush again looking for signs of humans.

"Ah, here's a hollow in the bank," Ike said. "Must be an old pit. Yeah, there's a piece of plank sticking out."

Marta came to look. *Another place with only an old plank left.*

Bruce said. "Harold as a boy used to walk up here at night and watch your boys out in the river spearing fish. He was so envious of them."

Marta said to Ike, "I read somewhere that your people chose sites at rapids for villages because it was harder for enemies to approach."

"Yes, but my people had many settlements and fishing sites all along the river, clear down to the mouth of the Snake."

"But is it true that it was Smohalla that chose the Priest Rapids place for that safety reason?"

Ike laughed. "Everyone wants to know about Smohalla. That does sound like something he would think of. Stay away from the white man, as far as you can get. An early non-violent protester."

"Didn't turn out well in the end. Do you know any stories about him?"

He gave her a thoughtful grin. "Are you an anthropologist by any chance?"

She laughed. "Does it show? Are you tired of them?"

He shrugged, "Some elders sure are. Maybe you could talk to my uncle Esau. He doesn't follow that Dreamer religion, but he sure knows history. Come up to the Rapids and he just might talk to you, can't promise. So...how about you, Bruce, are you an anthropologist too?"

"Naw, I work at a fish hatchery. And I'm not a manager, so don't get after me. I just do maintenance."

"Hah! Maybe you're tired of us tribal reps—always giving advice."

"You guys?" Bruce laughed. "It's livelier at least then."

Marta said, "Did your people resent the orchard settlers?"

"Well, not them especially. They weren't squatters; they'd bought the land from speculators. Where'd the speculators get it from? That's the story! You know, so many white people had already moved into the area before the fruit growers arrived. *I might as well take the opportunity for a little history for this anthropologist. See if I can do it like Esau!* The gold miners, the cattlemen, the sheepherders, the railroad, the homesteaders, the land speculators—all those people came before anyone tried serious orchards. And, well, that steam rising over there tells you the next bunch."

Marta waited for him to say more. But he turned to stare off into the brush. Neither Bruce nor Suki picked up the topic, though Suki recognized it. Marta wiped the sweat off her face another time and sighed.

"How did your people take this heat? How do they now?"

"You get used to it. But in the old days they weren't here at this time of year. They were up in the Cascades picking huckleberries and drying deer meat."

"Hey!" Suki said, "There's a guy coming this way!"

"We should be all right," said Ike. "This area is open for the reunion." *Oh no, it's Jason.* The young man walked up to them, glance around at the group, and turned to Ike.

"Hi, Ike. What are you doing here?"

"What are you doing here? More the question."

"I came down here to be alone and mobs descend on me."

49

"You mean the people down at the landing? You know I'm driving bus this year again for the settler's reunion. I have my pass, what about you?"

"Oh, I'm just looking around."

Ike touched his shoulder, and motioned him to come away from the others.

"What are you thinking of? They'll be really watching with so many people around."

"I forgot all about the reunion."

"Where's my kayak?"

"Over on the island, I'm camped over there. Don't worry, I'm leaving. I would be already gone, but…there's something strange going on."

"How's that?"

"There's a couple people over there, and they're up to something, seems like."

"They're probably just fishermen; they sneak over sometimes. You'd better get out of there! Go down the river and I'll come pick you up. Tonight."

Jason was quiet. "Well, maybe you're right…. No, Ike, they're up to something, not fishing. I had a look at their gear when they were sleeping. They're not fishermen; one flimsy fishing rod for show."

Ike saw his nephew as exasperating as usual and thought that probably hanging out down here had to do with the long-missing Arni. But he wasn't going to mention it.

"You need to pack up and leave tonight."

"A-h-h, okay. Do you have some spare drinking water, then? I'm about out."

"You shouldn't be down here, not even knowing where the springs are, huh? Forget the kayakers, they're nothing but trouble for you. Here…" And Ike dug a water bottle out of his pack. Jason thanked him for the water, nodded to the others, and turned back toward the island. Ike was frowning as he rejoined the others.

Marta said, "What did he mean, that kayakers are up to something?"

"Um…please forget you saw that young man, okay? He has no business being in this area. Only folks with a visitor's pass. But now we need to go back. Older people will be tired by now and ready to flop at the hotel."

They hiked back to the town site, mainly in silence, Bruce cursing to himself quietly.

"I couldn't see the plant," Suki commented to Ike at last, "but I could feel it. It has… a very negative aura. But I do feel there are good spirits around here too."

He caught her eye, nodded.

Marta, again suffering from heat, but keeping up, said, "Ike, I'm really glad I came, but why don't they have these reunions in the spring when it's cooler?"

"You're right, they should, in the spring. It's spectacular then, everything in bloom, all colors, for a few weeks. But that's the problem, the scientists say. There would be people tramping all over to look at the native plants then, and they're too fragile. They say there's plants that might soon be listed as endangered, about to disappear."

"And some things that need to disappear," muttered Suki, and he heard her and gave her another look but she didn't return it.

They found the rest of bus group waiting in the shade of the tall poplars near the landing. It was close to noon. Ike counted the group; three were still out somewhere. Bruce went right over to Leon to examine his foot.

"It's a sprain I think. You need to go soak it in the river, get it cold. Here, let me help you down there."

As Bruce helped Leon hop along, Ike watched. *I should have thought of that. He's a vet; was a medic maybe.*

Then the crowd saw a big kayak carrying two people coming around the south end of the island, headed toward them. They watched while the paddlers landed expertly.

"I thought they told us no one could come on this side except on the bus," a settler called to Ike. But Ike was already down at the water.

"Nice kayak! Are you folks all right?"

"We're fine," said the woman. "Why are there so many people here?"

"It's the annual settlers' reunion. They get special passes to come in once a year. You know you have to have passes to be on this side, and just for this reunion. And coming in by bus."

The two looked at each other. "We didn't know about any reunion," said the man.

Bruce walked over by the kayak. "Wow, look at this, Marta!"

Several others now came down to look at the kayak, and the paddlers hovered by it.

Ike said, "I'm sorry, but I think you'd better go back to the other side, before you get in trouble, or all of us. The guards may think you have some connection to this group. You could get the reunion coordinators in trouble."

The two stood by the kayak and said nothing. Suki came closer to Marta and muttered,

"The young man was right. These two do have something going on."

Ike waited for some acknowledgement of his point. After a pause, the young man said,

"We were just about to go down river. We wonder, though, do you happen to have any extra drinking water you could spare?"

Ike nodded, *second time in an hour,* looked around, and two people came forward and poured water into the kayakers' bottles. Bruce was bending over the kayak to look in the interior when the woman stepped in front of him and said, "Excuse us, we'll be going now. Thanks for the water."

Ike watched them push off and paddle back around the point of the island. *They are not heading down river.* But now he had to get the travelers back to the hotel.

"Wait, Ike, I want to jump in the river!" Marta cried.

Suki said, "Let's do it. Just a dip?"

"Sorry, I signed a contract and agreed to some things. Like no swimming."

"But you went in."

"I live here. They have to give a little."

"What's the problem," said Bruce. "Radioactive?" He looked out into the current.

"No, I don't think so. The junk isn't in the river yet, at least so they say. Just seeping that way. No, it's a matter of liability. You know, overheated old-timers, cold river."

Bruce stared out into the clear ripples, *so deceptive*. Suddenly, out of nowhere, but it wasn't from nowhere, Bruce had the vision, not the first time...*a child's corpse... floating down past*. With a cry he rushed toward the shore and saw it had caught on a vine. He reached out to the vine to free it, and saw there was no vine, no child, just a four-foot piece of drift wood floating by. Rage welled up in him, transferred to invaders of this desert river, and he forced himself to swallow his horror down. *Why was I on that other river? What did I think I was doing? What am I doing here? Why is that reactor still here steaming?*

"Bruce?" It was Marta, his anchor.

"Liability? Uh, yes, sure, liability.... Ha, a little late for that, I'd say." He rubbed his eyes. Ike stared at Bruce. *Is he okay?* Just then Leon came limping up the bank, leaning on a wobbly stick, in totally wet jeans and t-shirt, grinning.

"Hey, I wasn't swimming. I was soaking my ankle and I fell in!"

Marta laughed, it was so like him, her mentor. She looked at Bruce; saw he was back in touch. The last of the tour people straggled in, ready to return to air conditioning.

Ike called, "Okay, to the bus, really, folks. They'll eat all the food if we're late."

He checked on Bruce another time, saw that he was walking steadily and had offered the limping Leon an arm. He knew Louise would scold him some for letting an elder get injured. But Leon didn't seem like a guy who would sue, and they had all signed releases. As they waited in line to climb aboard the bus, Marta whispered aside to Bruce,

"Seems like you and I aren't the only ones angry about the Hanford Plant. I don't suppose there are too many Sukis around, but I am curious how many of the settler families agree with Orville."

Bruce turned with a frown, "Yeah, I'd like to know! And here I promised Harold I would concentrate on getting responses to his memoir. But my god, now that I've been to the old place, what am I supposed to do? Just forget what I saw?"

Marta saw his look of pain.

"Total devastation, that's all—except for the bluffs! Jeez, Marta, what did Harold expect from me? How did my folks stand it? I don't know how!"

CHAPTER 6

HISTORY LESSONS BY BUS

MARTA GRABBED THE seat up front by Ike, Bruce and Suki right behind her, but Leon went to sit by Roger. As soon as the bus was on the main road, Marta began to ease questions to Ike about the Wolf Rapids community. He didn't mind; it was part of his tour job to be ready with a little history. He told her what he knew about how some of the Wanapum had ended up there, that of all the mid-Columbia shorelines, the villages at Priest and Wolf Rapids were what they were able to hold onto. Many of the Dreamers had refused to go to the Yakima reservation, taking their chances at surviving with no government help, and no government bosses—for a time.

Marta saw that Bruce was staring off in space. *Well, who could blame him.* She would just go on talking with Ike.

"Is it true that Smohalla said something like this: *'My young men will never work. Men who seek wisdom must be able to dream and men who work can't dream.'*"

He laughed. "Something like that, yeah, famous words they claim are his."

"But all people have to work."

"Well, he meant not work for wages for someone else. Be independent, not servants. But, you know, they did have to work for cash to survive in a cash economy."

Bruce broke in, "Yup, like they picked strawberries for cash alongside my great-grandmother."

Ike nodded, "Cash was important. For a while we had quite a good mixed economy. In the twenties most families still left Wolf Rapids every spring, and some did stop at White Bluffs for the strawberries. They used that cash to load up on supplies, then they stored what they didn't need at their camp-ground we just saw, and went down to fish the eel and salmon runs at the horn of the Yakima River. They dried those, stored a lot, then worked in the hops for cash, then went over to the Cascades and hunted, picked berries, and dried enough for winter. Then they came back through Yakima and picked hops for more cash late summer."

Ike was always glad for a chance to tell a little of the region, and Bruce could see how pleased Marta was. They hadn't known they'd have a tour driver with so much historical information, and he broke out of his gloom.

"Oh, and then they must have gone back up to White Bluffs, is that right? For the fall Chinook run, when Harold watched the boys spearing fish."

"Right. And then home to their winter camps."

"Sounds like a good life, an interesting life. Impressive, the way your people adapted to such a mixed economy!" said Marta.

"Yeah, it worked for quite a while. But it was only a few families, not hun-dreds, or it wouldn't have worked, you know. Most went to the reservation. And it wasn't perfect here. They had to feed their horses with no land legally theirs, and cattle herds taking over. And they got caught in the epidemics like everyone. And their kids didn't have a school for a time."

Suki, listening to all this, broke in, "So how did your people feel when they were first told they must go to a reservation?"

Ike glanced over at her, was quiet a moment, then dropped his voice, "Well, maybe I shouldn't say this, but, well, how do you think they felt? How did your people feel about being sent to those camps during the war?"

Silence.

Oh-oh. Marta winced and quickly steered them back to her topic. "Do you think Smohalla was the influence for that passive resistance? I mean refusing to sign the treaty, refusing to go to the reservation. And the Ghost Dance."

"Well, he wasn't the only one. The original Sohappy, their chief, was also a Dreamer. Other tribes had Dreamers too. Maybe we already had a stubborn streak that way, and Smohalla developed it into a religion. I'm not the right person to ask."

Marta glanced at Bruce with a smile. *But he doesn't mind at all being asked questions. Well, he gets paid to. But why did he pick on Suki?...Maybe he didn't mean it that way.*

"So what are the Wanapum doing now?" she continued.

"There's just a few of us now up the river. The rest gradually moved over to the rez. And in my folks' generation some got talked into moving to cities for training and work, and became urban Indians. And some are still trying to fish, down on the lower Columbia."

"Yeah, good luck to them," said Bruce, "considering the success we've had restoring those runs. I remember Harold saying that one of the families fishing right near my folk's place got famous later. The Sohappys."

"Oh, that's David Sohappy. Very active in the fish-ins in the '70s."

Suki said, "But the fish-ins worked, didn't they? You did finally get back a good share of the fishing quota, so I've read."

"Yes, we did. So now the battle is to save the salmon themselves. But not with fish-ins, more at the conference table."

"I know, I'm taking a class in salmon ecology. Do you go to those conferences?"

"A lot, too many."

Bruce said, "Tell me about it. At the hatchery where I work there's sure a lot of frustration."

That was worth a laugh from Ike. Marta was enjoying the conversation even as it got off topic from Smohalla. Ike was interested that Suki was taking the class. Leon, too, had moved forward, happy to listen with no pressure to analyze it or take notes. It all stopped when an official looking car came up behind the bus and honked. Ike looked in the mirror and pulled over. *Oh boy.* He thought of Jason and the kayakers and how their activity could affect his tour job. A uniformed man walked over to the bus door and Ike opened it, recognizing the community relations man from the Hanford plant.

"Hi, Chuck."

"Hello, Ike. Have a good tour? Good. I won't keep you—I know these folks are tired. Will you do me a favor, though, and tell your own people, once again, they are not to hunt in this closed area, including on the west side of the road." He gave a polite smile.

"Well, you know we dispute that." Ike smiled back.

"I'm just doing my job. Pass on the message for me?"

Ike shrugged and kept his smile. Messages like that weren't his job.

"So, Ike, how's work going on your tourist attraction up at the Rapids?"

"Very well. Come take a look sometime."

"Thanks, I want to. I will." Chuck nodded and walked back to his car.

"They aren't going to stop people hunting, are they?" asked Marta.

"I never heard that question."

Marta hid her smile. For a while the three left him in silence to drive. The miles of brush stretched on. Bruce mused that what Harold had written about was just one chapter in the Columbia's history. There were thousands of years before that he hadn't really thought much about. The family had always had so many of their own stories to tell. He looked forward to going up to Wolf Rapids with Marta.

After Ike had picked up the other passengers at the Hanford town site and got them settled, Suki got up nerve to come forward and squat by the driver's seat and start the questions again.

"So, how many of the lost salmon runs are caused by the active nuclear plant do you think?"

"Well...maybe none right now. There's nothing leaking there yet. The old reactors are the problem. They will be leaking if they aren't already. But these salmon here in the Reach are right now the healthiest wild king stock in the river. Funny, huh?"

Bruce shook his head, "But you know it's a question of for how long? The radioactive waste is stored...what, ten miles away? And the tanks are corroding. There was grumbling about it at the reunion."

"There usually is."

"If that junk reaches the river it won't just kill fish," Suki said in a tone of finality. "And to answer your earlier question, Ike, about how people felt? My relatives down at Ringold and other Japanese Americans near here that got sent to the internment camps—I've never gotten to talk much to them. But I can imagine it would be like my own parents, how they felt."

"Uhh, I'm sorry, Suki, my smart-ass sounding question. I didn't mean it that way. I mean, I was serious. But your Ringold relatives never came back after the war. My family wondered why?"

"Well, all their trees had died of course. It was too much to bear, I think. And also because they got threats even before the war, from the Klan, you know, the Ku Klux Klan? 'Asians Not Wanted'. Stay on the other side of the river. So, after the war was over, well, it wasn't quite over. Not everyone acted that way; maybe most would have welcomed them back, but they didn't want to deal with that again."

That was news to Ike. He could hear the disgust in her voice and wondered how he had missed this for the tour bus history he'd put together.

"I hadn't heard that part, about the Klan."

"Well, you might add that to your talks to tour groups—the eviction of that group too? Almost two-thirds of the people that went to the internment camps were US citizens."

Silence swallowed them all again. Ike could feel her steaming.

After a moment she said, "It's okay, Ike. You know, I'm sure, that a lot of people are angry about the Hanford Plant. Like the downwinders, those people living downwind of the plant that have developed that unusual rate of many kinds of cancer. And they believe it's from radioactive iodine released into the air, and not by accident, and with no warnings. Is that true? It's what came out after the Freedom of Information Act, right?"

"That's what they say." *Do I want to be quoted in an article somewhere? Who is she? How does she know all this?*

Bruce felt his stomach clenching up. Uncle Harold hadn't prepared him for this sort of conversation. Marta did find more questions to ask about the Wanapum, but Bruce and Suki were silent. After a while Ike told his passengers that if there were seats left over, and they wanted to come tomorrow, they could. Several said they would, and lighter conversations started up again. Marta wondered about the settlers and descendants riding with them who came back year after year, no matter what pain they'd gone through. And the ones that had refused to come, ever, like Harold's wife. They didn't even want to see the bluffs? *I don't have a place like this that holds my heart...but what if I did? Would I want to be told I could go visit it for three hours once a year, and then sit around and exchange memories of the good old days?*

Marta thought the stories about pre-atomic White Bluffs were fascinating, even a potential study in community development, organization, and loss. And it was a history oddly ignored by academia as far as she knew. Bruce had been able to dig up very little information in print about the settlers that had been evicted for the Hanford Plant: mainly from one book by a settler descendant that drew mainly on weekly news from old newspapers. The rest of Bruce's information was all from his uncle's memoir, saved family letters, and family storytelling. How strange, she thought, that so little had been written about the evicted people. Instead, people had researched and published the history of the years after the eviction, starting in 1943: the building of the atomic plant, its thousands of workers, their town, Richland, and the plutonium they produced. And lately the dilemma of the radioactive waste and the downwinder charges had made the newspapers frequently. There were layers and layers of stories on this river.

Bruce broke into her thoughts, "It's odd, but isn't it just about this day in August that we dropped that bomb on Nagasaki? Harold told me some people that come to this reunion aren't so worried about the radioactive waste. They're proud of the role Hanford played, and like to take credit for winning the war. As if it wasn't our men we lost and all the other sacrifices, it was all the damn bombs."

She wasn't surprised at his tone; Bruce was open with her in his anger and disgust with more recent wars and regime changes. *So, he's been thinking about the reunion timing, too, that maybe it's not just the fragility of plants in the spring.* Suki said nothing but gave Bruce a long look. Leon, too, was quiet. None of the other passengers had anything to say on the topic, but perhaps they hadn't heard Bruce. After a few miles of silence, Ike slowed the bus to a stop and turned in his seat. Everyone looked up; some knew what was coming.

"I will take just a minute, folks. This is my little time on the tour, my part of the story here. Most of you know me. I'm Ike Jackson. My people are Wanapum Indians, a small tribe that lived on this stretch of the Columbia.

Our leaders refused to sign the treaty back in the mid-1800s, so we never got a reservation. To them it was impossible to sign away land that didn't belong to them to sign away, that didn't belong to anyone. You know—we just lived on it and used the resources of what we believed was God's land, a gift to us.

"Each time I take this job driving for this group, I think what memories you all have. I enjoy hearing them. You swam in the river as kids, worked in the orchards, and rode the horse, if you had one. You went to school here, played sports, got married here, and had kids here. You had a real community, a real life. I hear all about it from you at the reunions and when I drive out here. It's probably hard to find a community like that anywhere nowadays in such a beautiful place."

Roger, who'd heard the speech before, had his ear cupped by his hand to catch it all, and broke in, "Yes, you're right."

"So what I want to say is I respect how you feel about being evicted. I never saw these orchards but I have seen them over on the Yakima, so I can picture it. It was a fabulous scene, all a gift of the river. But I want to say also that when you look at those bluffs shining over there, and that great river, and this desert that looks empty to outsiders…but most of you know that really it's full of life…that my people lived here too. For thousands of years, probably way over 10,000. This is where they were, all along this river, clear down to the mouth of the Snake. Their biggest gift from the river was the salmon. We too, had to give it up, before you did, many, many fishing sites we depended on…almost all of them. And then gave up more at the same time you folks gave up your orchards."

Behind them, Marta heard a sarcastic call from the back of the bus: "And then, Ike, we had another fabulous gift from the river—the fabulous Hanford Plant."

And Dorothy's answer, "Orville, take it easy."

And her spouse's comeback, "It's part of the story isn't it?" He went on, "And you do have a place up at Wolf Rapids, after all, and your people did have the choice of going to the Yakama reservation. My folks got a piddling few dollars from the government for fifteen acres of bearing orchard, no choice. And sued to get a penny more. Highway robbery! No choice! And by our own government."

"I don't think the tragedy was about money," Roger said. "And thanks, Ike, for reminding us." He always thanked Ike when he took the bus ride.

Orville growled back, "Of course it wasn't just about money, I didn't mean that." Then he got the last word in. "Ike, I know what you say is true. But at least some people remember that you Indians got a raw deal. No one even remembers about us."

Ike looked as if he might say more, but instead nodded at Orville, always sure to get his message in, started up the bus, and they moved off down the road. Leon, who had picked up every word, sat back. *Whew.* Everyone else was silent. They moved on through the sagebrush-covered miles. Conversation began again in the back. Then Suki muttered as if to herself.

"Three evictions and two massacres. Quite a score."

*Massacres...*what did she mean, wondered Marta. *The Yakima War? And what else?* She wasn't going to ask now. The bus stayed mainly silent as they rolled into Richland, but many of the riders, including Orville and Dorothy, gave Ike thanks as they climbed off.

Back in the hotel, Marta did ask Suki, "What did you mean on the bus, about two massacres? I guessed maybe the Yakima War was one? What other?"

Suki stared at her, mouth tight. "You're so close to it you can step on it, Marta. Like a rattlesnake, it could bite you."

Marta felt scolded. She looked at Leon, standing by her, but he looked straight ahead. *It could bite me, two massacres...oh, of course.*

She wasn't used to being stupid and didn't know how to admit to it. Instead she nodded,

"Oh right, the bombing. Yes, it could surely be called that." She went on to ask Suki how she'd liked Ike's speech.

"It was good. I'd have liked it even better if he'd mentioned what I said, about the Japanese Americans that also got evicted. But I guess that would be too much in one message for a busload of tourists."

"But most of them aren't really tourists."

"Yes, they're people being nostalgic, or doing a roots exercise...like me. It was a good speech anyway. Ike is good at it. Too bad they can't clone him for all the bus tours through used-to-be Indian country."

Marta gave a surprised laugh. *Who is she anyway?*

⟶▪◉ ◉▪⟵

Ike drove his pickup back to Wolf Rapids that afternoon, planning to do the tour again the next day. *I'd better be prepared for more in-depth questions than usual.* But a small girl ran up and gave him a phone message. He read it and went looking for his uncle Esau. He found the elder sitting under a brush sun-screen watching three young men working on the roof of the new tule reed meeting house. The wind had torn a small section loose.

"How was bus driving?"

"Not bad. Some interesting folks wanted to walk up to the old campground at White Bluffs. A young guy named Bruce Wilder remembered his family having the orchard right south of it. He said his great-uncle told him of watching a boy spearing fish—David Sohappy, Bruce thought. He knew about him."

"Our claim to fame besides Smohalla."

"Oh yes, and the woman with him is an anthropologist who wants to talk about Smohalla. I passed her off to you. She'll be up in a couple days."

"Nephew, you know I'm tired of talking about Smohalla. I'll talk about Sohappy."

"Well, will you anyway? Because we need to encourage visitors to this project here, or the young people will lose interest. They can't all be heroes, Uncle."

They watched the young men working on the roof, stopping often to wipe off sweat.

Esau motioned, "I tried to tell them to not use nails, that it's supposed to be traditional. They said okay."

"So what are they using—doesn't sound like twisted roots."

"Big staples and screws." They laughed together, and Ike turned to the topic he dreaded.

"Also, I saw Jason."

Esau frowned, "Where? He said he was going kayaking over on the other side."

"Nope. He's camped right there on the island by our old campground. I told him to get his butt out of there."

Esau sighed, and pounded the dirt with his fist. "Is this about that boy Arni again? I'm tired of the spooky stuff. Such a smart kid, and acting so dumb. Is he okay?"

"Right now, yes. But there's a couple kayakers down there planning some kind of protest or something, he thinks. So he didn't want to leave. What if they talk him into something really dumb?"

"Maybe you should borrow a boat and go give him a good push downstream?"

"I sure would, but I just got a message about a meeting tomorrow that I forgot. They're planning a big lawsuit, you know. So, Uncle, I really have to go if you won't. Anyway, I need to behave on this tour job I've got; need to just stick to my bus in the closed area."

After a minute of watching the workers, Esau said, "No, I am not going to the meetings anymore. Well, maybe I'll walk down in the morning, and give him that push he needs. You can give me a ride to the turn-off."

"No way, it's too long a hike down to the island. How long since you walked that far?"

"I'll take my time. And maybe do some rabbit and grouse snaring."

"Wait, and I'll go with you."

"No, there'll be more follow-up after that meeting, there always is. No, you stay there. I'm going to look for him."

Ike, sighed. "You remember where the spring is? Yes? Uncle, you be careful, won't you?"

CHAPTER 7

PEACHES INTO PLUTONIUM

WAITERS WERE PREPARING the conference room for a buffet lunch when the bus arrived at the hotel and the passengers clambered off. Marta called to Leon that she'd see him in a few minutes and raced Bruce to their shower. Elena, the woman Leon and others had found so interesting, was one of the last off the bus. She walked with Leon as he limped into the lobby.

"I'm Elena, and you are Leon? I'm sorry you got hurt—is it painful?"

"It'll be okay. I just need to ice it."

"I can massage it for you?"

"Really? That'd be very nice, but...uh...not in the conference room, I don't think."

"In your room? Or mine?"

"Well, uh...maybe later, eh?" He tried to place her accent; he'd heard it before, he knew.

"Whatever you wish."

They reached the stairs, Leon feeling bewildered by her attention. *Asian, but where? What a beautiful woman.* She saw his confusion and smiled.

"I am a healer, well, that is what I do. A shaman. You understand?"

"Oh. Oh, I see. Thanks so much for offering."

She stared at him in a searching way. "You know that someone died out there?"

"What?"

"No, no, I do not mean today, but not long, long ago. I could feel it."

"Oh."

"Well, this whole place needs healing. It was beautiful up by great bluffs, but...."

"It needs a healing, yes, I'm sure you're right."

"You do not want help upstairs? No. I will see you later, then."

Leon wondered about what she'd said, that someone had died in the closed area. But of course many people had died over the eons. There could be an old Indian burial ground right near where she'd walked. *Another Kennewick Man to argue over, god forbid.* He stood and watched her as she went on up and thought the last few minutes were as interesting as the bus ride. He was glad he had taken time to trim his beard that morning. He realized he didn't know anymore how to talk to a woman like Elena, a woman with such powerful charisma. A shaman, a healer, she said. *Heal me, Elena!*

As Marta came out of the small shower stall, Bruce was waiting to get in, looking at the piece of shingle he had picked up. She toweled her hair and tossed out the question to see how he was handling it all.

"How does it feel now to have been right there? Your ancestral place?"

He smoothed the dry wood. "How does it feel? Well, what do you think?...Overwhelmed is the word right now. And damned angry at what was done to them. I wish Harold had been with us. He could have pointed out so much more!"

"But you can come back next year with him."

"And I'm going to."

"Good. I'm so glad we came; I could see you filling in pictures in your head when you looked at those old trees, and that piece of rope, and that shingle."

"I'm sorry that we about cooked you out there. I didn't know how it would affect me, being right there. So powerful, Mart."

"I survived, didn't I? Not the first time I've survived your adventures, right?"

Going on down to the conference room, Marta caught Suki and wanted to ask her the same question: how was it for you? But she decided that would be touchy, and instead changed her comment to how she felt herself.

"Wow, what a sight, those bluffs! What an experience, eh? And I'm full of questions for the settlers now."

"Yes, and I think I want to go back tomorrow if there's room on the bus."

"Uh…it was wonderful, but in 100 degrees? Once was enough for me."

Bruce came down the stairs bringing the memoir, and was about to follow them in when one of the settlers came out of the hall and turned his way. It was the man who'd made the vulgar remarks about Elena. *Shit, I don't want to talk to this guy.*

"So you're Harold's nephew, great-nephew I guess?"

"Yes. You are…?" Bruce decided not to hold out his hand.

"Walt Croaker. Your uncle Harold, some kind of a radical, is he? That must be hard."

"What do you mean?"

"The way he talks, not very patriotic, about this plant here and the way it won the war. He's always talking like a Jap sympathizer. People think he's maybe shell-shocked from the war? He must have suffered…that's it?"

Bruce exploded. "What? What did you say? There's not a goddam thing wrong with him. He was there, he saw what we did to those people. First hand! What do you know about it?"

"Hey, just a minute!" Croaker saw that Bruce's face was red, his fists clenched.

"No! You shut up just a minute. My uncle is the real patriot, and you're an asshole if you think you know more than him about that bombing."

"I see, I see…you're another." Croaker glared but took a step back.

Bruce knew he could end up hitting the man if he kept on. He wheeled to walk away just as Suki came walking over. Croaker looked at her, nodded, smirked at Bruce, and strode off.

Suki glanced after him and turned to Bruce. She had to take a chance on him—and now, she decided.

"Who's that person?" She motioned after Croaker.

"Someone…I don't want to know."

"Hum, okay….Bruce, do you have a minute? You know, those people we saw at the river? They are truly doing something besides kayaking, don't you think?"

He took several deep breaths before answering.

"Oh, the kayakers? Yes, I think so. They could have stolen that kayak."

"I hadn't thought of that. I thought it had something to do with the plant. If they did steal it, why would they stop off at an off-limits place by a road where we were?"

Bruce was calm enough now to pay attention. "You're right, and it was stupid to camp there unless they had some reason. So that young guy we met was probably right about them."

He waited, suspecting she had more to say.

"Bruce, I need to ask you something in confidence. Is that all right? Yes? Don't answer if you don't want to, okay? Or I can wait...a while."

Now what? He fought off his anger left from Croaker. "Okay, go ahead."

"You've been in a war someplace, right?"

What the hell? He glanced aside, felt more like backing away.

"No, no, I'm not going to ask about that. No, I just want to ask...how do you feel about that place, I mean, the Hanford plant?"

He took another deep breath. He could be forthright on that. "Well, bad, of course, for a few reasons. But the worst, what they did with the plutonium. I've talked to my great-uncle, the one with the memoir. He was with the marines that landed in Nagasaki a few days later."

He didn't know what more he needed to say, so he waited.

Suki whispered, "Oh. Then you understand. So, I need to get closer to a reactor. Where I hope I can see it clearly. I mean the B Reactor. It's why I'm here."

He stared at her. *What???* "You're here to get close to a reactor? Why? Are you some kind of investigative reporter?"

Marta, coming out of the reunion hall looking for Bruce, saw them and their intensity. *What's this, they're meeting?*

Suki spotted Marta. "Talk to you more later." And in a louder voice said, "Yes, sure, I'd like to take the bus tour again."

Marta called, "Hey, don't you two want to come eat? We paid for it."

Bruce decided to go on in with her to the lunch even though he knew he'd be too disturbed to enjoy it. Suki followed.

"Suki here was saying she wanted to go on the bus ride again."

"Oh? I think I'll pass."

They saw that Roger was already pulling chairs over again, and motioning to them. Bruce filled his plate enough to be polite and followed Marta and Suki to the table. While everyone ate, he tried to put both Suki and Croaker out of his mind and pay attention to the conversation. They were again talking about their times as children of orchardists, a topic he found out was the favorite around the room. If there were former children that didn't want to share memories of their times growing up, they apparently didn't come to the reunions.

Bruce recalled he had a job to do and paged in the memoir to find something on that topic.

Roger said, "Some families—like yours, Bruce—had Sunday picnics in summer. Under those locust trees still there, down by the river. What does Harold say?"

Bruce found a comment:

"There was always lots of good food at the picnics. The kids would be swimming, always, and a few of the grown-ups too, and some families had rowboats. The current was strong out in the main stem of the river. One of the challenges was to race, rowing all the way across. A few of us, as teens, even swam it. We had a boat with us— we weren't fools."

Orville laughed, "No, we weren't, not most the time."

Bruce paged in the journal, realizing it would be hard this way to find the random topics they picked. He would need to take time to mark sections and topics.

"Harold says his father had a rule: no working on Sundays except during harvests. He wanted picnics."

Roger nodded, "Yup, we'd see his father out swimming and boating with the kids, and I remember I was pretty jealous. Most the fathers were like mine and believed they couldn't afford to take any time off except in late fall and winter."

Thelma said, "The picnics were a needed break. Our mothers still had to make up the meal, of course, so they tried to get it all cooked the night before and have a Sunday off too. And some of them even swam."

Marta asked, "But you couldn't swim all year round; what else did kids do for fun?"

"Spring, summer, and fall, if we weren't harvesting there were always weekend baseball games. Some kids had a horse to ride, not everyone. Boating, bicycling, just visiting."

Orville nodded. "And we knew how to make some of the work fun. Like bringing rafts of driftwood down over Priest Rapids. That was a thrill, eh, Roger? Only for daredevils. But stove fuel to last all winter."

"How about catching the lambs?" Bruce had stumbled on that section.

"Again, lots of fun but for a serious purpose," said Roger. "We'd hear the sheepherders down at the ferry landing with hundreds of sheep, trying to put them on the ferry. Back and forth, can't you picture it—the dust and confusion? So some small lambs got left behind, and we kids were watching for them. We loved making pets out of those lambs."

"Not eating them later, Roger. I never could," said Dorothy.

Marta said, "Is there a section on the kids' work, Bruce? Farm kids are always working, aren't they?"

Orville cried, "Work? Speaking of sheep, Thelma, you girls always complained about the smell, carding raw sheep wool? That mild smell? Excuse me, but how about the smell cleaning out the outhouse, *peeyu!* I had to shovel it out and spread it on the pasture."

"Really?" Leon was surprised.

"Really. There was never enough fertilize in the area; not enough animals. Yeah, lots of fun."

Dorothy said, "My dad said no to that. So we had to raise hordes of chickens, not counting the pigs, for fertilizer. I sure got tired of eating chicken."

Bruce said, "Roger told us about crawling through the irrigation pipes to cut out tree roots."

"A happy day when we got too big for it." Orville shuddered.

"Pruning time. My own most disgusting work—hauling and stacking all those branches, thousands of them," sighed Dorothy.

"And girl's work never ended," said Thelma. "Especially laundry. On top of the outside work!"

Leon shook his head, "You surely must have hated it, all that hard work, and just kids?"

The four looked around, shook their heads.

"Hate it?" Orville laughed. "But we've been telling you all the fun we had! We just want you to have the whole picture."

Roger mused. "Even at six-years old, at harvest time I was picking up the fallen fruit. But we were let go for a swim break at noon."

Marta found the give and take interesting, but realized that Bruce wasn't getting much done for Harold, and he wasn't even trying very hard. *Well, it's not my assignment.*

She turned to Suki, "How about your family?"

"I wish I knew. I'm sure they worked hard, but I never met those cousins. I'm finding out about that life."

Thelma nodded and went on, "The grown-ups didn't just work-work either. I remember the women were always putting on something fun for the adults to raise money for a worthy project. Like all those box socials, Dot?"

Bruce paged, looking for mention of "box socials", and couldn't find it. *An index would help.*

Dorothy laughed, "Oh, yes, a big favorite. The men would bid on the boxes of our food—we'd try our best to make it real special—and we all had fun eating together and visiting. And, oh, the Saturday night dances at the Grange Hall! One family had a string band that played, and they were darn good, a big turnout. The Grange raised money that way. But you couldn't drink inside, and there were chaperones for the kids. And you didn't have to dance with any man too drunk."

That got nods and laughs, and Bruce, still in a mental stew over his strange encounters, knew he had to relax and listen. This was why he'd come, to see his folk's place, share stories with these people, and get the settlers' critique on the memoir. So far, these folks were just having fun. The other tables seemed to doing the same. *And what the hell does Suki want?*

"So it wasn't all just slaving away, even for the adults," said Marta.

Roger laughed, "No, heck no. Basketball all winter after we got the high school—both boys' and girl's teams. The parents went wild in the stands."

Dorothy said, "Oh, and we even had real talent shows in the winter. You'd be surprised how much talent there was in such a small place. And everyone went to Grange. Some men belonged to lodges, like the Masons and Elks, and many women went to the Ladies Club, mostly a sewing circle. But there was another one for so-called professional women—not that many actually were. But they did take up serious topics."

"Oh? Like what?"

"Like women getting the vote. Well, we won that one, eh, Thelma?" And she gave them a big smile.

Leon saw that Bruce was distracted, and through old habit he couldn't help picking up the interviewer role.

"So you had Grange doings, and the women and men had their clubs. And churches, of course? It sounds like a typical farming community."

Thelma thought it was about time some professor took an interest in their history, and turned to him:

"I don't know about typical—how many places were like White Bluffs and Hanford. But I know we had it a lot better than the women up on the Wahluke Slope, because our farms weren't isolated. Most everyone that wanted to could just walk to whatever was going on."

Marta thought Thelma had made a good point. She had read accounts of ranch women going insane with loneliness; no such problem here apparently. But she wondered why Bruce kept acting as if he had a headache.

When the storytellers took a break to return their empty plates and get iced tea, Bruce excused himself to walk around out in the lobby and clear his head. He finally decided Suki, wherever she was, must be a greenie activist or anti-nuke of some kind, doing a story on the plant. *That's gotta be it. Okay, I can help with that!* When he went back to the table, Roger said he'd like to hear more what Harold had to say. Such as about the orchard work. Luckily, Bruce already had marked a section on that earlier as it had so impressed him.

"Okay, listen to this:

'Harvesting was by far the hardest work we did. When people did get caught up with their own orchards, the ones that needed more cash

71

would hire out to the bigger places too. The rush never stopped—We had to make the train schedule to get the fruit to Portland or it could get overripe. In many orchards the grower might expect folks to keep picking up to 120 degrees, but kids at least got excused at 110. But my father had a heart; he always had all our pickers stop at 110.'

Marta groaned and Roger smiled at her. "Yes, it's true. Can you just feel those degrees up on top of a ladder? My dad passed out once, and so did my sister. Not up a ladder, fortunately. The luckier ones were working in the packing shed, so much cooler."

Thelma said, "Bruce, can you read to us what Harold says about the women and their work? Their other work, that is?"

He paged through the memoir, and luckily found a relevant section, wondering if the women would agree with Harold's recall:

'Women orchardists had a real challenge, I realized when I got older. Like all farmwomen, of course, they had to work too hard, especially those who were willing to do the outside work too. They did all the things other farmwomen did: cook on a wood stove, or for some, kerosene in summer, clean house, can everything, childcare, make and take care of all the clothes, care of the chickens, and many of the women milked. Then the work of the orchards, too. Many of them planted, pruned, picked, and even packed—hundreds of boxes, right beside the men. Some I knew, like my sister, helped with the spraying.

"What saved them, for my family and most of the others too, was their social life. My mother was gone out walking so much to one gathering or another that my sisters got annoyed with her. "Why is our house always messy?" Later the girls admitted that it wasn't dirty, just not all picked up like some houses. If Mother wasn't out to some group she was out in her prize flower garden. I think she was very smart; she knew how keep up her health and spirit, even when her husband was gone so much.'

He stopped and looked around for comment.

Dorothy nodded. "Smart woman for sure. My mother should have made note."

Thelma sighed, "We did take it for granted too much, all the work our mothers did."

Leon said aside to Marta, "Do you think old-time Wanapum women worked like that?"

Marta raised her eyebrows. Thelma heard him and answered, "Well, they didn't have to can on a hot woodstove, or milk cows, weed strawberries, pick apples, and stack prunings…"

"Mend, wash, starch and iron everything," added Dorothy.

"They tanned hides, and did a lot of very ornate beadwork I've seen," said Leon.

"Well, beadwork's more interesting than wringer washers to crank, eh?"

"I guess so. But now they've got both to do. Progress."

He got laughs. But the granddaughter, Janice, sighed; after hearing all she could stand of the routines of farm women, she stood up to wander around.

Dorothy said, "I had to beg her to come with us. These kids live in a different world. But they need to know who they are. She at first refused to come. 'Sit and listen to old folks for two whole days? Come-on grandma!' And she's a smart girl. But then I found out she had a big paper due next week in history class. Bingo! She agreed she could come, if I promised she could get her paper out of it."

Marta thought Janet could get more than one paper out of it, in fact she herself could. As the afternoon continued with such memories, she wished she could take notes, but was afraid it might close them down, and so little had been published about this group. In contrast, many people had written about Smohalla. She wondered if she would discover anything new about the famous leader, while this story right here at the table could be a great research topic. Why she chose Smohalla in the first place, she reminded herself, was that he was such an eccentric character, even for a spiritual leader. He had refused to support signing the treaty with the Washington governor; it meant signing away their lands for a reservation. Several chiefs had signed, feeling there was no choice, but others had refused. Smohalla had given them a faith to justify their refusal, a promise of spiritual retribution. That's what Marta liked, that defiance. Yet these were living people she was listening to today, with their own brand of defiance. *So strange, so little published attention has been given to these settlers.*

At 3 p.m. Louise called a break. "Folks, in the small room in twenty minutes a man from the plant is giving a lecture and showing slides about the Hanford Energy Works, for those who want to learn more about that. Otherwise you're on your own until supper."

Marta asked Bruce what he wanted to do. He saw Suki nearby and decided to avoid her.

"Hmmm, we could just walk along the river now that there's a breeze."

Marta was willing. After a few minutes of strolling through the green, maintained park, so different from yesterday's tour, Bruce stopped and said,

"This is all so interesting to me, what they're telling about, but it's probably because it's my own people. Might be boring to others."

"Not to me!"

"Yeah, but you're an anthropologist."

"But almost all of us Euros came from small farming towns at some point. We ought to be interested in our history, and it's right here with these folks. And I've read some of those family letters Harold loaned you. No one writes letters like that anymore; it's truly a lost art. So this is really special, and not just for the old folks." *So what's wrong with you, my love?*

"Yes, I am glad I came, but…why don't we go hear what the guy has to say about the Plant?"

"I thought you didn't want to hear about the Plant."

"I know, Harold said to skip it. Well, I'm already pissed off about it, and that Croaker idiot didn't help. I can't help thinking about it, so I might as well go and get good and pissed off."

"You will."

As they followed the crowd into the lecture, Leon saw that everyone from their table was along, including Suki, even though the plant offered much the same lecture each year, and many people did skip it. As usual, Chuck, the community liaison for the plant, was doing the lecture. He didn't like this assignment particularly, but it went with the job. He planned to skim over the history concerning the eviction of settlers, assuming that it would, be, like other years, a touchy area. Nor would he dwell on the bomb's effects on the Japanese population. He would talk about the Plant itself. The first part covered the development of the Manhattan Project, a search for a site for plutonium production, and why this particular site was chosen: the unlimited supply of clean water from the great river, the remoteness from urban areas, and the relatively small number of Indians and farmers that would have to be moved out.

He opened his slide show to a photo that made both Bruce and Suki cringe.

"Here's a picture of the Plant when it was operating. Eventually there were nine main buildings, built about five miles apart, close to the river, and some of them were reactors that produced plutonium, the biggest producer in the country. Think of that! It was an essential part of us winning the war, as it was used to create one of the two bombs dropped on Japan. It was the second bomb, and Japan after a few days surrendered. Probably many lives were saved through this Plant. The patriotic families that had to leave the towns of Hanford and White Buffs and the surrounding area made it all possible."

As he went on, a little muttering began, but when Chuck stopped and stared at his audience, they quieted down. Bruce, his blood pressure already rising, flashed back on a conversation with Harold.

"Uncle, weren't the families furious over being evicted? Wasn't everyone outraged? And then the bombs, the slaughter of civilians, my God!"

"Outraged, sure, over the evictions here. There were several lawsuits over the amount of compensation the government offered, and they did win a few thousand. Our family got $3,000 more. But Bruce, it was wartime, nothing was normal. And we didn't know, didn't make the connection for some time, what we were evicted for."

"Nothing was normal? What they did here was…more than abnormal, don't you think?"

"Bruce, at the reunion you can hear plenty of different opinions on that. But what I want you to hear this time is how it was to be growing up there. Take the memoir with you

and share it for me, get their reaction. Does it ring true? And what happened in '43 and '45, you can come to that later, after you have a feeling for the earlier times. You'll be glad."

"Okay."

Harold knew his nephew wasn't satisfied. "You know, I can't do anything about what the Hanford plant produced over fifty years ago. I wasn't even there for the eviction. I saw the bomb's result first hand at Nagasaki, yes, but, good god, I don't know how to write about that. . . . still hard to even think about it. I wrote about earlier times that I could make sense of."

Bruce understood, but now he had disobeyed and was sitting there, angry, even beginning to shake. *Should have stayed away from this.* He looked toward Suki, but her head was down.

The next part of the presentation was Chuck's specialty: more detail about the development of the Hanford Atomic Works, and the many thousands of people who came to work at what came to be known simply as the "Hanford Plant". He told how after the war the production had morphed to peacetime use, and of the years of political effort and fund-raising by Washington State that went into getting Reactor N built and producing domestic power by 1965. He told how the state went heavily into debt as the power and pluto-nium sales, including for Cold War military needs, couldn't cover costs of construction and production. By1971 all the Hanford reactors except N were closed down, and now it was as well. But a new domestic nuclear power pro-ducer was built and producing by 1984.

"You can see it out in the desert about ten miles northwest of here. It's one of two nuclear plants in the state. You probably saw some steam rising from it yesterday. And just upriver from White Bluffs if you went on the tour, more steam? That's one of the WWII reactors we are dismantling."

"Bout time!" came a familiar voice from the back.

Chuck was accustomed to this sort of interruption and went on.

"In 1977 trouble came to the national industry when a reactor at Three-Mile Island in New York experienced a partial meltdown and spewed radio-active material into the surrounding populated area. Domestic nuclear plants became less popular in America. Then the meltdown occurred at Chernobyl in 1986. Because of that accident, protests against nuclear plants have been worldwide, but they are important producers of power in many countries.

"The main problem at the old Hanford Plant is the safe disposal of its 177 storage tanks of radioactive waste. Hanford has about two-thirds of the plutonium waste in the country, that's 53 million gallons…"

At this point Orville called, his voice edged with sarcasm. "Excuse me, but I have to butt in and say we already seen these slides last year, and we know about the waste problem. We can read the papers, you know, and we know it's costing the taxpayers about one billion a year to take care of this old plant that will never operate again…probably. Great. What we want to know is what's being done about them 177 storage tanks that are leaking or soon will be, we hear. What if the radioactive stuff does seep down to the river? It could happen anytime, right? And now there's the new plant, same problem eventually."

Chuck shook his head, "Orville, the scientists don't think it's a worry, as the river current will thin the waste out so it's harmless."

"That's what you guys said about the radioactive iodine that you people, on purpose, released into the winds. Now you've got lawsuits from all those downwinders with cancer."

Chuck knew this would, as usual, be brought up. "We have stronger replacement tanks to transfer the waste to, and eventually will send the highest-level waste to storage elsewhere."

"But if no one will accept it elsewhere? Who would?"

"We will bury it."

"How deep?"

Every year I have to hear this, sure that Orville will be here just to bug me. "For permanent safe burial, it would be 2000 feet. Right now, we are transferring it to new double-walled tanks. They will be good at least fifty years."

"And then every fifty years replace them? And what is the actual life of this junk?"

"For plutonium unprocessed waste? 24,000 years."

"Wow. Well, you guys will have a job for life anyway."

Laughter erupted.

Chuck nodded. *And for me a job taking my beating for it, every damn reunion.*

But Orville wasn't quite finished. "Yes, and what if you don't get them new tanks all done in time; what about folks that still live on this river from White Bluffs clear down to Astoria?"

"Do you still live on the river, Orville?"

Dorothy broke in, "Mister, we can't afford a place on the river now. We've got a trailer over in Pasco. But we can see it, and we still care a lot about this river, and we're not the only ones."

"Folks, so do I, and we are working fast as we can on it. And as we get funding. It's expensive, all this storage, so write your Congressman. By the way, on to other topics, you all may already know there are serious plans about making a museum at the B Reactor."

Bruce had been frowning from the beginning, and now he twisted in his chair, his face red, his fist clenched. Marta heard him mutter "morons", and saw how Suki, next to them, had to close her eyes and bite her lips. *Damn, I knew we shouldn't have come. I am sitting here with a Japanese American, listening to a lecture that's a marvelously tailored history, and sitting next to a guy with his own ghosts who's about to blow up.* Marta reached her hand to Bruce's arm, but at her touch he sprang up and shouted:

"Excuse me! A museum! Really now! Is that how we answer? Is that all you're going to say about the bombs? About Hiroshima and Nagasaki? Maybe you don't know about it? Well, I can tell you more. My great-uncle, who grew up right at White Bluffs, was there with the Marines that landed a few days later...yeah, he did, at Nagasaki. 80,000 people had died or soon would. That's in addition to 140,000, mind you, at Hiroshima. And lots more later. They weren't all soldiers, not by a long shot. You folks want to hear about it?"

Bruce looked at the audience. The lecturer waited. Some of the audience got up and left. Others leaned forward as a young man called, "Let's hear it."

Chuck shuffled his feet, took a breath, and got himself under control and said. "I'm sorry, that history is not my specialty. After I'm done people can stay and hear what your uncle says. I'll go on now, okay?"

Bruce took a deep breath, "Yeah, okay, go on with your whitewashed story."

Chuck stopped the slides and kept his deadpan face. "As we've told you, we are trying to find a place interested in storing the waste permanently.

What would that involve for them, in addition to patriotism they'd feel; how much compensation would they want, and how could it be safer than storing it here?"

"So you're saying what? No progress?" Orville again.

"There was one place being considered, but it's run into protests...by locals."

"Well that's no surprise. Why the devil would anyone want it in their back yard? You know, you fellas have got yourselves, along with people that live around here, and in fact, you've got this whole region in a serious mess."

"Orville, you're arguing over my pay grade. To get back to my... the clean-up at the plant will take time, at least a couple decades to do properly, but I assure you, we will."

"I just don't get it," Dorothy picked up the message. "We can build the best bombs in the world but we can't figure out how to take care of the left-over waste? Maybe God doesn't like what we're doing. Do you people ever think of that?"

Chuck took a breath, *stay calm*. "It's a thought. Look, here is the address for you to write your concerns to. Public comment is always welcome." He handed Orville a card, who took it with a snort. Chuck passed around more cards and moved back to the slide machine. Three minutes later another voice broke in.

"Oh, by the way...how about all the throat cancer in the downwinders up north of us? What are they going to get in compensation? Better than us orchardists got for our places? I sure hope so."

Chuck nodded. He had to hear about downwinders every year; he saw some in the room. He knew they had filed a lawsuit against the AEC, but nothing further. After the audience got no answer on this, a milder voice began,

"Yes, I have a question. How do people apply for work at the plant? I have a son with a science degree."

Oh, it's okay to work there then? "Please have him visit the personnel department here in Richland." Chuck felt too annoyed to go on. "Folks, I'm sorry we have run out of time; I thank you very much. Goodbye, and do enjoy your reunion." *And screw this lecture.*

CHAPTER 8

VOICES EAST AND WEST

CHUCK PACKED UP his equipment, headed for the hotel bar where a colleague was waiting, and slid into the seat beside him. "Holy shit! That's it for me."

His buddy gave him a look and ordered him a beer.

"I swear that is the last time I am going to do that wasted presentation. Those people are not interested in the Plant and have no appreciation, really, of its history. This year worse than ever. All they want to do is bitch about the eviction—fifty-year old history—and complain about the fucking waste, yell about their cousin that's a so-called downwinder with cancer, and still they ask about how their kid can get a job with us. And now we have a guy who wants to tell us all about Nagasaki. Not that he was ever there."

"You do get some crackpots. Did you tell about the plan for a museum at Reactor B?"

"Are you kidding? I mentioned it. More shit thrown. It's destructive of my good humor. You will do the talk next year."

"No, no. I have no ability to stand up in front of a bunch of ornery farmers and keep civil. You are marvelous at it."

"You report to me, remember? Next year it's yours." Chuck gulped his beer. "Oh, there's Louise...I need to talk to her."

He waved the reunion coordinator over. "Hey, Louise, how's it going? Good?" He forced a smile. "Say, do you know that some people without passes got in on your group's outing at White Bluffs today?"

"Hello, Chuck. Yes, so I heard. Kayakers." She didn't smile back.

"My boss is worried about your program. I mean it's good, of course, but...things might be getting a little loose?"

"My program...loose? Chuck, you know I can't control who paddles across the river, for heaven's sake. Ike says they are probably college students. Their professors get them all steamed up about nuclear waste."

"The thing is I'm afraid my bosses may close the bus tours down if the reunions start encouraging troublemakers. We get enough publicity as it is lately."

She glared at him. "Troublemakers? Not from my bunch. Ike says those kayakers seemed to know nothing about the tour, just as surprised as he was to see them."

"I see. Louise, I'm just passing on a message."

"You know what? I've been doing this reunion as a volunteer for over ten years. Those bosses of yours can take it over anytime, or close it down, whatever the government wishes. My letter of thank you from Uncle Sam must have got lost in the mail."

Chuck had to smile. "Even Orville had his steam up more than usual today. If you could just calm him down, so we could finish to the lecture for those that wish...and there's another guy...a new guy..."

She nodded. "There's a few new guys, yes, and we welcome them. But as for Orville, he has good reason, as you know, even if it is fifty years old and he needs to move on. Chuck, I don't have to do this job, you know."

And with that Louise strode off. The men watched her go into the conference room.

"Whoof. She's not appreciated enough by the powers."

"Well true, but they do have other fish to fry. Ha-ha."

⊷═◉ ◉═⊶

Roger caught Leon as they were walking out of the lecture.

"I need to ask you something, professor. I know you read a lot, like history?"

Leon was caught off guard but was pleased to be consulted—usually. "Yes. I like history."

"I read something recently. I wonder if you've run across it, About WWII and Japan."

Leon waited and Roger went on, "I read somewhere that the Japan emperor had already decided to surrender before we bombed the second time, and we knew it. Have you heard that? That he just wanted to stay on as ceremonial emperor, which was all that he was anyway. But we rejected that, and we dropped the second bomb anyway? The one made here. And then we did let him stay on anyway. Do you think all that's true?"

"I think I did hear that. It's possible."

"No, that's not possible, is it? We're a Christian nation!" said Thelma, just behind them. Roger looked at her, eyebrow raised. "Leon, why would we do that? Why two cities?"

Leon had an answer. "I suppose to show the world it was no one-time thing, that America was the leader of the world now, and no nation had better think differently."

"So...two bombs? It just makes our history here even more...I don't know what. Well, actually, it was Harold that showed me that article. He'd cut it out. But he didn't want to show it to Bruce. We shouldn't put that kind of burden on young people, he said. A tragedy like that is for us old timers, since we can balance it with all our good stories. Anyway, I had to ask you, Leon."

They went back to their table to wait for the others, and Roger decided to keep on with his questions.

"You know there's something the lecture fellow could have mentioned, but I can see why he didn't. I know a guy who works at the plant. He told me something rather scary. I guess he trusts me—I'm not saying his name. Anyway, his job is to do inspections and he says there are tunnels all over under the buildings where they have metal waste containers, the ones corroding. What worries him isn't just the containers but the tunnels themselves. The supports are fir wood, and he's found dry rot in some of the supports. So what if they start caving after all these years? Like our early irrigation pipes that were made of wood. That tunnel wood may be contaminated too."

Leon digested the news. "Well, one more fact to tell us time is running out, eh?"

They sat for a moment on that thought; then Roger said, "Anyway, I hope you've enjoyed the stories so far—the happier ones."

"History can't be just the happy stories, right? But, yes, I am enjoying them a lot."

Leon thought that given he was stuck indoors with a sprained ankle, he couldn't have been better entertained, and he was impressed with Roger's historical information.

Bruce had walked out of the lecture knowing he had no specific facts to give the people about Nagasaki, just memories from Harold and his own anger. *Harold told me to stay clear of this stuff at first, but how? And he sure didn't know I was going to be cornered by someone like Suki.* He needed to get more antacid pills. Marta looked at his expression and thought they ought to bypass the snacks laid out in the conference hall. He was obviously too irritated from the lecture to be sociable, much less lead a memoir critiquing. She talked him into going back to the coffee shop. He was slouched in a booth with ice water when he saw Suki headed toward the stairs and decided to face it out with her. *If she'll talk in front of Marta.* He called her to join them.

"I hope you got something out of that lecture besides outrage," sighed Marta.

Suki's gave her a disgusted shake of her head as she sat down.

Okay. Marta shrugged. *I could have said that better.* Then she remembered Leon, and feeling partly responsible for his entertainment now that he was injured, she said she would see if he wanted to join them. As soon as she was out of range, Bruce began in a low voice.

"What did you mean earlier, Suki, that you have to get closer to the plant? Didn't you see enough now with those slides?"

She hesitated. This man wasn't any older than a grad student, but still, he had some understanding and could possibly help her. She took a breath. "You're angry, too. But I can tell you, Bruce, I'm a lot angrier than you! A lot!"

She looked around, took a breath, and began quietly. "I need to explain something, but please keep it to yourself, will you? I'm from Seattle, but... I, my family, we're from Nagasaki…. Yes, Nagasaki."

Her words went through him like a sniper's bullet. *Nagasaki, her family…oh my god.* The images that flashed through him were so sharp that he closed his eyes, and almost cried out. He couldn't think of a thing to say, just breathed hard to fight the clenching in his stomach.

After a minute Suki, staring at the table, whispered, "My parents were here in a relocation camp, but a few years ago, after my dad died, and I was in college, my mother went to Japan to be with her own mother, a survivor… who needed her. She's still there. I go to visit." She took a breath. "Well, a while back they gave me a mission. And I've put it off too long, way too long, Bruce. I've been too busy—I thought that, anyway, trying to earn a degree, and now another one. I…I won't say right now what their mission to me was. But obviously it's about the Plant. Specifically, Reactor B."

He stared at her, unbelieving, and new alarm surged through him.

"A mission? You're not thinking of…of something wild, like trying to break in, are you? Probably there's a high voltage fence."

She gave him a straight look. "No, I just need to get close for a clear view of the reactor. So, Bruce, will you help me?"

His stomach was in a total knot. *Why me? I know hardly more than she does about the area.* He saw her steely expression. It was like he had seen on soldiers going into battle.

"Suki, what's pushing you to do this? I understand how they feel, you feel, believe me, but…you need to get close? Why? I don't see how…how I can help."

She stared at him. "No one's pushing me, it's just something in me. I promised. The last time I was over visiting, it was so humiliating, that I couldn't give them any kind of report. I don't like myself for stalling all this time. So I'm here."

She stopped talking, and he wondered how he could reason her out of such a crazy idea.

But she began again, "Now, coming here to the river, and seeing that steam so close, I know I have to... to figure something out, or do my best. I can't just sit here and listen to happy stories. Just help me figure out how to get close enough so I can see the Reactor B building. That's all."

Close. How close? To do what? He shook his head. In the back of his head, like a chant: *Nagasaki, Hiroshima, Nagasaki, Nagasaki. My god, what good am I if I can't even help her, a direct descendant? As long as it's not murder or suicide. Oh boy, she sure picked the right guy.*

He saw Marta was returning, but without Leon. But not far behind her came the man who had accosted him earlier, Walt Croaker. Bruce braced himself as Croaker strode up to him, his face red, mouth clenched.

"So, Wilder, did your uncle send you to disrupt the lecture? Probably. Listen, we know him, he's either senile or an unpatriotic.... But you were a vet, should have some sense. Now...are you here just to make trouble? And you too, missy?" He glared at Suki.

Bruce was already fighting the shakes, but ready this time. *I will not be baited into fighting this shithead.* "Hey, I'm here to listen to history, not you. That guy was leaving out important history, whitewashing it."

"What? What do you know about the war? You weren't even born. You're just spouting off. Here I thought you were a vet to respect." He waved an arm at Suki, "...She's not from Nagasaki I don't think. Another one not even born then. What's she know? Jap propaganda?"

Bruce sprang up, fists clenched, head throbbing, and shouted, "You're the one that always wants trouble, seems like."

"Sure thing, I like trouble with guys like you." Croaker shouted back, his fists ready.

Marta, silent through all this, grabbed Bruce's arm. "Bruce, the desk is calling the cops."

Bruce saw he was taller by a head over the furious Croaker, who was also probably twenty years older, and looked out of shape. He held in an explosion, breathed deep, and barked a laugh.

"Aahh, too bad, the cops. Hey, I could kill you easily, Croaker. Easy, I'm good at that. But... why wreck the party, huh?"

He dropped his fists. Croaker glared a few seconds, shook his head, then stomped off, leaving the others in silence. Bruce, trembling, again wondered why Harold hadn't warned him about this freak. *Cool down!*

"I'm sorry, Suki."

"Oh, you're not responsible for jerks like him."

Bruce saw that Marta was furious too, but she would manage. He knew he needed to take a walk, alone, and she would understand. Suki would have to. He excused himself and headed for the green riverside park. *Why can't I just have a good time?* A gentle wind helped him calm down as he watched a mallard family near the shore, the ducklings always able to bring out a smile. Yet he was afraid of what he would do if Croaker said one more word to him. He had a purpose in coming here, and he couldn't let a fight with a psycho ruin it. Harold had warned him to skip the lecture. And Roger had urged him to share more of his uncle's memoir, so he needed to get on with that. After a half hour of walking the river path he felt the wind building rapidly, and decided to return to the conference room and try to get back in the spirit of the reunion. *I will ignore Croaker, I will ignore him.* But the issue with Suki, that was a different matter. Her request was too bizarre, and really, he didn't have to do anything for her. He owed to no one here—just to his uncle and Marta.

He returned to the hall and saw that Suki had gone off elsewhere.

"Oh, here's Bruce again," Thelma beckoned with her warm smile. "Dorothy asks that we talk more about the kids' life, for a paper Janice has to write."

Roger winked at Bruce, "Hey, what more does your uncle say about the kids' work? We always like to talk about ourselves as kids for some reason."

Bruce nodded shook himself from his thoughts, flipped through the memoir for more kids' activities, and once more had the luck to find a good one. "Here we go:"

'We kids always had work waiting for us. The girls had the house-work and cooking, canning, gardens, and babysitting. Whatever their mothers didn't get done, they did. Work was year-round for the girls, with no appliances. Cooking was horribly hot on a wood stove in summer. Wintertime wasn't so great either—the houses weren't insulated. And the girls helped outside whenever needed, no slacking. The boys, too, had all the work they could handle. Milk, help with the butchering, keep the irrigation ditches clear, herd cattle, any other fieldwork, the garden, pruning, spraying, training the grape vines. Some older worked in the packing-house. My dad even made me kill the pig when I was 13 because he said he couldn't do it—too soft-hearted for a farmer. And everyone age six on up helped with the harvests. That work didn't stop until the last of the apples and potatoes were sent away or put away in the fall.'

Dorothy laughed. "How'd you like that, Janice?"

"Well, at least they didn't have time to be bored." The girl grinned and reached for her notebook and, to Bruce's amusement, began to write. But when she decided to take a break and left the table, his good feeling left too. A noisy group had moved into the table next to them and he couldn't think. He slipped away again, leaving the memoir with Marta, and walked back into the park to face the wind, still angry about mad dog Croaker, but even more about the Plant lecture. *But that's all it was, just a stupid lecture.* Some settlers, certainly Orville, saw through it, knew the argument by heart, that the government had decided these two hamlets were filled with people barely making a living, and the feds were doing them a favor by buying them out for a fraction of what they were worth. He doubted many of the listeners agreed with that. Probably many of the settlers came to Chuck's lecture only hoping to hear good news about the radioactive waste, or to wait for Orville to start in on the guy. Yet, many didn't attend at all.

Bruce realized the steam he felt was what their folks had felt fifty years ago. Now for many it was probably just history. *So why do I feel like I have to help Suki?*

The wind was by now fierce enough to cool down his anger, but circling back to the conference a half hour later, he saw a large sign at a different park entrance and was angry all over again. "General Leslie Groves Park". So... a park on the Columbia, named for the general that had chosen White Bluffs and Hanford as the project site. *Oh great, a hero, a glorious hero.* Then, walking back into the busy lobby, he saw posters he had missed earlier that advertised the high school sport teams, dubbed "The Richland Bombers". Next to it was a photo of T-shirts for sale; on the shirt a drawing of an A-bomb mushroom cloud above the team's name. *My god, how callous can we get? Has Suki seen this? What do they have for school staff, anyway, to allow that?* He glanced around, then reached up and ripped a poster down, tore it, and stepped on it like it was vermin. For a moment it felt good. But when he was outside the conference room he realized how childish that was. If he wanted to do something about the name "Bombers" he had to start with the school office. And he had to have supporters. Now he needed to get back to what he'd come here for, and stop stewing over immorality and ignorance. He could ignore that steam up the river—a closed plant after all. *But not Suki. How's she going to get close to an off-limits building? Why?*

The generally happy settler recollections went on through the afternoon, interspersed with sharing of personal photo albums. Then it was dinnertime. The staff wheeled in the buffet on carts—the main dish was baked salmon—and everyone broke off to go fill their plates. Bruce took a little of the food to his seat to be polite and stared off into space. *How can these people sit in that so-called informative lecture and then waltz in here and carry on with their stories as if they closed off all that terrible history? And year after year. How can they? Only Orville seems like he can't just ignore the insult.*

"You don't feel like eating."

Bruce glanced up—Roger was sitting down by him. He'd tell him at least. "Yeah...to be frank, that lecture made me want to throw up."

"Well, try not to let it ruin your time here, Bruce. We've learned to cherish this time together. Most of these people we never see all year."

"Okay...yeah, I understand. Orville..."

"Yes, Orville's saying what probably a lot of us feel. But you know, there's others just want to forget it, just enjoy themselves. And quite a few think we did the right patriotic thing here."

"I think I met one...or I should say he accosted me. I wanted to hit him, and I didn't come here to be that way."

"I think I know who you mean—Walt Croaker, right? He has his own ax to grind. Just try to avoid him. And it helps to know his father spent time in a Japanese POW camp. Came home messed up I think."

Bruce sighed and nodded. *Great, Croaker's another one dredging up his family history.*

"So what did you do after the eviction?"

"I'd been drafted, like most the boys. Thank god I didn't see Nagasaki or any of that, or any POW camp. When I got out I was still just a kid, a kid a lot more serious than I left. So my folks saw to it that I went to college on the GI bill, got a degree in Ag, and became a county extension agent. Mainly helping farmers modernize and economize."

"How was that as a job?"

"It was great for me, working around the state with folks like the ones I grew up with—those still farming, or trying to. I retired a few years ago."

Bruce suspected he had been good at it. "You have children?"

"Two, one's a teacher, one's a county agent. But farming isn't at all what it was. Just look anywhere and you can see that. Frankly, I didn't want to be a county agent anymore."

Bruce nodded. He thought Roger referred to the industrializing of farming; he'd heard enough about it from Harold. And just like what was happening to commercial fishing, the bigger sharks would win.

He noticed that Suki was still off somewhere. *Fine, I'll be here.* He listened while the others ate and went on with their stories. After a length of time had gone by, and Suki hadn't returned, he started feeling nervous again and went up to his room to look at a map he'd picked up earlier. He saw that B Reactor was not anywhere near the place where they'd walked today with Ike. The line of reactors stretched all along the river north and west, and B was the last one in the complex. A highway went north to Wolf Rapids and beyond, but it probably wasn't close enough to the reactors for a view. How to get where Suki could see whatever she wanted to see?

Marta came looking for him and found him staring at the map. *He came to have a good time, and now look at him. Maybe we should leave. Go on up to Wolf Rapids, Priest Rapids. No, that would be a defeat.*

"I'm sorry, Bruce. You're angry, I am too. Hey, don't forget what you came here for!"

"I'm okay."

"Well, want to go for a walk?"

"I went for a walk." He slumped on the bed, then jumped up and paced around like a caged wolf. Marta tried to read some sections from a book she had found in the bookstore about the early homesteaders, before the orchardists.

After a half-hour he said, "I think I'll go get some beer."

"Uh...I want to get going early, if we're going anywhere tomorrow. You know, it's too hot later."

"Just a six-pack. I'll be right back."

She knew he'd be back; he hated bars. But he enjoyed getting a little drunk. She went down stairs, hoping to run into Suki and find out what on earth was going on. But she was nowhere to be seen, and Marta felt it was too interfering to go pound on her door.

Later that night, the beer gone, and Bruce still pacing around, Marta thought they could make love and he'd feel better. She put her arms around him with a warm hug that usually got a warmer response, but nothing doing. Pacing was tonight's action. He finally climbed into bed later, but turned his back. She thought what a special day it had been—until the lecture. *Oh please, tomorrow can we get back to the stories he came for?* But an hour later he was awake and tossing around. At last he decided that Suki's problem would have to wait until he had one more look at his family's lost home. At six he woke Marta to tell her he'd decided to go on the bus ride again if there was room.

"You don't have to if you don't want to, Mart."

She almost said she thought they had seen what was left to see at White Bluffs, but remembered how that simple piece of shingle meant so much to him. She told him she'd go, that the bluffs were surely something to savor again. And this was his project; hers would begin when they drove up to Priest and Wolf Rapids.

⊷⊷ ⊶⊷

Back at the island that same evening, Jason found that the kayakers had returned, and were deep in their own story, obviously with no intention of leaving. He decided to stay another night since he had enough water. Early the next morning he heard them still debating. Once in a while he caught a clear word that convinced him their topic was the Plant: "fence", "nighttime", "guards". They were planning something really crazy, something he might like to do himself, but knew better, and they were stalling. They knew they could get in big trouble. Another visit to their camp would be the kind thing to do, warn them.

He found them sitting with their gear in the dusk.

"Hello, again," he tried a friendly, not too friendly tone.

No answer. Just stares. Finally, "Hello."

"Ahh, please don't think I'm being nosy. I just don't see what the point is in you guys getting in big trouble. And you sure will if you hang out here."

"We thought you were leaving."

"I am. I don't like this place actually. It has ghosts. Well, it's true, I had a friend a few years back who disappeared down here."

"Oh yeah?"

"Yeah." He forced himself to go on, to convince them. "We did find him later...dead. Yeah. We couldn't see just how. Then, before we could retrieve him, he disappeared. See, he had this idea about the plant, that it was an evil force. And then my people found him down here, dead, outside the fence. And then a few hours later—gone, vaporized."

"Really? So...what's your point? We know it's an evil place."

Jason sighed. "Like I said. Well, I guess you will do what you want to do. I've warned you."

They stared at each other a while, and then, exasperated, Jason went back to his camp.

"What kind of freak is he?" Tom wondered. "But maybe he's right. He knows this place."

"Don't go chicken on me, Tom."

"Hey, I'll give this one more night, then I'm out of here, even if I have to walk out."

CHAPTER 9

GROWING A TOWN: WHITE BLUFFS

IKE WALKED INTO the café the next morning while the early birds were at breakfast. He had remembered he couldn't drive the bus that day after all and needed to apologize. Many of them had planned to go on the tour again. Marta was also looking them over: *tough birds*. She understood them wanting to see those special stretches of river and bluffs again, but how they could enjoy looking at those piles of torn up brush and planks she couldn't imagine.

Ike nodded hello to familiar riders. "I'm really sorry, folks, but I can't make it today. Unless Louise finds a driver, you'll have to settle for a van. How many planned to go?"

A show of hands told him a van wouldn't have room for repeat riders.

"But we wanted you to drive," said Marta. "What happened?"

"Nothing bad. Just another fishery meeting I had forgotten all about."

"We could go later," said Bruce with hope.

Ike had to say no. He needed the money from the tour bus job, and it was always interesting, but he was committed to the salmon meetings. There was the chance of a break through—a lone scientist cutting loose and saying, *Enough of this. We either restore the river to its natural condition or we'll have no salmon.* And another one, for once saying, *Quit worrying about your damn jobs and tell the truth!* He could always hope to hear that. And he would always hear his uncle Esau in his head, *You have to go to the meetings, Ike!*

"No, sorry, I'm always tied up later with more meetings—to talk about that meeting, right? And I'm real sorry to mess up your plans. But you'll come up to Wolf Rapids soon?"

Marta nodded, "For sure."

"Well, I'll see you then. Now I have to go. I have to pick up someone down at Cook's Landing."

Bruce said, "Oh, the fish camps there, Harold mentions them. That's where David Sohappy made his stand isn't it? I read when he had a net confiscated, he'd just go out and buy a new one. That's persistence."

Ike said, "Yup, but the treaty was on his side. And finally the federal court was too."

"He paid for it, though didn't he?"

"You mean his jail term. That was a sting, you know. And he knew it was...but he didn't expect to lose in court and he did finally. Different judge, different judgment. I admire Sohappy."

"Passed on now?"

"Yes, way too early. He got ill; maybe too much stress.... Well, I'm off. I'll see you soon though, up my way." He nodded and waved to the group and left.

"A nice guy...what were you talking about?" asked Leon.

"About the fish-ins in the 1970s. Remember? The Indians on the lower Columbia, and others up on Puget Sound. They finally got the feds to recognize their treaty fishing rights in the Judge Boldt Decision, 1974 I think. Remember all the uproar in the press?"

"Yes, I do! What a place of history, this Columbia, eh?"

Suki came over to their table, gave Bruce raised eyebrows and said, "So, no White Bluffs today." She sighed and left the cafe. Bruce looked at his cup and said nothing, and Marta was puzzled. *Is this undercurrent about Bruce, or about the story she's writing?*

"She was really counting on that trip today," she led.

"Huh? Oh, yes...she's got some story about the Plant she wants to finish."

"Well, I wasn't planning to go anyway," said Leon. "I need to ice this leg. I'll visit with more old-timers." *Will Elena stay, and do I dare bring up the massage again?...Hardly!"*

Bruce, toyed with his coffee, then suddenly smacked the table, spilling it. "I know what I want to do—rent a car and drive up the highway!"

Marta was caught by surprise. She grabbed for the napkin holder and began sopping up his mess. "You mean go on up to Wolf or even Priest Rapids? That would be great."

"No, no. I mean just drive up a ways and look around. You don't have to go. Stay and hear stories, why not?"

She thought a moment. *This could get risky.* "Oh, I'll go. Let Leon have the memoir then?"

"That's fine. So now I need to rent a car." He passed over the memoir, tossed her some cash for their breakfast and strode off. She looked at Leon and shrugged. *What happened to memoir duty? Turned over just like that.* They returned the conference room, and Leon, memoir in hand and glad for the duty, put on his reading glasses and settled into his professional role.

"So White Bluffs was an ideal place for new farmers, would you say? Or not?"

"Definitely not!" Thelma shook her head. The others all snorted or laughed. She looked at Roger and he nodded.

"She's right. They had the problems of desert farmers anywhere, but White Bluffs and Hanford had their particular problem, too, that no one was warned about: serious water shortages."

"How could that be with a river right next to them?"

Roger sat up straighter, glad to share more technical information. "The main source was from the Hanford Ditch and it was a mess for quite a time. You see, a small dam at Priest Rapids had a power line down to Coyote Rapids. That's where White Bluffs City and Orchard Tracts, the outfit they bought their land from, had a couple 100 horse-power pumps that raised water up to their private Hanford Ditch. That made enough gravity flow down to the new orchards, and it was supposed to guarantee enough flow for all the tracts they were selling. But it didn't work totally, not enough water at the south end for all the little trees. But Harold must talk about this... where's Bruce?"

Marta said, "He went to rent a car—to see the country again. Leon will have the memoir."

"Oh. But he can't get into White Bluffs by car. Only the reunion bus is allowed, better catch him?" He turned to Leon, "Well, anyway, that big ditch leaked badly from the start from prairie dog holes and the usual evaporation. Some folks downstream pulled up stakes. And there was another system, a coop, that pumped directly from the river at White Bluffs. But they had to barge in coal oil to run it and maintain their wooden pipes—those were the ones we had to crawl through. The bills to the coop members were hard for them, they couldn't keep up during the Depression. Pretty soon that system closed down and people had to solve their own water delivery."

Marta was impressed; Roger was a real source. "Didn't the government know there'd be problems with the big ditch leaking? It wasn't the first water ditch dug in the country."

Orville snorted, "It was a scam to start with."

Roger shrugged, "But it wasn't a government project, it was a private project. Anyway, everyone paid for their water, and I remember my folks paid their water bill before anything else. There were abandoned places around us where the water bills couldn't get paid."

Orville protested, "The government doesn't get off free, Roger. Don't forget its Soldier-Settler project out in the desert for World War I vets. Hardly anyone survived that pipe-dream."

Roger grinned. "Yup, a pipe-dream. Whoever dreamed up that project didn't know much about farming. Most of those vets weren't farmers either, and most did give up."

Dorothy said, "I think it was because they lacked the community way out in nowhere. My aunt was married to a vet who signed up for that, and he did know farming. They got a little house and barn, equipment, everything from the government. But she moved back to the river after only a year, said that wasn't living—way out away from the river, no social activities, too far to walk in. He followed her pretty soon, and he did well with a truck garden."

Roger said. "Yup, the community was what kept many of the folks going; that's what I saw later." He continued with the problem list. "Well, aside from water shortages—and that got better when they paved the Ditch—the dust storms would come and filled up the houses. Though that got better, too, as more land got irrigated and they got the alfalfa growing. But then the jackrabbits would come through, even more with the alfalfa, hundreds at a time. So they had to have those drives."

Dorothy shuddered, "Oh, ugh! Rabbit drives. They tried to make it fun, served food, even had live music. But it was nothing pretty—a fence and a line of men with clubs. Blood and guts everywhere, yuk."

Thelma said, "Some people just stayed home from it."

Someone said, "And don't forget the grasshopper invasions."

"Well, don't forget the spray problems," growled Orville.

"Oh," Roger shook his head, "You think I'd forget that? And specially for the kids, specially the coddling moth."

"And the fruit market, unending problem." said Thelma.

Leon, accustomed to studying Indigenous people, not for the first time wondered about the concept of western progress. It sounded as if these folks had ended up like so many cultures that had taken up agriculture—a high proportion of failures.

Janice was by now scrawling notes furiously and looked up, "Wait, what's that about a moth? I know what a moth is, but what's so bad about that particular moth?"

Roger sighed. "I can tell you, Janice. The kids did work hard, but we didn't feel abused, but we were abused, though, in one job we got passed to us—spraying the apple blossoms every spring. Our folks didn't know then; later they did find out, but they allowed it anyway—kids running the sprayers for the moth, using lead arsenic."

"Wow! That's poison isn't it?"

"Right. But it was the only way to stop the moth then. It curdles me to think of it now. My dad was out working, leaving me the spray job when I was about fourteen. We were told to wear masks, but it was already too hot by the time the blossoms were out. I'd start to faint with a mask on, so I had to go without. And my sister, driving the spray wagon—it was bound to blow back on her too. So, Janice, the spraying had to happen, but it sure shouldn't have been kids."

She gave him a gloomy look.

Orville said, "No, not kids. And the damn moth built up resistance, so a couple sprayings a season, then five, then eight, I think more—in one season."

Roger nodded, "Twelve."

Marta was silent in shock. Leon looked at her and nodded, pointing to the memoir.

Roger went on, "So Janice, finally they realized they'd have to switch to a fruit that the moths didn't like. Peaches, pears, cots, cherries. But the new trees took so long to grow and produce, like you pointed out, Leon. So no, the orchards were a beautiful way to farm, but not ideal for beginners."

Orville snorted. Dorothy poked him and said, "No. But for kids, overall, it was a wonderful place. I'm not just looking back with rosy vision; it really was."

But Leon pictured their youthful days as short intervals of fun surrounded by endless hard work and terrible problems, and he said so. He turned to the women, "So you don't think your old life's been romanticized a bit? People do tend to romanticize their childhood anyway."

Thelma shook her head. "You can't understand it, not being there. They don't have to romanticize it, people that live on a river. A river is romantic— that's its nature."

Leon stared at her. *Wow.* Two different versions of the same thing, by the same people.

But he realized he was used to that, and it made stories all the more interesting. He looked at Roger, who seemed lost in thought.

"You saw it from two perspectives, Roger—farmer, then county agent. Which is right, a great place or a difficult place?"

"They're both right."

⟶▬◉ ◉▬⟵

Bruce caught up with Suki; as he expected, she had been waiting outside for him. He told her his idea, that they could drive up the highway they'd taken before, look at the terrain, and see how close they could get to the B Reactor.

"If it's not close enough for you, we could cross over that bridge farther up the river, go down the east side. But the road is not close by B Reactor, either way. I have no idea if there is any view either way. Is that still what you want to do?"

"Yes, I have to try."

He looked at her closely. "If we go now and scope it out from the road, you can see if there's a view. Or a spot where you could sneak nearer the plant when it's getting dark. Because there's probably no way we'll get closer than the road in daylight. Okay?"

She nodded. "Yes. If you're willing. And check it out now."

She won't give up. But to be invisible sneaking through low brush, and in an unfamiliar place, even if in the dark? It would be a challenge; she surely realized that. Or if there was a good view on either side of the river, it would make more sense. But he couldn't go around asking for information and alert anyone to the mission, whatever it was.

"It's nothing for me, scouting around in the dark, but…what do you do, usually, besides write?"

"I'm working on graduate degree in ecology."

"Oh? A PhD, like Marta?" *But this doesn't seem like anything to do with a PhD.*

"Someday, very soon, I hope. Right now I have a part-time position, working on toxins."

"Toxins. I get it." *But why do you have to see the plant?* "I looked at a map, and it looks like at least a four-mile hike from the road to the B Reactor—I mean to its fence."

"I guess I didn't tell you, I'm a rock climber. So, eight miles round trip? Of course I can do it. I just need someone like you used to tracking at night in a desert, if we decide to."

Oh, I get to go too! Bruce looked her over. She was small but not delicate, in fact she seemed sturdy, in shape, very nice looking. So, a rock climber—meaning she liked danger. He stood there, his thoughts tumbling. *I can't say no. How can I when danger was my specialty?*

"All right. But if you really want me to go you'll have to do just like I say, as if I'm the lead rock climber, but in the dark, in the brush. Coyotes, snakes, scorpions, maybe cougars, guards, maybe…we don't know what. Can you agree to that, to let me lead?"

She gave him a strong look and nodded. He sighed. *Can't scare her.*

"Then I'm going to rent the car and get supplies for the ride, and go soon, to scout it out. Marta's coming too. You go buy food that won't spoil. And extra water bottles. We'll meet here in an hour."

Having made up his mind, Bruce went off down the street full of energy—the phony lecture, the revolting Croaker—he could swallow them down for a while with something physical to engage him. And he could put aside old settler stories, too, for now. As he filled out the paperwork for the car, a thrill went through him that he hadn't felt for a while, and he knew he'd missed it. *I'm not cured, am I?* He rented an SUV, checked all the needed equipment for safe driving, then drove it out of town a short distance to see that everything was working properly. The terrain along the highway north, as he remembered it, was nothing to encourage a daytime approach on the reactor. For sure, they would be hiking at night or not at all. *Unless we abort, unless I order it.*

He parked the car by the hotel, then went over the map again. Yes, B reactor was roughly five miles from the highway. Of course there would be a fence around its area. They would drive up and check out the lay of the land. If the idea turned out to be ridiculous, they could cross the river and drive down the east side highway up on the Slope, looking for a place to make a reasonable walk to a view spot. *Okay, Suki, that's about it.* He went looking for Marta and found her still talking with settlers. He interrupted them, telling her to please come up to their room for a minute. She followed him up assuming it was about the car ride, but when she heard his actual plan and the story behind it, she was aghast.

"You've got to be out of your damn mind! Why, why are you doing this harebrained thing?"

His face flushed as red as hers as he shook a finger back at her. "Out of my mind? You think so? Okay. But I'm going to do it. Marta, listen! I need to make a statement of some kind about that rotten plant. I don't know what yet, but I will. Suki needs to do it for her article. We'll do just a reconnaissance for now. You don't have to go."

"But of course Suki is going, so I'm going."

"And tonight too? When we really do it…maybe? It's up to you. You may not like it, but I know you won't like staying here either. Look, I …Suki is just an excuse."

"Or are you just her excuse?"

They marched up and down the room and raged on at each other. She saw he was going to ignore her arguments. "You know you could get arrested, sneaking in near the plant; of course you know you could lose your job, and for a magazine story?"

"So what?"

Then she knew, knew he had been missing that crazy fighter's life he'd only half left behind with that little chunk of his frontal lobe. But she couldn't bear that he was going to go off on this adventure with an attractive woman who had seemed sane, if a little odd. *But she's clearly as nutty as he is. Is that what this is really about? I'm not nutty enough for him?*

Bruce realized he had to tell her Suki's whole story, even though he'd said he'd keep the confidence. He didn't want his partner thinking there was something between him and Suki that wasn't. He went to find Suki, and finally spied her in the park by the river. She listened and soon saw that to get Bruce's help, Marta had to be included.

"Oh, go ahead, then, tell her. But Bruce, she has to keep quiet about this."

Bruce knew that would not be a problem when he asked Marta to please sit down and listen to a serious story. She listened, calmed down, and understood. She was there as simply an observer while those two had inherited entwined stories. How really incredible—Bruce's grandparents' own orchard land, and the river it lay along had been used to destroy a city full of families, including some of Suki's. *These two have found a common cause; that's what their intense looks are about. They feel this place far deeper than I ever could.*

Marta sighed, "It's okay, I get it." *But why this harebrained and illegal stunt? And I must be going insane, too, to wish to go along with them. Maybe I can argue them down if it gets too dangerous.* Then she decided she had to tell Leon the plan. What if they were caught, thrown in the clink, and he hadn't been warned? What kind treatment to a friend would that be? When Bruce was busy with his map, she hurried down to the conference room and motioned Leon to come out in the hall. Her trusted mentor shook his head at the tale.

"Well, you're not going to stop him, are you? It's just a question of whether you go or not."

He watched her steam, then said, "I can see this place has many parallels for him—the desert, the farmers driven out like refugees, the bombing, the destruction of whole cities of people, and now radioactive waste that hasn't been disposed of. And a victim family asking for help. A family with losses far bigger than his family endured here."

"Yes, I know. Nagasaki knocking on his door. He went overseas a romantic kid and came back an angry, guilty man. Leon, he hints he may even have been a mercenary for a time."

Leon tried to think of what to say; this was an adventure he had no precedents for.

"Whew! But you don't have to go. You don't have to feel guilty for stuff that happened at White Bluffs or Nagasaki before you were born. Or for choices he made or will make."

"Oh, I'm going, I'm going. And we're going to sneak in the pitch-black night through a desert full of poisonous snakes, to a place that is off limits, surrounded by guards with guns."

"Well that's what he did, isn't it? For years, that kind of thing? He's a warrior, let go from his life of action. Now, to sit on his haunches telling stories like an old man? Marta, my dear, you'll have to get used to life with more such impulsive notions if you want to be with him."

She sighed. "Yeah, thanks. I should've known you'd defend him."

"Just seeing the reality of the guy. So go, but don't feel obligated. You can always stay here and listen to stories." He knew she would go, of course.

Marta said, "You could do me a favor. I don't think anyone has done serious research with these settlers, and I'm thinking...if you'll keep some mental notes for me, I'll never forget it. And I know Bruce will be so grateful if you keep on with the memoir."

⋅⊷⊨◉ ◉⊨⊶⋅

Bruce picked up everything he thought they would need for the drive, including bug hats, rented a birding scope, and returned to the hall to find Marta and Suki and tell them to be ready to leave soon. Leon had rejoined the settlers, who had switched back to lighter topics: the fierce baseball, later basketball games against twin town Hanford, and small-town politics that were almost as good for blowing off steam. Thelma had commented that most of the time the population of White Bluffs (both sites) wasn't over 500 people, and could drop even to 300, depending on how the fruit market was doing.

"Everyone knew everyone, probably more than they needed to, through the grapevine. Most people believed when phones were finally installed that they were supposed to be used only for business, but of course the rule was broken, and people listening in could complain, like 'Get off the phone! We need the weather forecast!'—which came through the phone company."

Leon was not surprised that gossip was a main system of communication and control for such tiny communities. But after the town was split it must have had more of an edge.

"Hanford was even smaller. What was that town like?"

"Livelier," Dorothy laughed.

"Livelier! How's that?"

"Didn't I say they drank more, for one thing? And we were told not to go out with those Hanford boys. I did only once and never again."

Janice giggled. Dorothy touched her arm, "You don't have to put that in your report!"

Leon went on, "Those little towns sound like rather free-wheeling places."

Roger shook his head. "I can't speak for Hanford, but at White Bluffs it was a mix. Drinkers, sure, but many that never touched it. And some just made hard cider—plenty of that around. What they had in common was they all wanted to be living out in the country."

"What kind of people, I mean what background?"

"You mean what nationality background? I would say mainly British, some German, some Swedes. And Asians; they were not in White Bluffs, but nearby, like at Ringold. We got along pretty well for such a mix of backgrounds. There were some feuds. But in a small town with nothing much going on—except the ball games and watching your crops grow—little feuds keep things livelier. But moving the town—that was too destructive."

Thelma frowned, "Or taking up cross-burning."

Leon sat up. *The Klan?* "What was that about?"

Thelma looked around, was glad Suki was not present, and said, "The Orientals, we thought. My family never knew the whole story. There were a few Japanese families farming on the east side of the river and some people didn't want them moving over on our side. This was in the 1920s, I was just a kid. I don't know if it was locals or outsiders doing the Klan thing. Or if it was against the Catholics, or one Jewish family. But it didn't spread; I only saw that twice. My guess is that cross-burning wasn't popular."

Leon looked around, always surprises from this group, this history. He knew he'd never keep track of it all for Marta, and took a chance.

"Uh, I wonder, is it all right if I take notes? This history is all fascinating."

Roger shrugged, "Why not? We're glad to have people that are interested."

Leon said thanks, and got out his pen and tiny notebook. "Okay…then, aside from the moth-spraying, would you folks say White Bluffs was a healthy life for the children?"

Thelma nodded. "Very. Some came just because it was desert, trying to get away from the TB hitting the cities. Dry air was supposed to help. And the Spanish flu practically passed us by we were so isolated. Really, the worst health problem wasn't drowning, or sunstroke, or spray. It was TB in young folks—just what they'd come to the desert to get away from, and, sad, it followed them. Especially the teenage girls, right, Dot?"

Dorothy nodded, "It was the flapper craze, to get as thin as possible. Girls got caught up in it and some did get TB. A couple of them we knew died of it. Friends. Tragic. But I agree, overall very healthy for children."

There was a pause when Roger and Orville went to the bathroom, Orville commenting that the faucets didn't work so well anymore. Bruce went outside to check the temperature; had it dropped to something Marta could handle? The men were slow to return; Leon suspected a stop for a cold beer, so he picked a new topic for the women: "social problems", though he wasn't sure what would have qualified in those days. He waited for Thelma or Dorothy to speak up. The two women looked at each other.

Finally Thelma said, "Social problems? Oh...well, there were men who drank and then they'd fight, but I don't think they saw it as a problem. Probably their wives did."

Dorothy rolled her eyes. "And there were men who beat their wives, and everyone knew about it; most didn't approve of it. And a couple women were known to beat their husbands too. And beat their kids? In those days, you know, they believed the strap was necessary to raise kids properly, the boys anyway."

Leon thought this social behavior probably wasn't much different from rural communities anywhere in the country. He wasn't sure how far to go with this topic.

"How about...ah, unwed mothers?"

Thelma and Dorothy looked embarrassed, but after a moment Thelma spoke up.

"Girls did get pregnant sometimes, and it was called 'girls being where they shouldn't have been'. We did get the lectures on that! As for the boy—or man—he had to marry her fast or else leave town. We didn't have a lot of single parent families like today. And we didn't have things like burglaries. Well, I remember that some money seemed to disappear from the grower's coop once. That was a real shock to everyone. My goodness, stealing!"

Marta and Suki laughed with the others. The men had returned. Orville said, "Well, at least we didn't have drug dealers—no profit in it. Marijuana was growing wild all over the place. Well, a very weak strain...I'm told, compared to what's peddled today. And some young fellows, not me, would drink and fight, and go to jail for a night to cool off."

Dorothy said, "Don't forget, there was one bank robbery—in thirty years. And one murder, but it was by an outsider."

"So that was it for crime? Really?" Leon smiled.

"If you omit moving the town, moonshining, and things like that," said Roger. "But it gives the picture of a different society from today, doesn't it?"

Thelma looked around, "Where did Bruce go again?"

Marta was prepared. "Oh, there's a problem on his job. He keeps having to call, just the usual thing. And we talked about doing some birdwatching."

Thelma said to Dorothy, "It'll be too hot, won't it?"

Roger looked at Leon and frowned. *What about the memoir?* After a few more minutes he stood up, "My bones get stiff now. I'm going to take another break. Anyone want to join me for a beer?"

He didn't wait for an answer, and Orville followed him. Suki looked at Marta, *Can't we get going?* Leon left also, not with the beer drinkers, but to avoid more questions about birdwatching. Earlier Bruce had grabbed him out in the hall, saying he needed an idea for a cover in case someone got curious—a car parked out in the middle of nowhere. Leon had listened, realizing the plan was no crazier than what he did at Bruce's age, *traipsing around in a desert with a mediocre map, a canteen of water, and a book on edible plants and insects. Totally nuts!*

"So you need an alibi? How about this—you're birdwatchers. Try to rent a scope somewhere, and notebooks, and a bird book. And act wildly enthusiastic."

"But there won't be birds out in this heat. And how about later, when we go back. Bird-watching at night?"

"Sure. Owls…nighthawks. Or you're just waiting it out—to be there at dawn. Lots of birds then. Act like fanatics, you know, the harmless kind."

"Yeah…. Leon, I'm not sure I'm harmless."

CHAPTER 10

DESERT PLOTTERS

AN HOUR LATER the birdwatchers drove north on the same road the tour bus had taken into the closed area; no off-road excursions allowed. Marta observed the same brushy, dry-grassy desert, endless sagebrush, sometimes a few welcome cottonwoods, fences full of tumbleweed, and distant hills. They didn't turn off the highway, so there was no river-and-bluffs view to shock the senses. Bruce was quiet and the others followed his lead, but Marta, looking closer, began to see that the desert was not truly flat, but slightly rolling. Scattered among the endless gray-greens and dull yellows there were clusters of brushy plants with bright yellow, lavender, or white blossoms, many of them knee to thigh-high. She remembered that Ike had said they were immigrants. Before long they saw the active nuclear plant in the distance. Marta almost brought it up, then decided not to. There was enough tension in the car already. As for birds, it was too hot, she thought, until they saw a quail pop out of the brush and run across the road right in front of them, its flock of half-grown chicks scrambling along behind.

Marta cried, "Hey, so cute! Where's my notebook?" But she suspected that as birders they would appear likely fakes to any security personnel passing by, or to anyone else for that matter.

Suki finally spoke up, "How will we know where to stop when we can't see the river?"

Bruce passed her the map, "Here, take a look. See the bridge where this road crosses the river? Reactor B should be just east, downstream four-five miles. Maybe not close enough though. I can't guarantee you'll be able to see it, Suki. It depends on the lay of the land."

"I know."

"We'll park where we seem to be the closest."

More silence. Marta finally commented. "It's not so scenic, is it, this desert. When you get away from the river."

Bruce nodded. "It could be most of the Middle East. The river and its bluffs are what make it special, just like Harold says."

"But Thelma says the native flowers are outstanding in the spring. I want to come then."

Suki cried, "I just saw another quail!"

"Bird book!"

Bruce knew that if they would park and illegally walk around, they would see much more variety in plants and birds, certainly insects, and even animals. But all that would have to wait. They saw the brush began to move, and hoped it didn't mean, as Esau had warned, a possible sand storm coming. Then, up ahead, they spotted a car stopped, a man bent over by its side. Bruce slowed and pulled up to see if he needed assistance.

"Oh no!" Marta cried, "Can't we lose this guy?"

It was Walt Croaker.

Great. Bruce kept his face flat, his voice calm. "Hi. Need any help?"

"No, just checking the air in a tire. What are you folks up to?" Croaker came to the car window and looked the three over with his clearly faked smile. *Uh-huh, that Jap woman too.*

"Bird-watching." Bruce was about to drive on when Croaker leaned his arm on the window opening.

"Oh really? You're birdwatchers? Hum. So, do you folks really think the sage hen is endangered? Well, come for a short walk with me and I'll show you sage hens, lots of them. You're not in a rush, are you?" He stared at Bruce. "Oh... by the way, you hear about the endangered ruffled-neck turkey that's supposed to be hereabouts? Maybe you'll spot one. That one's gotta be saved at all cost."

Bruce nodded, "So...around here you say?"

Croaker gave him a sly grin, and Bruce felt a poke in his side from Marta.

"Well, actually, we do need to move along...so we can get back to the reunion events."

"Oh, I see...well, later then."

As Bruce started off, Croaker called out, "Have fun playing federal agent, Wilder. You don't fool me."

Bruce turned to Marta, "What did he say?"

Marta told him. He cursed, braked, and pulled off the road, "That's it, I've had it with this asshole. He wants trouble, he's getting it." He jerked open the door and jumped out.

Croaker was already running into the brush, Bruce plunging right after him, all his desert training surging through him.

Marta scrambled out of the car, Suki behind her, and yelled, "Bruce, never mind!"

He stopped, glanced at her, and shook his fist, "I'm settling this now!" And kept going, disappearing into the brush, a coyote after a rabbit. Scrambling through, he soon saw Croaker was much faster than he would have guessed, but he knew he'd outlast him. *I'll pound him till he's pulp. I told him I could kill him easy, now he'll believe me.*

Croaker's legs were magically faster than they'd been at age thirty, but after a hundred yards his smoker's lungs were shrieking. *Sonofabitch!* He tripped and fell. Bruce stopped to listen: silence. He couldn't see his tormenter through the brush. *Probably had a heart attack. What am I doing?*

"Croaker, listen, don't come near me again or you're a dead man. Hear me? Answer me!"

Flat on the ground, Croaker grabbed a breath and called, "I hear you, asshole."

"You will stay away from me and let me enjoy this reunion. You will do that! Answer me, or I'm coming for you."

"Okay, okay!" The voice came in gasps. "But I have friends that will take care of you later, Wilder."

"Bring 'em on!" Bruce waited. Silence. He turned and pushed through the brush back to the car. By the time he reached the two women—Suki standing frozen in shock, Marta in less shock than anger—he felt much better.

"I almost killed him."

Marta cried, "I'm grabbing the next bus out of here if this doesn't stop!"

"Fine. Go stop him yourself then. I don't start it, never have. Come on, let's go."

Heading north again, calmer, he said, "You don't see the whole picture, Mart. I had to scare him. He's after me for some reason, and we can't have him following us. I had a choice, stop him or cancel for tonight."

Marta begged, "So cancel then!"

"No way. Don't worry, he'll stay far away now."

Suki said, "What about his pals he mentioned?"

"Those old farmers?" Bruce snorted and drove on, one part wishing he'd beat Croaker up good, the other happy he'd stopped before he started.

After a minute Marta said, "I think he caught you on that ruffled turkey business."

"Damn! Should've kept my mouth shut."

"So what kind of agents are you guys?" Suki asked, half serious.

"Agents of Uncle Harold, carrying his writings. High security."

Suki shrugged and said, "I'm certainly finding out how many people care about this river and this area, all in their own ways."

"Croaker's ways are beyond me," said Bruce.

Marta waited for Suki to say more but she didn't. *Perhaps she's fishing for an article. Well, I'll give her a quote.*

"Caring about the river? I don't know about idiots like Croaker, but I'm sure the Indians care. They want to hold onto their culture, and that means the river and the salmon. And it's important for fishermen of all kinds. Thousands of sport fishermen. And the corporate farms and ranches, and any small farms remaining, and Northwest industry—they all need this river's power in a big way. And the barge companies. And the green groups, you know how hot they can get about saving the wild salmon? So I think you could say all kinds of people care about this river."

Marta wondered if she had come across as too know-it-all.

Bruce said, "Don't forget the scientists whose grants keep them going, and the Army Corp of Engineers that has the funding to keep it all pumping away for industry—the dams and all. And all those hatcheries, and their staffs. Even me. Like you say, they all see its value in very different ways."

Suki went on, "A lot of caring. But all those groups, and all that caring, and they can't force the government to get the Hanford waste cleaned up? That's pretty weird; that's not really caring enough is it?"

Bruce frowned, "True. But there is a real problem; someone has to be willing to be paid to take the poisonous junk, right? Why would they?"

Marta smirked, "Maybe some starving place, some third world country?"

"Sure," said Suki, "always a good answer."

Then she understood Marta was being sarcastic, and after a moment she added, "But what I think is that all these people, if they really care, if they don't want the nuclear waste in their river, then they have to build a huge movement against nuclear plants. I mean huge."

Marta listened to Suki, thinking she was beginning to understand her better.

Bruce said, "Yeah, but you know, it could be done. The Indians won their battle for dividing the fishing quota. That was a long, tough one, but they did it."

For a while Suki didn't answer, then she asked, "What about this guy Sohappy you were talking about? Is he still alive?"

"No, but if you want to know more, look up David Sohappy, and Billy Frank and their battles. It's quite a story." He thought a bit and added, "But what they won is just part of the salmon troubles. I hear about it every day at work. That was over twenty years ago and the runs are still weak. Lots of the reasons the scientists do understand, but not all. And of course it can only get worse when the nuclear crap reaches the river."

Suki kept going, "Then that means more public support, voter support."

Marta was impressed, and said, "When we go up to Priest Rapids, or Wolf Rapids, you might want to come along and hear the Indians' side of it. More for your article, whatever it will be. Or another one."

"Okay, thanks! I'd like to."

Marta felt envy. *I can't even make up my mind on my dissertation's direction.*

Bruce, by habit, flipped on the radio for the hourly news. After reports of local political battles and water shortages, a bright voice broke in with odds and ends of local interest:

"The Reactor B plant alarms went off last night about 9 p.m., but not to worry, folks, security reports that it was only an owl that had flown into the fence. End of owl. Hum, thought they could see at night!"

"So, electric fence," said Bruce, turning off the radio, "as expected."

Marta felt a chill. She definitely needed to understand this mission better. She certainly understood about the radioactive plant waste, and the fishery problems—she heard about them all the time, but not about why they had to drive up here just to see Reactor B.

"What magazine do you write for, Suki?

"Well, actually, I'm a freelancer."

"What are you planning for tonight? Do you have some kind of night camera?"

"No...I'll see pretty soon what I need to do."

Marta got the message: no more questions. Soon Bruce pulled over to the side and checked his map and mileage. They were as close as they could get to the B Reactor he thought. He could see steam but no buildings, as a rise apparently obscured them. He turned the car around to be facing toward Richland.

"Okay folks, time to become birders. Grab your field guide and note-books, and let's go find a spot to have lunch in the brush."

Marta took a deep breath. *Well, here we go, out into the furnace.* She was deter-mined she would not say one word about the heat today, and was relieved to feel the breeze. They put on their packs and hats, and she and Suki followed Bruce northeast. About fifty feet into the thigh-high sagebrush he came to a well-maintained barbed wire fence.

Bruce looked back at them, "Don't worry, this can't be the real fence. It's probably just to let people know this is government property. It's not live—just crawl through, like any dedicated birder would."

He saw that they certainly would not be trying to walk toward the plant in daylight—he had hoped the brush would be taller. He pushed through it until he found an opening where he told the women to sit down while he scouted for a higher spot for the view Suki wanted. He moved out soundlessly, crouching very low, and Marta mused that this was just what he had done, not so long ago, for a living. But she was puzzled as to what it could gain Suki—being near the reactor—if that was really why they had come.

The two women were silent as they got out the lunch. Marta decided that Suki needed to be more forthright.

"I think it's great if you do a story on this place from your perspective. Lots has been written about the plant's history, but nothing I know of, from your point of view—I mean from your relocated family, and your relatives in Nagasaki."

"No, I haven't found anything like that either."

Bruce suddenly popped up by them and stage-whispered. "There's a guy walking down the road toward us! So it's good practice for us if he gets curious about our car. Probably he'll go right on by. But just in case he notices us, be writing in your notebooks. Shhh…just write! And let's be eating too."

⊶⊨◉ ◉⊨⊷

That morning Esau had decided that he needed to check on his grandson Jason and the kayak. He asked his nephew Ike to drop him off at the highway fork that turned west toward Yakima. That would put him close to the old trail that skirted the reactors and continued all the way to the old campsite by the island. Esau expected Jason was at the island, but he also wanted to check along the reactor fences, just in case. While waiting for dark, he'd gone a hundred yards into the brush on the west side of the road and searched around an area where he recalled a spring. He found it in a hollow full of grass, creeping plants, and cottonwood saplings. Signs of jack rabbits abounded. Good, his alibi for being here. There was no running water, but dropping his pack, he dug with a stick until he created a hollow with some usable seepage. After that he set four snares and took a long nap under a shade he made from brush.

When Esau woke it was still hot; he had plenty of time before dark to look around for signs of game and plan his moves. He was determined to find Jason by tonight, unless he'd gone on down the river. The south wind he felt starting was going to bring more clouds, better for traveling unseen. He checked to see that he had his tiny flashlight to aid in looking for old trail marks on the long hike. Now he unwrapped some dry fish to munch on, drank a little water, and shouldered his pack. But as he was about to cross the highway, he was surprised to see a car was parked not far away. A few minutes later, he was standing right at the birdwatchers' clearing. *What are these people? Some of the reunion folks?*

Bruce was caught by surprise even though he'd seen the man on the road a few minutes earlier. *I must be losing my hearing.* He had decided that they might have to abort; they would say they needed to be off looking for birds again, just pack up and go back to the car. But now he saw the guy was an Indian elder, and was too curious about him and what he might know, and so instead they ended up introducing themselves and eating together. Soon they were talking about the missing grandson.

"I think we saw him yesterday," said Bruce. "He seemed to be okay then. He was down by your old campground. The bus driver was showing us around."

"Ah, yes, my nephew, Ike, he told me. You're from the family who lived right near our camp. Harold comes to see us during their reunion, but not this year. Is he okay?"

"He's okay, just quite lame, getting old maybe."

"A good man, I like him."

"He's why I'm here this time. He wrote something about his times in White Bluffs and wanted me to bring it to the settler's reunion."

"I'd like to read it."

"I probably can get you a copy soon. Well, we saw your grandson, and he talked to Ike for a while, and then he headed back to the island. There were some kayakers there, and he wondered what they were doing."

"Kayakers. So probably that's where he is. But I need to go by the reactor fences. He could be there too, and that's worse."

Bruce looked at Suki. *Another one needing to get involved with the reactors?* "Why would he go there?"

After a pause Esau shrugged, "A few years back something bad happened there.... I guess it still bothers him."

While they ate, Esau looked over the three. *So this is the woman related to the Japanese family at Ringold. And the Wilder man. The other is his wife or girlfriend, Ike said an anthropologist. Another one.*

He went on, "This area is no place to be wandering around. Some people might sneak in here to hunt once in a while. But young people these days have minds of their own."

He waited a minute again for someone to volunteer what their purpose was, but the three simply leafed through their bird books, made conversation about birds, chewed their lunch, drank water, and wiped sweat. Esau answered a few questions about local birds. Bruce saw he was not going to move on. He felt they were ridiculous to the old man, despite what Leon had said about "all kinds of birdwatchers".

Finally, after they'd finished the food and put the scraps away, Esau spoke.

"So... how can I help you? Looking for birds in this heat when, you know, they hide?"

Bruce smiled, *Okay, he's onto us.* Marta glanced at Bruce and noticed the look he always got when he was brewing up something. But Suki answered the elder first.

"Maybe you can help me. I need to find a spot where I can see clearly the B reactor."

She ignored Bruce's shocked look as Esau waited for her to explain more, but she didn't. Bruce, glaring at her, was struggling to control his annoyance, and Esau studied him for a moment before he spoke to Suki.

"Look at a reactor? You can't get close enough in daylight. Maybe at night you could sneak closer, but it's a walk."

Bruce shrugged. *There's no use packing up now.* "She needs to...see it. But you're right, can't get close enough in daylight."

"No, unless you want a lot of company," Esau grinned. "Another way, a better view, and easier if it's not too hot, is on top of the bluffs on the other side. There's a road part way, and then you can hike over to the edge of the bluff and see a long ways."

Bruce nodded. "I wondered about that."

"I did it years ago. I was looking almost right down on a reactor."

"But could you see the B reactor?"

"I don't remember—it was way off, but I think I saw them all. Probably they all look a lot alike. Lots of buildings and roads and fences."

Suki said, "Thanks for your help; I'm grateful. But it does need to be B reactor."

Esau waited. *What is her need? Sure not birds.*

Bruce thought a while, then looked at her. "You know, we are here now, so we should try this side and if it can't work, we'll try the other side, probably do that public side in daylight."

Esau nodded and looked at Suki again for a long minute, then went back to analyzing Bruce, as the others flitted glances at each other. At last he directed to him, "Seems like maybe you have some experience moving around in the dark?"

Bruce shrugged, "Enough."

"And I need to go that way tonight, maybe even as far as the island. There's an old trail. You could follow me part way, go by B Reactor if you want, but not all of you, it's too big a target. I won't go unless it's cloudy. But it will be."

Bruce was taken back. *Cloudy, that's good. But all of us, sneaking so many miles in the dark, through brush? A target, sure thing.* Bruce fought back warning shots: flashbacks that began to flood him. *First Suki, now this elder. Think, any way to make a good plan out of this?*

"You're going clear down to the island? Must be over ten-twelve miles from here, and then back again?" *This guy must be seventy anyway, what's he thinking of? Just worried about the kid? Talk him out of it. He could collapse out there and who'd know? And Suki doesn't have to go far at all.*

Esau nodded. He'd had time to think more about the trip during the day. Looking toward the distant invisible island, he stretched out his legs. He hadn't hiked clear down there in years...but his grandson. *Jason's in some kind of mess, I think. I have to go.*

Bruce frowned, hands sifting sand, thinking about the options. He refused to look toward Marta, while she shuddered at déjà vu that flooded her—*that time I knew I had to go out in the canoe with Bruce to rescue that dog stranded on a log jam in a river—here we go again.* She'd realized back then that Bruce was a rescuer. That was why he liked the job at the hatchery, trying to rescue salmon runs. Why he'd ended up on medical missions. Now this particular rescue mission could be expanding big time. She saw the excitement continuing to build in him. Since the dog rescue she'd had been on several rough, fast-paced hikes with Bruce, knew how they fed his spirit. *No use arguing, not when he gets like this.*

Suki finally said, "I am grateful for any help, and I don't have to see the buildings, just the lights. At night is okay, as long as I can see the lights."

Everyone waited on the others. Then Bruce flashed on a solution that pleased him.

"I have an idea, why don't we split this? I feel like I have to go see what those kayakers are doing. And I welcome the exercise, been sitting around like a toad too much the last couple days. I can look for your grandson at the same time. And you can help Suki."

Marta was caught by surprise. *How did we suddenly involve the kayakers? None of our business. This can't go right.* She tried to give him a questioning look but he went right on. She saw it was all an excuse for another rescue adventure. The reunion wasn't challenging enough.

Bruce made his proposal clear. "Tell you what, uncle, why don't you show me your trail over to the island, and if he's there I'll give him whatever message you want. And maybe you can find Suki a good view of the reactor easier than I could."

Esau mused. When it came down to it, he didn't really look forward to a twenty-mile or more round-trip. He just needed to find Jason. Once it would have been a day's hike down there, a little tougher coming back. This man, no doubt a vet, could maybe do it easier and in less time. He got up and walked a bit into the brush. *Ike says he seems okay, and he's from a good family. I can trust him. I could check the fence at Reactor B and this young vet could do the others.* Not positive it was a good plan, in a few minutes he walked back and nodded 'all right' to Bruce, and then to Suki. Marta stared at them all. *Oh boy.*

"I'll show you the trail." Esau began drawing in the sand. "There's nine reactors along the river, a few miles apart, but the trail cuts across this bend, lots shorter. There's one reactor about here, just up from where you were with Ike, our old campsite. Give that fence room, stay with the old trail, and here's where you can cross to the island—the head of the slough. It's dry now."

Bruce studied his drawing as Esau went on.

"The guards won't see you if it's overcast tonight. Jason's probably still at the island."

"If he's not there, check along all the fences on the way back?"

"If you want—it would be good. But I can check this first reactor. You could skip it and stay on the trail clear out to the road."

Bruce waited for any more instructions.

Esau pointed, "Have you noticed how much of this brush is covered with thorns? When you come tonight you'll be going through that. And deer ticks. So wear long sleeves and long pants tucked in like me, or you'll end up a mess of scratches and ticks. And take enough water. I guess you know."

"Sure."

Esau grinned, "Coming back, you'll look like war refugees...birdwatchers, maybe not."

"Can you show me the trail now, Uncle?" Bruce pulled his camo jacket from his pack.

Marta got the message she wasn't invited. *Too big a crowd.* She shook her head and glared at Suki. *Look what you got us into, and all for a story.*

Esau slid off through the brush, followed by Bruce. After two hundred feet he pointed,

"You see the trail?"

"Yeah, where branches are broke off."

"Pretty fresh, someone's marked it again. You can follow it all the way to the head of the slough. You've been there. You can make it down and back in maybe...six-seven hours, really moving though."

"That's fine."

Esau stood there a moment, staring out into the brush. *He wants to do this; it's important for him.* "Now tell me, if it's okay, why does that young woman have to see the reactor? Young people always want to get involved in things they maybe should stay out of. It's been a long time ago they made all the Japanese farmers leave here."

Bruce shrugged. "I know, over fifty years. But she's here now, and she hates what the plant was part of. Me too. Suki writes for a magazine, needs to see it I guess."

"There's lots of government photos."

"I know. But it has to do with her family in Japan. I said I'd help her. I need to."

"Oh, family. And you're angry about this plant too? So am I, lots of people are. Well, I need to find Jason…. So, okay, you follow this trail tonight and maybe you'll see him, give him my message to get out of there—now, or maybe he's got big trouble."

"Thank you, Uncle. So, this evening can we meet back at this same place? Let's say seven? I can make the car look broken down or something."

"Okay. But if the wind really comes up and a sand storm begins, forget trying to come back here, no way to see anything. Bad to be out then."

"Oh, I know about sand storms. What will you do then?"

"I know an abandoned shack across the road, not far. And I have a ride in the morning."

Bruce felt no reason to doubt the elder. He looked down what he could see of the old trail and felt confident. And he'd already been at the slough, a known destination. They rejoined the women and all pushed through the brush and fence back to the road.

"Can we give you a ride somewhere, Uncle?"

"No thanks, I'll be looking around." But Esau was already wondering why he had agreed to the arrangement. What if these people got in trouble? He watched the three go toward the car and followed them to speak his concern, when Suki turned and came trotting back to him.

"Wait, excuse me, can I talk to you?"

Bruce stared after her. *Now what?*

CHAPTER 11

SNAKE TALE

ESAU SAW THE great determination on Suki's face. *Now I will find out what she wants.* He waited while she took a deep breath and looked off past him toward Saddle Mountain, hoping she masked her nervousness over how difficult it was to talk to an elder she didn't even know about such a strange thing. She forced herself to make eye contact.

"Thank you for listening. I do need to find some higher ground, like I said, but it's not to take photos. It's something very important to me…. I hope you'll understand."

He waited. She turned away, then back to him, and he heard the tension in her voice.

"Your people camped and fished all along Hanford Reach and farther, Ike told us."

He nodded, "We got driven out again and again, and then again to make that bomb."

He had always wondered what the outcome had been for the Japanese farmers like the family at Ringold. *She must know.*

"So I think that's why you might help me," she said, and pointed east, "What's that over there? A ridge?"

He nodded, "A ridge, yes. I can take a look over there; maybe we can see the lights of the reactor. Is that good enough?"

"I think so. But there's more to this than just me. I made a promise to my mother and grandmother. Years ago."

"Ah. Those promises are important."

She took a long breath. "Do you mind, can we sit down, so I can explain better?"

He nodded and they moved away from the road and sat in the dry grass. She thought about how to phrase her request. He waited. She looked at the ground.

"So I need to ask you, Esau, I hope it's not sounding rude. Are you a Christian, or do you follow your old religion?" Now she looked right at him for a second. He couldn't help a little laugh.

What are these people up to, really? Nuke protesters? Some religion cult? Not much like the people Ike takes on bus tours.

"My religion? A mix I guess. And you, if it's not rude?" He smiled to take the edge off.

"Me? A mix...I'm not sure what. My older family in Japan, my mother's mother, still follows the Shinto religion—a modern version, I would say."

Esau was puzzled. *This is about religion, then.*

Marta, waiting in the car, looked back at them, but Bruce told her not to make them feel rushed, that they had hours until dark.

Suki went on, "I don't know much about Shinto religion, but I don't think you'll laugh at me about this. You've heard of Nagasaki, right?"

"Nagasaki? Sure, everyone my age here has heard of that place, that the plutonium for the bomb got made right here." He waited.

She forced herself again to look straight at him. "That's where we were from, my family...Nagasaki. My mother's there now with her mother."

His stomach did a flip. *So it's finally come home to us.* "Ah.... they were there when the bomb was dropped?"

She took a breath; she was prepared for this. "Yes, my grandparents. My mother and father were over here, in one of the camps. But her own father died, her mother got scarred, inside and out. Over 70,000 people died just the first year, many more later, and mostly civilians. And at Hiroshima. I guess you know about this?" He nodded.

"So...four years ago I promised my mother and grandmother to put a Shinto curse on this place for them. Not an evil curse, a blessing I think you probably would call it, a blessing for good, not evil. I've put it off way too long...maybe because I didn't feel sure of myself at all. But now I'm here."

He closed his eyes and breathed in the sage around them. *She is like my Alice, a warrior woman. On a mission.*

Marta, in the car, grew more concerned as they waited. She peered back at the two. "Is there more to this, that we're getting into?"

"I told you all I know."

"Okay. But there is more, obviously, going on out there."

"Seems so. But it's good. We are helping two people now, three counting Jason. Five if we get the kayaker kids out of there safely. I'm calling the shots now, remember?"

"Um." *Really?*

"Hey, this is child's play for me. You can stay at the hotel this evening, or you can stay by the road here tonight and wait. Look for hawks and owls."

"No way. I'll stick with you."

Esau, waiting for Suki to go on, thought her story believable. Quite a few ethnic Japanese farmers had been on the mid-Columbia, especially in the Yakima River area, before they were evicted and sent to camps. Before that, when he went to the county fairs he would see them along with the rest of the families showing their colorful displays of fruits and vegetables. So few had returned; he'd never met anyone from Japan after the war. *Why wouldn't they want to put a curse on this place? She's waited too long.*

Finally, he said, "You talk about evil. Lots of evil done in this valley. That bombing was probably the greatest evil. So...do your friends know about this?" He motioned at the car.

"They know I made a promise, don't know about the Shinto curse. The blessing. Today I've found out I can't get very close, but probably find a place where I can see the B reactor lights clearly."

"Probably."

Esau shrugged off the possibility that there could be some kind of trick involved; he didn't get that feeling. *She is what she says she is.* It was only a matter of deciding whether to help her or not. Helping her intrigued him, he had to admit; her promise, the spiritual side to it, he felt was genuine. There was right and wrong, and her people had been greatly hurt, whole communities, families, and many more to die later. *I know about things like that. Hanford Plant made that plutonium from our river, Chiawana water. Evil from our river.*

Suki went on, "Such terrible destruction there, so many dead, children too. Their wish is to carry this blessing out so that this place, this river, will never again be used for destruction, that no more people will be poisoned from what was made here, and the ones ill from it will recover, and the poison disappear forever, all of it. I've put it off and off. How to do this? So now I'm here, and on my visit to see them this fall, I want to be able to say I carried out my promise."

He was silent, pondering what she proposed.

After she had waited quite a while, she asked quietly, "What do you think? Can I do it?"

Shinto...I don't know I've heard of it, but the old religions have much in common. At last he said, "If you believe you can do it, you may have the power. *It can't hurt anyway.* We have medicine people that have tried, so far failed. But you have a strong spirit behind you I think. So you want to be able to see the reactor."

"I just need to see the lights. So, be on a ridge."

"Do you know the things you have to do, the things to say?"

Suki nodded. "The actions they told me are simple, and you don't have to say long rituals. My grandmother told me I'd know what to say when I am ready, that it's a universal religion, for any people."

He nodded.

"My grandmother says it needs a pure heart more than ritual. You get the strength you need for the blessing from your heart—and also from nature. She left it up to me, how to do this, but I didn't feel strong enough, I guess. I always found ways to be too busy. But this year I decided I had to try. So I went to White Bluffs, you know, on the bus with Ike, and we walked up the river...now I know what I will try to do—with your help."

"What about these other people with you?"

"They're just friends I met at the settler's reunion. They helped me by coming out here. I trust Bruce especially, because of—who he is. They helped me get the feeling of this place, the good and bad. And Ike did, too, on the bus ride; he speaks well."

"Yes, I hear that he does. So you just want me to find you a good ridge? I'll find the best one and we can go there tonight. And I should check that reactor fence anyway, the closest one, for my grandson."

She heard the "we"; he had said yes. She sensed she could trust him, maybe because of the way he would go through all this to find his grandson, and also that he was trusting Bruce. Now she felt she could ask one more thing, more difficult, from him.

"Esau, I feel like I also need something powerful from nature to help me."

"So…a helper spirit."

"Yes, and I know one here. I've felt its power—got charged with it yesterday, when we were walking with Ike. So I have another thing to ask you, to please get one for me if you can, before tonight. Or if not possible, soon. Then I know I can do the blessing. So…I need a bullsnake."

"A bullsnake!"

"Yes."

He was amazed. *A blessing, using snake power.* He sat in silence. *This is a strange meeting. Strange, yet she is sincere, and anything to clean this place is good. Has to be. A bullsnake, why not?* "Did they tell you to use a snake?"

"No, it just came to me when I saw it on the path; that's what I needed, that power. I felt helpless until I saw it."

Finally, he nodded, "Old religion always knows the power of snakes and you felt it." He thought for a moment. "When you do your blessing, can you pray to get rid of all the evil here, not just the Hanford Plant? For this whole area to be clean again?"

"Yes, I can do that, sure, I want to. Can you tell me what else happened here?"

Oh boy. Where to begin? She wants a history lesson? I don't think so…whew.

"So…to do the blessing you want to hear what happened here, besides what you know about. Well, lots of sad history since way back, the time of my grandparents. But now, the thing that bothers Jason—I will tell you, all right? It's best not talked about, but you could pray about it."

"All right."

Esau sighed, picked up a twig to stroke, wishing he could have a smoke, but not a good idea here. *She has trusted me with a lot. I think I can trust her.*

"A young man died down here, Arni was his name. He kept going down here. He was alone, a sort of wanderer, and came and stayed with us a while. Jason, just a kid, liked him. Then he was gone a lot and one day he was missing. Some of us came looking, and down here near the fence they found him. Not right at the fence, but close. We don't know what killed him, no marks. We didn't want trouble, so some of us thought they should move the body out of the closed area and say they found him out there. But when they came back in the dark, he—the body—was gone. Never found it. So, to many the place is cursed. It was already, so... even more cursed."

"And your grandson keeps coming back here now?"

"And it's one more evil thing about the place for him. He wants to get the whole plant taken out of here, and like you, get the area clean again. Well, you know we all do."

"Thanks for telling me. It's important."

"If you read any history of this area, you'll know other things."

"I can imagine."

"So...Suki...that's your name? I think you are on a good path. I can try to find you a snake. Male or female doesn't matter?"

She heaved a sigh that she had succeeded with her odd request, and finally smiled at him. "No, either is fine."

"A big one, I guess."

"Yes, but one we can carry a ways, and not hurt it."

Esau thought a moment, then said, "You know, what you are doing is all right with me, but I don't like these protests where young people get hurt and killed. And a year later everyone has forgotten what it was about except the suffering family."

"I am here to do is what I told you, nothing else. Oh, I might write a story about the river, or the settlers' reunion, for a magazine. But this special task is what I told you, not for a story, or to make news. It's for my family...and everyone. It's not connected to anything else."

"All right. I'll see you all back here this evening. And I'll go look for your bullsnake."

Suki smiled. "Thank you very much. I know you'll find one. I'll pray that you will. But please don't say anything yet to other people, okay?"

They stood up. He gave her a nod, waved at the others in the car, hoisted his pack, and disappeared into the brush. He had some waiting to do, and just in case, to create his alibi for being here in no-man's-land, he hoped he'd snare a couple rabbits. He looked at the sky, the clouds sneaking in. *What kind of energy is going on that all these strange people have moved in on the river?* He'd already heard about Elena being here again. But he had never heard before of the settler reunions bringing in such a mix. Ike, driving them, would have had big stories in that case. *Even Jason, and now me involved. Maybe even Ike—I hope not; Ike has other important work. Now my own—to find a bullsnake. But the pure heart, like she says, is where to start.*

Bruce was quiet and frowning as they headed back to Richland to wait a few hours, but Marta saw that Suki had a happier face.

"You might have more than one story from this trip, Suki!"

"It could be."

Marta thought that she certainly had much more than that to say to the elder.

"Well, I wish I was making as much headway on my research."

"Oh, you will find lots to study here, to write about."

Suki felt weak and opened her window, but the breeze was too warm to be comforting. She closed her eyes for a bit, and breathed in the smell of the sage. *All right, Mom, I did it. I've got a helper, two helpers, and I hope a third. I'm going to make good on my promise. You and Grandma will be with me and help me too.*

Bruce said, "I guess you heard him, Marta, only one person, for safety, going down to the island, less target. That's okay with you? You can stay with Leon for a change?"

"No! Why should you go alone? You and I are not a big crowd crashing through the brush. And you know I can hike."

"It's better I go alone tonight."

"No, it's not. If you find those kayakers down there...I'm more diplomatic."

He shrugged. That was Marta, no use arguing. But he wouldn't have wanted a wimp for a partner. If the long hike maxed her out, she'd learn from it.

"Suit yourself then. But I'll make you agree the same as Suki did, that on this trip I am the leader, and you will follow orders. Seriously! Do you agree? All right. I'll trust you on that."

CHAPTER 12

THE REUNION HEATS UP

BACK AT THE hotel in the late afternoon, Bruce and Marta removed their disguises, took showers, and rejoined the crowd, soon joined by a quiet Suki. Many of the settlers were focused on hundreds of photos of faces they were trying to identify. Leon had been reading the memoir, and a book he'd found in the hotel bookstore: *Kamiakin: Last Hero of the Yakimas*. As Bruce and Marta sat down he was asking settlers how they had gotten along with Wanapum families camped each fall just upriver a half-mile from the Wilders' orchard. The answers he got were various: "We never knew any", "I was scared of them as a kid", "Good neighbors", "Good to trade fruit for fish", "They used to be quite a few, then hardly any, sad to see". He thought they surely had more memories for people camped so close to the farms.

Then Roger was more forthcoming. "Their chief gave me two horses when I was a kid. My wonderful mare was gone, had been stolen by someone we found out later. I looked all over the county for her, no luck. But pretty soon we had two new horses. He just left them in our orchard, but they had his brand. One of the new horses was great. We took her with us when we left and the kids rode her for years."

Suki commented, "The chief must have liked you."

"Well, my family was always cordial, and his was in return. Just a few families were staying up there at the Rapids. Seemed like they were trying to hold onto their old life, and they made it work somehow."

Bruce said, "Yes, Harold writes something about that."

"Good. Can you look for it? Then, later two bigger dams went in, about the 1950s, I think, and those few Wanapums still wouldn't leave the last sites they had on the river. The PUD did the right thing then. Since they'd lost almost all of their fishing sites, it allotted them some property and better houses, and some got jobs working at the dams I think. That was one time being stubborn paid off. They're still there."

Leon knew there weren't many happy stories about the outcomes for Native Americans with the government, so he was glad to hear of one, even if a small one. Bruce and Marta listened and both were relieved that Leon seemed happy with his role in the story sharing. Bruce knew he would be too excited to carry it on with any sensitivity. He didn't even feel like sitting, and Marta couldn't relax either, worrying about what the evening excursion could bring. *Suki is off somewhere—getting ready to do what?*

Several tables had drifted back to talking again about their times as youth. The high-schooler, Janice, was moving around to various tables, all ears, and it amused Leon to see her taking notes just like a pro. Thelma and Dorothy, always storehouses on the old social life, were recalling how by the 1920s White Bluffs had expanded to include a movie house with silent movies, and there was even a marching band open to all ages. Leon thought his suburban life before college had been ultimate boredom in comparison, the life of a wolf pacing a cage. But though he much enjoyed the anecdotes from the settlers, he wanted to get them to say more about how White Bluffs compared with other western small farming towns. The memoir kept being put aside as they recalled the church denominations, the teachers, and who started successful businesses, who failed.

"Did you have a saloon?"

Orville spoke up with a grin, "Definitely a saloon, and pretty busy, but no so-called dancing girls. You had to go to Kennewick for that."

Dorothy teased him, "How do you know about that? And the men that were, you say, 'always working'? At Saturday night dances, there were plenty of men, for better or worse, dancing inside and drinking outside, eh, Thelma? So, Leon, are you coming to the dance tonight? Oh yes, your foot. Dear me. We need more men that can actually dance—without drinking."

She gave him a look. Leon saw she was joking, but persisted, "Any other non-drinking social life back then?"

She laughed, "Oh, I remember the camp meetings. Those preachers came in from somewhere. Anything from somewhere else was exciting. Big turnouts."

"I was forbidden to go," said Thelma. "My brothers could, but not me. My folks didn't say why, but I guess they thought girls could get carried away."

"I always went and I never got carried away," protested Dorothy. "Though the preacher certainly did."

Janice tried to control her giggles and get it all down.

Roger smiled and said, "Let's hear more what Harold has to say."

But Dot and Thelma were having such fun that Leon didn't feel right cutting them off. Suki became too restless to listen and left to walk in the park. Bruce was trying to act as if he were paying attention, but kept going outside to check the temperature, determined to leave as soon as it was cool enough to hike. He wasn't afraid of what faced him; no one was likely to get killed, and he welcomed a test of his night-stalking skills. The unknowns in his plan were what plagued him. He doubted that they were simply going to sneak down to the island and give Jason a message from his grandfather and return. What about the kayakers? He decided to go back to his room to think through the variables.

"Marta, I just can't concentrate right now. I've got to figure out some things."

Knowing that she would not enjoy watching him pace their room, she stayed with Leon and the settlers, and the memories kept coming. After more time with amusing recalls, Thelma asked, "Where did Bruce go? Still worried over his job?"

Marta shrugged, "I'm afraid so. I guess I need to go check on him, get him back down here."

She found him in their room at the window, watching dramatic clouds to the southwest.

"You're missing some great history. What you came for, Bruce!"

He blew up at her. "Quit bugging me! This is important too! Marta, don't you have...oh, sorry, sorry....Well, I was thinking we'd better get going."

His outburst didn't faze her, "Are you kidding? It's got to be 100 still."

He snorted, "The car is air-conditioned you know."

"Fine. So come get me when you're ready." And she went back to the conference room.

Leon was still steering, "So, the orchards weren't big profit-makers for most. But would you say the two towns, with such a mix of people coming from all over, that they did well as communities?"

Roger looked at Thelma and she answered, "I can't say for Hanford. But at White Bluffs, aside from the town split much earlier, we pretty much got along." She thought a moment. "Well, we did have our factions; some people resented the Masons controlling the few jobs on the road. And some people didn't like the saloon, and sometimes got it closed down, but not for long, until Prohibition."

Leon paged through the memoir, "Oh, here's what Harold says on that."

'I think generally the local people had a lot of tolerance for each other, even though they were such a mix. As one case, right before World War II Mormons came in to raise sugar beets. We had lost quite a few families due to the poor economy, and I think everyone was darn glad to see new faces. They brought new energy, fit right in.'

Dorothy nodded, "And they danced but they didn't drink."

Two important qualities! Leon kept his face straight and asked about Prohibition times.

Roger had rich recall. "Hard cider really took over for some families. The farmer next door to us did a big business out of his kitchen. We'd watch folks coming and going. I've heard you can get up to ten percent, but no one from our family sampled it, I don't think. The only alcohol we had was in our cough syrup."

Leon chuckled and scanned the memoir. "Harold says, '...as to the bigger picture, the loss of the grape market did hurt many families unless they made a deal with a big bootlegger. For the rest it was serious loss of income while waiting for fruit trees to grow.'"

Marta said, "So what do you think? Did less alcohol improve the communities?"

Orville laughed. "Some people thought so for sure. But there were other times when the county would vote to go dry, and the county across the river stayed wet. Then guys would just row over there for a bottle, and people wondered how they made it back alive, but they always did."

Leon laughed with the rest. "So...White Bluffs and Hanford survived Prohibition and no grape market. And survived their normal level of drinking, whatever it was, just switched to hard cider. And could survive even the river crossing while drunk."

Orville whooped a laugh, "Yup, in all the years only two people drowned, and they weren't even drinking."

Leon had by now decided White Bluffs couldn't really be called a typical small farming town; certainly not in the probably stereotyped impression he had of those places. He also saw that the group he was with produced a lot of joking remarks over what were often surely painful recalls. Perhaps it was because none of them—Orville excepted?—was truly suffering over it now. After all, everything had come to a halt fifty years ago. But it seemed that even if most of the families didn't find the financial success they'd planned on, even if they'd worked like slaves or sharecroppers, that while it lasted they'd enjoyed their community. The athletic wars with Hanford were for fun; the rabbit drives, well, fun for some. And apparently, they'd had no real conflicts with the neighboring Wanapum people. Somebody apparently had prejudice toward the Japanese farmers, or some other group, but crosses burned for only a short period. He suspected that smaller town Hanford wasn't that much different.

Marta listened to how Leon kept trying to keep their topics organized and yet not cut off the spontaneous flow of memories. She whispered *thanks* in his ear.

"No problem. I am thoroughly enjoying myself!"

"Do try to get them back to the memoir, though."

But the stories were interrupted anyway when Elena, the woman they had all wondered about, entered the room dressed in her unusual costume and went to the front. She looked at the crowd as if she wanted to say something. The tables, welcome for a new diversion, got quiet. Leon saw her give him a look. When everyone was focused on her, she began in a voice that was just right to cover the room.

"I'm Elena. I am so happy to be here with you. I will be doing a blessing of the river at eight o'clock this evening, and everyone is welcome to join me."

She had an accent Marta couldn't place. She saw that Bruce had come back to the hall and was watching from the doorway.

"That's nice, Elena," said Thelma. "What church are you from?"

"Not any one church. Ecumenical, and Indigenous."

Walt Croaker called out from the rear, "What's that? In…Indian, she says? Why is it always about Indians lately? They get enough attention. I thought we were here for us settler families."

Someone called, "Let's hear what the lady has to say."

Leon felt he had to respond to Croaker, "A blessing's probably a good thing. The Columbia needs it, in my opinion."

Croaker glared his way and stood up to point at Leon. "You people again? Roger, I don't know about your new friends. Why is this Wilder and his buddies here of a sudden?"

Roger stood up quickly before Leon could open his mouth.

"Walt, you've come here this year mainly to make rude remarks, seems like. We're glad to see Wilder and his friends here. He was in the military, defending our country, that's where he's been. And he invited these people, and we are enjoying them. It would be nice if they can enjoy us."

No one came to Croaker's defense.

"Well!" Croaker, feeling the continuing glare from Roger, a man with a lot of friends, sat down to continue his glaring.

Roger turned to Elena, "So, at eight o'clock you will do a blessing at the river?"

"Yes. It will be a good ceremony for peace and a healthy river." And she went to stand by the entrance.

Roger looked around nodded, "The river can use it." And after a moment the rest went back to their conversations. Leon waited until Orville picked up the dialog.

"To get back to the topic of the economy. Leon, aside from the World Wars and their high fruit prices, most families were not doing well money-wise until FDR got in and the New Deal."

He got a murmur of agreement. Croaker waved his arm in disgust and headed for the door.

Elena, waiting through this, broke in as he passed, "So, those who want to help this beautiful but abused river, please come."

Louise, meanwhile, had slipped into the room and was frowning and shaking her head.

"I wish people would check with me before adding things to the agenda. Your name is…"

"Elena."

"And what group do you represent?"

"Oh, no group. Just myself."

"And you're from where?"

Elena nodded, "I am from Seattle, but I am born far northeast part of Russia. Blessing rivers is one of things I do. I specialize in removal of toxins, includes radioactive toxins."

Leon almost laughed. This gathering was more unbelievable by the minute.

"Russian. I knew it!" It was Croaker, getting in his last word at the door, almost bumping into Bruce coming in. Marta jumped up, prepared for another blow-up as Bruce wheeled and followed Croaker into the lobby. *I guess I didn't scare him enough.*

"Excuse me, Mr. Croaker—Walt, is it?"

Croaker turned, "Yup."

"So Walt, what seems to be your problem? I came here to meet people, share stories, and have a good time. I brought friends I knew would enjoy it. I'd like to get along with you."

Croaker raised his eyebrows, "Oh really? You're here for more than old settler stories."

Bruce held onto himself, barely. Marta moved closer, saw his face turning red, and his jaw clenched. He kept his voice low,

"What are you here for, Croaker? More than just stories? Can I help you with that?"

Croaker's voice rose and he waved his arm, "I'm here to look out for these old timers, keep con artists like that Elena freak off them. I'm here to hold onto a fine history here. My father fought in World War II! What were you doing? Sucking mama's tit?"

Bruce stepped forward, fists tight.

Marta grabbed him and cried, "Stop now! The waiter is calling the police again!"

Bruce saw the staff staring at them, and realized that Croaker was a foot shorter and at least fifteen years older than him. *Maybe his father was a messed-up vet like me. Maybe childhood wasn't fun.* He took a deep breath, and another, and waved a hand. Once again saved, Croaker shrugged and walked off.

Marta was now quite ready to drive up the road and cried to Bruce, "Let's go!" But this time he was the one to delay, as he heard Louise in the doorway saying to Elena.

"Just a minute, Elena, I need to make a phone call and check with the government authorities here. These reunion bus rides into the closed area exist because of their gracious arrangement."

She turned to the lobby. Neither Bruce nor Marta said a word, simply nodded and went back to the conference room to wait with the rest. When Louise returned, she looked annoyed.

"Elena, sorry, I was told no, the agenda has to be approved ahead of time. Otherwise negative elements..." she looked pointedly at the door where Croaker had disappeared, "...could creep into the reunions, and they could cancel the bus tours. And we certainly don't want that. Elena, sorry but..."

"Very well." Elena turned to the listeners, and gave them a wide smile. It was not the first time she'd been closed out, and she could deal with it.

"So, I also plan to do blessing at Priest Rapids Dam tomorrow at 10 a.m. It is short drive. Please do come, everyone. The river needs you."

Another murmur filled the room as people started to leave again.

"Goodness!" said Louise, coming closer to Elena. "Why didn't you just go down to the river and bless it instead of trying to involve this group." She turned to Roger, "And why are people being so persnickety and emotional this year? I've never seen it!"

"Maybe it's the water?" Roger gave her a smile.

She snorted, then shrugged. "Certainly something's up their butts!"

Marta said in a soothing tone, "Believe me, the settlers appreciate all you've done all these years, Louise, to keep the reunions going. Even though I'm new to it, I can see how important it is."

Elena walked out quietly, and Louise watched her go. "Well, thank you. It's wearing me out lately. What is that woman anyway? I thought the hippy thing had gone its way."

Bruce said, "No, she's a modern medicine woman, what they call a shaman now." It was what Suki, returning in time to hear all this, had whispered to him.

"You mean like a witchdoctor? I would have thought they were gone by now."

He frowned at her, "Shaman sounds better. You know, I need to say this even though I'm a newcomer here. Actually, my job is on this very river." He took a breath. "Something has to be done about the radioactive waste, and Elena...I think she is trying in her way. Do you remember what happened at Three-Mile Island back in the 1970s? It was mentioned in the lecture today. It affected many families in awful ways. Like birth defects."

"Birth defects? Wasn't that just hysteria?"

"No, and that's part of the problem. Everyone's forgotten, or they just deny it all. But not Elena. They have their own radioactive toxins problem where she's from."

"No doubt they do, Russians! Well, Mr. Wilder, my job is keeping these reunions organized and happy, not international politics. And I can tell you that there are very important people that think our part of the Manhattan Project needs to be recognized more. There's serious interest now from historians in making Reactor B part of a big nuclear museum project across the country. Actually, I'd rather see a museum for the whole region, all of our histories, but maybe it's a start. But if a bunch of latter-day hippies and witches start descending on us with their weird ideas, that could sabotage any kind of museum."

Roger had come closer, "That's interesting, Louise, but a museum? When the real priority is the radioactive waste needs to be taken care of? This valley is more than a tourist attraction to a lot of us."

Louise glared at him. "I'm from here too, Roger!" And they watched her stalk out.

Roger shook his head. "She's a good gal. She works hard to put these affairs together, but she doesn't want to deal with the waste problem.... Well, shall we go get a beer?"

Bruce's head was spinning and he needed to be gone. "Well, thanks, but not now."

Suki had come back from a walk and had been listening to it all and asked Roger, "But is the museum idea for real? Or just a way to deflect people from the waste problem?"

"Oh, both, I think. There are people here who just love history, I guess you've noticed. And especially their own history. As for Reactor B history, well, over decades thousands of people worked at this plant, and many still do. Many more still live here. To them, that's the history of the valley!" He laughed, "Though that's strange to us from the old families. And for the Indians too, I would think. Well, come-on, a beer?"

Bruce knew that even though it was almost evening it was probably still too hot for Marta, so he did follow Roger to the bar. Leon, watching, motioned Marta and Suki to come with him. He felt more apprehensive of Suki's—now Bruce's—project than he had let on to Marta. He had almost decided he should talk to Bruce about the risks, but then realized this would be ridiculous. Bruce thought he already knew all the risks, and that was part of the attraction, obviously. Bringing it up would just make the scout in him angry with Marta for blabbing. Instead, Leon and Marta talked about Siberian shamans, quite a few of them women, and Suki listened.

Bruce gulped icy drinks with Roger, and grinned, "Elena's a new sort of intrusion for Louise, I guess. And that guy Croaker's something else. Are there always squabbles like this at the reunions?"

"No, nothing like this. Just arguments over whose memory is best on some affair at a picnic sixty years ago. Or if a certain broker cheated them. I told you I sort of know what's eating Croaker, though worse than usual this year. But I sure don't recall any Elenas!"

Bruce gave a big sigh. "It seems like this conference—for most of the folks—it's all nostalgia for the good old days. And you know that's mainly why I came, to read and hear the stories. But now that I'm here…well, I keep thinking about the river as it is today."

"Don't you anyway, at your job?"

"Sure. At my job it's the Columbia's other problems—the dams, the sinking salmon runs. And so many factions it makes your head swim. So I come up here to have a break, and it's a whole new set of issues. Of course I knew some of the Hanford Plant history, but we get stuck in our narrow worlds. Scientists are bad that way. I'm around them, I know."

Roger shook his head, "You know, these reunions are just for fun and keeping up some social bonds. Some folks here do belong to more serious groups. Like we belong to the Riverkeepers. If you want to actually get something changed for the Columbia you have to go to meetings like that, not social reunions."

"Riverkeepers? Oh yes, I've heard of them. Do you actually get anywhere?"

"Hummm, slowly. We get some spawning streams cleaned up, even seen some local runs come back, and that's pretty exciting. Well, for us anyway."

Bruce finished his beer and shook his head. "I don't have the patience for meetings. That's what my hatchery bosses have to deal with. And I think cleaning up a stream is great, believe me, as far as it goes. More power to you. But that's not going to fix the problem there," he pointed upstream. "That's going to take something huge. If we can't even fix a dam or rebuild some fish runs, how are we going to clean up a toxic nightmare? The biggest in the country! Arghhh! Well, people waiting…to go bird-watching."

He stood up. "So do you think Elena's blessing is going to help this river?"

Roger shrugged, "How can we know?"

"It's too…romantic for me. You've heard of Three-Mile-Island. I've read those people fought hard and long to get recognition they'd been hurt."

"Long and hard, yes, that's what it will take to clean this up. That's what I'm telling you."

The thought of it made Bruce's stomach clench. "The trouble is, I know myself. I…Well, I have to get going. *And, tonight maybe I'll find out just what it takes.*

He went to round up Marta and Suki, and at last they started up the road. Roger was left puzzled. Harold had never mentioned Bruce being a bird-watcher. And what about the memoir?

Leon went back to the conference room and looked at a thinning crowd. Throwing away the cautious approach, he pulled up his chair and pushed harder at Roger and his group.

"So, tell me, who actually ran the town?"

The question perked up ears and brought other people to stand by the table.

"The Chamber of Commerce."

"Nope. My dad said the Masons ran the town."

"They *were* the Chamber of Commerce."

"The Grange? No. And certainly not the churches or the school."

"Maybe nobody. We just bumbled along."

Leon had marked the memoir. "Do you want to know what Harold writes? Here it is…

'In my opinion, it was the women who held White Bluffs together as a community, through their clubs and church groups. The men were too busy out in their orchards and fields. The women kept us together, through projects like the traveling library and the baby clinic.'

Leon looked around. "What do you think?"

"Well, he's right on that." An older woman who was listening stepped up to the table and spoke with assurance. "Yes, it really was the women that kept the town going."

Orville laughed, "Harold's right. The men really were too darn busy most of the year to run even a dinky town. The business men were forever running their businesses, but that didn't make a real community; it has to have something more."

Leon smiled, "Thank God for the women, then!"

Cheers erupted from the female listeners and several of the men, and the rest laughed.

Leon noted that no one challenged it.

CHAPTER 13

A BLESSING

ONCE AGAIN BRUCE, Marta, and Suki drove the highway, this time seeing the country in twilight. Marta's head was simmering with the conversations from the conference hall. She wanted to hold onto every exchange. Bruce and Suki were silent until they spied what they thought was a sage hen running though the sagebrush.

"Oh, oh, here's our chance to play our role," said Suki, and got out her bird book. "It's true, sage hens are being considered for listing as endangered. Seems like everything is getting endangered around here."

Marta considered the comment. The original White Bluffs-Hanford settlers were definitely an endangered species. And the Wanapum before them. And the Nagasaki and Hiroshima survivors surely must have felt on the way to extinction.

When they arrived at their rendezvous point, Bruce pulled off near a clump of higher brush and turned the car around. He let the air out of one tire; later he could fill it with a repair kit he'd bought. They were lucky as no one came by and he hid the jack up in the brush and marked the spot. Now, if someone saw them, they would be just people walking to get help. They donned their bird-watching gear and made their way into the brush. The sun was almost down, and the clouds were thickening and lowering, as he had predicted. But the wind had abated, they hoped not for long, as they'd been warned that a still night meant a gnat attack. They sat down to wait for Esau, Bruce twisting, trying to be still. *I might be in jail tomorrow, but I'll bet I enjoy tonight.*

When it was almost dark, Esau emerged from the brush a short distance away, and saw the car with the flat tire. *Looks like we're going to do it.* He had left his pack, heavier than before, nearby. When the birdwatchers spied him they stood up, but he motioned them to sit back down with him. Marta, he saw, was there, apparently going on the hike to the island, and he wasn't going with them—their choice. He saw Suki's questioning look and gave her a nod and grin. Off towards the bluffs a coyote yipped, then howled, and soon others joined for a weird chorus.

"I love that singing," Suki declared.

Esau said, "They expect the moon to come out. I hope for not too long. But I have been thinking about this more…. None of you needs to go down to the island. Why should you for that silly kid? If no one hears from him, I can wait for Ike and go down with him by boat after dark tomorrow. It's not your worry."

Bruce, caught by surprise, raised a pleading arm, "Hey, Uncle, I'm all geared up to go, I'm looking forward to it! And I need to find those kayakers too."

Marta waved her hand in exasperation.

Esau nodded. He liked Bruce's spirit. *You want to see if you can still be the warrior.*

"What about her?" He nodded at Marta.

"She chooses to go too. She's a great hiker. No, I'm going. So, tell me what it looks like over there. Is there an electric fence around the whole complex?"

"Lots of fences—I don't know if they're all connected."

"Roads, you said?"

"Lots of roads. But you don't have to be close to any of that to get over to the island. The head of the slough is dry now, so you can walk right over."

Bruce looked around in the darkness. "Where's your backpack?"

Esau pointed.

"Well, we're ready." Bruce smiled and stood up, hoisted his pack; then Marta did.

Esau looked around and took his time answering. "I don't feel good about it. After I thought about it more." *There's too much evil in the place to fool around with it. But then, there's Jason.*

He finally said, "Well, turn back, then, anytime if it's not going right. Tell me you'll do that."

"I will, yes."

Esau nodded. "All right…good luck then. I am going to pray for you."

Suki said, "Be careful please; don't get in trouble for foolish kids."

She was relieved that they weren't doing this twenty-plus mile trek for her; her project was so easy by comparison. Bruce, for sure, was doing it for himself. Why Marta was going she wasn't sure, maybe hoping to talk him out of it after a few miles of switches and thorns. And snakes.

Bruce said, "If we're not back by daylight, Suki, don't go to the car. Just go with Esau?"

Esau nodded his approval. Bruce turned toward the trail, filled with energy, and Marta, saying nothing, followed. In a moment they were gone, and Suki and Esau were left alone in the creeping darkness. But they did not feel alone long, as a chorus of crickets soon broke the silence with such a racket they almost had to shout to carry on any conversation.

⋅⊷▭◉ ◉▭⊶⋅

Leon paged through Harold's memoir and marked topics he thought needed more attention, trying to keep his thoughts away from the trouble his friends were probably in. The planned reunion program was over, many tables now empty. Roger, Thelma, Dorothy and Janet were waiting to hear more from the memoir, while Orville seemed to be stewing over something. Leon turned to a passage he wanted them to hear and began again.

"During the Depression didn't folks here do better where they could raise all their own food? Shall we hear from Harold on that? Here it is:

'It wasn't just orchards here. Folks were like mad inventors—tried everything—alfalfa, melons, berries, potatoes—they had to! Very few that didn't raise gardens for themselves. Most people had a pig or calf, or lambs, and everyone had chickens. So mainly they ate well. But there was one family I remember that had decided to go for what looked like a simpler way, and put all their land in potatoes. So when the Depression hit, that's about what they ate.'

"Do you remember it that way?"

Dorothy grinned at Leon, "Sure. I had dinner there once. Potatoes with butter."

Janice, taking notes, giggled, "Wait, please, the Depression, when no one had jobs....What about stuff you can't raise, like...soap, and t.p., and bug dope. You had to buy it didn't you?"

Dorothy said, "Sweetie, we didn't buy much food even before the Depression. We raised it. Let's see....in hard times I got sent to the store only for sugar, salt, flour, rice, baking soda, tea—not much coffee or cocoa. That was about it."

"Uhh, t.p.?"

"Old catalogs, newspapers. I know, people joke about it, but true."

Thelma added, "And we had to buy cloth to sew, if we could afford it. Oh, yes, kerosene and soap. But we'd run out of funds in the winter, had to charge everything till there were strawberries to sell in the spring. The local storekeeper was hurting too, but what else could he do but let folks charge? So, sure, it was a hard time, Leon, but everyone was poor together then. That's the difference. We kids didn't have to feel ashamed of our made-over clothes."

Leon scribbled: *Depression times: Almost self-sufficient, grew their food. Remade clothes.*

"Harold writes that he and his siblings were actually glad that there were no jobs to go to in the towns, so their father was home with them most of the time."

Orville said, "Yup, the men were home more, could do more for their farms and their families. Then during the New Deal, finally, there was WPA roadwork for some men, the ones with connections."

Roger added, "And then when County Extension Agents were created, they came around and taught better farming methods. As a kid it got me interested in that work. But by that time most of the settlers felt they did have the experience, and some laughed at the so-called government experts."

Leon felt he didn't have the farming background to pursue it, and Roger, apparently one of the so-called experts later, left it at that. Leon still hadn't gotten one answer he was looking for: *Did they learn to be successful farmers or not?* Again he asked them, but got silence from around the table.

Finally, Roger said, "You know, small farming is just one problem after another to solve and some people like the challenge. So much to deal with in those thirty-five years. Every time one thing got fixed, then here came a new problem or more, and they had to find new answers. And they did their best, and some of them enjoyed it. That's farming. And I know some hated it, so they left. So if by 'successful' you mean all their bills paid, and money for retirement? No, not many. Able to just get by, yes, quite a few I would say, because they were still there."

Leon waited but got no more. He saw they didn't want to speak for others, how people might feel about that family's personal success.

Then Roger went on. "Leon, you being an anthropologist, would maybe look at the Indians, their earlier lives here, and I'll bet you would probably say they were successful? But someone else might say—well I won't try to use their words—but they might laugh at you."

Leon nodded. *So true. Define success? Surely a point of view.* He decided to let folks relax a little and asked Orville what he and Dorothy did now; were they still farming?

"No. We couldn't afford enough acreage with what the feds paid us. We've just a few pitiful rows of corn and grapes, just enough to say we're doing something useful." Orville looked at him, disgusted.

Dorothy added, "And drive around, watch TV, crochet. Boring."

Orville said, "She's right. Except when our kids and grandkids drive over to visit it's pretty boring. I miss the outdoor work."

Dorothy said, "What you're missing, really, is the old place on the river. You and all of us. Not the same."

Leon oddly flashed on the curse of the cheat grass invasion; it was symbolic for them whether they knew it or not. These folks were like the bunch grass, tough and full of value, he realized. But cheat grass, different versions, had overcome them.

⊷╾◉ ◉╼⊷

Suki, sitting in the brush with Esau and waiting for darkness, brought up what was most on her mind.

"The snake is okay, Uncle?" She liked using the familiar term.

"He's fine, beautiful and strong, over there in my pack."

She wanted to see the snake, but he advised her it would just stress it out before they needed to. So they waited there in silence then, each thinking about what faced them and the others. Mosquitoes swarmed in, and Esau was glad she had bug dope and helped himself. Even though he had agreed to go ahead with the plan, he thought again of the risks for the others, and that it would be nice to be at home with his wife, who could be over-zealous at times but always made sense. *Does any of this? But there is no way I can abandon this woman now.* He knew he needed to quit worrying, and think good thoughts about what they were going to do up on the ridge. At least they were trying to do something. He looked at the sky for cloud movement, then turned to Suki, who was staring off into the brush as if in a trance.

"You've seen photos of the plant?"

"Oh yes, the ones on the web. I know what it looks like. Ugly." And she pictured the stark gray structures, and shuddered. Something out of a dystopian movie, just no dinosaurs or weird humanoids marching or sneaking around.

"Yes...*think of something good*...Suki, what's that mountain in Japan they always show?"

"Oh, it's Fuji."

"Beautiful, eh? Is it a spiritual place?"

"Yes, sure. All the beautiful places in Japan have their spiritual side. But Fuji is rather touristy now I think."

"That's what they want here, our spiritual places turned into tourist traps. We need to stop it."

"But the Shinto shrine my mother takes me to is a lovely spot and quiet. Lots of people come there, but they don't act like tourists in those places. They are respectful."

She was still staring off, and he looked at her profile. *She's a good-looking woman. She's different from us, but not that different. And a strength in her something like Alice.*

Before long the clouds had thinned for just the right amount of visibility. Esau got up.

"Okay, shall we do it?"

She nodded, and Esau went into the brush to his pack and hoisted it, heavy with the snake, onto his back. "It's all right now, be calm, fella. Easy walk, easy."

They hiked a half-mile east, then to the top of the low ridge. The sagebrush was only to Suki's knees. The wind had picked up, and now the clouds thinned more, and the stars and full moon were brilliant. Suki, crouching beside Esau, was elated that from their elevation the many lights of the B Reactor area were so visible.

"This is perfect. Thank you!"

He eased the pack to the ground. "I've thought about this. In case this guy gets active, he's a very long snake to hold onto."

"I need to hold his head and point it toward the plant."

"Then we should keep most of him in the pack. I'll hold him in there and you hold his head out. Just keep him still with both hands at his neck. Will that work for you?"

"I think so…yes, that's fine. But not yet. We need to do a little Shinto first— wash our hands and mouths and drink water."

She got out her bottle and they did the ritual washing and drinking. Then Suki nodded toward the backpack, and Esau picked it up, opened it, and braced himself. As soon as he took hold of the bullsnake it started squirming, trying to flip. *Oh boy!* She reached to help hold the pack, while with one arm he managed to draw its writhing, hissing head out of the pack. He kept the rest of its long twisting body cinched in the pack while she grasped below its head, trying to hold it without squeezing it, trying to stay calm. She took a deep breath, trying to remember the next step. Neither had ever imagined such an act.

"Easy...easy now..." Esau muttered.

"Wait...sorry, you must take him for a moment." Esau braced himself more, grabbed the snake's neck from her, struggling to keep the rest of it in place as it thrashed around, while she recalled her instructions. She closed her eyes a moment, opened them, bowed twice, clapped twice, bowed again toward Esau and the snake, then held her breath as she reached with both hands and grasped its neck again. The snake's power surged through her as she held its head up, facing it toward the lights of the reactor. In the moonlight she could see the patterns on its skin as it hissed and tried to twist. Shakily she raised it higher. Esau watched her as he held the snake, both of them humming. She wasn't sure how long she could hold it, what words to use, and hoped what came from her was right.

"Beautiful, powerful snake spirit," she began softly, "power for good from all nature, help my prayer. Great snake, send your power...to heal all the families and the natural worlds of Nagasaki and Hiroshima.... Heal this great river, too, and the ground around it, and all the Columbia valley, and everywhere where there are toxins. And make the spirit of Arni calm and free."

Then she lost her nervousness as the snake calmed and the words flowed freely from her.

"And stop all efforts forever to reactivate the Hanford Plant... turn the radioactive waste away from the Columbia and to a safe storage...bring wisdom to the government and scientists to aid in all this, and turn their efforts to removing all signs of this plant from the area."

After a moment to catch her breath she glanced at Esau, saw that he was managing, nodding at her, and decided to pray for more. It came so easy now.

"I ask you, spirits of nature, to close down all such dangerous nuclear projects, to cause all people and governments to turn away from them. Until they know how to use them safely, and how to take care of the waste forever. Do all this for my family, all people, this river, and all nature." She waited a moment. "Great bullsnake, thank you for your powers, your *kami*, snake spirit."

Suki kept the snake pointed at the lights and waited more moments in silence, then nodded to Esau. Together they pushed it back into the pack, closed it, and set it down. The snake twisted for a time and then quieted. She then clapped her hands twice and took a deep breath. They stood wordless together, and she smiled with relief, so grateful for the elder's help. She thought she had carried out the ceremony as well as she could, and with a good heart. She wanted to thank him more formally. *How Bruce addresses him.*

"Thank you, Uncle, thank you."

"Did it go right?"

"I think so. Thanks to him. Wow." She looked down at the backpack, and took a deep breath.

"Wow is right! You put yourself into it."

"They told me I would know what to say. I just said what came."

They washed their hands and mouths again and stood a bit in silence. He thought she really had done well; the ritual felt right although he had never done anything quite like it.

Suki said, "We should turn him loose, shouldn't we, near his area? Where did you get him?"

He motioned east.

"So we should go down that way then? We can take turns carrying him."

"I need to go down to that first reactor fence, anyway, and check for Jason."

"I'd like to…"

He shook his head. *No. Who knows what's going on down there?* "It won't take long; you stay here, out of sight. I'll drop him off down near where I got him. It's getting cool, so you have my jacket. I'll be going fast so I'll stay warm. Just rest; don't let ticks get on you."

She wanted to protest, though she had no right to, and he felt her resistance.

"I'll be back in a couple hours or so. But if I don't show up by daylight, go over near the road and wait for Bruce."

"You say a couple hours or so?"

"Ahh, maybe a little longer."

"And if no one shows up?"

Esau thought it was possible that no one would, so many ways it could go. He looked up at the clouds moving back in, but no moon showing. He listened...nothing.

"Well, if no one comes in another couple hours...start walking toward Wolf Rapids. And your excuse is the flat tire, and that you're on your way to interview me. They'll believe you; everyone's always trying to interview me."

"I can picture that."

"Well, they should interview Alice, my wife. She gives a really good speech."

She smiled. *I'm sure you do too.*

"Wait, the car is pointed the wrong way. Uhh...so you forgot your tape recorder, and you turn the car around, and then you feel the tire is going flat. And Suki, you know Ike. He'll be coming from Yakima late morning, a green Ford pickup. You can catch a ride. Tell him about what we were doing if you want, you can trust him. But don't worry, I'll be back soon as I can."

He hoisted his pack and turned into the brush to disappear before she could say more. She listened. Silence. She picked up his jacket; it smelled of wood smoke and tobacco. Maybe like the grandfather she'd never got to meet. She sat down in the sand on the jacket to wait, not really worried about Esau, or about being alone, or about how long it took to walk to Wolf Rapids, but about her blessing. *Did I do it right, Grandmother?*

Esau moved off toward the trail. After a long crouching walk east, hard on the knees, he was near the B reactor fence. He sneaked closer to it; not a sign of Jason. The clouds came and went. The coyotes were quiet. The snake was quiet. Ever more regretting the agreement he had made with Bruce, he studied the situation a few minutes, then kept on going on the trail toward the next reactor, the snake still in his pack, half-forgotten as he worried about his grandson, and now the others.

CHAPTER 14

NIGHT HAWKS

BRUCE WAS ENJOYING himself as he and Marta scrambled through the dark brush. He didn't feel the scratches accumulating on his hands as he pushed along, soldiering again, the best of it. Whenever they came to a clump of taller brush he waited for Marta, close behind. Their good luck, the clouds were moving in more, but there was no blowing sand, and by the time they went past the first reactor buildings, they could see not just the lights but the dim outlines of structures. To Bruce it was almost too easy. When they had passed two more sets of building lights, and he guessed they were about halfway to the island, he stopped and sat down.

"How are you doing?" he muttered, gasping just a little as his partner staggered up.

"Oh fine," she panted. "I'll die before I let you leave me behind."

"Rest a minute." He pulled out a water bottle.

"My body's okay, almost...*pant*.... It's my brains I'm worried about. And... *pant*...how is it you...all of a sudden...an anti-nuke activist?.... We're here to dig into your old family history...I thought?"

He whispered, "It's not all of a sudden, you know that."

She wiped her sweating face on her sleeve. "Isn't this all about Suki? Her story?"

"Suki, and stuff I've been thinking about since we got here. You can't imagine...just seeing my people's place. Didn't you feel it?"

"Yes, sure, but...not like you do."

"Right...well, let's go."

"In a minute."

But he leaped up and plunged off into the brush.

Three hours later they were covered with sweat, the backs of their hands burning with scratches, their legs about to collapse, but he felt they must be close to the river. They spotted what had to be the lights of the reactor by the island, not far off, then a fence. After a rest, they headed around and past it, Marta dogging Bruce, a shadow. He stopped again to consider what might come next. *If anyone's at the island I don't want to surprise them—the kayakers might even be armed. I need to find Jason first, so a likely signal for him? Owl hoots?*

They broke out of the brush at the slough that formed the island, the reactor complex now close at hand through cottonwoods and brush. Bruce stared at the old gray walls of the main buildings, and felt sick with disgust. *Things we did to people, to Suki's family. I did my share. You fucking monstrosity! I'm glad she didn't have to see this.* He turned away from the sight and took deep breaths. Marta had kept quiet, sensing how he felt.

After listening for any action from the buildings, he gave two quiet *hoo-hoos*. No answer. Once more…nothing. *To the island then.* He crouched low and pushed across through the tall cattails of the slough, Marta right behind him. At the island shore he tried hoots again, and in a moment a dark figure popped out of the willows near them.

"Jason, that you?" Bruce called in a near whisper. No answer.

"Hey, Jason, we met yesterday. Near here…with Ike."

After a moment a quiet voice came back. "Oh, it's you guys! What are you doing here?"

They came close to him, a lean shadow, and Jason looked them over.

Marta whispered, "Jason, your grandfather…"

Bruce nudged her, "He asked us to give you a message. We met him out by the road."

Jason whispered, "Really? *Too weird.* Where is he then?"

"By now? Scouting around the B reactor in case you were there. He said tell you to go down the river tonight. That's his message."

"Yeah, I know. I've heard it before. But…there's more going on he doesn't know about."

"That's partly why we're here too. Just what is going on?"

Jason peered closely at them as the moon emerged for a spell, at their camo jackets and backpacks, both wiping their scratched faces. Clearly, they were not just out on a night's stroll and happened to bump into his grandfather. *What's their business anyway?*

The rest of the conversation continued in whispers.

"Why are you bothering with me? If my grandpa wants to come down here and lecture me, let him. Jeez, what a nice place to meditate I went and chose!"

Marta said, "You should listen to your grandfather. He knows what he's talking about when he says to leave. He knows what governments can do to people."

"You think I don't?"

"Well, he just doesn't want to see you doing ten years in a federal prison."

"Come on! For trespassing, ten years? Come-on! Okay, you are his messengers? So hike back there and tell him I'm sorry, I can't leave just yet…but I will very soon. Not to worry."

Bruce broke in, "Have you figured out what those people are up to?"

"What people?"

"Look, I'm concerned about those kayakers. I don't want them or you to get hurt doing something stupid."

"Maybe it's not so stupid."

"Meaning what?"

Jason stayed silent.

"You don't want to answer, it's okay. I can find their camp."

Bruce pulled Marta's sleeve and started to walk into the brush.

"Wait, wait, you might scare them. I've got them calmed down now so they'll talk to me."

"Look, your grandfather is waiting, wants to know what's going on with you."

Marta pleaded, "Jason, think about this more, what they're are up to."

"I did think a lot. Okay, I told them to leave for their own good. I thought they were gone, they took off, and then I hear them coming back. What the hell? So I sneak down there and listen, and I can't hear it all, but enough…I know it's about the plant, something they're planning. And I wonder what they can do? Like you read about protesters breaking into these places, or even blowing themselves up."

Oh my god. He's right. They were so spooky about their kayak, whatever was in it. Bruce whispered, "Well, if you're right, then you need to tell them their cover is blown, and they need to take off fast."

Marta added, "And you can go home, your grandfather will be relieved, and you'll be the hero. Because these kids could get others in big trouble too. But you can prevent it."

Jason was quiet for a moment. *My grandfather trusts these people? He must have.* "They may be asleep."

Bruce thought a moment. "Are they armed?"

"Nothing I could see. Who knows what's in that backpack?"

"You need to go wake them up, or I'll go … now!"

Jason sighed. "Okay, okay, I'll go tell them they need to come talk to you or…or you're going to turn them in."

"That's good. Do it." Bruce waved at Jason to go. He disappeared into the brush, but Bruce followed behind just as silently. Marta got out water and a kerchief from her pack and winced as she wiped at her scratched face. She tried to think of what to tell the kayakers—something they'd listen to, kids who obviously wanted to be heroes. Before long Jason was coming back through the brush, followed by the two. Their expressions, as before, were watchful, bordering on hostile. They were dressed to travel but didn't have any visible weapons. The man had the backpack.

Bruce came out of the brush near them and looked them over. *Just kids.*

He muttered, "Hey, guys, we met yesterday, remember? I'm not a cop or anything like that. I'm down here to bring a message to this young man here, that's all. But you've been here a while now in this off-limits place, and you're going to get yourselves in big trouble. We just want you to think about this a little more. I'm Bruce, this is Marta. What do we call you?"

The woman gave him a scornful look and muttered back, "Call us Mutt and Jeff. He's Jeff. And we don't need you to tell us to think. What are you then, if not a cop?"

"I'm…this fellow's grandfather's friend." Bruce began his argument. "Look, I don't like this plant either. It should have been cleared out of here long ago. And you are right, something needs to be done, and now, with the news of leaking tanks soon. So what's your plan?"

No answer.

Marta thought they had a small chance to get some sense into the two.

"You need to do something that really makes a difference, not just a brief splash in the news. But that takes time and numbers."

"Tell us more," said Mutt, as hostile as ever.

Marta's voice was edged with exasperation. "You've got to work with people who really care about the problem and get them organized, make it a real plan…"

"Sure, sure, but we don't have time for that," snapped the young woman—Marta guessed she wasn't more than twenty. "You're talking something for people with money and time and connections. We have to do what we can do."

Bruce shrugged, "Okay. I said, what's your plan?"

"Why should we tell you?"

Marta stared at them, chilled, and not just from the sweat drying on her.

Bruce, losing patience, whispered louder, "Then get the hell out of here before you get a lot of people in trouble! All the people at that reunion you saw? They're already being blamed that you're here. You were reported by someone, of course."

Mutt snapped, "Well, your friend here said he would do something for us, and then you can all go and leave us to our fate."

Marta and Bruce wheeled on Jason, "What? What are you going to do?"

"I just said I'd show them the trail to get close to a reactor."

Mutt said, "We want to go to B Reactor. You know its history, right?"

B Reactor again, wouldn't you know it. "Uh-huh. I sure do. But that's over twelve miles from here. A little far to dash back and hop in your kayak."

"So we compromised. He agreed to show us the trail as far as the next one over from here." She pointed west.

Jason said, "That's all I'm going to do."

Bruce swore to himself. *Damn kid.* "Okay, so say you're at the fence, the high-powered electric fence. Now what? What have you got?" He pointed at the pack.

"Something fast," said Mutt, with a show of pride. "That gets attention."

"A bomb?" Marta felt her stomach start to seize up.

Jeff shook his head. "Not a real bomb, just something…harmless…that makes a lot of noise and scares people. Just enough to make them think about what's coming next."

"Harmless. You hope it's harmless."

"I ought to know," snapped Mutt. "I made it."

Bruce was open-mouthed. *Unbelievable.* "From what instructions?"

"Off the Internet."

"Oh, great, great! Has it got a timer?"

"No, just a fuse. It's a simple thing."

"May I take a look at it? I'm familiar with such bombs."

She shrugged, handed Bruce the pack. Inside were a collapsible shovel, small wire cutters, a roll of fuse, and a package that had to be a bomb, or what they hoped was a bomb, but a "harmless" one.

Marta said, "Listen, there are better ways to do something. You know that."

Mutt shot back an angry whisper, "Not now, not for us. My god, you people, don't you watch the news? Don't you know this plant has a lot of the features of the Chernobyl plant? Right in our own country? This place, this waste should have been taken care of long ago, right? There are people building new plants every day that will have the same problem."

Bruce shook his head. "And you're going to fix that." *Whew, these are babies I've got here.*

He grabbed Jason's sleeve. "You shouldn't be involved. They don't have the expertise, believe me."

"I want to do something about the plant and I promised them."

Bruce tried his best to control himself to whisper, "Okay, here it is. You want to make noise and make people think. I understand. But you could just throw your pack at the fence, and I guarantee you all hell will break loose. Sirens, spotlights! You've sent your message. Your big problem is getting out of here. The alarms will go off immediately."

He waited for their reaction. Jeff seemed interested, but Mutt protested.

"That's not what we want. We want it to go off inside the fence. More of a statement."

She's invested in the contraption. "Okay, but what if the fuse doesn't work? Then you have nothing, a failed joke. So just throw the pack, hit the fence with it and you are sure to have what you want—lots of noise, lights, people running everywhere."

Jeff nodded. The woman frowned.

Bruce stared at her. "What's your other names. I don't like "Mutt" for this operation."

"Liz, Tom."

"Okay, Liz, we haven't got all night. We're right near this reactor, and someone's going to notice us, if they haven't already. *I'm talking too loud.* Jason can show you the trail to the next reactor. So, are you all packed up?"

The kayakers looked at each other, nodded, and she said, "Lead on... show us the next fence, and you can all split."

Marta thought there was hope. Jason was glad to turn the task over to Bruce; nothing about the kayakers gave him any confidence. They started off, following Bruce back across the slough, past the first reactor fence, and kept right on. Bruce saw that he didn't have to tell the kayakers to be quiet, and that his new team kept up with him easily. Well, they were younger.

"How are we doing?" He stopped to ask Jason, just behind him.

"Not bad, chief, not bad for a white man."

Bruce grinned. He'd been a cheeky kid just like that once. The real problem would be when the alarm went off. For now, it was just a matter of a long, cautious walk. The clouds cooperated, and they made little more noise than a pack of coyotes hunting. When they at last could see lights of the next reactor, Jason stopped. "Okay, the fence is right over there."

Bruce looked around, "This is still too close to the island. They could still figure out where you came from and get there fast. It's just a little way more to the next reactor. We'll keep going." He was feeling high on real action.

Jason looked at him, nodded, glad to be rid of any blame. "Okay, it's all yours, chief."

They made another quiet tramp through brush with no rest stops, Marta glad that they were at least headed back toward the highway. For now, if their luck held, just more scratches, more sweat, very tired legs.

When again lights ahead glowed faintly Bruce stopped.

"I don't see the fence," whispered Tom as he caught up.

Jason said, "Jeez, it's right there, ahead of us."

"That wasn't the deal. Take us closer to it."

Bruce felt the pressure rising in Tom's voice, while Liz seemed still calm, waiting. Jason said nothing. Bruce saw he must give more direction and support. He dug granola bars from his pack.

"Rest a minute, eat these, and drink some water now. We won't have time later."

While they complied, he studied the reactor lights, the clouds, and the visible stars' positions and thought some more." *It has to be done perfectly or we're skunked. Liz is calmer.*

"Okay guys, there's too many of us to go to the fence…. Jason, you and Tom stay here and be able to signal, so I can find you and the trail fast. Marta, stay with them. Liz and I will go to the fence. I know where it is." *Well, I'll find it.*

Jason shook his head, Liz nodded, Tom stared at her, and Marta glared at Bruce. *Damn it, you knew you'd do something like this. You knew all along.* But she'd promised to follow orders.

Bruce whispered, "I will give a hoot from the fence. Jason, you'll answer. We'll get your direction for our return. Then, we'll all act fast, and when the alarm goes off, you take off…don't wait. GO! Safer if we separate? You all know how to travel, I see that. Tom, show me which direction is the river; the path across to the island… good, you've got it. You and Liz will find each other and head down river fast. Jason, Esau says you must go down river too."

Bruce waited until they all nodded. He wondered how angry Esau would be when the fireworks started. Setting off an alarm was not part of the deal with him. And he knew, despite his orders, that the kayakers would need a ton of luck not to get caught. Jason would probably make it; so would he and Marta.

Bruce watched Tom hand over the backpack to Liz without arguing. Then he changed his plan. "Mart, we're too many for a retreat, so don't you wait for the alarm. Start now, back up the trail. Keep low, go like a bobcat. Wait near the car, but in the brush. You two wait right here. Listen for the hoot."

He gave his lover a little nudge, "You promised."

Marta saw he was going ahead with this madness. Furious, scared, she shook her head and turned toward the trail without a word. Bruce waited for the others to get oriented as to their escape routes, then touched Liz on the shoulder.

"Let's go."

Waiting at the trail, unable to control anything, Jason regretted his agreement with the kayakers each minute more. If someone got caught wouldn't it be his fault? No-no, these nuts had planned it all before he saw them. It was just a matter of which reactor. *And Bruce didn't need to come down here. No way my grandpa asked him to be involved.*

"What did I get into?" he muttered.

Tom heard him and said, "Hey, this was never my idea, you know. Liz—I can't tell her anything. We don't know what's going to happen here, do we? Anything could. It is better to separate, he's right. So I'm going to start back now, get all ready to head down river, wait for Liz there. They don't need both of us here, right? So I'm gone, good luck."

Tom turned and crept away fast, Jason staring after him. *What? Jeez, he's abandoning his girlfriend—some team. Well, one less to bump into when we run for our lives.* He squatted down, disgusted with himself, with the whole affair, to listen for Bruce, but heard nothing.

CHAPTER 15

PLOTS REVISED

SUKI SCRUBBED HER hands with sage leaves, trying to clean the snake odor. She prayed that the snake was fine, that it would survive its trauma. Bullsnakes were tough if they could chase out rattlesnakes. She tried to nap as she waited for Esau to return, but she was too restless, thinking about her actions. *Mother, did I do it right? Were we respectful to the snake?* The clouds returned and the plant's lights disappeared; she had been so lucky on the ridge. Esau had told her there were no big animals around to watch out for—*"Just coyotes—but they will like you."* She drew in the good smell of the brush and listened to the sounds around her. Even after the coyotes ended their concert she heard owls, and the crickets kept up their chirping with few pauses. She was relieved when the mosquitoes and gnats finally went to sleep. A bird silhouette swooped by. Small creatures rustled as they crept past her and a lizard crawled over her leg. *What's a little lizard, after a bullsnake?* She checked for ticks when she thought of it and didn't feel scared. Now the desert was cooling off, and she marveled at how fast it could change, glad to put on Esau's jacket.

Step by step, she went over the ceremony again and again. *Was the prayer right?* How could she know, except her gut feeling? *Is the snake all right?* She saw she needed to quit this kind of fretting and be trusting the natural powers around her. It was up to her to stay in touch. But she was filling up with worry, so instead she made herself concentrate on her annual trip to see her family in Japan that was coming up soon. She pondered what she would tell her mother. *"Mom, I finally did it."* And what will Mom say? *I should go with her to a Shinto shrine again, maybe more than one.* She thought ahead more, anything to stop worrying. She might even go to a university's environmental science department and ask what Japan was doing to protect its rivers and seas. And was there a museum in Nagasaki that dealt with the bombing? Of course, there had to be, though her mother had never mentioned it. She might speak to groups about nuclear waste; she had never done such things before, but perhaps she would. And then back here, she could speak to her classmates about the problems of the Columbia that they barely touched, such as the waste. She really could write articles for magazines. Thus, she entertained herself for hours, stretching her legs every so often, checking for ticks, wondering why Esau was taking so long. Finally she dozed, but only for short stretches.

The sky was lightening when she heard a car coming along the road from the north. It seemed to stop at their rented car; doors slammed and voices went back and forth. But they were not angry ones; they were asking questions. She crawled through the brush as close as she dared, and now heard people trying to get into the car. They sounded as if they could be the Plant security. After a short time, they drove away north again. She gradually stopped her tremors and settled down to wait again. Around her, busy spiders, dung beetles, and praying mantis began to wake up and go about their lives. A cry of some kind of bird. A hawk swooped past. She ignored the bird book in her pack and listened to small movements in the brush.

⊷▬◉ ◉▬⊷

Bruce and Liz crept up close to the reactor's fence and the debate began again.

"Okay, here you are, Liz. Now you can throw that thing, and we'll run like hell."

"But I want to be sure it sticks right to the fence."

He was exasperated again. "It's electric. How will you do that without killing yourself?"

She didn't answer. He barely kept from exploding.

"Liz, you need to act, now! Then we have to get the fuck out of here. Give it here!"

"Just a minute!"

"No, you're going to throw it. Or I am." He wrenched her pack away from her. "Now pay attention! Don't run through the brush when I throw it. You must crawl fast as you can, till you're out of range of the spotlight—it'll sweep through here…. Listen to me!"

She muttered about digging a hole under the fence, shoving it through, and lighting the fuse.

His next words burst out far too loud. "Liz, you don't have this thought out. The fence no doubt extends underground a ways. Why wouldn't it?" *She's frozen. Maybe she's suddenly scared after all. Sonafabitch.* He took several deep breaths, put his hands to his mouth and hooted and soon got a hoot back.

"Liz, hear that, that's Jason, where the trail is. Got it? I'll give you ten seconds to throw it. If you don't, I throw it. Either way, I'm out of here, gone. I mean it; you'll be on your own."

"Just a minute, quit talking, let me think."

"You had days to think at the island. One minute, that's it. One, two…"

⊷═◉ ◉═⊷

Esau kept pushing down the trail past the next reactor, and seeing no sign of Jason or the others, his concern grew. The clouds had moved in closer and made the trail almost invisible. What if Bruce and Marta had run into problems with the kayakers? What if they couldn't find Jason? What if they'd gotten lost after all? Suki, he felt, would manage fine if she did as he'd told. Jason would be okay if he used his head. But his own trek seemed ever more useless. When he stopped to catch his breath and dug in his pack for water, it woke the snake. *Oh yes, you! The pack smells…I should turn you loose, head back now.* But he saw a glow in the clouds; he was coming up on the next reactor. *Okay, check there, then I quit.*

A few minutes later he saw lights clearly but also heard sounds coming from that direction, and he soon recognized people talking. He stopped and listened…who could it be, plant workers? His grandson would never make such a racket. He didn't think Bruce would. *Trouble.*

He moved toward the sounds as fast as he could and still be noiseless. Stopping, he now recognized a woman's voice and a man's. *Bruce and Marta? Or the kayakers.* The volume was rising and falling. They sounded angry or upset. He moved closer. *It's Bruce; he's angry, and he's over too close to where the reactor fence must be.* He thought he must have misjudged the man. The woman? He couldn't recognize the voice. *The fools.* Then he heard someone coming from the reactor direction, rushing and stumbling past him a hundred feet away, heard a couple breath-catching sobs. Someone on the trail, headed back toward the road. *Not Jason, not Bruce. Marta? A mess. What can I do?*

Forgetting the snake, Esau moved closer to the arguers still going at it. *Way, way too noisy.* He squatted down to think. He saw now he should never have encouraged Bruce to go down where the kayakers were. They'd talked him, or maybe Jason, into something, and now they didn't agree. *Big mistake, all this; we all have to get out of here fast.* He crept more. A mist had come in, and the quarreling voices had moved, seemed to be even closer to where the fence would be, and louder yet. *They're about to do something really stupid…I have to stop it somehow.*

Then he saw how. He got down and crawled until he was right at the fence and pulled off the pack. Surges of argument swelled. *Do it!* He opened the pack and grabbed the sleeping snake by the neck and shook it from the pack. The snake twisted, writhed, and hissed but urgency made Esau strong. He grabbed it with both arms, spread them out, and with great regret and with all his might, he threw the snake at the fence. An alarm scream rent the air. A spotlight flashed on and started moving along the fence turning the brush bright. He dropped to his knees, grabbed the pack, zipped it, and began crawling, scrambling back toward the trail to the road, muttering,

"Goodbye, great snake, forgive me, forgive…you're the hero tonight."

Old joints, don't fail me now.

Rushing, crouching, dodging the spotlight, were the astounded Bruce and Liz. Far ahead was Jason, his path toward the island direct. Bruce headed toward the trail back to the road. Then he turned to see Liz veering off to the left, but not far enough. *She won't make it to the island.* He changed course to catch and redirect her.

Suki woke in horror at the screaming of the alarm. *Who did it? Why? Or maybe just another owl? Not likely. Oh, Mom, now what?* If they were in trouble it was her fault. Not the kayakers, the others.

⊷▭◉ ◉▭⊶

Marta had been scrambling along through the brush, her knees weak yet working, until she tripped on a root and fell, and right next to her she heard a rattling noise. *Snake!* She froze. The clouds had moved in again with a gusty breeze. It was too dark to see a thing down low, but... more rattling. She dared not move. *If I get out of this, I'm going to kill you, Bruce.* After long minutes, frozen, holding her breath to listen, desperate to pee, she realized the noise was coming in bursts tied to the wind gusts, and that it must be dried husks rubbing on brush. She collapsed with sobs. In a minute she was up, and finally she was at the path to the road, creeping and stumbling along again. At last she saw the light from the next reactor. *Good, I'll make it.*

But then the alarm screamed, wailed as if the world were ending. *Oh shit, he did it, he actually did it!* She saw the lights flash across the brush, but far short of her. She expected any minute to hear bullets whizzing past, and rushed again, faster, faster, fell, clambered up, and kept going, just going, not thinking. The alarm finally stopped blaring; the lights kept moving a few minutes more, then stopped.

For the next six miles Marta moved along in almost a trance state, all muscles on automatic, all brush scratches unfelt, no longer caring about snakes, no longer angry enough to kill Bruce. She almost ran into the barbed-wire fence in the dark and struggled through it; her camo jacket caught, and she simply ripped it loose. At last, close to the road, she knelt in the brush to really catch her breath, dug water from her pack and gulped it down, then splashed a bit of water on her face.

So where is Wonder Man? He should have caught up with me by now. She began to think ahead, that she had to get to the road, to the car maybe, and work out a believable alibi. Even with all his desert warfare skills she was sure Bruce had been apprehended. She reached the road, crept along toward their rented car, and raced across. She located the extra water bottle she had left in the brush. Then, satisfied that she had survived intact such a miserable trek, she moved back a few more feet and flopped down by some taller sage to wait. As she rested, her mix of anger and worry boiled up. *Exactly what I predicted. They've caught him, the idiot. So please catch Suki too.* She lay down, then sat up as she felt chilled. *Oh, damn, why didn't I ask Bruce for the car keys?*

Just a short distance from Suki, but out of sight, Marta waited. She listened to coyote choruses, a swooping bird, and small crawling guests until she became so used to them she forgot about snakes and stopped listening. When dawn streaked in the east, she heard the car come from the north, slow and stop, then voices, but before she could make a move it went back. Sure that Bruce had been caught, she prepared her alibi for the guards' return. She knew her face and hands were a mess of scratches. *A rape victim? A cougar attack? No, no, just a lost birdwatcher—no, I'm not lost, he is, my partner.* Exhausted, she finally dozed. When she heard a car coming back, it was daylight. This time she raised up to see it stop at the rented car. She was ready. Pulling her binoculars out, she brushed the twigs and grass off her clothes, smoothed her hair, and hoisting her pack, she pushed through the brush to two uniformed men examining the car.

Here goes. "Hello, hello!" her voice a mix of relief and worry—in fact, just how she felt. The men turned, wide-eyed.

She began, "Boy, am I glad to see you guys! I don't know where my partner is. Have you seen a guy walking along anywhere?"

She saw them stare at her scratched face. "Oh, I'm okay. No, I just lost track of my partner."

"Is this your car, miss?"

"Yes, it's our rented car. We were looking for birds. I lost track of him, so I came back here. She let her voice quaver, "He must be lost. It's been hours."

"How many hours?"

"Well, a long time."

"What's your friend's name?"

"Bruce Wilder. I'm Marta Stenoff."

"What was your destination?"

"Uhh, none, really…that is, we were looking for owls, you know, and we had the flat, and couldn't find a jack. So he got tired of standing around and… went off that way," she pointed toward the river. "We were supposed to meet back here hours ago. So he's lost, or hurt."

"And what were you doing?"

"The same." She pointed west. "Just looking around for birds. I got tired of waiting for him, and I couldn't get in the car so I took a nap over there." *Am I talking too much?*

"What about the rest of your group?"

"Umm…What group? There's just us." *Oh-oh, I forgot to mention Suki.*

"You thought you'd find owls with that? At night?" The other man— she was sure was the lecturer from the day before—pointed to her cheap binoculars.

"No, no. I was just using these daytimes, he's got the good scope. Oh dear… I'm afraid he's lost. And he's going to run out of water."

The radio in the security car crackled and one man went to answer it.

"He's got the car keys?"

"He must, I don't have them."

"Do you have your ID with you?"

"Yes…but it's in the car. Hey, I'm so worried about him—is there some way you can… search?" *I better calm it down.*

The man remaining, who indeed was Chuck, the lecturer, looked at her closely and went back to their car to confer with the other one.

"I've seen her before. I think she's one of the nutty birders, just like she says."

"It's the wrong time of the year for them. But she don't look like a terrorist to me."

Chuck walked back minutes later. "Okay, miss, they've found your friend. Bruce, right? They'll bring him over here in a few minutes. He is under arrest for trespassing in a closed area." *I'm not going to make this more complicated by telling them about his raving at my slide show.*

"Oh, I am so glad, so relieved…but…trespassing? Oh no, I told him maybe he shouldn't go through that fence, but he said it was just a cattle fence. Am I arrested too?"

"No, not yet."

"Oh. Uhh, closed area? For what?"

"The Hanford Energy Works. Actually that other side of the road is closed to the public too—Arid Lands Preserve. And an active plant."

"Oh, no kidding. Gosh, we didn't know…" Marta stopped. *Either we're trespassing birdwatchers, or what are we? No need to go on. This guy probably already hates Bruce for yelling at him at his lecture. Maybe he doesn't recognize me.*

He watched her swat at gnats. "You may go sit in our car if you like. We'll get yours open pretty quick, and one of us will change that tire and take it back."

"Oh, thanks, but I can sit here." She plopped down on the ground in relief. *Did I pass? Need to think. Why is he being so nice?*

Before long another security car rolled up by her. Bruce, in the back seat, looked over with a disgusted, exhausted look, his face telling her what hers looked like. She jumped up and ran to him, tried to open the locked door. The driver rolled the window down for her, then looked at her and unlocked the door, and she climbed in. Bruce smiled and showed her his handcuffs. She smiled back, trying to make her voice sound like she claimed to be, simply happy.

"Oh, finally! I was so…were you lost? So now you're arrested? This is a closed area they tell me! Bruce, I've had enough bird-watching for this trip!"

He gave her a sheepish look. "Yeah, this is embarrassing, sweetheart. First a flat, and I never did catch up with the owl I thought I saw. And now this. Uh-h-h, maybe we'd have better luck fishing." He tried for a humiliated laugh. "You look like a rape victim."

Marta thought he'd probably seen a few.

When the driver went over to the plant vehicle, she whispered, "One of those guys is the lecturer from yesterday. Did you argue…?"

"Hey, they have guns. I'm not crazy."

"This is the most harebrained…what made you think you'd get away with that?"

"With what? Nobody did anything! Well, just stood near the fence and argued. Shit, harebrained is right, to have anything to do with that madwoman."

"Did she set it off?"

"Hell no, none of us did!"

Marta stared at him. "Then what...?

"Shush! They're looking. Come-on, I did flush some kind of quail." And he motioned with his arms, grinning, imitating a flushed bird.

"Oh?" She spoke louder. "And gone for hours? You were lost, admit it."

Eventually they ran out of bird-watching comments and sat together silently. Bruce knew Marta was angry but he wasn't very worried about it. *She's survived my stuff before and she'll survive this.* He was more worried about how being arrested would affect his job at a federal hatchery, but more than that he felt sad and perplexed that his attempt to rescue some foolish people had gotten so botched. *Why did the alarm go off?* Had the plant staff heard their noise and set if off themselves? And he was depressed that his followers wouldn't obey him, that he hadn't been a better leader. Most of all he was humiliated that he hadn't helped Esau, and that Jason was now probably in worse trouble than if he'd been left alone. *Yeah. Big white chief.*

At last Chuck came to say the tire was changed and told Bruce that he would be arraigned at the county seat at Prosser.

"Jail time?"

Chuck was still angry at the way Bruce had disrupted his lecture, but he didn't want it to show; he was supposed to be able to handle disruptions. He shrugged and said, "Probably a ticket."

Bruce sighed, and Marta smiled as best she could through her drying scratches and swelling gnat bites and told Chuck that she would go with Bruce. Chuck apparently didn't want to recognize them. Why? Maybe he would have to describe the scene at the lecture to his boss and it would seem like he didn't manage things well.

⊶⊷

Sitting out in the sagebrush, Suki was munching crackers as the sun moved up the sky. She wondered how just long she should wait for Esau. She had already heard the car come down the road a second time and stop, then another car. She'd heard voices, one a woman's voice—Marta, she was sure. No Bruce. Before long she heard all three cars drive off south. *So Marta is in trouble. And I'm abandoned. Esau better show up.*

Suddenly he came rushing through the brush. She was so happy to see him, she wanted to hug him, but stopped; he was not smiling.

"Oh! What happened?"

He took her arm. "Come! We must get out of here, tell you later."

She stood and pulled on her pack.

"Get down, down! Crawl if you can." He pulled her to follow him and headed toward the road. She pointed—no car. Esau shook his head and motioned her to keep going. They scrambled across the road and along through the brush to the hollow where his snares were set around the water hole. He flopped on the ground, panting, and dug out his water bottle.

"Whew!" He wiped his face; his shirt was soaked. "I'm getting too old for this."

"I'm already there." She squatted beside him, saw that his pack was no longer heavy.

"You turned him loose?"

"…Yes."

"Tell me, what happened down there? The alarm!"

"I don't know." He calmed his breathing, looked to see if there was any new water he could drain into his bottle. *Nope.* "I never saw any of them. I did hear them, heard them arguing—Bruce and some woman, way too loud. Down along the fence. So when the alarm went off I beat it."

"Not good."

"No."

"And the car's gone, and they took Marta, and it's my fault."

"You had nothing to do with it, Suki. It's my fault, I think, if they got caught."

"No, not yours. You don't know Bruce. He proposed it first, going down there, and he had his mind made up. But how are you, Uncle? Your face—do you know it's all scratched up? Do you want something to eat?"

"Just water. Whew! Never went racing through the brush that way before, don't want to ever again. But now I need to check my snares; it's getting hot soon."

Oh, snares. Now? She wanted to feel that her/their duty was done, but something had gone wrong, and she had no idea what would come next. She must trust Esau for the next moves.

⊷⊨◉ ◉⊫⊶

At 9 p.m. the night before, Leon had gone outside to enjoy the evening air. He was beginning to see old White Bluffs as a whole, as a community, but even Roger had evaded his question: Had the orchard project been a success or not? Were the river communities themselves successes or not? He sniffed the sage fragrance blowing in from close-by, and the smell of the river, too, and thought that he was beginning to feel how it must have been to live along it sixty, or ninety years ago. He decided to start to write up the notes for Marta on what he'd been hearing. Someone needed to tell this missing story for the world and she would be a good one. He almost went for a last cup of coffee, decided it was too late for that, and climbed up to his room. But without intending it, instead of notes he began jotting down thoughts about the earlier people on the river and the contrast with the later ones.

Before the orchardists, and the earlier homesteaders, were the Native Americans, who pre-contact surely would have suffered few of the problems these settlers described. Yes, they'd had dust storms, and pests, but disease, pre-contact, was limited, I suspect, in the healthy desert climate. Was there even need to fight other tribes over fishing sites on this long river? What serious problems were here with all those salmon coming every year? And they traded it for what they lacked. Then, after the Spaniards, horses and long-distance buffalo hunts. But salmon were the true base. The Columbia's Indigenous culture survived for many thousands of years through the river and its salmon. The white settlers survived less than a hundred years, and most of them less than forty, because something happened to the Columbia, that had never happened to any other river before.

He stopped, thinking that it was likely that few of the small orchard-ists were able to find new ground after their eviction, for when the war was over, the other huge change, giant hydro projects like Grand Coulee, kept on expanding, and irrigated farmland prices went to the moon. On the way here, he'd seen miles of tracts owned by just one family, or one partnership, or more likely, a corporation. People that "came in with money" as the settlers put it. A very different life, nothing like that of the early settlers, and theirs was noth-ing like the Indians'—except for one quality: everyone's total dependence on the Columbia. He began to write more.

CHAPTER 16

ROAD TALK

SUKI AND ESAU stood by the intersection of the highway to Yakima. At almost eight it was getting warm. A quail family marched across the road with a hawk soaring, eyeing them. Suki forced herself to ignore last night's gnat and mosquito bites, and the collection of beer cans and plastic bottles in the ditch, by watching for any special sight like a pheasant or grouse. The backpacks, split rabbits tied to them, attracting flies, hung nearby in the brush. Esau told her that they simply needed to watch that the flies didn't lay any eggs, or they must flick them off. She was tired and thirsty, and they were almost out of water; she hoped they hadn't missed Ike. Esau had walked to-from Wolf Rapids more than once from the Yakama reservation, but this morning he felt he'd already done his exercise for the day. Suki asked him for more detail about what had happened at the reactor fence and got a vague answer. He hadn't seen Bruce, no. Had he taken care of the snake? He repeated, yes. But then the alarm had gone off and he'd gotten out of there fast. She tried to get a clearer picture.

"Do you think Bruce somehow set off the alarm?"

He didn't answer as he pointed to a car coming fast from the Richland direction. It slowed and stopped by them, and, surprised, they both recognized Elena, the shaman. She was dressed for a ceremony.

"Do you people need a ride?"

Esau told her no thanks, that they had one coming, and she nodded, smiled, and drove on as if she had an engagement.

"What's she doing?" he wondered.

"She's going up to the dam to do a blessing of the river."

Suki described to him what had happened at the reunion, and of Elena being told no blessing by her, no thanks. He pondered that there must surely have been a surge of evil forces in the valley to bring a busy traveling healer like Elena back, as she had been in the area only two years before. *It must mean something…well, of course it does.*

Suki peeled off his jacket and handed it to him with thanks, and even though she felt embarrassed to be demanding more of him, forced herself to make eye contact and to ask, "Do you think my blessing could work, truly?"

He thought about his answer. "I haven't done anything like that before, but it felt right to me. There's much power in this place, good and bad, and you can't pretend it's not here. We know that your blessing felt good."

"But the good and bad here. Can I ask, how long bad?"

He gave her a critical look. "Not just fifty years, you know. At least a hundred fifty years."

Ah, he wants me to have a longer perspective.

It was not easy standing and waiting in the ever-stronger sun, and Suki decided to sit down away from the road. Esau kept looking around, though there was little activity now—several kinds of butterflies flitting around the flowering brush. A little squadron of dung beetles marched by. Suki wished Esau would sit too; she wanted to get to know the elder better. But she soon decided there were too many dung beetles to deal with and stood back up.

"I wonder, why so many?" she pointed at them.

He stared at the army marching and frowned. "Never seen that many, and all on the move."

They continued to stand, and shift their feet, and wait, and feel the air getting hotter. She began to think they really had missed Ike. Esau was too quiet, maybe thinking the same. She decided to quit being shy and think of questions to ask to pass the time. She was taking a class, "Writing for Publication", and one assignment, which she had put aside, was to carry out an interview. She certainly should be able to do this with such a kind man. It was a chance to practice, at least; she'd have to ask him first if she wrote anything up.

"Esau, do you mind, can you tell me what it was like around here when you were young?" He didn't answer for quite a while, understanding why she wanted to know more about the area of her blessing. *How to give her the picture? He made a broad sweep of his arm to the east, then south.*

"We fished all along the river when I was young, not just here. Then for a while the government closed that down. Then some white politician with a heart complained, and they reopened a section, just for our own use. How could our little group hurt the salmon runs?"

He liked to tell history to the kids; they needed to know. Now she did too. But he had more stories than the Hanford Plant.

"Do you know where Bonneville Dam is? Above there was Celilo Falls. That was the big time of the year for us, a huge fishery, many thousand years our people were fishing there. The Falls—the salmon had to jump them to make it up to their spawning grounds, do you know? Hundreds of us used to go there—no, thousands, from many tribes. We traveled there from all over and set up camps during spring and fall runs of red and king salmon. Men built platforms of driftwood out over the river, by the falls, and men and older boys stood out on them with long dip nets."

He stopped for a time, lost in the scene. "You've maybe seen pictures of it?"

"Yes, I think so."

"Good. They would stand out there over the falls on those platforms with nets on real long poles and net the salmon coming up, and the women cut and dried them. That dried salmon can be good all winter. And they pounded a lot into meal that's so valuable. You can mix it with dried berries and fat, pack it in bags, and live on it. So good for traveling too. Everyone wanted to trade us for that rich meal.

"But we weren't just catching fish. We looked forward to that time at Celilo all year. There's nothing like it now, nothing. When the first king salmon arrived, we had a huge ceremony welcoming them. Prayers of thanks, feasting, drumming, dancing. The Washani, they were the leaders, and David Sohappy, from up at Priest Rapids; he came back from the war and he was a main one. Then after that big welcoming, the fishing and drying and smoking them, and visiting, games, races, more singing, drumming, dancing, courting, gambling, trading, everything…. Pretty soon I was a young guy out there on a platform, learning how to balance on it and work that dip net."

He paused again and she waited.

"Wow, Celilo Falls! You know, I was so lucky to be at the Falls when salmon runs were still the center of life…I mean for all the tribes along the river. You know they still are so important for many. No place like the Falls… but somewhere."

He seemed to be finished. She nodded, "Celilo Falls, yes! I have seen photos. Amazing—guys out there on those platforms! To be part of that, yes, you were lucky."

"But now, for many, it's casino jobs on the rez—that's all. I can't go in casinos—I feel demons in there. Well, there was gambling back then too, but it was different. Casinos, what a come-down. But, Suki, the Falls—what times those were!"

He didn't look at her and she saw his eyes fill, and she sighed.

"That's a real picture, Uncle. Do you tell it to your grandkids?"

"Yes, but maybe not enough. They never saw the Falls. Ike, his generation, never did. The camps are gone, just a handful left down there. Now the river's just reservoirs for dams. The dam operators think they own the river. The government."

Suki thought of the class she was taking in salmon ecology, and the discussions about salmon run recovery efforts.

"Can we get it back?"

"The river? The salmon? Maybe, if we honor them again."

Honor the river, yes…. But not what's planned for an honoring here.

He was so willing to talk, and they had nothing to do but wait, so she decided to keep going. There was so much she wanted to know.

"Did you hear about the plan to make a museum out of Reactor B? A historic monument?"

Esau shot her an angry look. "Oh yeah, we heard. Another tourist attraction…." His tone was no longer nostalgic.

"Hah! Suki, what my people really want is every piece of this Hanford plant removed! And the new one too; it's going to be more of the same problem. Radioactive waste! It all needs to go, down to the last piece of concrete!" He glared at her, "And if they want a museum, then one for this whole area, not just the cleaned-up story of Reactor B. Do you see that mountain over there? Saddle Mountain they call it. It's one of our sacred mountains, but the government took it over. It's theirs now, they think, another preserve. But what if it ends up having a place to buy water, then chips and sodas, then pretty soon microwaved stuff. Then crowds and trash. And this area next to us where I got the rabbits, it's a military training site, used to be our horse pasture." He stopped and sighed. "Lots of history here, Suki, good and bad."

"And thousands of years."

"Millions! See those humps over there, they call it basalt, from volcanos near here. Where are the volcanos now? Evicted, maybe. We could talk all month!" He looked toward Saddle Mountain, and she studied his profiled face and hands, so tanned, dried, and lined by sun and wind, and thought how remarkable it was that she and this elder had crossed paths. *How could my mother and grandmother have foreseen this meeting?* She waited for more as he began to pace around. She squinted down the road to Yakima…something coming? No. A heat mirage.

Esau began again, seeing that his audience was intrigued. "So, we're going to have our own heritage center and tell our own history of the valley. You've heard about Kennewick Man? The ancient bones found near here? Some of the anthropologists, they don't even want us to have the right to claim our own ancestor. They want to prove he's some kind of wandering European or—what? From China?" He looked at her, eyebrows raised, "Do they just like to argue? Or do they want to prove they really can claim North America is theirs?"

She smiled, "Probably both." She'd heard about Kennewick Man and the arguments. Most everyone in the Northwest had.

"Anyway, we're fighting to get him back, and other treasures. We'll have our Wanapum Cultural Heritage Center. This valley doesn't belong to the Hanford Plant. Never did, never will!"

She nodded, delighted with his passion. Why would anyone want to be associated with the Hanford Plant? Though it seemed many were pleased to be.

"I heard about your plan for a center from Ike."

"Yes. It's coming along slow. But the PUD is helping with our costs, because they put dams in where we used to fish. But I just don't understand the government minds. A museum to that bombing?"

"There are museums that recognize the Holocaust, you know. But not to glorify it."

"The Holocaust? Yes, I've heard of that time. A European tragedy. But this reactor museum will be to glorify the place...what it did."

She nodded. *Here is a person who can really understand my feelings. Where did he go to school? Or is he self-educated?* "Uncle, if the reactor museum idea does get a go-ahead from the government, you'd be good on that planning committee."

"Yourself, maybe." He kicked at the sand and shook his head. "Meetings! People don't really listen to us at the fishery meetings, and I end up angry. Alice, my wife, should be on any planning committee. She has the patience."

Suki had never met traditional Indian elders before, and she looked forward to meeting Alice. Was she a patient version of this outspoken man?

"That's good, Uncle. I can get frustrated at meetings, too—have to work on patience."

After a minute he asked, "Your family, are they farmers?"

"No, not in my lifetime. Earlier sometime."

"These big irrigators all over here now, they're another bunch that think the river is theirs! We started with small ones; now look at them! To them the river is like one of their machines."

Suki was beginning to see the whole picture he carried. But having no experience with the region, knowing almost nothing about irrigation, what it involved besides water, she tried to think of a corollary in the Puget Sound region and the issue of the ownership of nature. *Ah, the clams.* She'd recalled a scene with their neighbor who had a beach house down on the lower Sound. She had heard him bragging to her father as the two converged over their lawn mowers, how he had been inspired to hire a man with a front-end loader to go in and dig up the clams on the beach in front of his place. In the spring, before the local Indians could come with their shovels and get them. He'd bragged how he'd sold almost all of them to a cannery. Her father had just listened, hadn't said anything to the guy. Later he told Suki, "Those clams were not his; the beach below the highwater mark belongs to the state for all to share. Even Indians." She caught his sarcasm and knew her father was right, as they often went clam digging and knew the regulations. And this man probably did too.

She asked Esau, "Who does the Columbia belong to?"

He looked at her. "To God, don't you think? We can use it if we take good care of it…" he waved his arm, "not turn it into something else."

They were quiet then until another car came zipping up from the south, pulled to a stop, and the Plant employee, Chuck, rolled down his window. He looked them over through his sunglasses. Suki recognized him and her heart started hammering. *Here it comes.*

"Hello folks, what are you doing way out here this morning?"

"Hello! Just rabbits." Esau smiled. He, too, recognized the man, though he didn't know his name. Chuck looked at two furry carcasses dangling off Esau's pack and another off Suki's. He sniffed and smiled a little.

"Oh, yeah. They should dry well…. Where's your shotgun?"

"No, no gun…snares. We're not hunting, we're snaring."

Chuck just looked at him.

Esau smiled. "Anyway, we have traditional rights to this area. I know you don't believe that, because you're told different, but it's true."

"Hum. May I see your ID please?"

Esau gave a half grin. "I don't carry it for snaring. I'm Esau—you know me, eh? From Wolf Rapids. This is my niece, Suzy."

The guard looked at Suki in her dark glasses, smiled, and waved it off, "Oh, yeah. Esau, Suzy…from Wolf Rapids, sure. How did you get down here?"

"We caught a ride real early this morning."

" Do you want a ride now?"

"No thanks. My nephew's coming soon and expects us here."

"Okay. Uh...Did you see any people hanging around here earlier?"

"No, no one. Just a car with a flat." He pointed.

The guard nodded, gave each of them another look, said goodbye, and drove on.

"You're good at this," Suki let out her breath.

"Have to be. He knows this empty area can be the best hunting and trapping. Deer, and elk sometimes. I even got a bobcat once. And we are to stay out."

An hour later they were tired of waiting for Ike and began thinking of walking up the road, only to see Elena coming back, headed south. Again she stopped.

"Are you two really all right?" This time she barely smiled.

Suki answered, "Hello, Elena. Yes, we're still just waiting for a ride that's coming." *I hope.*

Elena gave them a searching look. "Then I'll see you later."

As they watched her disappearing into the distance, Esau said, "Something didn't go right for her, I guess."

By now Suki had built up the nerve to ask him more regarding the Hanford Plant history.

"You know why I am curious about this place. I wonder how people here felt about the bombing of Nagasaki, I mean the part the Plant played?"

"Huh! It was all top secret, what was going on here. We just knew what we lost—so many camping, fishing sites."

"But then, after it came out in the open?"

He thought for a while. "Over fifty years ago...it was hard to know what to believe. Many guys my age joined or got drafted. I wasn't; some kind of heart murmur. Well, you know we were patriotic, defending our country. We believed the Japanese brought the bombing on themselves by starting the war. We didn't have any picture of what the A-bombs did. Later on I thought about it, how can you get revenge on civilians that way? But what I remember of that time is we had so many problems of our own. Japan was far away and the bombs meant the war was over."

"Over, but the effects not over."

"Yeah, the effects. I think I found out first from Harold, you know, Bruce's family. We were neighbors. He came to see us after he got discharged. He was there, right after the bombing, yeah, at Nagasaki."

"Yes, Bruce told us." *So you've talked to an eye-witness!*

Esau thought he had talked enough. No, she acted like she wanted to keep going. She probably was a writer, too, and this was a good opportunity to get some facts across to the public. But he decided they should start walking; it was better for talking than just standing on his sore feet. Suki saw he was not too tired of her questions, and when would she have this chance again? After a night and half a day, they weren't exactly strangers. And he really did need to be in on any museum planning for the Hanford Plant. He and Harold both.

"If you don't mind, I am interested in this place as you know, and I wonder what was going on here after the war?"

She wants to know more history, okay. He looked toward the mountain again.

"I went to the Yakama rez for a while. But too many problems there, nothing I could do anything about. Some young guys went on Indian Relocation to the cities, but I didn't want to. When I was a kid I got sent to a boarding school. Enough of that. My cousin David Sohappy came back from the Army, and pretty soon he went down on the lower river. Like I say, he chose the spiritual way, and a few of us went down and we built homes we could use year-round, not just seasonal camps. We wanted to live the old way as much as we could. You know, we still believed the salmon were a gift to us to use—to eat or barter, as we always did. But now it's cash you have to have, at least a little, and fish cops was always arresting us if we got caught selling, and took our nets." He laughed. "We'd just go get more nets and find more ways to sell a few salmon. It was a bare living, but a good life mostly."

"So you had other things on your mind, not the Hanford Plant."

"Yeah. But the Corps was putting in more dams. The future was electric power, not salmon, not us, and those year-round camps down on the river were in the way of dams. So the evictions began again, more battles. But at least we finally did win something in federal court. I think you heard about that?"

"Yes, Ike told us some of it, how the treaty tribes won half the harvest."

"And the state fought that, too."

"I heard. It was the state that evicted you from your camps?"

"No, the BIA. We're supposed to be on the reservation if we want land to use. To them, on the Columbia's banks we're squatters. Forget treaties. More electric power is what the government wants to sell. Dams…and nuclear. I don't know how they can be blind to the risks of nuclear. Anyway, we had to clear out of homes we made down at those camps. And we came back here, Alice and me, and the kids."

She thought about all the battles that had gone on over this river. And evictions, always evictions. Japan must truly have seemed far away. She hoped he didn't mind; she had to ask him more as they walked along up the quiet, ever hotter road. She wanted to understand this place.

"So you started thinking more about this plant when you were actually back here, living right up the river?"

"Yeah, and of course when we started to hear about the dangers of these plants everywhere. You know about the downwinders? Well, we're right on the edge of downwind too, Suki! On the edge of cancer maybe. Living so close to this place, you can't help thinking about it…. Look, those dung beetles again. Maybe it's a message of some kind." And he pointed at another troop moving past.

"What…a message?"

"We, I mean anyone who listens, gets messages; we need to pay attention to them."

"Yes, for sure."

They were quiet then, both thinking about messages. He offered her a last swallow of water. She shook her head; she was okay.

"Well, messages. When we won on salmon quota, that was a message. That we can win if we fight hard enough and have the right allies. I was even up at Nisqually with Billy Frank for a while. He'd worked on getting allies. I saw more real fighting for fishing rights. And so we won."

Esau stopped then and looked at Suki. *Enough history for now.* "We were lucky. They could have made us disappear too."

She had to think what he meant by "disappear too". *Us, last night? Or, like the young man Arni? Or, his people…like mine?* But Marta had said that Smohalla believed the whites would disappear if the people followed the Washani way. Did the people still believe Smohalla? She asked him about that.

"No, no, by the time I came along no one believed the whites would disappear. Too many," he laughed. "They were going to just keep coming. But he was right about reservations, that we Wanapum would do better to hold onto our camps here on this part of the river and survive on our own. And a few of us have."

After she saw he was really through talking, she said, "The river was a huge part of life wasn't it? I don't have memories anything like that from an old culture, never will. It would be good if you tell more people stories like that, Uncle. It could make more people listen about this river, what it used to be, but maybe that it still can be—like you say, if it's honored. You know, I 'm taking a college class where we talk about this, except they don't say 'honored'. They say 'restored'."

She realized she was fortunate that Ike was late, allowing her to hear history that linked so much to her own life, even though so different.

⊷⊨◉ ◉⊨⊷

Sitting in a salmon management meeting, Ike felt exasperated as usual. A federal judge had been on the Columbia salmon case for years, ever since the State had refused to obey the federal court decision that the treaty tribes would get 50% of the salmon harvest. The feds had taken over salmon management for the state, a Columbia River Intertribal Fish Commission had been formed, and the four tribes had been hopeful. They had sent representatives to meet with the State fishery managers, the Army Corps of Engineers, and other groups concerned with river management or shrinking salmon runs, and Esau was one of those appointed, with Ike his choice to learn the job. Ike remembered how he'd at first been charged with energy. But none of the work had rebuilt the runs, and Ike expected that 50% of nothing would be the picture soon. Last month Esau had declared he would attend no more; it was all Ike's.

Today, the members were debating again the many ideas for restoring the once great salmon runs. One much used strategy that hadn't entirely worked was raising more hatchery fish to release. But one time, when a manager proposed to increase their survival rate by trucking or barging the baby salmon down the river to release them in the estuary, it had been the last straw for Esau; he announced it was an abuse of nature. Raising the level of the water from the reservoir so the juvenile fish could pass safely over the turbines was another solution, something Esau could agree to. But that was a hard sell, much opposed by industry representatives as it would lower the amount of power produced, and hence the price raised. Ike had observed that sports fishermen seemed to blame whatever group most vulnerable for the missing salmon. Earlier it had been the Indians they blamed; now it was commercial gillnetters, who didn't seem to have near the sports' political power. The majority at the meetings favored continuing a workable compromise: hatcheries.

When that morning Ike had been asked for his opinion on rebuilding runs, he gave the answer Esau and other elders always gave: the river habitat had to be restored to its natural condition. Then the fish could maybe make a comeback. But the managers shook their heads; that would be a long, expensive process, if even possible, and federal funds for fisheries were being cut. As for cleaning up sections of streams to resurrect them as spawning areas— small, worthy efforts carried out by volunteers like Roger and Thelma? Ike respected their efforts, but knew they could never restore the whole abused river. And so the arguing would continue, and meanwhile they would continue a workable compromise: hatcheries.

At coffee break, fed up, Ike walked outside for a smoke. He was sorry he'd missed the second day of tour bus driving because it was such a contrast to the fish meetings. Just driving, answering questions, giving simple lectures, and sometimes getting in a swim. The worst thing that could happen was one of the passengers getting hurt, or sick, or bringing alcohol, or the bus breaking down, and those events were rare. He'd especially enjoyed the last trip because of Harold Wilder's nephew being along, and the two women with him, both full of curious questions. He'd looked forward to more of that, and hoped to have good answers. Such a contrast to these meetings! He should have told Esau he needed the money, that he needed to drive another day, but the elder had the last say.

Ike dragged on his cigarette and turned to his more personal concern over his two pre-teen daughters. They were in a good home with Esau and Alice, but he knew they very soon had to move to a place with a high school with decent college prep. Starla was already going into seventh grade and so bright. He thought of a recent question from her; *"Dad, why do you think the salmon research doesn't get enough money, or do they just not use it right?"* He couldn't stand the thought of such smart kids working in casinos or making earrings for tourists all their lives. He saw that the salmon loss was going to take years to fix, that his daughters' generation would inherit it, and they would need to have degrees to have a voice. Just what he hadn't done when he could have. Where could the girls go, how would he pay for it? BIA college grants were just a start. But he had no answers to those questions either.

He found a phone to call Esau. *What can I say at this meeting that hasn't been said fifty times?* But Esau was out looking for Jason. He talked to his other mentor, his aunt Alice.

"Auntie, do you know anyone I could lease a gillnetter from next spring? I need to make some money."

Alice had come in from wind-drying salmon that Ike and a cousin had caught with a subsistence net downriver.

"Maybe your uncle Will? He can't run his boat anymore. Stop and see him. But commercial, Ike? Are there enough salmon left to make a living?"

She was probably right. He went back in the meeting to find more business introduced to make him despair. A national organization of sport fishermen had proposed reducing the salmon quota for the commercial gillnetters on the lower river, their goal being to close them down entirely. And these were small fishermen, including some of his relatives. The dam operators and their political supporters loved the idea, as they would be off the hook, at least for a while. It was likely to pass. Would the federal judge think it was a solution?

As Ike drove home, he pictured, as he often did, what fishing on the Columbia must have been in Esau's youth. He doubted he would ever see anything like it. Then, when he stopped overnight at the rez to visit his uncle Will, he got no encouragement.

"You're welcome to my boat and permit if Tommy doesn't want them, but drift gillnetting is going to get killed by the sports before long. Then, maybe even setnetting."

He thanked his uncle and said he saw his point. *If Tommy doesn't want the boat, why do I?* He went back to his other issue, a better school for his daughters, and how to get Esau and Alice to understand.

⊷▻═◉ ◉═◅⊶

As Esau and Suki waited for Ike and kept walking, the elder decided he would take the opportunity to tell a little more of the area history and other issues on his mind.

"You know, about the river, it's the source of everything for this valley. It's why the salmon are here, and why my people were here, and many still are. Our grandparents told us about this very old river, its powerful spirit. Their grandparents were here, and theirs, because the river and the salmon were here. Then the Spanish came and we got horses. That turned out well. But then more Europeans—trappers and fur traders—and they used the river too, to travel. Then gold miners. Then along came armies, to get us out of the way, and then homesteaders and cowboys—thousands of cattle, and then sheep herded through this valley, eating up the bunchgrass, trampling the river banks, nothing left for our horses. And us herded too, to reservations. And more dust storms than we ever saw. Then, next chapter in that history book that never got written: life on the reservations. But then the small dams, and the fruit orchards, and steamboats, and then the railroad. All because of the river, Suki! And another chapter, our kids sent off to boarding schools to get messed up. But we, a few of us, we stuck it out, right up the river here."

Hey, I heard this version of the area history not long ago, didn't I? " But also…right here…" and Suki pointed back where they had been the night before.

"Yes. The next chapter. The government picked this place for the Plant, too, only because of the river. Our Chiawana had lots of water for the reactors. There's another one built later, still operating near here, did you know that? Because of the river. But lots of people—those orchard people, your people, my people—all evicted. But the Hanford Plant gets built—new people coming in, thousands for bomb-building, bombs to drop on other people. The Yakima War was nothing! So now here we are, today's chapter. Now we have the big government dams, and the huge wheat ranches that need canals for irrigation, and barges to send the wheat somewhere. Maybe to Japan? And power for those huge cities and factories across the mountains. All history because of this river, Suki!"

She realized where she had heard a shorter version of this—on the tour bus. *So this is where Ike gets his lecture!*

Esau was going on: "I think about all my people lost. But then I think about those upriver tribes that lost all their salmon, all of them, when Coulee Dam went in. Then Chief Joseph Dam—I don't think he would be too happy about it named after him. Those dams are too tall; the salmon can't get over them. And the government knew that, but wanted that power."

She nodded, felt dazed trying to take it all in. He saw she was listening, and it felt good to have someone, someone not an Indian, so interested, so he continued.

"So then more dams, why not? But also we need to save the salmon, so now we have the hatcheries, cheaper than fixing anything about the river. And we have big ranches now up on the Slope, with miles of irrigation canals off the river to feed them. They call it 'agribusiness' at the meetings. Very important business, but it sure pollutes the river. And now the nuclear waste is starting to leak toward the river. So that's where we are, and it's all because of the river, all this history. But it's no longer a natural river, the gift our god gave us."

Suki, used to taking notes in college classes, and empty-handed, was afraid she'd never retain all this. "Yet the river's still here. I saw it yesterday looking good."

"True, and wild salmon are still here, in the Hanford Reach. One natural place saved. Thank you, Hanford Plant. Funny, huh? But I mean the spirit of the whole river, how a river is supposed to be. Downriver it's just a big canal, hardly moves. I've seen it. It makes me angry and sad."

She looked at his now scowling profile as they strode along the dusty pavement and thought the fishery managers should have listened more to him. But, actually, what could they do? The dams were built to produce power for places like Boeing and Kellogg, and could be a benefit for any small farmers left. Any big change in policies for dams, she had learned in class, was going to take more than just scientists' or Indians' or greenies' arguments. Most important changes of any kind took major movements. She'd learned that in history classes.

"What was the worst of all those changes you told me?"

"Worst for who?"

"For you, for your people's way of life."

"Well, it's all one. One way taking over from another way, isn't it?"

"Oh…sure. Are people angry about it all? I'm angry about some of it, I guess you know."

"I could be angry about a whole lot. But, Suki, people destroy themselves with anger. I almost did. Now I'm just going to be angry about stuff going on right now, about needing to fix it, and it's not getting fixed. That's a big enough pile for anger."

"But how about the future?"

"Well yes, of course, that's what everyone cares about, their children. We can't make more messes for them."

"But we have—the radioactive waste. It's going to seep into the river."

"I know. That's one of the things that makes me maddest of all."

Suki shook her head: *A crash course like I've never had!* "That was a real sweep of history…and politics…you just gave me, Uncle." *Mom, you would love to talk to this elder.*

CHAPTER 17

WOLF RAPIDS

Esau wondered if Ike had gone to Ellensburg, where he was hoping to pick up more trucking jobs. Suki wondered how far it was to the bridge, a reach above the Plant where there should be drinkable water. But she didn't want Esau to worry about her so she marched along. Their talk was interesting enough for now to counteract the heat and thirst and nagging worry about her friends. *Or what were my friends, maybe no more.*

"What do you do now, Uncle? I know you don't just snare rabbits and look for lost boys." She glanced at the carcasses swinging on his pack, hoping it was okay to tease him, and gave him a kidding smile.

He grinned back. "I told you...or didn't I? We teach cultural history at the school, Alice and me. You just got a small piece of it."

Aha! They picked the right guy! "And I liked it! Kids don't get that in regular classes. Thanks very much for all the history you've given me."

They were quiet then, marching turned to plodding. But then she saw the dung beetle army again, this time moving along the same direction they were.

She pointed, "Maybe this is just something these bugs do?"

But Esau shook his head; no, he'd never seen it. It had to be something special. After a while he felt like going on with his history lesson. *Why not, if she likes it?*

"I was thinking, this valley has seen so many relocations. Must be something special about this place, that everything has to be relocated from here. Our own people, most of them, gone, and then all the Japanese farmers, gone, and then all the orchard people, gone. And most of the cattle and sheep ranchers, gone. And then almost all of the plant workers. And now most of the salmon, gone someplace. And now Kennewick Man, dead thousands of years, and still they have to relocate him too. Must be trying for some kind of record!"

He stared at her, waiting for a response, then added, "Maybe they'll try again with us Wanapum, what's left of us."

She grinned, "Only if you get in the way of something."

"Well, won't they find something? More bones, or something juicier?"

He had her laughing again. Jokes with a lesson: a whole new teaching method for history. He dug in his pack and offered the very last of the water he had gleaned from the spring, telling her he had strained it through his neckerchief. She hesitated; the backpack was so reminiscent of snake.

"This water is a little smelly now, but not radioactive," he smiled.

"How do you know?'

"I guess I don't."

Suki handed the jar back, then retrieved it and drank. *Snake power versus radioactive.*

"I'm worried about my friends and your grandson, Uncle. And I am not sure about my blessing, because I'm not a real Shinto person. I just said what seemed right, seemed from nature."

"Nature was there for you. You joined with it, so it was right. As for Jason, he knows how to go fast through brush. He'll be okay, but I don't know about the others…. Ah, here comes our ride at last!"

An old pickup was rumbling up the highway to stop by them. The driver flashed them a big smile through the open window and she recognized Ike. She wiped off her face fast as Esau placed their packs in the back.

Ike wrinkled his nose, "Hummm, pretty smelly, Uncle. Not just jackrabbits…. uhh, isn't that…snake? Have you taken up hunting them now?"

"Beats hot dogs."

Esau squeezed into the middle as they climbed in. Ike looked over at Suki more closely and nudged Esau,

"So, I see you found a new girlfriend. Do I know her? Can't we leave you alone for a day?"

"They just seem to find me." Esau gave a twitch of smile.

"But did you find Jason?"

Esau frowned. "No. I sure tried to—I walked half those fences, but I didn't get to the island. Something set off the alarms, so...time to leave. I'll get some sleep and go back down."

"No, no, I will if he doesn't call today."

Ike looked at Suki and tried to remember her name.

She smiled, "We've met, Ike, on the bus. I'm Suki."

"Oh, sure. Your relatives were from Ringold, and you were with the Wilder guy. How did you run into my uncle here? Out chasing rabbits too?"

"Bird-watching."

"Well, you're lucky. He knows more about birds that just about anyone around. Snakes too, maybe."

She saw he really liked to tease and sniffed her sleeve. She listened as the men switched to annoyed talk about the fisheries meeting, then about what was to them a false solution: hatcheries. They soon reached the Vernita Bridge, and Ike slowed to a stop. They all climbed out, and Suki was again facing the great river and across it the shining, transfixing bluffs. *To look at that every morning!*

Ike watched her. "I didn't get to take you on another bus ride, so there it is. You need to save something of this river besides toxic steam."

He remembers. "I do, I will! I just need to drink some of it. And wash. Can you wait?"

He nodded and she pulled off her boots and socks and waded out to douse her face and arms and saw Esau and Ike doing the same. She went back for her cup, waded out again to offer it to Esau, then to drink and drink, and was so grateful for their tardy but marvelous rescuer. They all admired the shining bluffs for a little longer.

Esau said, "And they don't belong to the government either. It just thinks they do."

Suki nodded. As they climbed back into the truck, she spotted another dung beetle army, this time moving past them toward the bridge. But Ike said they should catch the ten o'clock news, and her attention switched to the radio.

"More excitement from the Hanford plant today, but again it turned out to be more comedy than anything. Two birdwatchers were picked up for trespassing last night, and two kayakers were also arrested for camping at one of the islands by Reactor N. That's a no-no as everyone from around here knows. It was a busy night. And in the middle of it, another animal on the fence set off the alarm. They haven't said what kind. The critters just won't learn."

Ike glanced at Suki, "An animal? ...Or birdwatchers, maybe?"

"Maybe. I hope not." *But if not an animal, it has to be Bruce.... or the kayakers.* Esau didn't say anything, so she decided not to. As they drove on, and the men continued to talk about the fisheries meeting, Suki tried to pay attention and thought that the dialogs Ike reported were what Esau had described— frustrating or worse. Then, like a floodlight's flash, she interpreted the radio news: *Another animal?* A sick feeling swept through her. *No, no...that couldn't be.*

But now they had arrived at Wolf Rapids village, and Ike pulled into a parking area among several old trucks. Dogs—some loose, some tied—sent out a racket of barking. People outdoors stopped what they were doing to see who had arrived, recognized Ike's truck, and hushed their dogs. Ike got out and looked at Suki. *She's unhappy...or is she just tired?*

"I can wash your pack, Uncle. How about yours?" He looked at Suki's.

She shook her head. "It's okay." As he walked off, she climbed out and glared at Esau.

"You said you took care of the snake?"

He glared back. "I didn't say it right, I'm sorry...I meant that the snake took care of us. I didn't have much time, and I had a choice.... Suki, a fight, a shouting match, going on right at the fence! Maybe my grandson could have been close too. I had to stop the yelling! It was the snake or your friends."

She stared at him.

"I had to move fast...well, I sure did. The snake is the hero, Suki."

She felt like crying, and then she was, she couldn't help it. "Bruce is arrested, and the snake is dead. What have I done that's worth a damn thing?"

He frowned, "Oh, Bruce will be okay I think. I'm real sorry about the snake, believe me. What could I do?"

She was silent. After a moment he looked at her, "Don't you Shintos believe in reincarnation?"

"Esau, I don't know." She choked back her tears. *What right do I have to be angry; I risked all these people. Calm down.*

"But you believe in prayer. We must pray for the snake, to reach peace, and then maybe it will understand. Yes, it will, and it will return."

She looked at him and saw he was serious. "I...I hope you are right."

But he felt she was too upset to listen. "Well, come over and look at what we're doing."

She followed him and saw the almost finished tule reed building. She thought it was an amazing structure with its symmetrical construction of reeds, apparently a replica of a traditional building, and big enough to hold many people. But she was too upset to walk over and really study it. She knew the young men working on it would be looking at her, wondering, and eventually one would come over, and she'd need to explain herself, how she happened to be there. She felt she couldn't explain anything right then.

Nearby Esau's house, under a brush sunscreen, a woman with long gray braids, wearing a loose light dress and an eyeshade, was sitting on a reed mat. She looked up from a book. Esau chased off the curious dogs and took Suki gently by the arm.

"Come meet my wife..... Hey, Allie...here's someone I met down the road. She had relatives at Ringold."

Alice stood up fast for an older woman, and looked at Suki, surprised, and reached for her hand. "Oh! Was it the Hayashis?"

"Yes. Did you know them?"

Alice smiled, "I remember them. Good growers. But they never came back...too bad.... Well, you look tired, sit here, and you must be thirsty, can I get you some cold water?"

She glanced at Esau, went into the house, and Esau excused himself and followed her. Suki sat down and prayed, "Dear bullsnake, you sacrificed for us and we deeply thank you. We honor you..."

Soon Ike came back and also went in the house, but in a moment came back out.

"How you doing, Suki? You must be wiped out."

"I'm...okay." She saw he'd changed to a fresh T-shirt, faded turquoise, with an Indian sun design and a message from a tribal conference, and wished she'd had the chance to change—*so sweaty!* She thought Esau must be telling Alice about their doings, so Ike soon would know it all, if they had the usual family grapevine.

"Esau can tell you about our night if he wants."

"Well, you were in good hands. So, I need to drive down the other side of the river real soon and look for Jason. Can you stand me for another ride, back to Richland? No crawling through brush for rabbits or birds, just riding along, and a couple places to check out the river for him."

She didn't have a better plan and thanked him, knowing she was too upset to be much of a visitor. "But I'd like to change my shirt."

"Sure, just go inside. We'll be leaving soon." He went back to the building crew, Esau soon following. Alice met her on the porch with a smile and a glass of cold water. Suki gulped it down, wondering how they kept it cold, then saw the freezer.

"It's from Ike," Alice beamed. "Sure is nice."

Suki changed her shirt with relief, and the two went back out to sit under the sunscreen. Suki tried to converse, but had lost her energy for interviewing and couldn't get beyond complimenting the meetinghouse. She looked around more. The village appeared to be very small, ten or so buildings were all she could see. She wondered what people did for a living in order to stay here.

Alice broke the silence. "Thank you and your friends for helping my husband, Suki."

Suki was embarrassed. "No, no, it was the other way. Didn't he tell you?"

"You must be tired."

"Yes, but I'm okay." *But I'm not.*

Suki watched Esau over by the building crew talking with Ike. *Our adventure last night must be quite a story to tell, and more we don't even know.*

After a moment Alice said, "The farmers my family knew most were your friend's family, so close to our fall camp. I remember them—good people, beautiful orchard. I remember how they let us pick fruit there and we gave them fish."

"Bruce has a great-uncle Harold who remembers all that."

"Harold, yes. He stops by here in the summer, but not this year. I hope he's okay."

"Bruce says he's just lame. He can't walk around like he wants to."

Alice smiled. "Tell him come anytime. Maybe he can't walk but he can always talk."

Suki started to tell her about Harold's book, but Alice said, "Right now we are worried about our grandson. We told him to stay away from that place." She sighed and pointed south. "That whole business needs to be cleaned up, removed. And that new plant too."

"Yes, I agree…. Well, I'm sorry we didn't find Jason…. Esau helped me a lot though." Suki choked up and couldn't keep talking.

Alice at last put a hand on her shoulder. "You feel bad, about the snake, I think? But it did what it was supposed to do, what it was waiting to do."

Can I believe that? Suki stared toward the cultural building project. *I'm too confused to know what I believe.* She mumbled, "I am very, very grateful to your husband …he helped make it a good ceremony."

"He helps any good people." After a moment she said, "But something else is going on too. Do you know the medicine woman Elena?"

"Oh, yes! Did she do a blessing at the dam?"

"She was here. She said the boss stopped her, that there were security problems, and told her to leave." Alice shrugged. "Maybe she scares them. And she told me some kids with a kayak are going to get the trouble that they planned for, but what they're doing isn't going to really help."

"I wonder what will help, then?"

"Prayer, she said. And we've prayed a lot. But you know, sometimes I wonder if this river, this valley can ever be fixed. It's part of something so much bigger, these problems."

Suki nodded. *What can I add to that?* "Yes, for sure. But I'm too tired right now to think of—the bigger thing. And I…well, Bruce, the Wilder man, I think he's one mentioned on the news, arrested for trespassing."

"Well, don't be surprised if nothing happens to any of them." Alice gave her a strong look.

"*Really?" How that could be—nothing at all?* But Alice didn't elaborate, and Suki was too bewildered to ask for explanation. She begged off from more talk, "I'd really like to visit more another time, when I feel more…myself. Bruce and the others want to come up here soon, and I can probably tag along."

Alice saw Ike coming their way and stood up. "That would be good, see you soon then. And stop worrying, Suki, you did well."

Suki stood up, relieved to go with Ike, but noise over by the building site made them all turn that way. Two young men were arguing and pushing at each other, along with yelled insults.

Ike shrugged, "Those kids—they're supposed to be part of the crew. Some elders sent them over here from the rez to get straightened out. Auntie, I don't know where they got it, but they'll use it up fast. They'll be back to work by morning."

Alice nodded, "Don't worry about them, they'll be okay. We aren't building this just for tourists, Suki. It's also to give these young people something positive to do around their culture, work they can feel proud of."

Suki sighed, "I know. Goodbye for now, then…oh, before I go I need to say a word to Esau."

She found the elder and took him aside.

"Uncle, I need to say, no matter how this…comes out," her throat tight, she croaked, "you alone made it possible, and thanks. I did…carry out my promise."

He nodded, "You did. And you folks helped me. I could've made it down to the island, no trouble, but the trip back…I picture myself twenty years younger, or thirty." He reached in his shirt pocket, "Here, this is for you. I found it yesterday when I was waiting for you folks."

He handed her a folded six-inch piece of dry skin that a bullsnake had shed. She took it, stared at the patterns, felt the scales, felt tears coming again. She looked at him, nodded, rolled up the snakeskin, whispered thanks one more time, and turned to Ike's truck.

CHAPTER 18

WHO CARES ABOUT A RIVER?

LEON HAD STAYED at the reunion tables all the previous evening, then was up late, hoping to see his friends return. Finally, he told himself that the project Bruce and Suki had planned would have taken much of the night and to stop worrying. Finally, he managed to sleep. But by eight the next morning, he felt certain that some snag had occurred, or they would surely have been back. He listened to local radio reports, but there was nothing about the Plant or birdwatchers. An hour later he stuck his head in the reunion hall and saw it was half empty; people were heading home. Limping into the cafe, he noticed Louise talking earnestly with the Plant lecturer, and sat down to watch them for a sign of news.

Chuck had called Louise at 8 a.m. and insisted he needed to meet with her very soon. She was annoyed. She had never been summoned in such a way by Plant staff, but agreed to meet him in the hotel lobby. When she found him waiting, she was prepared to object.

"What's going on, Chuck? I was about to have breakfast."

He wasn't surprised by her testy tone; he hadn't wanted the assignment, but it went with his job. He asked if she wanted to sit with coffee, got her answer—no.

"Louise, I'm sorry to bother you, as I know you are busy. But there is some odd activity going on in the Plant area, and I've been asked to talk to you. It may be nothing at all, probably just an animal, but we must have the necessary security, right?"

"So, go on, Chuck."

"So, I must…we want the reunions to continue, of course."

"Of course. So…" she recognized the threat, "go on."

Chuck sighed. Why was this kind of task always dumped on him? The recent lecture scene had been bad enough.

"Louise, are there any people at the reunion this year that seem different, or upset over anything? Anything at all that you notice in the attendees?"

"Chuck, for heaven's sake, you know we have characters who are different, and some with axes to grind that go back to 1943, and some even further back. And we have old timers that are jokers, and some that are even getting a little senile." *And let me handle this.*

"But are there some new people, not just more old settlers deciding to join in? Their children? Or others not related?"

Louise thought of Elena, and Bruce and his friends immediately. She was going to take care with her answer. She had invested a great deal in years of successful reunions, and she didn't want them ripped away from her or beset with more rules. *What's behind this? Someone wants my so-called job? Wants to move in on a volunteer?*

"Why, I don't know. I have to think."

Chuck waited. She stalled, still a little angry with this year's people who were acting like a bunch of young bulls, even older ones like Orville who should know better, and cranky Croaker. Nothing new there. *But now we have the weird Elena, and that anthropologist who keeps limping from table to table.*

"Chuck, I will get back to you. I have your phone number."

He knew he was being put off. "You have a great program. We can't have it attracting trouble makers."

"There are no trouble makers, just people with their memories, and maybe a few new ones I'm glad to see."

"But who is new? Is there a person who seems to be an angry guy, a vet maybe, but also a bird watcher?"

"I don't know about angry…some off-season birdwatchers, I think so."

"Is there a woman who claims to be a shaman?"

"Oh…yes, there's Elena. She just wants to pray for the river for heaven's sake, and I told her the Plant said no. That's odd, is there a rule about prayers now?"

"Well…Louise, I appreciate your help. Call me please."

"I will." But she had no intention of doing so, and she was pretty sure he knew that. She was a third-generation settler, like Harold, but from ranchers that had run cattle on open range in the desert outside White Bluffs, some of the last of that breed. She and a few other ranch kids had ridden a school bus to get an education at White Bluffs or Hanford when they weren't called on to help herd or corral. She'd told at the reunions that at home she'd worn coveralls like her brothers, on horseback most of the time on weekends.

Louise watched Chuck go to his car and was angry with the Plant bosses. She was also tired of hearing endlessly about the good orchard life at the reunions, and she'd reminded the folks at last year's reunion of her own family's history, and that the federal government had gradually taken over the valley's open grazing areas, one after another, just like all over the West, and put up fences not to be crossed: the Hanford Works, the Saddle Mountain National Wildlife Refuge, the Arid Lands Ecology Reserve, the Military Training Area Reserve, the Wild and Scenic Rivers reserve, and Rattlesnake Mountains to the southeast, another military reserve. And now the newly approved National Monument to include Saddle Mountain and the Hanford Reach. *Ye Gods! All schemes for taking away the peoples' land. Walt Croaker is obnoxious but not all wrong. Not to mention that the ugly Hanford Plant buildings should have been torn down and hauled away long ago.*

Now the government was talking up a permanent museum at a reactor. But why not a museum for the whole valley's history? A lot of people asked that. From Louise's memories of what the life of the area had been for a child, she privately, and sometimes not so privately, had sympathy with the folks that today were so angry at the feds. And she believed she understood how the Wanapum felt. Now they were all told the same: "Keep Out". *No, I will not help the feds chase down hunters, or bird-watchers, or poachers, or Indians, or miners, or ranchers, or anthropologists, or Sagebrush Rebels…even witch doctors!*

But whom should she contact about Chuck's message, the threat there? She saw Leon sitting in a booth alone and started to walk over with a smile. But then she saw Roger and Thelma come downstairs and go over to him, so she stepped outside to enjoy the morning air and wait. Chuck—he was just doing what he was told to do.

⊶⊷

Ike and Suki were both silent as they headed toward Richland. She thought he was waiting for her to say something, and there was certainly a lot that could be said, but where to start? She felt she must talk in order to stay awake. But the roar of the truck was annoying. And it was hot even with the windows open. No frills like air conditioning. It was too odd to be driving down an empty desert road with someone you'd known so briefly and say nothing. Ike had been somewhat talkative when he drove the bus; she needed to encourage that side of him. She was sweating, and she saw he was, but he didn't have the rank smell white men had. *So it's true, his people did come from Asia, my authentic research!*

He saw her grinning. "What?"

"Oh, nothing." She couldn't help laughing; she couldn't tell him her research success. *But keep talking!*

She had expected they would see more of the river, but from the bridge the road had turned away east, and rising into a mix of irrigated stretches and shrub-steppe.

"Why is the road headed off this way?"

"They didn't want the public driving along the bluffs where they could look down on the river and the reactors. But farther downriver there's a couple boat launches—you've been across from one—where you can't see the reactors, and it's open to sport fishing for a ways. We can turn down there and take a look for Jason."

Another silence, so Suki begin again, "I liked talking to your aunt and uncle."

"Oh yes. I'll bet Esau talked your head off once he found you were interested. He's a natural historian. Alice is special too. Esau calls her a warrior woman. Maybe like you?"

So he was going to tease her, but she wasn't up to it.

"I didn't ever think of myself that way. But everything is new to me since I came here."

"New to you, old to us."

"Well, it's not exactly all new to me, you know…all this." And she pointed in the direction of the river and plant.

"Uh, yeah…sorry. I…." Ike was embarrassed. He had been thinking he needed to be more forceful at the fishery meetings and now he was overdoing it with her again.

"It's okay."

Esau had told Ike why she was so upset, and that it had been no silly adventure for Suki. Ike respected someone who would try to do something about that haunted place, but he felt he also had to respect her privacy. Before he could think of a topic that wouldn't circle back to her worry, she began talking again.

"I learned a lot from your uncle."

Ike smiled and nodded. "We all do. That's why the school hired hm for the cultural classes."

"Yes, he's so knowledgeable. Kind, too."

Ike then surprised himself as he blurted out what he was feeling, "Yes. But now he's refusing to go to the fishery meetings where he's needed. And I can't really fill in for him. He has the voice, you know, the authority as an elder I don't have."

Suki thought about it, the authority of elders, and her own mother's wishes, at last carried out.

"I would think he'd be great at meetings."

"He is. But they're frustrating and drag on, and they don't seem to listen much to him. And he disagrees with management, especially hates that we're raising most of the salmon in hatcheries now."

"Oh yes, the hatcheries. Bruce works at one."

"Yes, and he hears a lot of the debating. Some of our people accept hatcheries, to make the best of the situation. How else will we save them? But others like Esau say we have to rebuild the runs a more natural way. Restore the natural river. He's right I think, but either way, it's very hard to bring a run back after it gets below a certain number."

"Too few to survive, I know. The instructor talks about it in the class I'm taking—salmon ecology."

"Really? You and I do have something to talk about! Esau's almost always right, but sometimes he expects too much. He gets disgusted when the scientists can't see the whole picture."

"But you know, I've learned that they have to deal with NOAA Fisheries, a huge federal bureaucracy, and the dam operators, and Congress, on top of the states' own management. And the fishermen, especially the sports fishermen can be very vocal."

"Yup. Running fisheries is a job I'd never want." *But do I want my daughters to have it?*

"The Columbia sure has its share of problems."

He anticipated the direction her thoughts had gone. "Suki, I know, salmon runs aren't the only worry on the river. But what you were doing last night—it's all tied together, including all that," and he waved his hand out the open window.

She looked out at the vast irrigated fields of the Wahluke Slope.

"How is it...all tied together? Besides water."

"I don't know how to explain it better than that: water. I need to think just how to get it across, for those meetings."

"Tell me when you get it all together? I'm interested."

After another mile she tried a different topic. "Ike, what's that crop out there?"

"Lentils, irrigated from one of the dams."

"Do your people grow lentils?"

"Are you kidding? We don't have land, remember? Not the Wanapum. No, not much chance to be big ranchers. It's even hard to feed our few horses."

"I didn't see any horses."

"Well, hardly any left. The Army took the pasture land."

"Oh, yes." *That was part of Esau's lecture.*

"Uhh, sorry to sound so cranky; those meetings do that."

She wanted to hear more about the area, but the botched blessing kept swamping her mind.

Ike read her expression and felt sorry for her. "Suki, Esau says you did your blessing very well."

"I want to believe that, and now I just feel sad. And I'm the only one not in trouble. What else did Esau say about it all?"

"He said the snake was a hero."

"A dead hero. What else?"

"That it...did more than just die. You don't believe that?"

Why not tell him. From that talk he gave on the bus, I know he's a thoughtful person. "I don't know what I believe. That's part of my trouble right now."

Ike pondered for a while how to respond. He decided it was something she would have to work out for herself. Belief wasn't anything you could just lay on someone.

She went on, "Maybe if you believe something strongly it is true for you. That's where I wish I was now."

◦═◉ ◉═◦

Roger and Thelma walked up with smiles and a "Good morning!" for Leon and asked where Bruce and Marta were, and Suki? Had they all gone home? Leon offered the bird-watching alibi, and that they were for some reason late returning.

Roger frowned, "Cars do break down. But someone would come along and help them."

Leon didn't know what to respond.

"Shall we go look for them?" Roger wondered.

"Not yet... well, maybe I'll go look in an hour. My ankle—I can drive well enough now to rent a car. I know you folks need to get home."

Thelma nodded and said, "Too bad you couldn't get around more, Leon, but it's the wrong season anyway for your specialty. So do come back in April. The true native flowers—I could name you about twenty kinds— orange mallows, blue camas, yellow bells, wild iris...come, and we'll find them for you."

"I want to do that, for sure." *Twenty kinds, not counting the exotics.*

"Oh, we missed you down at the river. That woman, Elena, decided this morning to do a blessing after all. She said it wasn't the Plant's business to tell settlers what they could and couldn't do in a peaceful way. We agreed, so we went with her, a bunch of us."

"And I missed it! What was it like?"

Thelma answered, "It was beautiful. A little breeze, people being quiet, looking at the river. She drummed and said a prayer, and sang in some language. I don't know if it helps, but it was truly beautiful, all of us down by the river. Actually, I believe it does help because it makes people think about the river more. Most of them come here just to socialize, and talk about the past, and they need to think more about this area as it is now."

"I agree, much as I enjoy their stories."

Roger said, "I hope we see Bruce before we leave, but if we don't, please tell them to come next spring. Are you going back in for a little while? We thought we would."

"Oh, for sure."

Before Leon could follow them, Louise, still waiting, strolled over to him.

"Hi! Where are your friends? I wanted to say I'm glad they came. I hope they haven't left?"

"They're just out bird-watching, Louise. They'll be back."

"Oh, good, I can still catch them." *So, Bruce and his gang probably went into an off-limits area and were spotted. Then that's what all this is about! I can handle it.* Louise thanked Leon, and after a few friendly exchanges and an invitation to come back next year, she went home. Her planned program over, normally she would have a day of relaxation. Not this year apparently. Perhaps she should just unplug her phone for now. Later, thinking about Chuck' message more, she thought of another rebellious group, the downwinders. If there was ever a bitter bunch it was those folks—all kinds of cancers, probably from radioactive iodine, and a lawsuit in progress. Maybe a bunch of them were up in arms. She added them to the list of suspects she wouldn't report. *But I am getting tired of uproar.*

⊷⊨● ●⊨⊶

During another mile of scenery viewing Suki tried to file in her head Esau's history of invaders to his homeland in order, from fur trappers to reservation bosses to fishery managers. How about missionaries—did he mention them? She wanted to hold onto it all, but felt she couldn't be writing notes. It could seem too much like an anthropologist. Or a reporter.

Just talk about fish, that's best. "So how was your meeting?"

"Are you interested?"

Yes, talk about something besides last night. "Well, I'm working on a PhD in ecology, and we study rivers and oceans, and, so, of course, fish."

He glanced over. "Hey, we really need you! Someone with the right degree, and interested in this river and its fish. But also its people? The ones living here for thousands of years? Does that get time in your ecology class? No? *Ugh, I'm still being cranky!* Well, it's no secret, I can say there's sure to be a lawsuit by the tribes when we get it all together. So… your class is following the salmon problems?"

"Yes, but the class is too academic, not talking to people really involved."

"Lots of chance now—if you could stick around. You know, we asked Jason to go into fisheries science. I know it's part my fault he dropped out. I wasn't keeping close enough to him."

"Hey, I understand him. I know how slow it is to wade through all the general courses before you get to your real interest. Ike, lots of people drop out in frustration. Didn't you go to college?"

"No, I was set-netting down on the lower river, something I really liked. Then the next thing I knew I was drafted to attend fishery meetings."

"Oh!" *I wonder what he really does for a living; you can't make much from meetings.*

"What else do you do now, besides the tour buses?"

"What's available, what I can find. Something that doesn't drive me crazy with boredom. I wanted to try commercial fishing, but it's…not doing so well lately."

Keep talking. "Do you like driving?

"No, not especially. I do like the tour bus."

"I wanted to take that tour again; you helped make it interesting. So, how about Jason. What does he want to do?"

"Something big, not baby steps like planting salmon eggs in a tributary."

Suki looked toward the invisible Columbia, annoyed that they were driving along not far from it, and yet she had hardly seen it after coming all this way. She thought there was plenty of "big" available on this river, both from what she'd heard in class and in her short visit. But who was she to tell Ike that? And she also knew the jobs on the river didn't pay much unless you had at least two degrees.

"Well, if he wants to do something big for the salmon, he needs to get back in college." *If we find him I could talk to him about that.*

⋙ ⋘

Back in the conference room, Leon saw Croaker sauntering his direction from his usual table on the other side. He stood listening, then pointed at Leon's notes.

"What are you doing, professor, writing a book?"

Leon gave his automatic smile, "No, I write about plants. This is just for my own enjoyment; great stories, well worth remembering."

"Come and hear my stories then."

"Sure thing, I will."

Leon wanted to invite him to sit down, to defuse him, but it was Roger's table, and he saw Roger was sitting back, arms folded, mouth tight. After a moment Croaker nodded and walked off flexing his fingers as if he had arthritis. Another interesting character, Leon thought, then turned to Dorothy.

"Can you tell me more about Hanford. I mean the old town. How was it different from White Bluffs?"

"Oh, Hanford! Life would have been boring for the youth without Hanford, our only sports competition! I remember one girl transferred down there to high school when she got suspended. She said it was much more fun there."

Roger mused, "The towns actually were quite different. It's odd how two little places just eight miles apart could have their own personalities."

Leon wanted to hear more but saw Croaker motioning him to come over to his table. Roger shook his head, "He's just going to bait you, Leon, in front of everyone, for a show."

"Oh…. I'll go over just for a minute. I'll avoid the bait."

Croaker was sitting at a table of middle-aged and older farmers. As soon as Leon reached them Croaker smirked,

"Where's your pals?"

Leon regretted his move, gave his stock answer, "Out bird-watching. Maybe I can sit with you a bit later? I'd like to hear your stories."

Croaker snorted. "What do they know about birds? Probably Wilder never shot a duck in his life. A birdwatcher? What a laugh…I know what he's doing, him and your other fed agents. Hey, do you know he tried to kill me earlier? Yep, it's true!"

Leon was speechless, finally getting out, "When was this?"

"Out the road, on his spying mission. I'm in better shape than I thought; I outran him. And I'll let him be for now, for the sake of this reunion. But this is a message for you to pass on to him: he'll hear from me and a few others when it's over. We don't like nosy feds."

This is too bizarre. "You must be pretty fast to outrun him." Leon saw the other men at the table giving each other the eye.

"Have to be, Professor. Country's full of feds. You know, it used to be you could hunt anywhere around here, now all preserves, preserves, each year more of them. Now it's the sage grouse we must save for posterity. So, we close off more land, and have more spies to catch us using the land supposed to be our reward for taking it away from the Indians."

Croaker turned to smirk at his friends.

Leon saw Roger was right. If he wanted to hear anything valuable from Croaker, it had to be when there was no audience. He kept his face straight, "See you later then," and left before the talk got any crazier.

Back with Roger, he shook his head, "You were right, what a nut case. Tries to act like Bruce is a federal agent for some reason. He can't really believe that; why is he being so hard on him?"

"Croaker does that, finds fights. I'm told some of it started with Bruce's grandfather. Wilder was good to his neighbors in many ways, but he let them know when he thought they were wrong on something. Small-town petty wars."

"They were wrong, like on what?"

"Well...for instance, something Walt's been grousing about this time, I guess because he sees Suki here. It was the relocation of the Japanese farmers that lived around here. Wilder spoke up early about that being wrong, and Croaker's father thought it was right. But there's other issues now, and some people do agree with Croaker, like that the government is setting aside too much land with no farming or ranching allowed."

"How do you feel about that?"

"Why, it depends on the location. I think making the Hanford Reach into a monument is good. It's a beautiful place full of nature. We don't need any more huge wheat ranches, do we?"

Croaker had turned back to his group once Leon was out of earshot and snorted,

"Studying plants, that guy? Sure. He's another agent nosing around, I'll bet you any amount. When he reports, they'll list more plants as endangered, just like the birds, and we can stay out of more land. Just wait."

One of the farmers smiled. "A federal agent? That professor? How do you know that, Walt? What's your source? Sagebrush Rebellion, or whatever you call them?"

Croaker snorted, "Look around you. These Jew scientists on government payroll think no one can see through them. And bringing in a Jap sympathizer, and a Jap even, to our reunion, and trying to make an issue of ancient history—a bomb, fifty years ago. And even a hippy witchdoctor! It's a, what you call a diversion, all so we won't notice what's happening here right now!"

"Walt, really..."

Another man grinned, "You see plots everywhere. I think Wilder's just another guy looking for his family history, maybe the same with the Japanese woman. And professors are naturally just studying something. That's their job."

Croaker snorted, "Well I'll tell you what, they're not birdwatchers. I saw them out the road and he really did chase me to kill me! They're out there right now to try to find another bird they can call endangered. They don't care about the people that pioneered here, never will."

The oldest of the men laughed and slammed his fist down on the table. "How did he try to kill you? By taping your mouth shut? Common, Walt, small farming is frigging dead anyway, no matter what they close off, or open up. Dead, D-E-A-D dead! Walt, you're fighting Washington D.C., the whole damn U.S. government. Go get yourself a beer, pal, and cool off."

CHAPTER 19

CHIAWANA OR COLUMBIA

THE ROAD STRETCHED on, and Suki fought her eyelids' droop. She had listened and talked for hours with Esau, and now with Ike felt compelled to keep on talking. But at least she'd get material for that journalism class. *Strategies for interviewing, #1: Keep them talking.*

"So what do you do besides go to fish meetings and drive the tour bus?"

"Oh, I have my two girls to look out for. Though mostly Alice and Esau do. I drive trucks full of produce from here to Seattle, I fish, I pick apples or hops if I'm really broke. I'm trying to learn to drum and sing—not often asked so far. Hey, I do what Indians do."

She laughed. "Yeah, like I do calligraphy and geisha dancing. Don't put me on."

"I'm not! Driving a loaded truck over the pass at rush hour is pretty challenging. So is fishing. That's funny, huh? I got caught up in the salmon problems, and now I can't find time to fish? But I have no PhD in fish to boss fishermen around. I'm useless at those meetings."

He shrugged and laughed, and so Suki did too. "And you want Jason to get degrees."

"I do. There are enough guys like me—no, there aren't, not that will go to those meetings. But so that's what I do. And what do you do? Besides take classes?"

"I have a graduate assistant job that goes with the classes. It's in a lab. We get samples of river water to study, measure different kinds of pollution, organisms...that sort of thing."

"So this river should interest you many ways."

"For sure. We talk about the Columbia often."

"And here you are."

"Yes…but it will make it a lot more real, especially if I get to see more of the actual river. Not just more sagebrush."

"You'll see more soon."

And you seem a lot more real than guys in my classes. Though that could be partly me not paying enough attention to them. She took the chance of seeming nosy, as he didn't seem shy.

"You have children. A partner?"

"Daughters, nine and eleven. No partner now. We stay with Esau and Alice. I'm very lucky the girls can be there with them. Great grandparents."

She tried to imagine growing up in Wolf Rapids. "It's a very small place, where you live. I wonder how it would be for teenagers."

She couldn't see his eyes through his dark glasses, but saw the frown. She thought, not for the first time, that he was quite handsome.

"You're right, not exciting enough for young people, so they tell us. We don't even have a high school. We do try to do cultural classes and other things with them."

"Yes, Esau told me." Suki decided that was enough in personal questions since he didn't return them. But the scenery didn't easily provide interviewing practice for her, just more acreage of some kind of grain. She took another chance on the next question. *What if it cuts him off? But it has to do with last night.*

"I hope you don't mind me asking, what about the missing boy that made Jason go down to the off-limits area and get so many people involved?"

"Yeah, dumb. Oh…the boy Arni? Oh, I think that's just how people like to make up spooky stories."

"But he—his body did disappear?"

Ike sighed, "He's one of many missing people. I do not know why he died, but I don't think ghosts took him away, or whatever. I think it was the plant security guys—they didn't want more publicity. And elders are distressed that he didn't get a proper burial, so he's a ghost down there. One more harmful thing, as if the place needed more. But for Jason, it's all just an excuse, I think, for quitting college. He's too modern a kid to get pulled into ghost stories."

I guess it's not my business. "Hum...he wouldn't be interested in things like a museum?"

"Hah. You mean ours, or the one for the Hanford Plant? Suki, the Plant museum, if it happens, the big star will be Reactor B, of course! It would be like, for my people, a museum glorifying Columbus."

Wow! Like Esau, he really wants to speak openly. She thought Ike was not much older than her, no elder she had to be careful to be respectful to. She could tell him about the lecture.

"The guy that gives the lecture for the reunion—he said something interesting. The general that chose this place to begin the bomb project? He made a statement that what they built here was, quote, *'a great venture into the unknown, greater for humanity than Columbus discovering America.'* How's that for shaping history?"

Ike snorted, "Oh yes, I've heard that famous insight! He should have been on the ship with Columbus, been right at home."

She laughed. "But museums can be good, don't you think? Teachers skip over a lot of heavy stuff, so museums can help kids. Like yours will be good for that."

"Our heritage center will be, for sure. Smart kids aren't satisfied with just skipping over stuff. I try to tell my girls the whole truth about things."

"But it's like people I've talked to that were in the internment camps. Many would rather not talk about it. And most people I've met in Japan don't want to talk about the bombing. Too, too painful, just move on—can't blame them. But there is a museum in Nagasaki I've wanted to go to. My grandmother that's there doesn't want to take me."

"Yeah, I can understand that. But we are doing more about our cultural history, like that tule reed building you saw. It will be part of our heritage center."

"It's amazing. So for Jason, your center would just be another baby step to him?"

"I don't know, that's my problem. I haven't kept close enough to him."

"Well, now you are... I mean you're looking for him anyway."

Suki watched a section of bright green irrigated land emerge from the dull sage, Ike explaining it was alfalfa, and that the farmers could sometimes could get three harvests from it in a season. She remembered what Harold's memoir had described, a wide border of miles of color along the west side of the river, and even some on the east—orchards, gardens, flowers. Gone. And soon they were back in an un-farmed section of tans and gray-greens, and the most interesting sight was the moving cloud formations of every shape and size. She pointed them out.

"I know, one of our regional specialties."

The clouds, and a few weeks of spring flowers, she mused. *Really, the only reason to want to live here, to make it your home, is the river, and if you could be right near it.* But then she thought that was her own prejudice, that there were people that loved wide-open spaces, just as there were people who loved vast expanses of salt water. It's their home so they love it. His people didn't have to irrigate to make it beautiful for them.

"Do you want to live here always, Ike?"

"No, not really. I want to be somewhere where there's opportunity, especially for my children. You can't live on pretty clouds."

"It was the salmon? That's it?"

"Pretty much. The difference between a bare living and a rich one. That's why…oh, here I go again, into bitching about fishery management. Skip that. So tell me about where you live, what's beautiful to you there."

"Everything, really, of the natural country and Puget Sound. But it's getting way too built up. You've seen it, I'm sure?"

"Yeah. Oh yeah. I see Seattle too much, truck driving. I can't stand it."

He really is on the cranky side today. Fishery meetings, or Jason, or what? She ran out of topics, closed her eyes, and tried to picture something reassuring in the happenings of the last twenty-four hours. She thought of her mother and the Shinto shrine her mother had taken her to.

The pine forest, the winding flagstone path, the cooling breeze, everything green, and then appearing—the moss-covered simple stone shrine, the stone basin of clear water. The shrine, covered with scraps of tied paper —messages, prayers…but then…a snake moving out of the low brush, its head she recognizes… the bullsnake…. She shook her head free of the images. This was no help at all.

"Ike, what is the Wanapum name for the river? 'Columbia'—I wonder how your people like that, if they connect it with the great Columbus?"

He laughed. "Our river is the *Chiawana.*"

"*Chiawana.* I'm sure you like that better."

"At least they didn't decide to re-name it after that general."

"At least."

More miles of silence, then Ike broke into the roar of the truck. "Suki, I understand what you and my uncle were doing, but not why your friends had to go down to the island and get mixed up with those kayakers."

"Oh, Bruce said he thought it would be too far for Esau to go. But really, he was already so angry about the Plant. He just wanted to do something to protest, I believe. But really, I'm the one that started it all."

"How was it you?"

Suki sighed. "You weren't there, listening to me talking him into it in the first place. But your aunt said nothing may come of it all. Why does she say that?"

He shrugged. "Well, she knows things. Alice is someone to listen to."

Suki wished she could have talked to her more. Alice had shown strong feelings about the Plant too. How could you live at the edge of it and not? Hoping to help her stop worrying, Ike tried the radio for some music from Richland, but it wasn't working, so he began to tell her about issues at the fisheries meeting. She felt herself slipping, and resorted to saying "uh-huh" or "oh" whenever he paused. Finally, he stopped.

"I think I'm boring you."

"No, no. I'm just tired. I'm listening."

"Well, it's what I do…meetings. Why don't you just sleep; you were up all night."

But she couldn't. How could she snore away as they drove, with her friends in trouble? Last night seemed each mile more foolish. She did have to think about something else. She liked this man; he challenged her.

"What do you think about besides salmon, and this river?"

He laughed, "Is it that bad? Hey, I think about other things. My family, bills, how long this old truck will last, the state of the world. What do you think about?"

She sighed, she'd asked for that. "I understand more now, about the... *Chiawana*. A much broader perspective, I guess you could say, from when I walked into that reunion."

"Doesn't that include helping it get back to being a natural river, a river salmon can live in?"

She tried to focus on what that would entail, and how much it would be fought, how much it would cost. He would surely have ideas on returning it to a healthy river if anyone would.

"How about the scientists? They do care about the salmon, don't they?"

"I think so. But most of them don't want to say anything too upsetting to the places where they get their funding, like saying—like I always want to say, like Esau does, 'This hatchery program we are spending so much money on is crap.' You can't talk that way and get anywhere."

"No, probably not," she laughed. It reminded her so of her own communication issues. *Anyone living near here would surely worry, you would think, about what to do with the radioactive waste before it seeped into the river? And no one seemed to have a solution. Did fisheries scientists even talk about it? My instructor hardly mentioned it.*

⊶⊷

Leon was trying to think of the best way to wind up the reunion conversation. He supposed he could just thank them all for Harold, close the memoir, thank them for himself, Bruce, and Marta, and say goodbye. *No, that lacks something.* He thought there must be a passage from the memoir itself that could be a good closure, and he looked at pages he had marked as special. He was interrupted when Orville turned to him.

"Hey, you're an anthropologist; you must know something I've wondered about."

Leon dreaded such entrees, but he smiled and waited.

"Well, what do you think? Is Kennewick Man from Asia, or Europe, or where?"

Oh my god, can I ever escape this? "Oh, I think he came up out of the ground. And I think we should have left him there."

The settlers looked around at each other. Roger grinned as he saw Orville's puzzled face.

Leon sighed. "I'm sorry. I'm just...it's one of the stupid debates anthropologists are always having with each other. As far as I know Kennewick Man is from right around here. Well, excuse me, I think I need some ice water."

He limped out to the café, ordered the water, and leafed through the memoir, chagrined that he had been sharp with people kind to him. Voices from old debates swirled in his head. It was why last spring he had told Marta, to her dismay, that he wouldn't be on her dissertation committee. He felt he could no longer maintain the objectivity social scientists were supposed to honor. Hence, his switch to plants—easier there. His ex-colleagues could go on arguing about who Kennewick Man was and how many Native Americans there were at the time of Columbus' landing: 1,000,000, 10,000,000, or 100,000,000? What killed them off—introduced disease, loss of subsistence, or their own unwillingness to adapt, or to adapt by becoming white people, but as impoverished farmers, or crop pickers? He thought about those on the Yakama Reservation, forced to give up their fishing sites, and a lot more, for government commodities.

And what did these white settler folks here give up? Harold said it was everything they couldn't pile in their one allowed truckload paid for by the government. Unless they could afford a mover for the rest, and many couldn't, he suspected. But their families were intact, and their pride. They drove away with those at least. Back to his task, he paged in the memoir for something from Harold's point of view that would satisfy his listeners as a closing for reunion conversations. But it should also be a good section for them to offer some critiquing—what Harold had asked for, and had gotten little of. Partly Bruce's fault, partly his own.

-->|=@ @=|<--

Suki, rubbing her eyes, reflected how for Ike the Columbia was a daily problem, while for her the river had meant only one thing for her at Richland: her promise. Then, after she'd listened to Esau, then seen the river again and waded in it at the bridge, she had a much deeper view, but still she had put aside any thoughts of salmon management. Now, here she was, back in class.

"So, your people favor lawsuits now? But lawsuits are expensive, Ike, and will they work?"

"They have at times. Nothing else has so far."

"Aren't there lawsuits going on now involving the Hanford Plant? The downwinders, and something about the waste? Do you think they'll get anywhere?"

Ike thought it was interesting to talk to a woman so determined to be serious. It was like being in a college class as he imagined them. *But of course she's serious…that's why she came here in the first place. How serious can you get?*

"Hard to know. But, yes, I favor lawsuits, Suki. We've carried out lots of debates and lots of fish-ins but they only made a difference when someone actually went to court. We've learned from the greenies' mistakes and wins. And we need those guys too. We have the treaty, and the big environmental organizations have the money. And so do some sport fishing organizations, but they're hardly ever on our side."

"Is it about who gets how much? How much of the annual quota do the Indians actually take?"

"Huh! Back in the '70s when the runs really started down, the fish scientists said it was just two to five percent. Now we have rights to fifty percent and the right to joint-management. But the biggest problem now is not who gets what percent. No, it's how many salmon survive to get up river and spawn, and how many smolt make it out to the ocean."

"Yes, I did hear. But lawsuits, could we use them, such as to dismantle Bonneville?"

He laughed, "Not a chance, Suki. Have you any idea how many big industries use Bonneville and Grand Coulee power? We can't close those big federal dams. But maybe some smaller ones…. Hey, you're the person, not just Jason, that should go to the meetings. I'm serious!"

She frowned. Meetings? Was he saying she couldn't get off by just doing a blessing? *But fisheries aren't the major issue on the Columbia right now. Hardly. Maybe to him.*

He went on after a minute, "And sorry if I sound preachy, but restoring fish runs—that's part of a bigger question, isn't it? About how humans relate to the river, the natural world. Like is it our plaything, or to get rich with, or are we a respectful part of it? Indians always bring that to the table, as you'd expect."

She smiled. She could hear Esau again. "That's good. It should be right there at the table, every time. So you really do think about things besides salmon."

He looked at her almost too long, even for a straight road. His tanned, beardless, somewhat Asian features, but different, were so attractive. His bare, smooth arms looked so strong. *I hope he doesn't think I'm flirting. Am I? That's not why I'm here, no way.*

But he stuck to the subject, and in softer voice, "Well, I'm not saying you should do what I do—drive from meeting to meeting. If you want to help the river and the salmon, you need to finish your degree, one you can bring to that table. But the problem of peoples' beliefs, it's sure bigger than just salmon survival, but that's where it really gets brought out to me. And then also driving the tour bus, and getting to hear the settlers. It's made me think more about all the questions around this river…and valley."

"That's just what's happened to me, but it's all happened in only four days."

"Whammo!"

"Yup, whammo."

They had passed out of the farmed area and back into sagebrush now. Once more she was gazing out at the dry August vistas, so different from her green Puget Sound, when Ike turned into a narrow road off to the right, and they were soon winding down, down through the bluffs. And then, suddenly, they were at the east shore, back to lush green banks and moving water. A startled heron, a bird she'd always liked to watch on the Sound, went swooping up and away. A pair of mallards went rushing upstream. Again, she marveled at how fresh this big river smelled, and how the water was so blue-green. She was pleased to see that they were right across from the old White Bluffs site with its tall trees that they had walked through just two days before.

Today it was quiet—no boats, no sport fishermen, a small derelict building, and the east side's old ferry ramp. They climbed out and walked down to the shore, and she looked at inviting water.

"Ike, 'I'm so thirsty! Can I…'"

"No, no! There's water in the truck; I know it's not cold but it's safe."

She was embarrassed that she'd even considered drinking that water. But she was about to plunge her face and arms right in when Ike pointed across and upstream.

"The reactor steam, like you saw on the bus trip."

"Ah, yes." *I should have come to this spot in the first place for the blessing!* But, no, this reactor wasn't the right one; it had to be B reactor. She turned to look up the slope behind them.

"I want to hike along up there sometime. And I want to see it again from the other side. But I think of Bruce walking around his family's old place right across from us, and I saw how he felt. I know that's why I thought he might help me. All he saw at this beautiful spot was loss."

"Oh, I don't know. Bruce saw the bluffs, too, didn't he? Doesn't Harold, when he comes here? Sure he does."

She shook her head and sighed. "And now Bruce is…"

"Hey, I'm thinking he's been through worse than last night, or today, whatever that is."

He turned and walked slowly down the shoreline. She watched him, shook her head, wondered if he didn't understand. She stared at the clear water flowing past, no sign of the radioactive fluid threatening to seep down to the shore. *No sign, but it's coming.* She thought of the deer they had seen the other day, just across from here, then a phrase for the article she wanted to write for her journalism class: *A shockingly beautiful place, the Hanford Reach, full of wildlife, spawning Chinook salmon, shore birds—ironically protected from humans by the proximity of the Hanford Works, the plutonium producer….*

She stopped the thought as she stared at the water moving past with the smallest of swirls, not a hint of all the big issues swirling around it, just a peaceful stream, and was thinking of taking off her boots when a shift of perception swept through her, and questions tumbled over her. *What am I doing here? What is this all about? I'm an alien here! I did what I said I would do. I'm done. This is a real river, not a symbol, and that steam plume across from us, behind the brush, is coming from a skeleton. Whatever I did or do, nature is going eventually to cover it. It'll be gone...gone. I'm making up a story of my own.* A flood of anger hit her, toward her mother who had forced this misbegotten venture on her. *What does it have to do with me, really? This is just a big river, nothing more, a river flowing by in a desert.* Images from the previous night seemed a weird fantasy. Then came her mother's voice, crying out, *"Daughter, the smoke! Why is that thing still smoking?"* She shook her head, *I'm hallucinating,* and yelled back in Japanese, *"Mother, it's steam; they are cleaning something. I did what I could! Stop!"*

Ike looked back at her, calling, "What?"

She jerked away from her mother's voice. *He's no hallucination.* She strode over to him, angry, pointing at the steam, "That...it's giving me the creeps, Ike!"

He saw the fury in her tight mouth.

"Okay, yeah...you want to leave? We can move on in a minute."

He was looking through his binoculars, up and down the river. At last he turned to her.

"I understand, Suki, believe me."

"Do you?"

"Yes. You know, don't you, we have our own history around here."

"You think it's the same? Really?"

"You should come visit again and stay a while. Find an elder willing to talk to you."

"Oh...well, I already know two of them."

He nodded and she took a deep breath and another. *I can't be blowing up at him. He had nothing to do with this mess. Nothing.*

Ike was now peering at the island. Then he studied both shores once more.

"No sign of anyone."

They stood a while, their tongues quiet. She drew in the smell of the real river and recovered from her moment of disoriented horror. *Time to talk about something besides horrible histories. Think again of what Harold has written, that it was this river and the bluffs it created that made the place so wonderful for humans. Wonderful for any of the people who lived along it.* She moved her hand along the flow of the current. *I need to understand all this better before I lecture people.*

"Chiawana, Chiawana, I like the sound. What do you think, that they are making this into a national monument? A good move?"

"As long as they really clean it up and don't make it into some commercialized tourist place. We don't want that at Saddle Mountain, or Rattlesnake Hills either," he pointed northeast. "They're sacred places. Know what I mean?"

"Sort of. At Nagasaki I visited a Shinto shrine with my mother a year ago. Shinto—that's what the snake ceremony was from."

"Did you feel the spirit at the shrine?"

"I…I think so. But I can't say…except that the ceremonies must be good because they call on nature. I felt in touch last night, but today I'm not sure, and I want to be. I'm too westernized I think."

He smiled. "Yeah, I know that feeling."

He saw her frown as they stared together at the river, neither of them at the steam. And then he surprised her and himself, too, by reaching for her hand.

"Let's go. We're supposed to be looking for someone."

His hand was warm, friendly, but *Oh!* a jolt shot through her. He glanced at her, dropped her hand, "So…Jason?"

CHAPTER 20

SEARCHINGS

LEON, STILL WITH no sign of his friends, felt too worried to sit and converse. Back in his room he looked at the photos in the books he had bought. He thought about all he had heard and read for two days. He concluded that the Indians of the mid-Columbia surely must have had a more successful economy than the settlers he'd listened to. The orchardists could talk all day about the orchards and animals and flower gardens and active communities they had created on the beautiful river, but it was all completely dependent on the fruit market unless someone in the family had an outside job or had come in with money to keep it all going. They'd admitted that the majority, the smaller growers, had never made it financially on fruit except when there was a war and shortages to raise their prices. He really wanted to dig out the settlers' view: was the orchard project truly a success—until forcibly closed down?

At eleven he took the memoir back downstairs, but didn't see Roger and Thelma and went into the café. No one. Maybe they had left. He was looking absently at the menu when he saw Elena coming toward him. She was wearing her ceremonial outfit again and carrying a pack. *Such a beautiful woman, and I turned down a massage? What a fool.*

"Hello, Leon, and so where are your friends?"

He gave her his stock answer: looking for birds.

She raised her eyebrows. "What do you think of it all?"

"The reunion? Very interesting, the conversations."

"Ah yes, you are anthropologist. But I mean what do you think of this Hanford Plant and... role, even today?"

"Very disturbing, of course." *You are disturbing, my dear.*

"Yes. The downwinders, ones with cancer, you know of them? They asked me to come here last year and do prayers for their healing, but I couldn't—too busy. But this time I do come, and now I am blocked. And blocked again, at dam. Well, I am doubting can I heal major outbreak of cancer, I tell them. But I must try, eh? And go to source! Leon, how can prayer hurt anything, I wonder? Why I am blocked?"

He raised his eyebrows.

"And Leon, you know, I am ordered to depart, up at dam this morning. So I come back here and do the blessing, and people joined me."

"I heard. I'm sorry I missed it."

She smiled in a quirky way. "You missed more! When I am still at river two men in uniforms come to me and wish talking. Well, I am not citizen, you know, so I talk very nice to them. They want to know who am I, and what am I doing. I explain. They ask to see my I.D. and my passport. All familiar, this."

"Really!" *Oh, oh. Does this have something to do with some missing people?*

"Yes! I stand there, and think I am to be arrested. For what? For praying in public park? In America? Really? No, it must be that I tried to do blessing at dam this morning. I thought dam was public property. My goodness, I am so much threat! But then police give back my papers and thank me, and they leave. But others are arrested, you know. Not about me, I think."

"I'm very sorry you were bothered." Her being interrogated—it couldn't be good. But she broke into his thoughts, back to her searching mode.

"Do you believe telepathy, Leon?"

He flashed on old experiences in Australia. "Yes, in some circumstances."

"Well, then you must use your powers for safety of your friends."

"Yes, I'll try. Do you think they're in trouble?"

"Well, something disturbs these authorities!"

He nodded. She stared at him and he knew that it was more than a sexual attraction he felt. Yes, she was beautiful, but she was calling on more than that.

"I'm certainly glad you weren't arrested. It's good you keep doing your work. We... do need you here. We need you very much. Uhh, yes, and by the way, you speak very good English."

She shrugged and frowned, "English...Russian...Chukchi...Yakuts...not big problem. The problem is other language inside us—we not listening to."

She stared at him more. "Your friend, Bruce...he needs prayer. He suffers too, tries to heal."

He saw her eyes as deep dark depths. "That's true." *And I, Elena. I too suffer.*

"I will do what I am able. And early this morning I did see another, your friend, Asian woman, Suki is her name? Another one looks for healing. She was far up that road with elder Indian man."

Now what? "Oh, really? Hum. But how was it that you almost got arrested at the dam?"

"Well, they say I trespass. The dam is not public place? So now, instead, I will drive up other side of river, across from steam we saw on bus tour." She pointed upriver. "I learn there is fisherman road to shore there, good place for a blessing."

She suddenly sat down by him and gave him another intense look he couldn't turn away from, and she was certainly reminding him of Indigenous Australians he had known.

"What do you think, Leon? Do I have powers to help? Am I real?"

"Real? Yes, oh yes...and you have powers I'm sure."

"You need to open up your senses and then you will also...have power."

"Power? Yes, I must try." He felt he was being inadequate for a so-called researcher, for a friend, even. But then he'd always felt inadequate in the deserts of Australia; he just hadn't been prepared for that feeling at an American settlers' reunion.

She nodded, smiled, "I will see you again sometime." He nodded back, and before he could think of more to say she stood up and walked to the exit door. *Wait!* But when he limped as fast as he was able to the door, she was gone. Again he'd moved too slowly. *Damn!* He'd felt for some time that his senses, as she put it, had been closed off. And he no longer had a wife to set him straight on that. *You said you'd see me again, Elena. Sometime.*

He hoped Thelma was right, that Elena in her own way would cause people to pull themselves out of the past and think about the problems of the river today. Or was this group too old? Maybe it would have to be their grandchildren, and few were at this gathering. But who would be able to return the river to what it had been? What could work? Prayers? A start, sure. He bought a sandwich and went back up to his room. He searched for local news on the TV, then the radio—no luck. He again tried to piece it all into some sense. So Suki was on the road, after being out all night, but not with Bruce or Marta. Who's the old guy with her? And who was arrested up by the Plant? Predictably Bruce, but where was Marta? He always knew the plan with Suki was a bad idea, but who could stop Bruce? You had to be able to pull concerned people together to talk, not just go rushing off. *I should have been able to do that. I missed the chance, if there was one.*

⋈ ⋈

Ike and Suki drove on silently for a while after they left the river, passing more seas of sagebrush on the right, grain on the left. Her arm brushed his; a shiver went through her, and she eased away. She recalled his comments when he was driving the tour bus, and smiled again at the echo of Esau in the whole conversation today. She felt she could ask Ike questions, as she had Esau, but more easily, and then even talk of her personal concerns. She remembered again the interview she owed to that class, "Writing for Publication". Because of Esau, she'd felt she could do this interview of a virtual stranger. Now, if she, so groggy, could only remember it all! But she also had to remember Ike had something immediate to worry about, a missing boy. No wonder he was quiet. Still, she needed to talk again or fall asleep. *Keep on talking.*

"Ike, did you know that the government used its Indian reservation idea again to make the internment centers for my people? It's where that brain-storm came from."

"No, I didn't know. And most of them American citizens, I've heard. But at least it wasn't for that long…like forever."

"But some of my people didn't know where to go when they were released. They'd lost their homes, and a lot of leased farmland. And some of the coastal towns didn't welcome them back. You can imagine what it was like, maybe, from your own history?"

He nodded, "I sure can. And your family, Suki?"

She told him that yes, her parents had been in a camp as young people, and her father had caught TB there, was never very strong, and had died too young. Her grandfather, in Japan, had died in the war; she'd never met him. Her mother was back in Japan now to care for the grandmother.

"I try to go there at least once a year. I'm an only child; I need to keep close to them."

"Do you have children?"

"No, not even a partner. I'm concentrating on school; a PhD takes everything."

"You're at the UW? Going for a PhD? Wow. But not an anthropologist like Marta."

"No, I told you, ecologist."

"I'm relieved."

She smiled. "And you, have you always lived at Wolf Rapids?"

"No, my senior year in high school I was in Spokane. My elders thought it would be good for me to experience life in a bigger town, bigger school. But it was wasted. I wanted to get out and work, make money. So I passed the GED exams and left early and went fishing."

"Commercial?"

"Subsistence, it turned out."

"What will you do next? Any more tours?"

"Well, tomorrow I begin driving truckloads of hay to Seattle for a couple farmers over at Ellensburg, alfalfa hay headed for Korea. They are all hot for beef cattle now."

Cattle. Alfalfa. She felt her train of thought slipping again, fought a yawn.

"And your own parents?"

"They died in a car wreck."

"Oh, I'm sorry. *My God, so many dead parents.* Did you ever live on a reservation?"

"I did for a while. But it's better for my kids where we are. Well, you saw those young guys they sent over, drinking. But we control it pretty well. But now my girls are getting older, and I see they could be like you—women with degrees! But for that they need a good high school."

"Yes, sure. But the drinking problem is not just on reservations I'm sure you know. Many people at the university drink too much, even binge drinking, and don't even have what I'd call serious problems—like how to buy groceries or pay the rent. Yet they drink too much."

"I think they have problems, just different ones." Now a new worry; he hadn't thought about such a problem at college, and how that could affect his daughters.

"Uhh, I guess…. I hope the driver isn't as tired as I am."

"I'm fine. Don't worry, go ahead and sleep."

"No, no, I need to stay awake. I can sleep later."

She soon began again, "I liked what you said on the bus the other day, the little history you gave us, about the river and the area. But right now my worry is not just about this river, though it is special, but also about nuclear plants in general. Like there are people in Japan that want more reactors built, can you believe it? And they already have many. But others there want them all closed down, of course."

He fumbled in his shirt pocket for a cigarette. "It's always that way. There's always factions. Come visit Indian country."

She ignored the smoking; at least the window was open. "Wolf Rapids looks too small to have factions."

"Well, that's what they hoped."

She had to keep it going. "Back to the river, I've read that the Columbia, the *Chiawana*, goes from one court case to another."

"Yup. But, like I said, the tribes have a good chance to win some. You know, we have broken treaties on our side. So it takes time, and we can't make the river exactly as it was once, but we can restore a lot. And there are other people that will work with us."

"But how many are also putting action about the threat of nuclear waste right near the river on their agenda?"

"That's a good point." He rubbed an eye. Actually, though he denied it, he was getting tired. He was used to driving tired, but not to carrying on heavy conversation as well.

After another mile of sagebrush and silence she said, "When I go to see my mother and grandmother soon, in Nagasaki, I want to be able to tell them something good, something positive besides my blessing, my one messed up effort. Can you give me ideas?"

Ike thought she was the most intellectual woman he had ever had a long conversation with. Did you learn this in college; would his girls learn to go on like this? If so, they would be great on a fisheries group, *blah, blah.*

"Well… jeez, Suki…You want me to give you some good news? I sure don't have any about the nuclear waste problem, wish I did. Let's see…"

"About the river? Anything?"

"Well…not this river, but the s'Klallam tribe that's working to have a dam torn down over on the Olympic Peninsula, on the Elwha River? I think they're going to win. It once had a great king salmon run that's going to be restored. That's something very positive."

"Oh yes, the Elwha. We did talk about that in class."

In a minute she drooped again, and her arm again touched Ike's and she straightened up. Still, she liked the feeling of that warm, smooth arm. She wanted to hear more what he had to say, and she was sure she didn't want him to disappear from her life at the end of their drive. She waited while Ike tried to think of something else "positive" she could pass on to her relatives in Nagasaki. The windows were open, but the air too warm to be refreshing. He was still thinking when he felt her on his shoulder and saw that she was finally asleep. He then noticed the sand starting to move, the wind picking up.

Very soon his voice woke her with a jerk. "Hey, here's the road down to the Ringold boat launch. I need to check for Jason. Do you want to try to find your family's old place?"

She sat up, shook off embarrassment, thought quickly, and knew she wasn't up to viewing another scene of dead fruit trees.

"I don't know exactly where it was. But it doesn't matter. You know, it's the river, the whole area along it, the stories connected to it, that have meaning now for me."

When they stopped in the parking area at the riverbank, she climbed out with him into the rising breeze. She was amazed to see dung beetles again, but only a few. She pointed at the line scrambling along, making their weird trail.

He nodded, "They sense a sandstorm coming; time to take shelter. I hope we beat it."

But before she could comment, he pointed, "Look!"

Down the river was what appeared to be a canoe or kayak. He grabbed his binoculars and trained them on the tiny shape. "Yup...I'm almost sure it's him."

"How can you tell?"

"His shape, the way he moves the paddle...and headed downstream."

"He's okay then?"

"I need to find a phone and call home. Then we can speed on down to Richland."

Suki could see how relieved he was. While he was gone she walked down to the river. She trailed her hand in the water and felt her puzzled worry ease off a bit. At least here there was no ominous steam to invade her. She pulled off her boots and socks, rolled up her jeans, waded out, and bent to bathe her face and hands. The chill of the water was a blessing.

Chiawana there's still so much good in you. There has to be—there's salmon still. And great snake, your spirit may live, Alice says so, Esau does. Ike says it does if I believe it, and I know what else he's telling me—if I do more, you live. What can I do? What counts?

She swept her arms in the slow, cool current, then splashed it up over herself. *Ahhh, Chiawana, you do live for sure. You were drawn into evil but you've survived. You have great power to heal, and many people want to renew you, make you clean again—people like Ike and his family, people at the reunion, fishermen, scientists, environmentalists—many people. They need to come out of their separate dens. I'm half-out...right now I'm just crawling, searching. Help me!*

She was crouched, combing her fingers through her wet, snarled hair, when suddenly a huge spray of cold water hit her back. *WHAT? Ohhhhhh. How did he sneak up on me like that?* In a flash she was scooping water and returning the attack. *Splash, splash,* her delighted gasps turned to hysterical shouts of laughter: *YOU, YOU!* Drenched, she swung her arm and drenched him back. *Splash, splash!* And again! Neither of them could stop laughing, swatting water back and forth. But then Ike stopped, poised to listen.

"What?"

"There's a boat coming. Let's get out of here!" He grabbed her arm.

"Why?"

"If it's a Plant boat they could know my truck. We don't want to talk to them."

He switched his hand to grab hers and they rushed, dripping, back to the truck and jumped in. He started the engine and turned up the road at a normal speed. But then, as he looked back, he ran over a rock, a sharp one he'd seen as they drove down, and then forgotten.

"Shit! I'm supposed to know how to drive." He crept on up the road, while the boat passed on by without slowing.

"That was a Plant boat all right."

And they saw that the kayak had slipped out of sight around a bend.

Suki said, "They probably they never even saw Jason last night. It was still plenty dark when... the alarm went off."

"Maybe so. Well, I couldn't call anyway; no one I know was at home."

"That's a relief, anyway, to see him?"

He let out a long breath. "No kidding. Now I just hope he can stay out of trouble for a while."

Once out of sight from the river, he stopped to shed his wet shirt. Then, thinking of her feelings, decided to leave it on, but took off his sunglasses to dry them on a rag. She gazed at him, and took off her own wet glasses.

"I like your eyes—good to see them," he said on impulse, as he reached to dry hers.

"Oh? I like yours too. *All this hiding behind sunglasses.* And I like your braid. Is it...?" She wasn't sure how to ask.

"To make a statement, I guess. Like at the meetings. You know, that we exist, that our culture exists."

They grinned at each other and replaced their glasses. Ike looked around, saw the wind was still rising, and started the truck, "We don't want to be caught in this. No more sightseeing. But that was fun in the river?"

She laughed, "Ye-e-e-s. And wonderfully cooling. More fun than I've had in a long time."

"How come no fun?"

"I have to get my PhD, and soon. It's been going on way too long."

Now speeding down the road and happily cooled off, he said, "Once when I was wasting time in Seattle, I ran into a Japanese folk festival. There were guys in loin cloths and headbands striding along, chanting and pounding on a really huge drum."

"What did you think of it?"

"It was fantastic, powerful! I was surprised; I pictured Japanese men always in suits and ties, carrying briefcases."

"You saw our traditional stuff, and no festival is good without it. Like your people, we try to hold onto it."

"I had no idea. Well, stereotypes in our heads, huh?"

"Yes, for sure. So, how about Japanese women? How do you picture them?"

He grinned, "Same problem, I guess. My information is just from the movies—uh, till now! Let's see, I saw an old romance from the war, and I remember the women walked funny because they had long tight skirts. Auntie Alice was with me that time, and she said it was probably to keep them from running away."

"Hum…. At least not bound feet like in China; Mao did get rid of that anyway. But peasant women everywhere have to work hard. Nothing to bind them from that!"

He laughed, liking the light side she had to balance the super-serious.

Now she felt she had a right to ask, "So your people in old times didn't have any such controls on women?"

Another super-serious question! "Hum, just worked too hard, I think. Still do, a lot of them. You could ask Alice."

He has such a great smile. "You don't know any Japanese or Japanese American women besides me?"

"Just the TV news reporters, not exactly knowing someone."

"Not very exotic."

"No, but neither are bus drivers."

"No, but you sure were interesting compared to other bus drivers."

"Oh, good. I worked hard on that speech."

They both broke out laughing.

"So what are your stereotypes about us Indians?"

Suki thought of the most obvious, "Cowboy and Indian movies, a lot of naked men on horses running, arrows flying, whooping and hollering. The stereotypical-equivalent of a crowd of Japanese men in business suits and briefcases, running for the train, pushing at the closing door, sometimes yelling curses."

"Perfect."

Actually, she thought he was probably more uninformed about her background than she was about Native Americans. At least in an anthropology course she had been assigned books to read about them, though they were almost all by Euro-Americans. It would be interesting to find out more what he knew about her actual culture. They were silent for a while, lulled by the roar of the engine, when bump, bump, bump, the truck started to swerve. Ike swore, they came to a rough stop, and both climbed out into glaring sun, blowing sand, and a flat tire.

"Great. An old tire. Probably that rock I ran over."

Suki glanced, glad to see there was a tire in the back. He rummaged for tools.

"Ah, here's the jack. And the spare is good, just got it fixed in Yakima—I must have known. This won't take long, Suki."

"How are your other tires?"

"Hum…good question." Suddenly he cried, "Oh, no!"

"What?"

"The tire iron, it's not here. Oh, shit." He dug around more, no luck. "I should have checked that before I left…the guy must have used it, forgot to put it back."

Suki waited for him to come up with a solution. *Start walking? Drive on to town on the flat tire—how many miles? And now there's no breeze at all.* The river was out of sight, with nothing but grain fields or desert rippling off into the distance. No traffic, no shade, not a good place to be stuck. At least there was a full water jug.

"Don't worry, a car with an iron will come along soon. More time to talk, right?"

She shrugged and grinned, "Sure, talk some more." But her topics had dried up. He stared down the long road, trying to calm his disgust.

"Let's see, talk...but Suki, your conversations are so serious. Are you always that way? No, a minute ago you were not. Well, let's find some rocks to brace the wheels, be ready for rescue."

They found rocks, positioned them, climbed back in the truck out of the sun, but found out they had at last truly run out of talk. They closed their eyes to wait for rescue. Even the sandstorm struggled to stay active, and the dung beetles kept marching.

Chapter 21

MORE SHAMAN APPEARANCES

AT THE REUNION Leon continued making notes for Marta, right down to the hawks that grabbed the chickens, as the storytellers couldn't help wandering off into their treasured storehouses. He still enjoyed it but felt he must push the group a little more before everyone left. He looked around the table.

"Folks, you've said so much about what a good place White Bluffs was. And probably Hanford, too? Your folks had the problems of any farmers, but these places were so much better in many ways you've told about."

His listeners nodded, and waited. They were tiring and had decided to let him lead.

"But now, as to the problems you've also described, what were the very worst ones?"

"We already told it, I think," said Roger. "The poor fruit market—except during wars."

"Well, you did, yes. But aside from that?"

Orville sighed, "We already mentioned another big one. What year was it that they admitted the damn codling moth had won, and they started pulling out the apple trees?"

Roger shook his head.

Leon said, "I don't know the year, but I just saw something here..." he paged through the memoir:

'My grandmother cried as they cut down their apple orchard. It was what the family had started with, back in 1907, planting fifty little apple trees. Now firewood. It was such a personal defeat, destroying those trees, a heartbreak for many families.'

Dorothy sighed. "Lots of crying as they cut down those trees. It was definitely one of the worst things, like he says. It took years to get other fruit producing."

Leon thought of the acres of black stumps they had seen on the bus ride the day before and how people had reacted. *But those were not the moth's doing; those were the final slaughter, '43.* He waited for more of "the worst".

Roger finally spoke, "At first it was the water system problems. Some people at the lower end of the Hanford Ditch lost a lot of trees early and gave up. I think after the ditch finally got paved another big problem was lack of paying jobs except at harvest. Men having to leave home to find work when they found out that even with orchards full of fruit they just weren't making it. My dad was one of them gone so much. No welfare or social security then."

Thelma said, "How about the time we tried to sell direct to the retail stores?"

Roger nodded, "Oh, yes, there's a problem for you, Leon, although it wasn't the worst problem. I guess you'd call it a political problem. Harold must talk about it?"

Leon had earmarked a comment on that experiment, but Roger went on.

"Some of our folks decided to can their own fruit and try to sell direct to retail markets, cut out the middle-man. This was in the late 1930s. They chose very high-quality tree-ripened fruit, created their own pretty label, and took their samples around. Delicious fruit! And the sales were going great until the big fruit canners came on like a sandstorm. I don't know why folks thought they'd get away with it. That great idea lasted only a season."

"What happened?"

Orville exploded. "Ha! The big canners, Libby for one, just went to those retailers and said, okay you want to buy your peaches and cots that way? Fine, then you just get your grapefruit, oranges, pineapple, bananas—everything that way. So, end of experiment."

Dorothy sighed, "They worked so hard, and it was going so well. They were sick, just sick."

Leon made a note, thinking how discouraging it must have been, but hardly surprising. The orchardists had been naïve.

Thelma said, "Of course, of the worst things, that terrible time you've already heard about—very early, 1913, the Milwaukee building the tracks away from the town and splitting us up into factions."

Orville nodded. "Everyone angry, I mean some not even talking for decades."

Leon couldn't get any more "worst things" from the group, and he realized that definitely wasn't their favorite topic. After a silence Thelma proposed they all take a walk through the park down to the river.

Orville said, "Yes, enjoy it while we can before it gets too full of crap."

The peacefully flowing river did its magic and brought them away from considering worst things, past or future. Soon they were looking at huge swooping pelican flocks, and as they walked they spotted a gorgeous male Chinese pheasant, Roger commenting that he knew for sure it was one of the introduced species, probably by would-be hunters. The breeze was just right, the river was not yet "full of crap", and they returned to the hall refreshed, the men with a stop-off for beer.

⊷⊜ ⊜⊶

It was hours before Ike saw a car emerging to the south, and pushed Suki awake. They clambered out to signal and it slowed.

Suki cried, "I can't believe it, this is the third time today!"

"Who is it?"

"Elena! She passed Esau and me this morning. She was headed for the dam, I think. Then she came back down past us again. And now she's here."

Ike peered. "A cross-country, car-racing shaman, with a tire iron for a weapon, I hope!"

Elena stopped, rolled down her window, and gave them a bright smile. "Hello! Can I help this time?"

Suki wanted to hug her. "Yes, you really can."

"Well, good. So far, this trip I did not do very well. What do you need?" She stepped out of the car and Ike saw her in her regalia for the first time. *The famous Elena, and I hardly noticed her on the tour bus. Wow. She's as elegant as Wanapum women dressed for a powwow.*

"A tire iron, if you have one." He felt almost humble.

She eyed the flat tire. "Hello, Ike. Yes, right under the back seat. Of course, I checked before I left the rental place."

"Of course. And I did have one, but someone took it." He saw her smile was teasing this time.

The three ignored the blowing sand starting up again, and he had the wheels exchanged in a few minutes, Suki admiring his shoulders and arms at work. She marveled that she normally never got to see men doing actual physical work. The crisis over, she decided to ask Elena if she knew where her friends were and who was arrested.

"No, I see only you...oh, and anthropologist, Leon, and kayaker on the river, down near the bridge. You might know him. But your friend Bruce...could be in trouble. Well, actually, I was one almost arrested, but they let me go, I do not know why, but maybe I could be worse problem, eh?"

She closed her eyes and put up a hand toward the wind. Then she looked back at Suki.

"It will not blow too hard. But yes, you know your friends have problems too; they need our prayers."

Suki sighed, "I am praying."

"Good, you keep praying for your friends. So Ike is finished with tire, now he can help me."

"What do you need?" He wiped off his sweaty face.

"Tell me how to find certain road down to this river, and one more time I will do blessing—you see I am dressed for that. Then I will be done with your Chiawana...for this time."

Ike put the tire iron back, and got another teasing look. But after he described how to recognize the river road, Elena gazed around.

"Did you notice this?" She had spotted a troop of large insects crossing the road, moving eastward. All three stared.

Elena spoke, "Ike, is this normal?"

"No, I don't think so, not so many."

Suki frowned, "Ike, we saw them first where we were waiting for you. Then again at the bridge, then again on this side, and now again!"

Elena said, "Ah, you see they are leaving this area." She bent down and saw they were big black beetles with two bulbous shells for a body, the hind shell with folded wings, and sporting very long hind legs.

"What do you call them?"

"Dung beetles," Ike explained their normal work. "Smart bugs, but no dung balls today!"

Elena picked one up and looked it over as it waved its legs. She put it down carefully and pointed at the troop passing.

"Ah, you see, they give up here...it is too dangerous for them. They flee poison that will seep to this river, and they give us warning. Suki, you want to help river, this whole area, and your friends want to, and of course Ike does. You need to think more about way that can be done. We cannot just march away like beetles."

Suki sighed. "I agree."

Elena stared at her more. "You do much searching today. You will find him. But I think you search inside yourself too. And that is good, we need to." She held up her hand to Suki and moved it slightly.

"I feel strong spirit in you; you must use it, Suki. It is there for you." She dropped her hand and continued, "Today I saw how I also need to do much more about rivers. We cannot live without them; have you thought about that? But they must be clean, natural rivers. Am I right, Ike?" She turned. "He knows. But we lose rivers if we do not take care of them. Ike, your people used to know, they yet must know. Call on that knowledge, that power, yes?"

They both stared at her, then nodded.

"Well, I am going now to Chiawana. And then to another important river, Klamath. I will pray for you both. So, good searching."

"Thank you, Elena," Suki said. They watched her climb in her car and drive on up the highway. Suki commented,

"I knew those beetles meant something. Elena's a little stagey, but she's not just a show person. She came up here all by herself to do a blessing, no audience."

Ike nodded. "And she had a spare, a jack, and a tire iron. Doesn't just count on prayers…or luck."

Suki smiled. "Well, you had a spare and a jack—and water."

"Ha, I'm not a medicine man yet. And my luck hasn't been so good lately…till now."

He did not return her look. In a few minutes they were on the road south again, and Suki was on her second wind to keep the conversation going as the sagebrush view slid past. After a few minutes of engine roar and otherwise silence, she started again,

"Okay, can we talk some more? I want to stay awake, but I don't want to bore you."

"You're not boring me, believe me."

"So what do you really like to do for fun?"

"Oh, fish, hunt deer, hike around, swim, go boating, camping up in the mountains…sometimes to powwows. And goof off with my kids."

"Pow-wows. I've never been to one."

"You might find it interesting. A lot of costuming, drumming, singing, dancing, socializing, gambling. And some serious stuff mixed in too. I like to go once in a while."

"I should take one in sometime."

"And you?"

"I like the outdoors too. I used to go with my father and mother before he got too sick. We went clam digging and berry picking. And sometimes we'd rent a boat and go out in the Sound and fish, though we didn't catch much. There aren't even many clams left in the Sound I don't think; it's pretty polluted."

She stopped talking as a memory swept through her of her father.

The three of them had driven up to Lake Sutherland in the Olympic forest and rented a cabin for the weekend. It was when she was about nine and a time when he was feeling

fairly well and able to hold a job that wasn't too strenuous, and he liked to get out in nature on the weekends. After they'd gotten settled in the cabin and were looking out on the long blue lake surrounded by evergreens, he said to her, "Let's go fishing." He'd brought hand-lines, and they rowed way out into the lake, trolling the lines and lures behind. He was teaching her how to row, and she felt so proud when she got the rhythm going and could feel the boat streaking through the water. She was proud again when she caught a small fish of some kind. It was a perfect day for her out with her dad, and exciting when wind came up, and he had to take over the oars. Rowing back through the chop she remembered him saying, "I love this."

She cherished this memory but always teared up, thinking how by the time she was a teenager he couldn't do things like that anymore. She shook herself free of the memory.

"But, back to the river, and the promise I made to my family. I've carried it out, but not how I'd hoped, not like it was supposed to be. Now, since being down by the river again, I don't feel as if I've done what I could. And Elena… pushes me even more. I'm sure not going to solve the nuclear waste problem on my own, but I feel there's got to be more I could do, you know, to make this river, this area, clean again."

A thinker, all the time. "Well, I believe you're right."

"But I have to be realistic, Ike. I want to do something that a small, unimportant person can carry out. Something I can tell my mother. Right now… it overwhelms me. But maybe you could give me an example, something that an ordinary person could do? You must have talked on this level many times, right? Over salmon run rebuilding?"

Okay, no more joking. Of course he had examples. But something that she'd like to do? Small projects that would mean something? He was quiet for a while.

"Well, okay, here's a project I thought of for myself. Something different from forever meetings. I don't know if it's what you mean, or if I could ever do it though. There's a museum down the river at The Dalles, a pretty good one. But in their display on river history they have a long string of photographs that show a certain white pioneer family. It shows that family's great army of horse seines, and gillnetters, and fish wheels. And all for salmon. Huge seines, many men, eight or more horses hauling on just one of those seines full of salmon! Just this one family! What we'd sure call an industrial operation today! Who knows how many more families doing that? But not one word in the display about how this kind of harvesting affected the Indians that lived along there…to say nothing of the salmon! Not a word. Well, I'd like to fix that, put in the missing story of that display."

Suki saw the connection he'd left for her to find. "And so if there's going to be a Hanford reactor museum, I should do whatever I can to be sure that it covers that whole story. How that bomb, the plutonium that made that bomb, affected the people it was dropped on?"

"Yes. The story most people don't know, maybe don't want to know. And they should have a hard time refusing if you went to that museum planning committee. But you also have to have the so-called credentialed people to back you up. Like we always have our biologists with us now when we go to meetings."

"A great idea, a museum that tries to tell the whole truth. Thanks, Ike. But I know, I do need the credentialed people, people from Nagasaki. I don't think I actually know any that are here in the U.S."

"So find them, I bet you can."

She didn't answer for a while, then, "Okay, that's sure a real example. Can you give me another idea like that?"

I'll never get off easy, I can see that. "Well, I can give you one I've thought of for Alice and Esau. When they teach cultural history of the valley, I think they could expand it, and talk more about the Plant, and what it was meant for, and what it did. They could even talk about the bigger picture—nuclear plants and their problems."

"Another great idea! And that's something you know they would do? When I see my mother, I want to be able to report things like that, other things that can really make a difference, as well as my blessing…if it did."

She saw such practical thinking was easy for him. Of course. This river and region were not just an academic topic for him.

"Since I came here I keep thinking about things so differently, Ike. And it's…disorienting. Have you had talked about this before?"

He shook his head with a smile, "Not quite like this."

But is it such a weird conversation? Suki thought that mainly they had been talking about their families, their work, the environment. Normal topics. The men in her class did talk about the environment—protecting whales, trash on the beach. But more often it was yesterday's football game, their new computer. There couldn't be so many boring men, or was it a version of natural selection running backward? She smiled at the idea. But Ike was involved in something real, even though he complained about it. Minutes later she was falling asleep again against his shoulder and didn't mind.

Ike didn't mind either, though he was surprised how attracted he was to Suki. It wasn't just that she was a pretty woman—he knew plenty. But was she always so serious? But, of course—she, like Elena, had come here on a mission. He wanted to say that tomorrow, maybe, they could continue this talk, but remembered she was leaving for home and her classes. And he had a hay truck to connect with, and whatever else that Esau thought of.

CHAPTER 22

THE MEMOIR CAPTURES IT

BACK IN THE conference room after the river walk, Leon paged through the memoir and waited for any more recalls of the settlers' "worst experiences" or a more preferred topic. They looked around rather wearily. Roger broke the silence finally saying,

"Well, there was a group at place called the Klondike up the river who'd made it big on the real Klondike and came to the valley to retire, and they could afford to have a poor market. Others, each year a new challenge."

Orville nodded, "But far worse for the folks up on the Wahluke Slope. I knew some. That homesteading program, what a joke. The government knew they would end up abandoning their places."

"You really think so?"

"You bet I do. People would give up when there was little rain for years. They'd go bust and then the government could grant the land to the railroads. And once a track was in, the railroad could sell lots for little towns, just like White Bluffs. We saw it! One more government scam!"

Leon glanced at Roger, who raised his eyebrows.

Orville saw it and smiled. "I'm not talking about your outfit, Roger. The county extension agents were okay in the main."

Roger shrugged and smiled, being used to Orville. "You know there were a few homesteaders right on the river, too, and smarter, or luckier. Some of those families were still there when our folks arrived. They didn't have the advantages ours had—no steamboat, just rafts, no irrigation system, just waterwheels, but their animals were out on the bunchgrass. And there were families, or outfits, with big herds out there in the desert. Louise can tell you about that life. But one winter it got terribly cold, and they didn't have hay stored—they'd never needed to—and they lost most of their cattle and went belly-up."

Leon marveled again that the West was full of such stories, but he'd never heard any of this from eastern Washington. The west side somehow won all the attention.

A woman who had been standing there listening spoke up. "But back to the worst part for us, you left one out. I think the women worked way too hard."

Leon nodded to her and flipped to a short comment by Harold he'd tagged.

'My mother grumbled once, and it was not like her, really, at least not in front of us. She told us we could have just stayed in a town and bought our milk and fruit and other food and been better off, and not near so much work for the women.'

Dorothy voiced her agreement. "It was much harder for the women than life in a town, but they stayed with it. I guess for us children."

Thelma looked at her, "For their husbands, too, I think. The men would've been working hard somewhere, anyway, wouldn't they, Dot? And nothing to show for it like those orchards."

Leon thought again that Thelma always brought something a little different to the table; she focused on beauty—or in the case of the Klan, its opposite. A young man that Roger knew slightly, Keene, who had been standing there for some time, broke into the talk.

"But if you want worst things, what I think? The worst was our government letting the valley and river be taken over for a project to bomb and destroy and mutilate thousands of civilians."

The others all turned to look at him. He was a local college student: white, tall and thin, with a ponytail, stylish glasses, and a *"Make Love Not War"* t-shirt. Roger and Thelma already knew him from years as volunteers with 4-H.

At last Thelma spoke quietly, "We didn't have any idea, you know, till much later."

Roger said, "You're right, though, Keene. And we survived our troubles—pretty much."

Leon waited for more. It was first time he'd heard anyone at the reunion, besides Bruce, make such a bold statement. He smiled at the young man, who nodded back. Leon wanted to ask, *Well, what about the government taking the land from the Indians in the first place?* But then he thought not. He didn't feel he had the right to drop that on them. And what was the point? All of America had been taken. *I could lecture a couple days on that.*

As Keene left, Dorothy looked around at the others and said, "He has a point. But Leon, for us, you mean the worst thing for us, the people at White Bluffs and Hanford? Well, this: they took it all away from us! That's the worst!"

Leon stared at her fierce expression, then wrote down and underlined: *Worst? "They took it all away from us."* It seemed to be the repeated history of the river.

Dorothy stood up, "On that, time for the women to have a break!" She marched out, followed by Thelma and a few others. Leon got up and stretched while Roger and Orville drifted back to farming anecdotes. When the women returned with smiles, he tried to steer them all back to the part he thought most unique: the community.

"Okay, you've told me most of the worst problems, so tell me again now, aside from farming problems and marketing, and too much hard work, would you say White Bluffs and Hanford were successes as towns, as communities? And if they were, how did that happen?"

Roger sat up straighter, glad to swing back to the positive. "Leon, I'd say yes, our folks were a success in town-building anyway. A real mix of people coming together and building a town out of pretty much nothing! They did get help from outside for the post office, churches, and schools. And then later the county agents, and the WPA. But mostly our families created the towns by themselves, like all the small local businesses they started that made things work, like the newspaper, the little stores, the movie house, the Co-op, the sports teams. Some people that came in with more funds built a cold storage and larger packing sheds and hired people."

Dorothy said, "Things like the baby clinic and the traveling library never would've happened without lots of volunteer effort. It's hard to get volunteers like that these days."

Orville nodded, "That's the way things worked back then."

Leon jotted notes fast, then flipped to the memoir. "Here's a comment from Harold that surprised me:

'Quite a few families were able to send their youth out for college or some kind of training, even in the Depression years. College was so cheap then, and they often got scholarships. I think those folks, or maybe their kids, saw farming wasn't really going to make it.'

Thelma said, "It's true. White Bluffs, and I'm sure Hanford too, raised kids that became teachers, engineers, scientists, secretaries, politicians, lawyers, artists, researchers—you name it. And a few stuck with farming and made it somehow."

Leon sat back and pondered. "What makes people stick with small farming anyway? It can't be just because the crops can look beautiful. Even orchards, beautiful as they are…"

Thelma gave him a piercing look, "Leon, it's hope! They're always hoping next year could be better. You don't ever think it's going to be always the same. You can hope. A bumper crop coming! Or a war, God forbid. But now can you read us more from Harold?"

Leon took her suggestion. He had saved some of Harold's final comments and been waiting. A few people still scattered in the room had by now come over to stand behind them listening.

Leon looked around at them. "Okay, here's what Harold writes near the end, sort of a summary, looking back at everything for his family. I suppose much of it could be the same for others. You can say."

'My father had been the big promoter of the move to the desert. He wanted his kids out of the smog and the TB ravaging the cities. He was used to laboring with his hands, and he'd always loved growing things, so orchards seemed like a good move. He knew he'd have to keep working out for a while, and his wife's parents were also used to working hard and were willing to get the orchard started. What my father didn't factor in enough were things he didn't know much about—costs of farming, irrigation problems, the fruit market, the brokers, and so many different pests that could attack. All that was new.

'He, I should say they, were able to overcome so many problems that came up. There was no high school at first at White Bluffs, so they sent us kids out to high school to live with relatives, or to families where we worked for room and board. When we did get a high school, the community made sure we had good teachers, and that our kids won whatever scholarships were available. When the coddling moth ruined the apples, my father and others switched to other fruit.

'The families had always caught their fuel from the river—that never had to change. When a power line came in, my folks made do with one light bulb, so they could read or do homework at night. When Prohibition ruined the grape market, out came the grapes, in went some other fast crop, like melons. Later when the local water coop went broke, our neighbor was able to keep the system going for a few farms, and he never charged the widows.

'When prices were poor, they formed a local fruit-canning coop, hoping to break into the market. That idea got killed real fast, but later some young fellows figured out how to bypass the broker and take pick-ups with boxes of fruit across to the west-side highway fruit stands and sell direct to them. They got a better price; it was so smart. So mainly the growers kept solving their problems, just enough to keep going.

'During the Depression my father couldn't get work for cash, but my mother kept working out for other farmers—berry picking, packing shed, and even became a bee-handler. Like the other women, she was always sewing clothes, making over clothes to look like something new. When the families ran out of cash the storekeeper let people charge till the next harvest. So they made it through the Depression.

During any hard times people did leave the valley, and that was usually sad for everyone, but others came in to make a go of it, and the town would grow again.

'My folks and the others in White Bluff had learned how to survive, make-do, fix just about anything. The one thing they couldn't fix was the lousy fruit prices, but wars fixed that for a time. But then came the Manhattan Project and they were trapped. A gigantic secret government project, and everything closed down, everyone evicted. They couldn't fix things that time.'

Leon paused for comments. He thought Harold had done well summing up what they had been telling about for two days.

"He could have been a lot harder on the government," said Orville. "Aside from that, I'd say he told it right."

After a silence, Dorothy broke in to talk about the eviction. She said it was the older people that it affected the worst. The listeners agreed. They had gone mainly to other small Eastern Washington towns and somehow adjusted to living on what was now called "old age assistance" and local part-time jobs. Roger commented that only a few were eligible for social security when it came in. He knew only a handful that could buy another productive farm with the pittance they'd received from the government. One woman listening remembered how many older people had died soon after leaving.

Roger nodded, "Many were well along in years, of course. But it may have been partly that the young people's energy had kept them active, and they'd all gone off—drafted, or for training, or work."

After waiting for more comments, Leon said, "I'll go on with Harold?"

'In spring, 1943 I wasn't there; I was in the South Pacific. With no warning the order came to leave our homes, giving families ninety days. My dad wrote us, the ones not at home. "If you want to see this place one last time, try to get back here." My sister was the one who made it. She was there to see the bulldozer come into our place and knock down the fence.'

Leon stopped. No one said a word, so he continued with Harold.

'My parents were luckier than some. Over on Puget Sound they found a very small rundown farm and an old empty house they could afford that he could renovate. I don't know how many were able to find personal solutions so good. What would never be good was what their old place and the others had been used for.

'I met many of the settlers later, and some of the elders were just lost. Younger people didn't suffer so much because they went on to other ventures, as young people do. I became a construction worker like my father, and I had to move from place to place in the Northwest, leaving my family like he did. Some of those places had beautiful settings. But I never was able to live again in a community like White Bluffs. They are hard to find.

'I don't think my father ever got over it. Not just the eviction, but when he found out some time later what their White Bluffs place was used for. My mother, being so social, managed well with new friends, neighbors, and clubs. But he was quite silent most the time. No more jokes at the dinner table. He spent a lot of time alone out in his garden and little orchard, a few chickens, and went to church once in a while. Once I tried to talk to him about Nagasaki, what I'd seen there—I had my own nightmares. But when I waited for him to say something, he finally just said, "Harry, I can't talk about it...I can't. Not right now." I never brought it up to him again. It wasn't easy for me either, but he had put 36 years in the place, to have it taken and used that way.'

After another silence around the table and from others standing there listening, Roger said, "I think a lot of people, later when they knew, that it was beyond what they could deal with. I try to imagine what he felt when he landed a few days after the bomb, just a kid. And not even knowing the connection yet with White Bluffs. I know the shock it was when I heard later."

Janice looked up, "I think it was very wrong, the whole thing. War is wrong."

The wisdom of youth, Leon smiled at her. He suspected the others had things they wanted to say, but perhaps right now it was too much for them, as they stayed silent. They were probably used to leaving the reunions with happy thoughts, and Harold's last words had brought clouds. He looked around at the faces of five people that he had grown fond of in the short time with them. These people had fought to overcome an incredible array of problems—real killers, some they couldn't ever control. So it was all for beauty, healthy kids, and promise? Too bad Marta was missing all this. He wondered how the conversations had gone when, ninety years earlier, so many Wanapum had debated whether to go to the reservation, and some had rebelled and stayed behind at the river. That couldn't have been easy either.

Leon decided he didn't want to leave the people with gloomy memories when they had plenty of happy ones to balance—the ones they wanted to remember. *And that's why they come here. We need to wind this up right for them.*

"Folks, you've told so many wonderful memories, too, of your thirty plus years at White Bluffs. I took notes for Marta as well as for myself. I know you're getting tired, need to go, and I need to digest all this! So now, before you take off, each one tell me what was one best part of that life for you that made it special."

After a moment Thelma said, "Probably this isn't what most people would say, but to me, it was the beauty overall. I mean the natural beauty— the bluffs, the river, the gardens, the orchards, all of it."

Orville said, "Yes, and of all those, it's got to be the river. We wouldn't have been here thirty plus years, not even a day, without the river."

"Yes, but once we were here, the healthy life for kids—most important of all!" Dorothy cried. "How can anyone disagree with that?"

Leon wondered, were they going to debate it? But Roger broke in.

"To me I think the very best for me was what our folks built of the natu- ral place, the community itself. I know there was the town-moving issue, but aside from that they got so much done as a community working together. All the good food for those kids, Dorothy, and the natural beauty of the orchards,

Thelma—that's what they themselves created. Yes, I know they couldn't have without the river. But they learned how to live on the river. They did all that and they didn't quit, they kept going."

Leon thought a moment. "So, Roger, are you saying the best part was not just the beauty of the river, but also the beauty of the people?"

"You could put it that way."

Leon felt he finally could quit. It was a strong start on topics for Marta to explore later. He put down his pen, took off his glasses, and looked around with a big smile. *Done.*

Then Orville stood up, "I have something I want to say. Been on my mind a while."

He straightened his suspenders, shuffled his feet, and cleared his throat. Leon grabbed his pen again. *He wants this recorded!* Everyone got quiet. They'd heard Orville grumble remarks at the reunions, but they'd never seen him stand up to make a speech.

"Dorothy and I come here because we want to remember all our parents did to make it a great place." His rumbled voice carried across the room, and the people not already listening came over or turned their chairs to hear. He saw he had their attention.

"And we come to see you all, and we talk about our past, and we all enjoy it. But every time, all we hear from the Hanford Plant is how they can't figure out what to do about their frigging, s'cuse me, toxic radioactive waste. They finally admit they let some of it to the sky—and we got the downwinders crying with cancer. And now they say it will start to seep in the ground toward the river. And they can't give it away, no thank you. It's costing us over a billion a year, us taxpayers, cleaning up this mess. And we sit there and listen to the bullshit, and for over fifty years we argue about whether we needed to drop that bomb on Nagasaki or not. Whether we needed to drop two bombs! And should we stockpile more!

"Then Walt Croaker over there, another issue..." Orville pointed. "He reports to us on how much more land will be set aside by the feds to protect birds, flowers, and bugs. And then we go back to talking about the good old days. Even today."

He stopped for a breath and Dorothy muttered, "Good, shorten it." He put his hand over hers.

"And now we hear that there will be a museum made of Reactor B. How much will that cost? You younger ones here may not know that Reactor B is the one that was making the plutonium for that Nagasaki bomb. But the reactors turned to domestic energy later all make radioactive waste for us too. And so it goes. And I want to say I am disgusted, and I don't believe I'll come to another reunion unless I hear some of you—and that includes me—raise a little hell and get this settled."

"Orville…"

"No, I'm coming to it, Dot…Our families, and many others no longer here, were given the shaft. I hear the government finally has decided to apologize to Japanese Americans that got sent to relocation camps. That's good. So what happened to the apologies to us and to the downwinders? Why no museum planned for us? Why do we just sit here, year after year, like…we're a living wax museum?"

That got a few quiet laughs, and it energized him. "And how about the Japanese families? I know, we rebuilt Japan. But did we ever apologize to those mutilated families?"

"So, okay, the past is past. We will never know how many lives were forfeited by the Hanford Plant, here and in Japan." He stopped to catch his breath, face red, but plunged on.

"What we need to do…what we need to do, is demand no more lives will be lost to this mess up the river. What has been done for the downwinders and their families? And I would like to know what was, or is, being done to help the descendants of civilians in Japan who got burnt up or all messed up. Maybe that was compensated—I'd like to find out. I do know we here didn't get properly treated. I don't care about compensation for myself; I want the families here to get some recognition, besides a museum for a bomb."

"Okay, Orville," a man finally broke in, "what is it you want us to do besides complain to ourselves like always?"

"I know! So here it is! For those of you who agree with me and are tired of excuses, I'm saying you are invited to meet at my house at Pasco next Friday evening at seven, and coffee will be served, and we can decide what we as taxpaying citizens want to do. If you need directions to our house just come over here for a minute. And pass the word. Okay, that's all. I'm sorry I didn't bring this up earlier—it just came to me as I boiled here."

Dorothy called out, "Just come on Friday and we'll all figure out what to do."

Thelma said, "That's right. We'll be there."

Orville nodded, "Okay, I'm done. Hope to see you." And sat down, still red in the face, his shirt wet with sweat.

Roger said quietly, "Well done, buddy." He was in shock.

Leo looked up from his scribbled notes, "Whew, yes! Orville, that should have been recorded."

"That's your job!" Orville began giving directions to his place. Leon looked around. He saw a few listeners walking out; some were laughing quietly, some frowning. More were coming to the table.

Leon muttered to Roger, "Is this usual?"

"Never. Never saw it coming."

Orville left to wash his face. When he came back a few more people thanked him and got directions for his meeting. But soon the crowd was thinning again. After some lighter comments Orville, Dorothy, and Janice excused themselves and shook hands around, "Time to go—till next week—our place!"

Leon told Janice she would have a fine report, and she beamed.

"I will! Like nothing my teacher's ever seen!"

After they were gone, Roger turned to Leon, "Well, aside from that grand finale, what did you think of our reunion?"

Leon couldn't begin to tell him all his reactions. He thought it was good karma from bad, that he had come here, possibly only listen a while, then to walk around and look at some desert plants, instead had been sadly stuck inside for days, then to have a fascinating time with these elders. It was an encounter he knew he'd cherish a long while.

He said, "Orville just now, he was incredible. Aside from that, it was all very, very interesting. What a rich life you had here! It's been a real experience for me…in many ways. I really thank you and Thelma and the others for letting me be part of it."

Thelma smiled, "Come over in the spring, and we'll show you those native flowers. You've got our phone number."

Roger got up. "When you see Bruce, tell him I sure enjoyed hearing Harold's story. What we heard so far, I think it's great the way it is. Tell him to make Harold come next year and bring it again. If he can't walk around, I'll sit with him—I mean it. He really needs to publish it."

"I know. But he says someone else will have to. But why don't you call him and tell him yourself? And tell him about Orville's meeting?"

"I sure will."

Roger and Thelma were barely out the door when Croaker reappeared looking jaunty. Leon had no escape handy. *Looks as if he has yet another ax to grind.*

"Hello, Professor, how did it go? Did you find out everything you wanted to know about the folks of this valley?"

Leon gave him a neutral look, "Oh, I wasn't actually here for that, you know. I study Indigenous peoples' use of plants. But I enjoyed visiting with the settlers very much."

Croaker sat down across from him, half in the chair. "Plants, huh. Indian plants? Hey, they only ate fish. Now they eat microwave stuff like me. Indian plants! Ha-ha. Well, berries. But maybe you've learned from these old settlers what it took to run a real family farm, back when it was still allowed?"

"I got a start."

"And I hope you aren't really part of what's going on, that more and more land is being scooped up for so-called research projects. Yeah, Orville's right on that—public stay out. And to hell with farmers, except huge outfits that aren't anything like farms we had here."

"Yes…I understand what you're referring to."

"Yeah, I'll bet you do." Croaker rummaged for the makings of a roll-your-own and sat down to make a smoke. "Politicians are all crooks—that's all I need to say on that. Anyway, please tell your buddy Bruce something for me. I respect veterans and I'm sorry I got rough with him, almost beat him up. I just don't like the company he keeps. Tell him if he really wants to help this valley get back to what it was in his family's time, he should drop these loonies of his and check out the Sagebrush Rebellion. Have you heard of that outfit?"

"Ahh, I think so."

"Well, tell him—I was going to. He needs to find out what's really going on here. But pretty soon we won't have all these loonies and government agents buzzing around us like hornets. They may soon have their funds cut off—if not their peckers, hah!"

"Oh…really? How is that?"

"Huh, I'm just a big mouth…Ha-ha."

"Walt, you ought to talk to Bruce more without an ax to grind. You're both for the small farmers, you know."

"Hum. I dunno. See, if we don't do something this valley is going to be run-over completely by Mexican version farmers. They come up here to pick crops and then they find ways to never go home. That's the real future, and I don't think he gets that."

Leon shrugged. *What's the use, why waste his time. He's got it all locked in.*

After a moment of silence Croaker said, "Well, good research to you, Professor, but remember what I told you; it's us real farmers that are endangered, not a silly weed. Research us a little more before you write anything. See you again maybe."

Croaker stalked off. Leon took another long breath. *So why be surprised by this raving? Small farmers everywhere have taken a terrible beating the last few decades. Willie Nelson understands that. Sagebrush Rebellion, eh? Be interesting to talk to them sometime.*

Later, out in the café looking over his notes of Orville's speech, Leon heard the radio at the desk being turned up for the local news and half-listened to the usual amused delivery.

Then he almost choked on his mouthful of coffee.

"…*A lost birdwatcher was found wandering in the Hanford closed area early this AM and coincidentally two kayakers were found in a closed area on a nearby island, all of these people apparently unaware they were trespassing. All were taken to Prosser to be arraigned. And again, another animal ran into the fence at Reactor B, set off the alarm, and gave the security staff more drill practice.*"

The announcer went on to other news.

Oh boy. Thank god Croaker went out the door. So... three people arrested...two kayakers and who? Bruce, Marta, Suki? He had no influence on Bruce or Suki, but obviously he'd done the wrong thing to encourage Marta to go along. Trespassing... it normally wouldn't be a felony, but he didn't know what it could involve with the feds. Now what...bail? He went back to his room to count the cash he carried as an old habit and wonder what to do. He checked the local TV channel again. Nothing of significance. He waited for a phone call, or something. Finally, he lay down on the bed and drifted back to a sentence he had not read to the whole crowd, but just to the two women. It was a statement in the memoir that Harold quoted from his sister, one she had made much later, long after they had left, all their buildings had been torn down, the trees burned. *"Dad should have known better."* She was talking about the enterprise he'd jumped into back in 1907. He recalled how Dorothy had asked Thelma about that remark, how to take it: *"Dad should have known better? What should he have known?"* And Thelma's reply after a moment:

"Well, sure, he should have known they would have had an easier life in a home in or near a regular town, not trying to farm. They still would have had a cow probably, and for sure chickens, and a garden—they always did have those anyway. They would have had an indoor toilet, maybe. But they wouldn't have had a refrigerator, or a car, or a freezer, or an electric stove, or a modern washing machine, or a big house. No one did that they knew. And they would have been short of funds anyway; they always were before they went to White Bluffs. But they wouldn't have had flies crawling all over them at meals, dust storms filling the houses, killing themselves at spraying, pruning, and picking times. And no brokers cheating them. But they, and we, Dot, wouldn't have had all the luscious fresh fruit and berries and vegetables to eat. And no huge showpiece flower garden. And no horse. Maybe no Saturday night dances. And most of all, no wonderful river to play on. I guess that's not *knowing better.*"

Leon reflected that all kinds of daring adventures in living—usually by men, or men dragging their families along—were, in hindsight, at best brief mistakes, but more often causes of financial ruin, broken families, broken bodies. If no one was maimed or abandoned, or dead, well, it was indeed a great adventure. If not terribly happy, if likely to fail, it was still a courageous project, or, if really lucky, even an advance for mankind. Explorers, warriors, romantics, inventors, racers, entrepreneurs, crusaders, revolutionaries, missionaries, pioneers, empire builders—good lord, all men and often women who could not just stay home and do their jobs and raise their family. *Where would we be without them, knowing better? Great observation, Thelma.*

Chapter 23

RECAPPING

Leon's phone finally rang at 2 p.m. "Hi, Leon. It's Marta, have you heard?"

"Oh, I sure have. Where are you?"

"At the county courthouse at Prosser, not too far from you. I'll explain later. Uh, I'm short of bail money, only have $100 cash here. No checks, they say. Do you have $400 on you we could borrow? They'll let him out as soon as they get their cash."

"Yes, I have it. Just one person?"

Marta sighed. "Yup…Bruce. At least that's the only one I'm dealing with right now."

Leon was soon in a shared cab to Prosser. He was glad Marta, so far, wasn't charged. He didn't know what a dissertation committee would have to say about such shenanigans. It certainly wouldn't have the appearance of objective investigation. He'd been on many such committees and never encountered doctoral candidate arrests in the course of research. As for Bruce, he'd asked for trouble. But Marta and Bruce would survive as a couple, he was pretty sure, having seen their dynamics over a couple years. She would scold him for some crazy impulse, he would sulk a short while, apologize, and it would be over. Jail time was a new level however. How could he help— beyond the bail money, beyond nagging Marta to decide on her topic and get on with it.

At Richland Ike poked Suki awake. "Hey, we're here!" She rubbed her face; they were outside the hotel. *Now I have to face the music.* "Ike, I learned a lot on this drive, and I'm glad."

"Me too! One of my better drives down the river."

Suki got out of the car, but plunged on: "So…let's go for another educational drive someday, when we don't have to look for Jason."

"Sure thing. What are you doing early tomorrow morning?"

Really? "Well, not that soon. I have to see Bruce and Marta about something. What are you doing tomorrow?"

"Wearing my truck-driving hat, picking up a load of hay at Ellensburg in the afternoon, taking it to Seattle."

Seattle. "Oh, well, call me whenever you want to. Maybe you'll think of another great idea— for me to work on. But actually, I already have three papers due. They're late; I hate having incompletes."

"What papers? If there's any on salmon, I could help you get it done fast. I'm your walking encyclopedia on salmon!"

Maybe he could! "Well thanks! I'm happy for any help!"

She gave him one last smile, and went into the hotel. Ike sat there for a moment. *What to do now? Oh yeah, Jason.* Then he saw a human form farther down the block, sunk against the wall. He climbed out, went to look at the man, leaned and touched his cheek. *Just sleeping, drunk. I know him. He'll be picked up in no time.*

Ike shook him, "Hey Jimmy, you have to wake up…. wake up!" He managed to pull the fellow up to his feet where he swayed and looked around.

"Oh, hi, Ike. I'm too drunk. Uh, can you take me…?"

On her way through the upstairs hall Suki went to the window and looked down. Ike was helping someone, obviously drunk, into the truck—rescuing the guy like it was part of his normal day. *Is he another rescuer, then…like Bruce? Am I just another someone to be rescued? No, Ike, don't think of me that way.* She watched him drive off and dragged herself on to Bruce and Marta's room.

Ike headed toward a friend's house, with a passenger on his shoulder again, but thinking about Suki. *Well, that was different…but what was so different?* They had talked about the same things his people covered at home or, more likely, at the fishery meetings. *An intelligent, pretty woman. Serious, maybe too serious? Women are usually happy enough to hop in the sack with me, but I didn't exactly get that message, not today. And she was too tired to even talk she said. Not hardly. What's she like when she's not tired? What's so fascinating? Besides her being a young, smart, pretty woman?*

He dropped the man off to a resigned relative and drove back to the hotel to make his call home. Alone at last, he was able to capture part of his attraction to Suki: she'd asked good questions, and he had given decent answers, and gotten sincerely thanked for them. *For once!*

Suki got up her nerve and knocked at Bruce and Marta's room but got no answer. She went down to look in the conference room and saw hardly anyone there, so she postponed the pain coming and went to her own room to try to sleep. Two hours later, she tried knocking again, and Marta heard, rose slowly from her bed, and opened the door.

"Oh, here you are, Suki. How'd you get here? Well, come on in. How was your bird-watching? Better than mine, for sure. You know Bruce has you to thank if he loses his job over this!"

Suki went in, staring at Marta's scratched-up face. "Marta, you must be even more tired than I am. But Bruce...is he okay?"

"In Leon's room; he bailed him out."

"What's he charged with?"

"Trespassing. He's okay...got tired of my raging and Leon's comforting him."

"Oh. But how about you? You're all scratched up. Do you have some salve or something?"

Marta flopped back on the bed and closed her eyes. "Oh, never mind me, Suki, I'm fine, just wiped out. Yes, just trespassing. Dumb inexperienced bird-watcher, in the middle of the night, out wandering in the brush miles from his car? Really now? But they seem to want to believe him, and me. I'm not even charged...yet. Sit down if you like."

Suki, tired of sitting so long in the truck, kept standing.

"Just trespassing? I've been so worried. What about the others?"

"Who? Jason? Don't know. The kayakers? Who cares? Idiots! And now Bruce is taking the heat for them. We saw them getting arraigned, caught at the island, I guess. Off limits, trespassing, I think. If so, I don't get it."

Suki mused. *Maybe Alice is right, that they could sweep it all under the rug.*

"Are they bailed out?"

"I don't know, don't care. But guess who else we hear was being interrogated, almost arrested? Elena! Remember Elena? Trespassing."

Suki burst out laughing.

"What's so funny?"

"They must think a major attack is being practiced!"

Marta hooted, "Of course!" She stared at Suki a moment, then at her own scratched hands,

"I feel like you haven't been fair to me, Suki."

"Oh?"

"You let me believe your interest in White Bluffs and the Plant was that you were writing a story for publication."

Suki felt embarrassed. *Why did I do that?* "Oh…. Well, I could, actually. But right now I have deadlines in classes to write papers for. Marta, I'm sorry for all this. Still, I never asked Bruce to do more than to just go with me to a ridge to stand on, and not even near the reactor."

"But he never would have dreamed up the whole thing if you hadn't pushed him."

"Are you sure?" Suki felt cheap to debate it. *Isn't she right?*

Marta sighed and slumped down on the bed. "No. He does like…challenges." *Like riding horses down into the bottom of Grand Canyon in mid-summer. I got heat stroke that time.*

"But, until now, never taken to jail for godssake. That I know of. Oh, Suki, I know it was a normal thing for him, wanting to help you, and it just turned into something more out of control than he expected. Though he should have, with those dingbat kids."

"He's a good man, Marta."

"Yes, if you want to live a life that's one big drama after another—I guess I must."

"I hear you. Well, uh…I'm bushed; right now I need to get some sleep. You too? Well, I am sorry, Marta. His job…I should have thought more. I have some anti-biotic…would you like some?"

Marta shrugged and closed her eyes.

Suki sighed, "Well, see you guys in a couple hours?"

"You can go see him now in all his scratched-up glory."

"No, I'm too tired. Later I will." Suki wanted to be at her room where Ike could find her without knocking on all their doors.

Later that evening, Leon brought beer, cider, ice, and chips to Bruce and Marta's room. Suki and Ike, dust washed off, arrived to find Bruce—hands and face the same mass of scratches—explaining how he, a desert warrior, got caught by the plant guards. He had circles under his eyes from the hours without sleep, but he had waved off Marta when she started to fret about his hatchery job. He was happy to repeat his version of the night for Suki and Ike's benefit.

"Well, there I was, trying to figure how to get Jason and those idiots out of there when the alarm started screaming—WHAT! How'd that happen? I'd already ordered Marta to go back, and I took off, but I see the kayaker, the woman, she's moving fast but veering off from the direction to the island. Damn, she's going to end up too far down where she might not be able to get across the slough—I have no way to know—so I go after her to get her oriented. Finally I make it back to the trail, too much delayed. I never did see the others."

He smiled at Marta and got a resigned look in return. In truth he was humiliated that he'd not handled things better, but he wasn't going to show that to everyone. He went on,

"So then I hear a boat roaring down the river. I think, oh no, they'll probably check the road, too, right away, and see the car. And I think I'll look more like I'm really lost if I don't come out too near the car. So I head more south through the brush and I'm walking back up the road when some guards come by. '*Hello, sir*'. Oh no, it's that asshole lecturer."

Suki shook her head, *that guy too?* "So why did they arrest you, just walking on the road?"

Bruce shrugged. "I thought at first I did a good job—a lost guy looking for his girlfriend—didn't realize how scratched up my face was. But some other personnel went downriver with the boat I heard. They must've caught Liz and her pal at the island. The ones with me talked on their radio, and they guessed I must be involved with the kayakers, since I guess I looked like I'd been thrashing through brush quite a ways."

Bruce stopped as if he were done and began picking at thorns in his hands.

"But why did the alarm go off?"

"Damned if I know! Not me, not the kayaker with me! I finally just admitted I trespassed by going through that barbed wire fence near the road, but that's all. I had to be guilty of some illegal act for them to get credit and move on."

Marta thought he had actually come up with the best alibi possible. He had to go back to court tomorrow morning to plea, and he'd lose his job, no doubt, but she would say no more on that. Seeing Bruce was done for now, she looked over at Suki.

"How did you and Esau come out so well?"

"Oh, we were stopped too, but we were on the road and we had our alibi—rabbit snaring. We even had rabbits, and I was Esau's niece."

Leon studied her. *Esau? Ah, the Indian elder.*

Marta said to Ike, "Where is Jason anyway?"

He shrugged, "I haven't located him yet."

Leon was trying to piece it all together. "But how did the alarm go off, if you swear you didn't do it. And, Bruce, her pack, if she didn't throw it at the fence, where was it? Surely having that with her meant a more serious charge than trespassing."

Bruce shrugged. "Who knows? I saw them at the court, but couldn't talk to them. The alarm...maybe an animal?"

"Is that likely," Marta frowned, "two times in two days?"

"How do we know? Maybe every day. And I don't know where Jason or Tom was when it went off."

Suki sneaked a look at Ike, but he was staring at the floor.

Leon waved in disbelief, "And then there's Elena. But she's okay too. She did a blessing at the river here in the morning, though I missed it. Then, she almost was arrested for trying to do one at the dam, she told me. And this afternoon she was headed back upriver, determined to do another blessing."

Suki grinned at Ike. "We saw her, up the river on the east side."

Leon shook his head. "Amazing." *Does she teleport? Such energy!*

Marta thought that the whole night and day were beyond amazing, even for Bruce. She sat there, like Leon, trying to put it all together. Suki and Ike were silent. Bruce, after all, had been trying to help Esau, so Ike wasn't going to criticize his efforts, and certainly Suki wasn't. In the silence all around, Leon finally asked if he should order some fries or something for everyone. No one answered. Bruce got up and started pacing. *How am I ever going to explain this to Harold? I totally screwed up what he asked of me. And how did I help anything?*

Then he turned to Marta, "I need to check on the kayakers tomorrow morning. If no one's bailed them out, I need to take care of it...somehow."

"Why? Can't this ever end?" Marta muttered.

Suki, remembering Alice's advice, broke in, "You shouldn't worry just yet. Maybe the Plant will drop the whole thing. Maybe they want it just to be an animal on the fence again."

"Why? Oh, I get it," Marta smiled, "because there could be copycats lurking out there?"

"Oh, of course!" Leon chortled. "Can't you picture bored college students, delighted to jump into such high jinx? An army of kayakers!"

Everyone grinned, picturing that scene.

Ike, knowing the Plant history, said, "Yeah, they could want to cover up the whole thing."

Marta mimicked, "*What was that? Oh, just an owl again.*"

"Anyway, I do have to see if they need bail," said Bruce. "I like their gutsiness in a way."

Marta shrugged. *Of course!*

Leon shook his head. He thought he'd never been involved in such a comedy in all of his South Pacific investigations.

"What, Leon?" Marta didn't want any more loose ends.

"Oh, nothing. I'm just flabbergasted at the energy swirling around this river."

Ike shrugged, "It's always been swirling around here. But not like this, never at any settler reunions I've been connected with."

The conversation lagged as the birdwatchers' energy faded. Bruce stopped pacing and sat down with a loud sigh. Suki was trying to signal to Ike that they needed to talk. *What should we say about the alarm going off?* Leon was thinking about Marta, her situation. Bruce was still trying to figure just where he'd lost control of the operation. *The alarm???* Marta was wondering if she'd have to look for a job. Then, the radio music they had left on low volume stopped, and the local announcer came on:

"Breaking news! We have a person here in the studio with a special local news story. He just walked in here a short time ago.…. here he is."

Bruce grabbed the volume control. A youthful voice came on. *"Hello. I'm Jason. I want to confess that actually I was the one who set off an alarm at a reactor last night, and I take responsibility for it. I did it because the …."*

The radio went silent. A few seconds later music came on again.

"Oh no, that damn kid," whispered Ike.

A different announcer voice broke in:

"Oops! Please excuse the interruption. There was supposed to be a joke, but darn it, we got the wrong tape. That was an April Fool's joke from last spring! Ha-ha. Sorry, that was not actual news, folks. So now back to some old-time music. Remember? Driftin' Down the River?"

The song began. No one laughed, but there were several groans.

Ike said at last, "Well, I better call Alice, my aunt. She's by far the best at getting young guys out of the slammer as needed."

Marta made a face, "Maybe Bruce can use her talent."

Laughter exploded, but Bruce was pacing around again. "It's not a joke. Look at us! Eight people, nine counting Elena. You'd think we could've actually done something that made a difference. There is a real issue involved here, after all."

Marta nodded. *My love, you've found a cause.*

"About…you mean the waste?" Leon asked.

"About the waste, the valley, people that live here, the fish, the river— the whole damn world of this river. You know I've worked on the river for years…that is, I did. I can't just drop this."

"You won't be alone." Suki gave him a nod and smile.

After another pause in the room, Bruce looked at Marta with a gleam that signaled his moving on to a new adventure.

"Well, Mart and Leon, I guess this reunion's over. Do you want to go up to Wolf Rapids tomorrow, like we planned? After my conference with the judge? Hah, if there's car rental in town that will still rent to us."

Leon said, "Oh, I can rent a car if you're all recovered? Will it be okay to visit, Ike?"

Ike, jerked back from his thoughts, nodded. "Oh, more than okay. My folks are fond of Harold, and Bruce is his nephew, and so Bruce's friends, all of you, will be very welcome."

Leon smiled. *So that's the way it still is.* "We can probably find a car that can be dropped off in Seattle. So we can drive straight on home from there. Anyone else want to go? Suki?"

"I can't miss it, more stories."

Ike smiled at her, "You've just started to hear the stories from this valley."

The meeting broke up, most of the crowd headed for sleep. Suki went to her room to wait, hoping Ike would come soon, but wishing just as much to sleep. He went outside to smoke, wondering what Jason was facing. Did he think he would be believed, that the guards are as dumb as that? No. They would go back along the fence and find lots of footprints, and who would be making all those footprints? Not just Jason! And the closest group of still-angry people? Just up river from the Plant a few miles. Jason could be taking this on himself as a false trail to protect his relatives. Smart! He decided he wouldn't tell Suki his thoughts about footprints; she was feeling guilty enough. He finally went back inside the hotel to call Alice, explained the situation, but then asked her if she could drive herself down to be with Jason at court, if needed. He reminded her of that truck-driving job in the afternoon he couldn't afford to lose. Then he went back upstairs to Suki.

"I caught Alice. She feels quite sure she can get Jason out if he's arrested."

"No kidding? How about bail? Bruce needed it."

"She'll have it."

Suki smiled, "*No wonder Esau calls her a warrior.* I want to ask you if we need to tell the rest about why the alarm really went off?"

"I think it's up to you and Esau."

"Well, I don't want to have to go into the whole thing. I don't mind that Esau told you, but…maybe I'm just too confused right now. And my blessing doesn't matter to the others here, not that much."

"No. Probably Esau would be happy to say nothing."

She nodded. "I'll see him tomorrow; I can ride up with Bruce and all. I guess I might miss you if you are off driving truck."

They looked at each other, neither wishing to end their long day of conversation.

"Ike, thanks again for offering help on papers. I'm going to Nagasaki in a few days, makes it even more of a crunch."

"And then?"

"Then I have a couple weeks and start another term."

"Well, if I call you about a fisheries meeting, will you try to come?"

"Hey, I'm hardly credentialed like your scientists. I'd feel a little out of place. Well…how about a trade? You must come to my class that covers salmon issues. Soon, because it's ending. We've never had a single serious fisherman come speak about salmon or river problems. And we've never had a tribal representative. We just talk about them."

"Me, at your class? I'd feel more than a little out of place with all those college students."

"But that's the deal—a trade?"

She and Esau would sure get along. He sighed, nodded.

She felt much better. "Ike, believe me, you and Esau are more aware of some things than the PhDs I listen to, I'm serious. So, you've got my number, about the paper. And I'll wait for you to call me about your salmon meeting. I'll be real busy but I do want to stay in touch with this river."

He gave her his warmest grin, and before he could stop himself reached for a quick hug.

"It wants to stay in touch with you." Then he left to find a bed for the night.

⊷⊷▣ ▣⊶⊶

Roger and Thelma, on arriving home, rushed to let their cat out, get irrigation going again for their small garden, and pick corn and grapes. Everything had survived their absence, barely.

Thelma said, "It was so good to have new activities and new people. Weren't you getting a little tired of the same program? But I wonder why Bruce was gone so much of the time. Harold never said anything about Bruce being a birdwatcher, did he?"

"No." He didn't say that he didn't believe it.

"Thank goodness Leon took over; what a nice man."

Roger came over with more grapes for the basket and told her he agreed. Thelma went on, "And the other new person, Elena, I liked her too. Some people didn't of course. But will her ceremonies work?"

"Who knows? The other person that really surprised me was Orville: I hope he gets a good turnout for his meeting."

He went back to picking, then stopped to look at her. "You know, I'm glad Bruce blew up at the Plant lecture. People come to the reunion year after year, and I think Bruce was the first one to really challenge Chuck."

"Chuck's just doing his job as he's told."

"I know, he's got a script to follow. And it was great to have Bruce with guts to challenge him. It's time, don't you think? By the way, you know that kid, Keene, from the McGinnis family? When we were leaving he caught me, said he goes to college at Pasco now, and there's a student group that's planning a demonstration about getting the river cleaned up, back to natural."

"Well that's positive!"

"New generation, new ideas."

Roger picked out a melon and they headed for the house. "But you know, the task we had was to critique Harold's memoir, and we spent most of the time just talking, not critiquing. How's Harold going to feel?"

"Well, Bruce took off, and it wasn't all our fault that Leon liked listening to us. Anyway, you call Harold and tell him how great his story is."

⊷⊷▣ ▣⊶⊶

"Things could have been worse," was Bruce's weak assessment as he and Marta finally dragged to their room and pulled off their clothes for sleep.

Worse? He's finished at the hatchery, and if he can't find a new job fast, I'll have to start looking, and another semester gone, eating away at my deadline. But she had no energy to say one more word to him. When she didn't answer Bruce's silly remark, he knew more was coming—her silence was scarier than her scolding. But it was his nature to move onward, and soon he was asleep. Marta before long dropped off as well.

Leon fell asleep over trying to finish his notes for Marta. He felt that at least he'd been some help there, and had a fine time, and made new friends. Tomorrow, Wolf Rapids. The next day, back to teaching classes. His ankle seemed to be a lot better. As for the so-called bird-watching adventure...*Did I ever do such crazy stuff? But then, I was never a green beret or whatever he was. But they may need help. And Elena? Elena...Must admit I'd like to see more of her and her blessings even if she doesn't need help. So who's crazy?*

Suki was just dropping off when a vision of Esau emerged. *It is night; the moonlight shines on the sagebrush and on the snake wrapped around his waist, its head turned to his. Esau smiles as it licks his face, and he says to her, "You did good." She wants to believe him. She tries to give Esau his jacket to wrap the snake like a new baby. "No, you need it," he tells her, "the snake doesn't." Then he hands her the discarded snakeskin he found. "See, this is yours."*

Suki forced herself to wake and get up; this was not resting. *I must see him tomorrow.* She went for a drink of water, but then, back in bed, and again asleep, now Elena talked to her, handing her a glass, *"It's Chiawana water, Suki. It's all good now, drink!"* Then her mother popped up with a pleading look, *"But whatever you do, stay in school."*

She couldn't help laughing out loud. When she dozed again, she dreamed she was swimming peacefully in a warm river, and then she and Ike were splashing each other and laughing wildly. In the morning she recalled it all and wondered what her mother would say about these linked scenes. Probably: *Watch and listen for something more.*

CHAPTER 24

APOLOGIES AND LESSONS

AT 5:30 A.M. Suki's phone rang. It wasn't even light and Ike, apologizing for waking her, explained that he was still in Richland and was hoping she would ride with him early to Wolf Rapids. She could catch her friends later when they came through.

"We can talk on the way, more from last night and important to you, and, see, I might miss you at Wolf Rapids. You know, I have to leave there early in the afternoon."

What's going on with us? What does he need to tell me so urgently? Groggy still from the day before, she didn't want to have to decide anything new. She explained that she'd like to talk more, but had told Bruce and Marta she'd would ride up with them, because she needed a private time to apologize to Bruce. After Wolf Rapids they were all going right on to Seattle.

"I don't know when I'll see Bruce again."

"Well, you don't know when you'll see me again either."

Oh-oh. I thought he was coming to my class? "But we'll see you at Wolf Rapids today, won't we? We're going up there as soon as Bruce gets back from dealing with the judge."

"I might have to leave too early." *So she'd rather ride with them?* "Okay, Suki, here's what I was thinking, that it is a good time for me to help you with a salmon paper. And we need to talk more about a museum at Reactor B, what needs to be included in the exhibits that they could easily leave out. You can guess?"

"Okay...sure..." *Really, Ike, all this so early in the morning?*

"And today is also your chance to talk to Esau and Alice about you doing a lesson or two with their class, tell the whole story of the Plant. I think it's important that the kids know it. You are perfect to do that, and I know the kids will be interested; I know my daughters."

She shook her head to clear it. "Oh, sure, those are good ideas. But…they take some planning." *And how will I work all that in on top of everything else?*

Ike did not give in, and eventually they agreed that she would meet him at Wolf Rapids, and after planning out a few kids' lessons with Esau, if he agreed it was a good idea, she could ride with Ike to Seattle (in the hay truck) and on the road they would figure out how she could do actually do the classes. Perhaps she could catch rides with him to-from Seattle. He would also help her with a salmon paper, even get it all roughed out. She decided he was serious, that he wasn't just flirting; it was too complicated for that. At least she'd get to talk to Esau again, and get a start on one of the papers. She knew she did want to see him again, just not right now at 5 a.m.

"Yes, I guess it can work."

"So, what's the subject of the salmon papers then?"

"You'll love one of them: 'Describe issues on the Columbia that affect the survival rate of salmon smolt.'"

"Hey, piece of cake. I'll give you everything you need."

Everything? So is this a courting proposal, too, or am I just imagining things? "Oh, thank you. I hope I catch you later today, if not call me soon."

She knew that his promised "everything you need" was not possible, not for the paper; she would need to quote some published authorities to make it scholarly. But she was relieved they had an agreement; quoting him could make it more than a routine paper for the prof. After a goodbye, she tried to go back to sleep, but of course failed.

Ike drove home, the road seeming longer than usual, monotonous. He spotted an eagle soaring overhead. *Uncle called her an eagle for her searching ways. Are we searching or dancing around or what? All I do is just drive the darn tour bus, and now look. Make a presentation to a college class? Help her write a paper? Butt in on Esau and Alice's classes? Is it just the beginning? Of what? I wasn't even looking for a woman, not really, but… she sure draws me.*

Bruce came back from his hearing with the news that the fine for his guilty plea on trespassing was $200, already paid by Leon, no jail time, and six months' probation. Oddly lenient, he thought. His boss probably wouldn't be.

Leon rented a car and the four were soon on the road, but Suki was frustrated. Bruce was driving, and riding in the back with Leon, whom she scarcely knew, was no place to talk to Bruce about the trouble she gotten him in. She would need to do it at Wolf Rapids and now wished she'd gone with Ike earlier. As the scenery whizzed past, they ignored it, their minds jumbled with the events of the last few days and the bizarre outcomes. All four agreed they needed to come back to the next reunion, though their reasons were not entirely the same. Bruce was quiet, still angry with himself for his failed mission. He also had wakened that morning to realize what Ike already had—that the guards would soon find the footprints of several people, not just one, at the fence. Probably the incident was not really closed. But for now, he must drive; he and Marta had flipped a coin for that. Her job was to keep him awake with a stream of talk.

At one point she turned back to Suki, "We've been wondering all this time, can you tell us what made the alarm go off? Did Jason really do that?"

The snake, twisting in my hands, hissing, pointing...my prayer. Oh, I'm so damned sorry. She finally answered, "No, not him. Actually a snake did it."

"A snake."

"Yes."

"How did you find out?"

"I'll tell you sometime."

Marta sighed. *She still wants to be mysterious.*

Suki had her own question for Leon. "What do you think of Elena?"

He cleared his throat. "Well, my experience with shamans is only in Australia, but probably they have universal talents and purposes. And I respect them."

"But you're a scientist."

"Well, science has failed me a few times, I can tell you."

"She said several things to me about healing the Columbia."

"Yes, she's serious. She's on her way to another river now."

"But she's into prayer, and that's good, but…is that enough? The way the nuclear plants are still sprouting round the world? Chernobyl didn't even stop them."

"I know, oil is expensive, coal ruins the air, dams mess up rivers, so engage in something worse yet. Well, I agree, Suki, prayer isn't enough. But we have to find our own roles. I'm sure puzzling over mine after this weekend."

"So do you think we have a duty of some kind? I mean about nuclear plants and their risks?"

She really is serious about this. "Absolutely. You can't see that steam and not know it."

She marveled at how so many different kinds of people seemed to agree with her, or at least understood her. Had Bruce and Marta told him how the blessing had gone, the part they knew? Probably, and he wasn't privately laughing at her, she felt. Of course, many people would laugh if they knew how things had actually gone.

After a while Leon said, "It's too bad you missed most of the time with the settlers. But you could read some of what we talked about." And he leaned forward and asked Bruce if Suki could read the places he'd marked in the memoir.

"Sure, I've got to give it back to Harold, but, if you can read in a car, you can have it now."

Marta handed the memoir back to her, and happy to catch up on what she'd missed, Suki paged back to one of Leon's marked sections. In a few minutes she knew what she should do—let her mother read some of it, the last part. Bruce gave her permission to copy out the section, saying he knew Harold would be agreeable, and she got out her long-ignored notebook.

When they arrived at Wolf Rapids, Suki saw Ike was still waiting. As soon as they were parked he took her aside. His look was urgent, she thought. She wondered how haggard she looked. He explained that he had only about an hour, and that Esau was interested.

"He does want to talk to you; Alice left real early to get Jason. And then, would you please drive with me, instead of Bruce, to Seattle? Is that still okay?"

"Yes, but I've been wondering, will kids want to come to a class now? In summer?"

"Something new! Nothing much new happens for them. Tomorrow they'll go berry picking up in the mountains, or some of them downriver fishing, but that's only for a few days."

Once Ike had introduced the others, and they'd had a view of the tule house, they left Leon engrossed in the construction details. Esau had greeted them warmly but ducked Marta's tentative question about Smohalla.

"We've talked enough about Smohalla all these years; even he is tired of it!"

He nodded to Suki, and she explained she would be with him in a few minutes. She took Bruce and Marta aside.

"I've been waiting to apologize to you guys. I'm so sorry how all this has turned out for you, Bruce. I really didn't think it through enough ahead of time."

Marta walked off a short distance; she felt it was their scene. Bruce acted surprised, then shrugged.

"Never mind, Suki, probably it was all for a reason. I've had time to think more about what I want to do. A two hundred bucks fine is cheap for that."

"But your job, Bruce."

"I'll get a new one; one I like better. And I see what I need to do in my free time is just as important as any job I could get. I have some ideas."

Actually, he wasn't sure of any of this. When did his life ever get simple? When would his projects not take a piece of his hide? But he was damned if he was going to have Suki feeling guilty for him. She had carried out a somewhat reasonable plan; his was the wild one. His was the one that needed repairing.

"Thanks, Bruce, that means a lot to me."

Suki saw that task as completed. Ike, standing off to the side, was pointing at his watch, so she went right to Esau. A few minutes before, she had seen Ike's daughters very briefly. Cute, lively, deeply tanned and barefoot girls, they both had Ike's infectious grin, but one had her black hair in braids and the other had hers in a short bob like Suki's. They were close in age and wanted to be different from each other she guessed. And these girls would be the sort of students she would face, if Esau said for sure that he and Alice wanted her.

The conversation went easier than she expected, with Esau looked pleased.

"Ike already talked to us and we think it's a good idea; the kids would like a new face. We can make it a couple hours on Saturdays or Sundays. You should do it as long as it makes sense for you and the kids."

So it was just a matter of planning. *Now I can't back out.* Esau gave her a picture as to how the classes were organized with the students sitting in a half-circle on the floor of the meetinghouse. She shouldn't expect them to talk much at first, but a few of the bolder ones would break the silence when she urged them. He assured her they would all be very interested; why wouldn't they? Who else had a ring of ghost buildings in their backyard? Then he was embarrassed.

"Of course you have seen such things too? Or is that city all rebuilt? And the spirit…? Well, we can start planning now, and you can finish with Ike if you ride over with him."

Oh! All arranged. The new teacher has some catching up to do.

Together Suki and Esau outlined the topics. He suggested she start briefly with WWII; the kids knew something about that from regular classes.

"So, the bombing of Pearl Harbor?"

"Yes, but can you tell them a little about why Japan did that? Kids these days are always asking why, why about everything."

"Okay, I'll try.…But it's complicated. And then WWII, and they have covered that enough, you think? I could talk about the internment camps."

"The camps? All of them! You know, it would be good if Bruce could come up and talk about his people getting pushed out, along with us. And Suki, you could tell why they chose this place for their great experiment. Lots of rivers and empty deserts around the country."

"Okay. But building the bomb… I can't tell them anything technical like that."

"Never mind, these are not high school kids. They can get that later."

They finished more of the outline, but suddenly Esau motioned Ike over.

"Good enough for now; Alice will be glad that we got this much done."

He took on the faraway look that Suki was already familiar with that signaled a story or lesson coming.

"You know, I don't understand how we started out being one of the most unknown places in the world, and now we are one of the most famous. And if they make a new museum of that Reactor B we will be even more famous. Even though another group says it wants the museum for the whole valley. And there's already another museum just up the river, too, did you know that? For petrified wood. All that's on top of our own center here we hope gets finished. Because maybe we'll be petrified pretty soon, too, with all the chemicals going into the river! Yeah, a whole valley full of mummies—Kennewick men, and women, and kids even. Need a big museum for all of them. I'm already beginning to feel kind of hardened myself."

Ike exploded and Suki choked. She finally got out, "I hope not, Uncle. And I hope I'm not going to add to a pile of mummies!"

Esau smiled. "We won't let that happen. And your classes will be part of our living heritage place here."

Ike stopped laughing and broke in, "I do have to go, Uncle. Where are your things, Suki?"

As he went off to get them, Esau got serious. "When will you come back?"

"Soon as we can work it in. I'm going to Nagasaki soon, just for a short week."

"And they will be going fishing and berry-picking anyway, most of them. Then we can start up again."

"I have no car, but Ike said he'll try to give me rides. Oh, can you put him in the outline too? He can talk about salmon habitat."

"Yes, let's do that. Ike is a smart boy, the best...well, he's not a boy, he's a man."

She felt a blush bloom as Esau glanced at her, then off toward the meetinghouse.

"He notices you too."

She kept her face calm and went off, a happier person yet, to tell Bruce of her new job and, therefore, her change of ride.

He gave her a puzzled look, then a bright smile, "Oh! A great idea!"

Suki and Ike were a topic as soon as Bruce's smaller carload left for Seattle.

"Did I miss something, those two?" Marta queried. "Oh yes, they had a long, long drive down the river."

Leon mused, "Not the river of golden dreams. Remember that song? No, you wouldn't. Bruce, I've been thinking, whatever you want to do about the river and the nuclear waste problem, barring actions like storming fences, you'll get my support."

"Well, thank you. What kind of support were you thinking of?"

"What do you need most?"

"Hum, aside from ideas…traveling funds, I guess, unless I find a well-paid job. Funds to go to meetings, much as I don't usually like them. I'm hoping these could be different."

"So, meetings."

"Well, at least not throwing bombs! Conferences, peaceful demonstrations…you know."

Leon nodded. "I'm sure I can help a little with that. Just say when."

He went back to his own plans. He had classes tomorrow he'd hardly prepared for. And he'd need to put in a good word for Marta with her dissertation committee. He glanced at her; she was deep in thought.

Bruce, of the three, had nothing waiting for him in the morning except a phone call to his federal hatchery boss, and most likely, his suspension. But he was not in turmoil over it. For when he was alone, he, like Suki, was nagged by an old promise, one he'd made to himself.

Dear family I hardly knew, wherever you are now, you dear souls that hid me, took care of me, until I could take care of myself, out there somewhere, gone from me probably forever, but you're with me, believe me. I told you I would do my best and I haven't. I have to do better, I will. This is my life now you gave me.

Chapter 25

SALMON AND HUMANS

Suki climbed into Ike's truck without a look toward her friends, her stomach fluttering. He gave her with one of his flashing grins, "Did you see? New front tires?"

"Wow! How'd you manage that so soon?"

"I borrowed them, got to replace soon as I get paid."

"But we're switching to a hay truck? I thought truckers aren't supposed to have passengers."

He shook his head. "Suki, I'm not a Teamster. This is a fly-by-night deal with a small rancher that pays in cash. He saves, I make."

Soon they were driving north along the east side of the river toward the cross-state highway. Vast fields of summer grain, most of it harvested and stubble, again dominated the eastside view. They passed by a few desert hamlets surrounded by green oases and orchards. But the west side of the river was desert. Their own scene was more of the already long conversation by truck.

"Why doesn't anyone farm that side?"

"Remember how I told you we lost our horse pasture? A nuclear plant and a military training range now."

Horses evicted too? Oh yes, Esau mentioned that.

"So your people used to be all along here? Who lives here now?"

"Now people can be anywhere with irrigation—if the feds haven't taken over. But who, aside from big grain farmers and fruit growers? Well, quite a few Mexican harvest workers who came up and decided to stay and a lot have been here three generations now. I went to high school with some. They've been through many things my people have."

She felt she needed to apologize again. "Ike, I should have gone with you this morning. I was too groggy to think."

"It's okay, it worked out. I had time to do stuff. I even have a place for us to get dinner in Seattle, with Esau and Alice's daughter, where I stay over. So while we drive, we talk about baby salmon and you take notes, rough out your paper. It's overdue, you said? Too much fun over here, huh? So, after the truck is unloaded tomorrow, well, if you can get away, you drive back across with me. You have a laptop like all the scientists? Good, maybe you can finish it right in the truck."

"Sounds almost possible."

"Sure. Then you do the class with the kids, soon as we can get them together. We overnight with Esau and Alice, then on the way back to Seattle, with another hay load, you can really finish it. How's that?"

"Oh! That would be a relief."

"But if the hay truck isn't ready to go back yet, I'll drive you back home in this one."

She gave him a long look that he pretended not to notice. "So...we stay over with your aunt and uncle? Their house looks rather small."

He grinned. "On air mattresses in the front room. See how modern Indians make do!"

She saw he was half-joking, half testing her. *So, his girls' mom, not around at all? And this is about make do...or make out?*

"I need to think, Ike." It sounded a little thrown-together, not exactly the romantic scene she had to admit she'd half-hoped for. But it seemed as if he really was trying to help her.

He said, "Okay. You don't have to, of course, but it's a way to get to your class with the kids. And that way you could go to a meeting of the Reactor museum planners, if they actually have one, on one of your trips. If you decide you want to be involved there."

"Hum...I might."

"Well, just an idea. You said you wanted some positive ideas of actions ordinary people could do. I don't think you're ordinary, but you could do it anyway. Someone needs to."

This is like the next scene yesterday, but sped up...a lot. Looks like I will know him a lot better by the end of this week.

They passed what Suki could see were apple orchards, people busy in them. Ike told her the other fruit was finished for the year—pears, peaches, and cherries. They passed a feed lot and her comment was "yuk!" She was quiet while they transferred trucks at Ellensburg without incident, and was again introduced as one of the cousins, this time not rabbit hunting, but headed for college. She thought Ellensburg a pretty town, another lushly irrigated place in a desert. She hoisted herself up into the cab, and once she became accustomed to the roar of the big engine and the high perch, she decided they could finish planning out the lessons for the culture classes, and that went well, but there was another complication.

"You know, very soon I'm going to Nagasaki to see my family. So there's a break then."

"It's okay. You're sure to have ideas from there to talk to the kids about."

It was a good thought. "And while I'm gone, you could fill in for a class, couldn't you, about salmon problems?"

"I guess. Esau will want me to, and, yeah, I'll try to be there, but I've got to look for another job too. This one will be over soon."

"He keeps you pretty busy?"

"Yeah. He has a list of stuff in his head, everything other folks should be doing, not just me, but I'm a favorite."

"So Ike, what kind of job would you like?" *Here we are, back to the road conversation, just louder. But I do need to know this man better, don't I, beyond fish problems and Hanford waste problems?*

"Well, not desk work. Outdoors. And with other people, I guess."

"Fishing."

"Well, sure, I do really like subsistence fishing, set-netting. It's fun and productive. But Suki, commercial means always worrying about your gear, making the right move, your load—if you'll make a profit. Anyway, salmon runs are in trouble, as you know. And no way am I ever going on one of those factory ships. I talked to guys who did."

"You like truck-driving?"

He laughed. "No, not really. It pays the bills. I don't want my daughters working in 7-Elevens, I want them with degrees, like you, and like my cousin Doreen in Seattle. She's a registered nurse."

She turned the topic back to him.

"Maybe you could take college classes, get a degree, and work for Fish and Wildlife on salmon."

He shook his head. "Uhh, you know, I think I'd be angry so much of the time over no progress. I'm sure that's not good for you to work at a job that keeps you angry."

"No. How about forestry then?"

They were now climbing up into hills with scattered pine. He looked at her. *What is this? Oh, just another time making conversation.* "Maybe I wouldn't get fed up so much. I could learn to talk to those trees you think?"

"Or you could be a guide for river-rafting groups."

She heard the edge in his voice: "And you could be a job counselor, right? Hey, I'm mainly concerned about my daughters. So for now I'm going to drive trucks, and look for the next job."

He's getting annoyed. I need to stop this. She decided to enjoy the scenery and wait for him to say more. He pulled out a cigarette, looked at her, and put it back. They talked about the scenery.

But sometime later, as they climbed toward the pass, he said, "So, yeah, Suki, I'll do a class on salmon troubles for the kids. I like working with kids. Maybe I should have been a teacher; I can act like a teacher." He put on the professorial voice he regularly heard at the fishery meetings.

"Okay, Miss Matsuda, let's talk about your paper. What problems do young salmon face?"

She giggled, took out her notebook and pen, waited for him to say something. He didn't, so she started with what had been in the back of her mind lately.

"Professor, I've been thinking about what Esau told me of the old days fishing at Celilo Falls. He painted such a clear picture for me of what that life was like, and it seems there were plenty of young salmon then, even with so many canneries operating."

"Yes, he tried to paint that picture of Celilo at the last meeting he went to, and talked about our responsibility to rebuild the wild runs and care for them. And I saw that, except for a couple of us, the scientists were just waiting for him to finish, fiddling with their papers. *'Haven't we heard this Indian lecture enough times?'* They showed they were pissed when he told us that we were insulting the salmon to truck them down the river. Of course, he saw that and told me he wasn't going to any more meetings, said he wasn't making a difference. Though one guy did stop him later and thanked him."

"I'm glad one was polite anyway. My instructor, my other instructor, talks quite a bit about the efforts to rebuild the runs."

"Hah! Miss Matsuda, we've been talking about that at least since the 1970s. So, to your paper? So to start, salmon are so unusual; that's where a lot of people get off track. They see them as just another fish. But they're a lot more. They're not the only fish that goes from the ocean into a river to spawn, but they're so needed by humans, and such good eating, and pretty easy to catch. So there's the human impact for thousands of years, hundreds of settlements along the rivers. But really, it's only a short time ago that humans started wiping them out. How come?"

"More people came."

"Well, there was lots of Native people, lots more than now. It was something else, too."

"Hum. Commercial fishing came in, and canneries…"

"Yes, go on, Miss Matsuda."

"And, uh, then all the logging and other industries the Northwest started, and bigger farms, and they all pollute the rivers."

"True. But how do farms harm salmon?"

"Well, feedlots drain into rivers sometimes, and fertilizers' pollution."

"What else?"

"Oh, insecticides. We were assigned to read Rachel Carson. But I think the destruction of stream spawning areas from logging must be much worse. The insecticides and toxins can clear out, but a stream would have a hard time fixing its spawning gravel."

Ike gave her a faked frown, "Miss Matsuda, you already know all this stuff. You didn't need this class, I suspect. Hum, anything else hurting the juvenile salmon?"

She gave a know-it-all look. "A growing population that goes along with industrialization, I believe."

"Correct. Never stops. What else?"

"The dams of course, to power industry and irrigation. And big dams stop the spawners from going upstream."

"Do you know the dams also stop the juvenile salmon from going downstream? They get pulled into the turbines. How can we stop that? That's a big issue now; the operators know they could raise the level of the water and let the fish pass over, so why don't they?"

"No idea."

"It reduces the power output. Everyone wants that power. And when there is less being produced, no surplus, and the price goes up."

She scribbled notes. He turned to her. "Excuse me, is this a graduate course?"

"No, I just wanted to take it. It sounded interesting, and I will be all done with my required courses—except my dissertation research class."

"Ohhh, you're in the same boat as Marta then!"

"Yeah, funny isn't it. I didn't even know her."

"Well, the salmon problems—it is interesting. Until you get sick of the debates. Oh, did your class talk about the effect of drought on the rivers? It's more a problem in California, but headed this way, the scientists say."

Thus, the lesson went. It was true, Suki did already know much of this, but she was enjoying her class more than usual. And it avoided her other demanding topic, the man himself.

She began again, "The other instructor says there are problems for salmon out in the ocean too, but harder for us to do much about them."

"Right. So we need to concentrate on what we can fix. See, you have the picture. But then someone says, '*Oh, this is serious, we must rebuild the salmon runs*'. And they built hatcheries and brought in Atlantic salmon eggs to raise and release. Soon there was hatcheries all along the coast, easy fix.

At least they use local eggs now, but it's still not a good solution. Why, do you think?"

"Not sure. Do hatcheries really weaken the fish?"

"Eventually. The scientists say the fish from different rivers are separate stocks. But hatchery fish coming home can interbreed with wild stocks. Then the stocks don't have their normal diversity, they're weakened, like for fighting diseases. And that keeps happening, so pretty soon there are fewer and fewer separate stocks, and more chance of a disease wiping the runs out. That's the theory. And the offspring aren't as hardy with the hatchery fish mixed in. Hatchery fish are weaker because of the way they're raised. That's what Esau gets so outraged over, the hatchery solution."

"But what else could they do? I learned those tall dams planned with no ladders killed off a lot of stocks and the easiest, cheapest solution was hatcheries below those dams."

"Yes, that's the popular answer."

She nodded, jotting down more notes. *This is sure more interesting than the classroom, and at least this paper will get written, only two more to go. But, hum-m-m, an air mattress in the living room?*

He saw her frown. "What?"

"Nothing, just thinking."

He went on, "There's a lot of disagreement about hatcheries; not just Esau. But they do produce a steadier run of fish in the short run. How else can the salmon industry overcome all the problems they have now? Problems much tougher than maintaining hatcheries."

"What's the biggest problem?"

"You tell me."

She shook her head, "Too many. Maybe funding?"

"Yeah, that's one. The feds keep cutting the fisheries budget. Miss Matsuda, you did know this already."

"No, not at all. And it's more authentic coming from you."

"Well, I wish more people recognized that, with all my credentials."

She giggled, and waited for more questions, and he knew he could easily list more problems. How many did she need?

"Out in the ocean, Miss Matsuda, out in the 'donut hole'—that's the international zone—more problems. How're we ever going to fix problems out there? One place that we are not the boss, we, the federal government. Hatcheries are so much simpler, and cheaper, and faster."

"And to Esau it's all evil by humans. Do you agree?"

"Pretty much, yeah. Evil or stupidity."

In half an hour of writing fast Suki had enough rough draft for the paper. She needed only to flesh it out and quote some authorities. And quote him too—that was the good part. Now she saw that Ike could help with the last salmon paper, with its more challenging topic. And it wouldn't be a collection of quotes from other peoples' reports, but from someone who lived it.

"Thanks so much, Ike."

He smiled. "Nice to be appreciated."

"I don't understand why you feel useless at the meetings. You know what's going on."

"Because they don't really listen. Or I can't express it right."

"Well, it's true, the scientists I've listened to have their own jargon. You can feel excluded. I'll feel at home with the kids because I can talk in regular English."

He knew what she meant. The scientists had a serious English problem, especially the social scientists he'd tried to read.

Before long they were over the pass through the Cascades and starting down into evergreen covered foothills, the kind of country she knew as home, that she had hiked in earlier years with her parents, and loved. An hour later she was impressed at how skillfully Ike drove the big truck along the freeway in the insane rush hour traffic, never the time to be arriving in Seattle, and due to his waiting for her. She commented on his calmness.

"Well, I'd never survive as a truck driver if I let it get to me, right?" In fact, he did not enjoy it, but he tried to avoid griping—except, lately, about fisheries management.

They made the rest of their way to the city center, dropped off the truck at the port's secured unloading area, and walked to look for a cab. He was quiet now. She thought about his plan for a return trip, doing a cultural class with the kids, overnighting with his family, riding back, and all this time, most of it alone with him. She was nervous, but she liked him too much to say no.

"About next weekend, I guess I'll say yes, I can do it. I said I would, and how else am I going to keep such a schedule? And, sure, I can sleep on an air mattress, too, it's nothing."

But she was thinking of other possibilities as she got up the nerve to catch his eyes and give him a small smile.

They finally spotted a cab. Arriving at his cousin's place, they found dinner waiting and quickly heated up. Doreen apologized that the meat was only chicken. Suki hardly tasted it but complimented the seasoning. She glanced around the apartment, noting its private bedroom, full kitchen and bathroom, and even a small deck, and observed that Doreen was supporting herself well—even her own car. But no kids. Ike talked with Doreen about their connected family and fishery news, and Suki mainly listened. She caught Ike looking at her in quick glances; it was easier to read him with sunglasses put away. *This isn't about salmon papers.*

Doreen said, "What are your classes this summer, Suki?"

Suki, her thoughts elsewhere, had to think what they were. "Oh…Writing for Publication, Pacific Salmon Ecology, Freshwater Microbiology."

"Wow, that's too much for summertime."

"I know. Classes are over next week, and I'm taking incompletes. Then onward on my dissertation. I need to have that all done and accepted by next summer. And get on with life."

"Dissertation? Ugh. No fun. But I survived college somehow; and you'll make it."

But Suki was thinking of the night before them. Did Doreen have air mattresses?

They were barely through with the meal when Doreen sprang up. "Oh, I forgot! I need to go pick up some quilting squares from a friend. But it's across town, so it could take about an hour in the traffic."

She motioned to Ike, "But I need to tell you something from Esau," and he followed her into the kitchen.

"Oh, thanks," Suki heard Ike mutter. In a moment the two were back.

Doreen smiled, "Just save the dishes, Ike, I'm sorry." She got her coat. "So, Suki, do you want a ride home now—I can drop you off—or would you rather stay and visit with Ike and he can take you when I come back?"

He's set this up! She didn't dare look at him. "I think I need to stay. He did promise to help me more with a paper on salmon that's due."

In a minute the nurse was out the door. Suki stood up and couldn't think of anything to say. Ike grinned, "What shall we do, the dishes? Or more on your paper, or...I know! How about another water fight? I'm very sweaty."

"Oh...like the shower? Better find her mop then."

He found the mop. Suki saw there were two fresh towels out. *Who was the master planner?*

"So, together?"

"Uhhh, yes, okay."

The shower was even more interesting than the river fight with the discreet looks from each. Drying off, Suki took a breath and said, "Which was more fun, the shower or the *Chiawana*?"

"Well, we can make improvements on this one, right?" He pulled her to him and gave her a long-awaited deep kiss. *Wow! Wow!* In a flash, floor mopping forgotten, towels scattered, they were in the bedroom, on the bed, wrapped around each other. *At last, at last.* The sunset had broken through the clouds over the Olympics, and now it was a bright orange streak the length of Puget Sound, but they didn't see it. No scenery, no roaring truck, no salmon lessons, just warm, naked, tanned, eager bodies moving.

Doreen was slow to return. Traffic, she had explained, gridlocked. They'd had the time finally to get to know each other beyond talk and had even taken care of the dishes by the time she was back, knocking on the door. They both had their jackets on, ready to leave. She glanced around and gave their embarrassed expressions a diagnostic look.

"Thanks for doing the dishes, guys."

CHAPTER 26

TRIBUTARIES

FOR THE OTHER travelers returned home, the next days were filled with their own questions. Bruce faced his hatchery boss with a story about birdwatching gone wrong. The boss assured him that with his good work record, and most charges dropped, he would probably be hired back when there was a new opening at a hatchery. But Bruce wondered when that would be with the fishery budgets, both state and federal, forever being cut. Meanwhile, when he wasn't job hunting he, and sometimes Marta, too, went for hikes in the foothills. But that relief only lasted for a day each time. He had never been a TV addict, and Marta worried for his and her own sanity when she watched him pacing their tiny apartment, ever tinier. Unlike her family, his own parents didn't agree with his ideas on war, nuclear weapons, or foreign policy in general. After the reunion, even more than before, Marta was his support as he tried to figure his next move.

"I can't stand this—doing nothing!" he cried as he marched the room.

"Well, I can't stand watching you!"

"I still think their intent was right; they just didn't have their strategy all thought out."

"Who? The kayakers? Ridiculous! They'd never get public support that way."

Bruce knew she was right, but at least the kayakers had cared enough to try to do something. He was glad to get a call from Roger that he and Thelma were planning their stream-clearing projects for fall, and Bruce and Marta were invited to join them on one soon. Bruce was quick to say yes. Roger also reported that Orville had chaired meetings of his new protest group, and that the group planned to prepare a letter to the Atomic Energy Commission, to be signed by as many people as possible, demanding action on both the Hanford Plant waste and the downwinders' case. They also talked about asking for an apology to the White Bluffs/Hanford evicted families. But when the group converged for their second meeting, Roger said they slipped back into their habit from the reunions of reminiscing about the old days. Finally, Orville, frustrated in his new role, declared he and Dorothy would draft the letter, and the group could review, correct, and pass it. Then Orville wanted everyone to try to get signatures from everyone else who'd been evicted.

Bruce wondered how that would work. If the other settlers didn't actively help with the letter would they feel invested enough to get signatures? How many cared that much about the downwinders unless they were their own relatives? How many thought hard about the problem of the leaking waste? How much influence did Orville and Dorothy have? He had no idea. But at least they were trying to do something for their old community, their river, and their valley. So he had to as well.

Leon went through his cataract surgery and was back to his routines of researching indigenous plants and teaching graduate classes. But he, too, was unable to put aside Orville's speech at the reunion and his own need to take more action. His notes from the sessions he had passed onto Marta to use however she wished. He went on Roger and Thelma's first stream renewal project of the season, one in eastern Washington—his choice. Long ago he had stood on the banks of Australian streams, and the muted colors and blazing cliffs of the Cascades' desert side were a powerful *déjà vu* he now wanted more of. The less startling things—*rabbit brush, cattails, willow-thick banks, quail, herons, sand, dragon flies—all different, yet so familiar,* had their power in the recall of his sensual delight back then, a young researcher on his own and in love with it all.

Now, here he was, picking up plastic and aluminum waste, and to save salmon runs, not human communities. But he believed it was important, for him as well as the fish. He felt out of shape, knew he'd ache the next day, liked that, and was sure his time with Roger and Thelma was more renewing than the stream or the salmon probably received. Tramping around, he looked forward to the Columbia's flowering desert next spring, happy he'd be able to clamber along the banks without a stumble.

Thelma, dragging her own trash bag along the bank, told him about the letter Orville planned, and Leon, surprised, said he wished he were doing more about the waste issue. She was glad that someone who had never lived along the Columbia cared that much, but then realized the Leon was looking beyond just that particular river. During another conversation, resting on the river bank, Roger asked Leon to explain what Bruce, Marta, and Suki had been up to when they had disappeared from the reunion for an afternoon, then again that night, and the next morning, too.

Leon put him off gently. "Well, I feel it's theirs to tell; I don't know the whole story myself." *And that is the truth.*

Back at work, Leon stayed restless. In the past, after such a rich session as he'd had with the settlers, he would have been full of ideas for follow-up research or action. Preserving Indigenous knowledge of plants was important, but was it enough for the rest of his days? He'd liked being with the settlers so much. Then he thought of another way he could contribute to the Columbia's history, if not its rehabilitation. He was sure Harold's memoir was important, not just for these settlers' history but for the whole history of early irrigation in America's western desert. Knowing Harold still refused to take on the task of looking for a publisher, Leon called him and proposed that he could take care of it.

"I want to pay to have the memoir proofed and printed as a paperback, and have it ready for the next Hanford-White Bluffs reunion, at about $12 a copy. A deal, Harold. You can add an addendum if you wish."

"Addendum?"

"An up-to-date at the end."

Harold was pleased but skeptical. "Me, a published author?" But before long he agreed to it and that he would go to the reunion next summer, no matter how many aches plagued him, and sign copies. And after some pushing he said he would think about reading from it to a small group.

"But not a whole packed room, Leon. I'd panic!"

Harold had already called Louise to feel out her reactions to the reunion and to apologize for any part he'd unwittingly played in any uproar. She assured him that he was not at fault for the strange events, but that she meant it when she'd said that never again would she coordinate a reunion. Yet when she heard the plan for his memoir she was quick to reverse.

"Wonderful! Well, in that case, of course I'll be doing it again." Bigger crowds would surely come, energized by a new agenda. For every story from the memoir five new ones could pop up.

⊶⊷ ⊷⊶

Four days after dropping off the hay load, Ike and Suki were headed back east with an empty truck, her first salmon paper turned in. She had two more papers to write to avoid incompletes. That morning she had been up at six waiting for him, wondering what he had done those four days, wondering if she should care so much. She still couldn't believe she had hopped eagerly in bed with a man she had known for all of a bus ride, a short hike, several truck rides, and the next thing she knew...*This is crazy, I'm crazy. All I know about him is that he's good looking, he's a good driver, he knows how to change a tire fast, I like his family whom I've known for parts of three days, he knows all about salmon, he's got two kids, he needs to find a job, and he can be both very serious and very funny...and he's incredible making love. And that for some reason he's latched onto me. This is not like me; I must be sex-starved! Well, I am...was, this we know. He probably is not. No, I don't think so.*

So what's with him? He wants me for some reason, and I want him. Is there some deep Jungian thing going on? His people have been victims of war and social violence and so have mine? And all the business that has nothing to do with sex...I don't think. He's talked me into teaching a class to some kids, and go to a museum planning meeting and fishery management meetings, neither of which I've been invited to—I just show up. More road trips, and sleeping on his uncle's living room floor with him. And I seem to have said yes to all of it. Well, I did ask for it didn't I; I did ask him for some ideas of things I could do.

And what does he do? Drives me around, keeps me company with long discussions, lots of them about salmon, helps me write a paper, tells me I can be a teacher, tells me I have to make a government committee listen to me, and talks about his two cute, lively daughters. And makes love when or if there is a place to, sort of, accommodate us.

She again wondered if, for her, the attraction could be partly how their families' and peoples' histories crossed paths. But they had been very different strands. Maybe the attraction was the differences as much as the similarities. *A flesh and blood global social history course we are, the flesh part is important, isn't it! But courtship in a truck? That's what teens do.*

Ike, for his part, was surely hoping it had been as great for her as it was for him. *I'd like to pull off and park right now, go for a second act. No, that could seem pushy, especially with me being in control of things right now, fifty miles into the mountains. No, gotta stick to the agenda. She's real special, many ways.*

Thus, driving over the pass they were mainly quiet. Suki had to force herself to stay focused on the class she was to present the next day to pre-teens and teens. She, who had never taught a thing, had only given a few short talks. He was holding her hand as he drove, something illegal for a trucker she was sure, and talking about the berries that grew up on the higher elevations they were roaring through. He was saying that she'd have fun when she went berry picking with him and his girls, and he wished they could stop right now and check on the berries, but didn't have time. *He's thinking about berries? After last night?* Finally she finally got up nerve to ask a question bothering her.

"Um…Do you always carry a condom in your pocket?"

He broke out in an embarrassed giggle. "No. Doreen gave it to me before she left. Yeah, I know. But she's a nurse; it's her job to think always about health and safety, right?"

It was her turn to smirk. "Good thing someone was." *I am not going to tell him I have an IUD. Not now. He likes to tease; I can just hear him coming back to me, 'Oh, do you always have your IUD with you?' But it's not the same, and he wouldn't understand that.*

She decided to change the subject back to the great scenery they were passing through, and commented that truck driving wasn't all bad, something different to look at.

He shrugged, "It's okay when it's not the rush hour. Wait till you see the vine maple changing, if we're still making this drive next month. Stevens Pass is even prettier, but too long for truck contracts." In a moment he went on, "Uh, Suki, your question...I guess that sounds like I'm a thoughtless guy. Actually, I did call Doreen, you know, to ask if I could bring a guest..." He gave her one of his smiles that made her heart flutter.

"I see."

A few miles later she posed another question she had held back too long.

"If I'm not being too nosy, uh, sorry, but where is your girls' mother?"

"Well, she's not in Wolf Rapids. She's off somewhere with another guy, been quite a while...years. Believe me, Suki, that's over."

They arrived at Esau and Alice's with no more on that topic.

The class area in the new meetinghouse was ready for them. Eight students rushed in to sit in a circle on the cool earth floor, and as Alice and Esau had predicted, before long questions began: "When did you come here?" "Why is Japan so small on the map, but was so powerful?" "Why weren't the Germans and Japanese put on reservations when they lost a war to us?" "Why are those buildings sitting down there doing nothing?" "Where is your family, Suki?"

She was glad she'd been warned you had to be prepared for anything. She loved talking with the kids and felt the cloud over her botched blessing fade a little. The next week, headed for Nagasaki, she would have some things positive to report to her mother. Well, not everything.

Dinner was special too. Esau and another nephew had been to the lower Columbia and set net half the salmon they needed for winter. Some were now in the new freezer Ike had bought, the rest drying out in the wind. Topping the dinner menu, the salmon was a wonderful change from hasty microwave meals Suki relied on.

Esau, as usual, enjoyed teasing her: "You are from Japanese culture and you don't know how to fillet fish?" And of course, "When are we going to go rabbit snaring again? It's not so hot this week, so you'd like it better maybe?" Sometimes he teased her until she couldn't stop laughing and she had to walk away. She wasn't sure how much she was allowed to tease him back. But when he stopped kidding she was quiet.

"You are so serious, Suki. Yes, when you were born, I think when you came out the first thing you saw as they were washing you was an eagle flying past. That eagle never smiles; she is always searching, searching."

She knew it was true; she needed to lighten up sometimes, and Esau, even more than Ike, saw to that. The family took her to a potlatch celebrating the re-opening of the meetinghouse. She endured more curious stares and answered polite questions when people heard she was a college student interested in the problems of the Columbia. And especially the dangers from predicted radioactive leakage from the plant. Do whatever you can, people told her. She gradually relaxed but was too shy to dance to the singing and drumming with the others.

She found Ike's girls, Starla and Judy, friendly but quiet. They asked questions about college life; clearly they were being pointed that direction. Once in a while she caught them looking at her curiously: *What does this woman have in mind with our dad?* But outside of the cultural classes and evening meals, it was hard to engage them for long, as they were off with other youth.

"They're normally noisier. They're just being respectful to you," Alice said.

Ike watched all this in a half-bewildered state. *All at once I'm in love? I sure must be. But what do I have to offer her, besides free rides and advice? I helped her very little with that paper. It was a joke, really, but she thanked me as if it was important. What do we have going, really, besides love-making? Salmon? A nuclear waste problem? Crazy!*

And it could all end soon when his truck driving jobs ran out, and her ride-alongs, with their excuse to be together, the classes, would also end. With these questions pushed to the background, the week's routine repeated for the two: hormone-filled truck rides, much talk, an exhilarating class with Wolf Rapids kids, fall class registration for Suki, job-seeking by Ike, and for both, too short nights. Suki had no solution better than the air mattress in the family living room. *If only I didn't have a roommate, but I can't just kick her out. She wouldn't go.*

⤜▪ ▪⤛

Marta was hugely relieved when Roger finally called to tell of the next stream-clearing project, this time on a tributary of the lower Columbia. Of course they would go. The memory of their time on the eastern Columbia banks brought her no pangs of nostalgia, but she knew that for Bruce it was right on surface. Deep in her new research topic, she scarcely was available for conversation, while her man stewed over his failed projects: He hadn't done what he was supposed to do with the memoir, he hadn't saved Jason or the kayakers, he'd passed on Suki to Ike and Esau, he hadn't seen the school administration about the name "Bombers". At least cleaning up a stream that was part of the Columbia system was something he and Mart could do together.

Their stream was in the western foothills, running through Douglas fir second growth. Many of the western wild coho runs were gone, and the stream-clearing job was part of an experiment to see if they could be brought back using hatchery fish. The volunteer crew was to copy the procedures of a salmon specialist that came along with them to show cleaning up of human and logging trash, then redistributing normal woodland debris to rebuild the ponds that coho liked for spawning. Bruce had sloughed off his malaise the minute they reached the work site. Both he and Marta felt right at home in the western slope's evergreen forests and rocky streams, the banks covered with ferns, or thimbleberry and salal brush.

Marta kept looking around with new eyes. "I can't believe we are right now connected to that same river."

"I know. But everything connected with the Columbia seems…complex."

Bruce checked with the scientist in charge, "Can we be sure that baby salmon or salmon eggs will get planted here?"

"Absolutely, well, almost." He explained that the managers got to each cleared stream as fast as they could with incubators or smolt. It was a matter of money more than anything.

Oh, of course, factory boats are priority in D.C. Well, it's healthy work, anyway.

When Roger and Thelma took breaks on the stream bank, they joined them and heard more stories of old days at White Bluffs, but even more of their concern about what was coming for the Columbia and the region if the waste wasn't taken care of.

Once back home, Bruce was pacing again. "Mart, I need a real job. I need some money."

She agreed, but already her head was back to her own project, as she knew her committee chair would ask her: Why is this a good topic for research? She argued it to herself to be prepared: *The 1907 orchardists truly were an unusual group. They were not traditional farmers; yet it was neither a religious, nor socialist, nor utopian community. They were not homesteaders; yet very few were well-off. They were novice irrigators in a desert, and without government subsidy—even the diversion dam had been private. Then, after thirty-seven years to be suddenly evicted. It was such a unique history.* They scheduled another meeting with her committee, and after a long discussion it did give her permission to change her topic to: "Early Desert Irrigators on the Mid-Columbia: An Experiment Aborted." Elated, she plunged ahead.

Of everyone that had traveled to that 1998 reunion and ended up as bird-watchers, or worrying over them, Marta was now the one with a clear view of her path forward. But she kept her eyes open for Bruce at the campus job-listings board. Soon she came home with news that the local community college was looking for an experienced instructor for an outdoor survival class. Bruce was out the door before she finished talking and had no trouble getting hired. After two days of feeling things out, he proposed new challenges for the class far beyond the standard curriculum: making tourniquets from grass or roots, identifying the most dangerous of various scorpions. The students asked, "Where did you learn all this stuff?" He decided to just smile and say, "Where do you think?" And he took them through tracking, snares, fire-making, shelter-seeking, weather forecasting, signaling, finding directions, camouflage, first aid—everything but bomb-making.

⁂

Ike was happy with how Suki's meetings with her new students were proceeding, but half his mind was on how to find ways to be with her beyond the long-distance drives. He thought about Seattle, and he didn't care for the picture of life there for himself. He knew he couldn't afford his own place anywhere near there without a steady job for the winter. When they were at Wolf Rapids and she talked with the kids, he half-listened, pondering commercial fishing again. But with no encouragers, he decided he would instead apply for work at one of the hatcheries. *Fish and Wildlife sure owe me something don't they?* But Esau let out a howl when Ike broached it to him.

"What? No way I could stand that! I know you want work, but no hatcheries. You know they're a lot to blame for missing salmon. And don't take any reservation job! Our people fought to stay here for good reason."

Alice nodded, "He's right, nephew."

Ike wasn't going to go against family that had provided him a home for years, and now for his children too. But later Esau reminded him that they needed to add to the kids' classes about rebuilding salmon runs, and that Ike should take care of that.

Ike kept his voice calm. "Okay, Uncle, I'll try to be a teacher, and then your part is that you will go to fishery meetings again?"

"I'm too busy now, I really am. No, it's yours now."

Having lost that argument again, Ike decided the next time he and Suki were visiting that they should walk along the river where they could talk privately. It was still quite warm, but she'd learned it could be below zero in the winter, and as they walked the bank in the wind now growing cooler, she again marveled at the extreme contrast between the west and east sides of the Cascades. Yet people had made each side their home. She asked Ike how they had stayed warm in winter here? He laughed, that they had managed it like any desert people, that they had made sod houses half sunk in the ground, and he would show her one soon. Finally, she felt she had to ask more about the girls' mother, and was relieved that he didn't seem to mind.

"Where is she? Traveling around. She's from the Yakama rez, a professional powwow dancer, always on the go. I tried it for a while but it wasn't for me. Yeah. So when I quit it after a couple years, she met another guy that's into that. And taking little kids along with her never did make sense. I was glad to keep them, with a lot of help."

"So do the girls see her?"

"Oh yes, whenever she's near us she'll get over to spend good time with them. It seems to be all right. I'm so lucky that Esau and Alice wanted them."

Suki thought that was enough of questioning. But was he looking at her as a surrogate mother for the girls? No, not possible; as an outsider she would be last place to look. The girls seemed fine where they were. No, it was as she'd first thought, that what he saw in her was simple sex. Or…something more serious.

On their way back to the house, Ike stopped and stared down the river. She spotted what he was peering at: a thread of what he'd earlier said was steam, drifting up from a reactor.

She cried, "Damn, how I hate seeing that!"

"I know, me too. We have to get rid of that dump. But do you always have to think about it, Suki?"

"Not always." She put her arms around him, closed her eyes, and they pressed close. But then she opened them to see Starla and Judy sneaking along the slope. The girls suddenly came whooping down like warriors in a cowboy/Indian movie, circled them brandishing stick spears, then went rushing off again with echoing laughter.

Suki laughed at their comedy. "Ike, your girls make me happy."

"You need to see more of them then?" His look wanted an answer.

She gazed off into the distance, then back to him. "Could be."

The girls came galloping back, asking them to come look at their new hideout. Ike said no, he had some stuff to figure out, but Suki said yes, and ran off with them.

Standing alone on a rise looking down at the river, Ike thought again how strange it was, that this great river had been home to millions of salmon and thousands of people for hundreds of generations. Now this section in a short time had become the only stretch where wild king salmon thrived, right alongside that fortress of evil! If it had never been built, there could be no wild kings spawning on the mid-Columbia; humans, or something, would have wiped them out.

What a strange twist! And we have to repair all this, however we do it; it's my home. But I know I can't stay here; my daughters can't stay here. We can't live on ghosts of salmon, or even healthy ones. I have to find place where there's a living for me. And now, more complicated—where I don't have to drive across mountains every time to see Suki. She puts life in me, like waking up—her beauty, her spirit. And she needs me; I feel like she does.

He walked down to the shore and reached for a handful of the smooth, rounded stones left from the glaciers, and one by one pitched them into the river, each with an insight.

So… (one stone) The salmon and the river problems. The next generation, my kids' generation, will be still working on them, will have to solve the messes humans caused.

(another stone) Suki's projects are simpler. She'll have no trouble with the kids' classes, and either the museum people agree to what she wants, the whole truth about what the bombs did, or they don't. But if she succeeds, truth can spread.

(another) And the even bigger issue—the future for nuclear energy, including the messes it can make. Ten years from now people could still be arguing about them. But maybe the students here will be the future scientists working on safer kinds of energy—like wind. Sure got lots of that!

(another) My girls will inherit all this, have to be able to fix it all. So they have to go to college; they had to have the credentials. So… I have to take that under-the-table trucking job offered me in Tacoma. I might even have to give up subsistence set-netting. Even give up the fisheries meetings—that won't break my heart.

(a last stone) I want to be near Suki, somewhere.

He decided he would find a town with a good high school, not a big city, but near her campus. There were many little towns in driving distance as long as you avoided rush hours and he knew that routine. There were even towns close to a reservation, so there were bound to be Indian kids enrolled in their schools, kids the girls might even know from visiting at powwows. He could find a place to rent before next fall, even sooner.

Esau and Alice would be sad—that was a hard part. But they had other grandchildren that would be happy to fill the empty space. He could take the girls back home on a weekend, like once month, and they could have the culture classes then, too, if the kids were still into it. *Suki, we could be together a lot more. It's not perfect, but it's what people do.*

The girls and Suki returned, out of breath from racing.

Judy was curious, "What were you doing, Dad?"

He smiled. "Figuring things out."

"Good things?"

More smiles. "You bet."

They all walked back, and Ike, ready to propose his plan, kept Suki from going into the busy house. She listened to him, eager for any idea of how to have more time together. Then he proposed they could share a household.

Suki was caught by surprise. *Become a household? Even part-time?*

"Gee, Ike, I do want to be with you more, but let me have time to think… that's a big step." *And he wants me to leap right into it when I can't even keep up with classes now!*

"So is it, uh, something you've had problems with before? I mean a live-in boyfriend?"

She felt herself blush. "No. I haven't even had a live-in boyfriend. I knew I had to stick with my studies. I owe that, more than you know. And then grad school—no C grades there. Have to be better than that…or get out. I've never been so far behind as I am right now. No, I just know what can happen—from friends. I don't want you to end up hating me, buried in books and papers, ignoring you and everything else! But I'm so close, just my dissertation. I have to stay with it, finish!"

"That's crazy, that I'll hate you."

"I've seen it. It's not about you, it's me, my problem! Until I get through this, get that PhD."

He was let down. *She's being cautious…why? She doesn't have to change, just do what she's doing. Or she's just by nature cautious, a thinker?*

"What will you be doing, I mean when you're not truck-driving."

"I'll be where I want to be—with you and my kids, and we can go to Wolf Rapids whenever you can. Visit, and do the classes."

"What else?"

"Well, what do you want to do?"

"No, not me. I'll be buried in a computer, and books, and papers, and deadlines. I mean, what will you have to keep you engaged."

"Suki, I won't bother you."

"That's not what I meant. You haven't lived with a grad student trying to graduate. You need a challenge of your own to be working on, your own. Not me or your kids or their homework. *And I can't tell you what.* Something that you'd really like to do, your thing be busy with, and then maybe you could stand me, buried over in my corner. I've seen how it is with Marta."

He didn't answer. She came close to him, took his hand.

"You know I love you; I sure don't want it to sour. But I have to get that PhD. Then a job. I'm sorry if I sound so…driven. That's the way it gets."

She waited for an answer. He stared off toward the river. *So much for my ideas.*

"All right. I can think about it. Truck-driving can get pretty driven, too, you know."

He'd tried to end it with a joke, but thought she was making a deep pit out of a prairie-dog hole. He realized she must have reason to be so insistent, and that it might have something to do with her coming trip to Nagasaki, her obligations to family. *I sure know about that.*

⋆⊷ ⊶⋆

The rainy season on Puget Sound started too early, only mid-September, and brought the usual flooded streams. Cleaning them came to a halt for a time for Roger and Thelma and anyone else they recruited. The woods were so wet Bruce's students grumbled, and skipped class. At home he stared at the sheets of water running down their windows. Marta saw the signs of seasonal depression he was prone to.

"What are you brooding about, Bruce? Is this about the Columbia?"

He turned to her, frowning, "Tell me, why do people have to screw up the Columbia and every other damn river—and the people living by them, of course? And not just rivers. I see people trying to fix all the other messes we've created, and everywhere we're busy making bigger messes."

"I know, I know. I'm too much living in research of the past. And I agree, we do need to try to make a difference. How?"

298

"How...How? Jeez, I suppose by cleaning up the messes? Little ones, maybe even some bigger ones. *Like I promised.*

He gazed out through the mist toward the gray-green foothills, and past them to the grayer mountains that divided them from that other world, so different, to the east. A desert, like all the others he couldn't get out of his blood. *I ended up hating deserts, though not the people living in them. But now I've been to the desert my own family loved, and I think I can get over hating them.*

He looked over at Marta and her piles of books and notes. "So...are you with me?"

"I'm here, aren't I?" She smiled.

"Yes", he squeezed her hand, "and thank you."

She grinned. "So can we at least try to stay out of jail anyway?"

He gave her a hug, "I'll do my best."

CHAPTER 27

PORT RADIUM / NAGASAKI

HEARING THAT SUKI was leaving soon for Nagasaki, Bruce agreed to try to get Harold to cover the next Wolf River kids' class: the eviction of the White Bluffs-Hanford settlers in 1943. Harold protested that he wasn't there, but would do it if someone who had experienced the eviction would go with him. A call to Orville and Dorothy got a yes, and Bruce said he would provide the transportation. Suki was relieved that her trip wasn't going to stop a thing. A group of her students waved to her as she and Ike began to drive off, and she looked at their grinning, tanned, healthy faces and thought that they were what Ike's and her own children could look like. *If there ever were such. Oh, why am I thinking this way?*

At Ellensburg, the new hay load was ready to go, and this time they had something different to look forward to. Ike received some pay and after the hay was unloaded they were going to be alone in a cheap motel room on Aurora Avenue for the night. The next morning he would take the truck back while she flew off to Japan. As they started west in the big truck, Suki was thinking about Japan and her mother, and what she wanted to do there, mixed in, as usual, the kids' classes, papers due, and the man beside her. It was too complicated, the logistics alone. *And do I really have to get involved in the museum issue too, on top of everything else, when I 've already carried out my promise?* She hoped to get new perspective on it in Nagasaki.

He broke into her thoughts, "Suki, I've been saving something to tell you."

She held her breath. Oh? *Please, nothing personal, not until I get back.* "Bad or good?"

"I met a guy at the fishery meeting in June."

She let her breath out. *It's about fish, of course.*

He read her mind. "And it's not about fish, not really. He's from Canada, way up in Northwest Territories. A guy about forty-five or so. He was sent down from his tribe to see what we're doing about rebuilding fisheries. They have lake and river fisheries, not salmon, but big trout and white fish. And they heard about us. He also wanted to hear what tribes around here are doing with cultural restoration, and with tourism. So I told him about what we're working on. They've had hard times, but then a few years back they finally got a land claims settlement and some self-government. Like Alaska Natives? He's from a place called Great Bear Lake, up in the Arctic. Ever hear of it? No? Then he asked me if I knew anything about Hanford. Turns out, there was a big uranium mining operation up there at their lake. Some of them worked at it."

He went on to describe the place, then glanced over; her eyes were drooping. They had not slept much the night before with the air mattress arrangement, although it had been a perfectly good mattress.

"Hey, don't fall asleep yet! Do you believe in coincidences, that are somehow...special?"

"Yes, sometimes."

"Well, the place was called Port Radium, and that mine produced uranium in World War II. And the workers carried the radioactive ore in bags on their backs. And of course, they ended up with a polluted lake and river; the lake's still polluted. And with so many outsiders working at the plant their fish stocks got real depleted too. Then a few years later the local people began to have a high rate of cancers they never had before. There had been no information to them about that risk, but he says many scientists later claimed they had warned the Canadian government. But the government says there's no provable connection with the cancer rate. Sound familiar?"

She was wide-awake now. "Oh boy, too familiar, the whole scene! Port Radium...never heard of it."

"Me neither. But it seems it got to be quite a story in Canada later. It was top secret like Hanford at the time. But you know that some of the Hanford workers and other people, the downwinders, are suing our government over the radioactive releases into the air. And this guy sure wanted to hear about Hanford because of their own problems with that. But there's more, Suki. They found out a while ago that probably some of the Port Radium uranium was turned into plutonium at Hanford. And that does make sense, Hanford being the biggest plutonium plant."

Suki was for once speechless. She tried to picture it: a great misty far north lake instead of a great river, another mysterious war production place. And Indigenous people living there, their home, some of them to end up working at the mine, sick from it. And very likely the uranium went into the bomb for Nagasaki? She felt her gut clench.

"Ike, how very strange, this guy just appearing!"

"Well, he came to talk about fishing—he didn't just appear. But he was on his way back from Japan; he was part of a delegation they sent to apologize about the part they believe they played."

"No kidding? An apology? Really?" *Has the U.S. ever apologized? I've never heard of it.*

Both of them were quiet until Suki said, "Did any of your people work at the Hanford plant?"

"None that I know of. They brought in outsiders."

"How about the orchard folks?"

"I don't know. But I can't picture that, they were so angry about it. But the people at Great Bear Lake were not removed. They worked there...and they paid for it."

"One more people that paid for it."

"Yup.... Well, I told him a little about you, and he wants to meet you. I've got his phone number. Do you want to talk to him?"

"Of course! Here I am, about to go off to Nagasaki. I'll call him when I get back."

At last they were rumbling down toward the docks. They got freed of the truck, and headed in a cab to the motel. It was basic: a bed, a bathroom, and a T.V. They ate the lunch Alice had sent along, took another shower together, and for once were all by themselves a whole night, the lumpy, squeaking bed a little heaven.

Later Ike wrapped his warm arms around her. "Wouldn't you like to be together more?"

"Yes, I would, I really would, believe me! Maybe you haven't observed how it is between Marta and Bruce. Not that you're like Bruce, but I can sure see myself in Marta when she's spaced out on her note-taking. Think about it while I'm gone?"

The next morning Suki was on her way to Japan. After seeing her off, Ike headed back across the mountains, pondering the task she'd given him, hoping that the news of the apology from Great Bear Lake had made her feel better, and hoping for another hay load.

⊷⊨◉ ◉⊨⊶

Bruce, still waiting for a break in the dreary rain, was rescued from his own blue funk by a call one evening from Leon. After the usual "How are you?" exchanges, Leon got to the point.

"Bruce, I've gotten too academic I think. You know, what I was able to do at the reunion, and now getting out the memoir—it's all useful. But there are so many threads to those stories that tie right into the present day. Tell me, in your opinion, what's most important that people can do, I mean about the Hanford Plant, or maybe I should ask—nuclear plants in general?"

Bruce, phone to his ear, began his usual pacing.

"I know, I know, it's overwhelming."

They both were silent; Bruce paced. Then he said, "Hey, Leon, do you want to come with me to an anti-nuke meeting? I mean an actual big organized group, not a rendezvous in the bush?"

Leon wondered. *Would I be of any use?* "Bruce, I admire you, that you find ways to respond to that whole bizarre scene."

"You didn't see all of it. Be glad you didn't."

Leon knew that part of him wished he had. And he flashed on Elena inviting, exhorting people to come together and pray for the river. *But I'm not a praying person; I'm a...recording person. Yet how can you just sit and record, record—with that stuff seeping toward the river?*

303

"You bet I'd like to go with you. Just give me a date, time to arrange it."

⇥▱◁▱⇤

Suki spent a week in Nagasaki, all she felt she could spare with two papers still overdue. Among her gifts to her mother and grandmother were the dried snakeskin Esau had given her and a swatch of dried sage. She told them the whole story of the blessing, and her mother took her girl's hands in her own with an encouraging gaze, and spoke in Japanese.

"You carried out the ceremony just right, daughter. Just continue to do whatever you can for that river and that strange place, and those people that still live there."

The grandmother nodded. "The snake did its work; its spirit will be there."

At another point, Suki asked, "I know you are needed here, Mom, but will you come and visit sometime?"

"I'm not sure I can. We'll see." And she glanced at her own mother.

Suki found out her mother had gone to see the delegation from Port Radium.

"It was a big affair; I couldn't even get close. A very good thing, very solemn, but heart-warming. Please call them as soon as you get back and thank them."

The grandmother said, "So far away, long ago, but they remember. What human feelings they have!"

"I know, it was so good to hear of them. And yes, I will call them. I'm sorry the U.S. hasn't done this. It really must. I feel as if I should…"

"Suki, you did what you could, did it well."

"But Mom, they've built a new plant near the old one, it's operating with the same problems."

"Daughter, you know we have those plants here, too. And yes, with some of the same problems, I'm sure. People are not learning. But you can't fix everything. You need to stay with your studies now. Make that first."

Suki read to them some of the section she copied from Harold's memoir. And, just as she expected, they were very interested to hear about these people, their lives, and their feelings. Suki had much to talk about with her mother and grandmother after a whole year, but her thoughts kept jumping back to questions over the Chiawana-Columbia.

"What more can I do, Mom?" She hadn't mentioned the planned museum for the Hanford Plant—it would be too much.

"It will come to you. After you have your degree."

She doesn't want to give me any more tasks. "Then what can I do for you, Mom?"

"Just get that PhD, that's all. I'll be very happy then. Your dad would be so happy. I know you will get a good job."

Finish my degree, job. That's all.

Suki gradually passed on some of the historical wisdom from Esau and more from Harold's writings and Ike's ideas to the two women. She told of the fun she'd had teaching pre-teens. She told about Bruce and his need to "do something", and about the other people she had crossed paths with, all because of her promise to do a blessing. She didn't tell the whole story, not of Jason and the kayakers, or of Bruce's arrest; she'd decided it was too complicated.

Together Suki and her mother walked out to two parks with shrines where her mother was a caretaker. Suki envied her job. She felt the spiritual presence in the shrines and their beautiful natural surroundings, but still didn't feel she knew how to connect it with everything else lately bombarding her. She didn't know how to ask her mother what Shinto spirituality was for her, a woman mainly raised in the U.S., or even more, to ask her grandmother. They chose easier topics while they cooked Japanese food that Suki so missed. The women told family history that Suki hadn't heard before. They watched TV and talked about the current news in Japan. Suki noticed the two women avoided talking about the bombing and its aftermath unless she brought it up. She knew there was still much anger in the city over how the survivors had been dealt with. Her mother told her it was nothing they wanted to burden her with more than they already had.

Stirring inside through all the visiting was Suki's confusion over Ike. How much was her excitement over the man himself; how much was his way of challenging her with ethical projects. And how would they ever have more time together? She scolded herself: *just let things take their course.* Her mother noticed Suki's preoccupation. After three days she asked a routine question for mothers: had Suki found a potential husband yet? After all, her daughter was close to thirty.

Suki just smiled. "We'll see, Mom." But later she asked in English, not wanting to include her grandmother, "What do you think of me with being a man who is not married, just a little older than me, healthy, good looking, but has two school-age daughters he is raising?"

After a moment her mother answered, "That could be all right if you all really care for each other, and that you are ready for teenagers when that day comes!"

Toward the end of the week, at Suki's request, her mother went with her to a Nagasaki museum dedicated to the effects of the bombing. It was the first time for Suki, as her mother avoided the place. Her grandmother, still embarrassed over her scars after all these years, didn't like to go to public places. Suki's mother explained that many of the scarred victims felt the same way—the exposure too embarrassing or humiliating. The museum exhibits showing many photos of victims' bodies were gruesome. Suki saw how troubled her mother looked, gazing at them.

"Do we really need people to see this, Suki? It's done, over."

"But it's not over! There was a Cold War going on just a short time ago. Probably there will be another if governments don't change. People need to see this kind of display, isn't that so? That the story mustn't be lost?"

Suki was now even more determined not to abandon the argument over what the proposed Hanford reactor museum must include.

Later she got her mother and grandmother laughing over what Esau had said about the proliferation of museums and their stories. But their laughter stopped over Esau's joke about mummies. *Oh no, Grandmother's seen people that look like that!*

"I'm sorry. It's not funny for you."

Suki was sorry to leave them, all three of them in tears, and at the same time felt so urgent to get back to her unanswered questions that she was glad that her excuse of fall classes waiting forced her to the plane. Then, on the plane, she felt sad for the short time with them and regretful for the things she should have said and hadn't, knowing she might not see them again for a year.

CHAPTER 28

WHERE ARE WE GOING?

IN SEATTLE LEON sat looking out his window, the rain still pouring down. Why had he, a desert dweller all those years, avoided Eastern Washington until now? And why did he feel so unsatisfied since his trip? He had done a fair job of facilitating. He had turned over Harold's memoir to a proofreader friend and was waiting. His classes were under control. He was waiting on Bruce.

His thoughts kept going back to the Columbia, still under the spell of the stories he'd heard and Harold's writings. He sensed he needed more work related to that time, though he wasn't going to get involved in research—it was Marta's project. Then one morning it occurred to him he could write an introduction for the memoir if Harold approved. But that wasn't all he wanted either. He needed to write something about the whole experience of the Columbia, if only for himself. And maybe something about the tule reed meeting house, but for that he needed another visit. He cleaned his new glasses, and, a computer-resister, he picked up his pen and scratch paper, and printed.

"Seattle Times, Dear Editor" …. How strange, he thought, that he'd never in his life written in such a way—to confront. *Well, it's time.*

The Wanapum lived and prospered on the river for eons. Then settler families were recruited by investors for a brand-new project that was based on an ancient technology: hydropower for irrigation. Small farming. Then in just three decades hydropower was central in a rage for industrial development as well. (I saw it start up in Australia—hydropower, a great example of humans dominating nature through technology.)

He paused, saw that he had fallen back into his habit of writing what popped into his head, then later to turn it into something concise, even publishable.

We humans seem to have an adventure-dream nature easy to recruit for such speculative projects. In some cases, hunger, as much as dreams, forces us. But according to the White Bluffs settlers, they didn't move to the Columbia to ease their stomachs' growling. They were not homesteaders, nor were they, as in Australia, released convicts or their descendants, or immigrants fleeing persecution, or refugees needing a roof and food. They were, like Harold's family, lower middle-class folks looking for someplace healthier than a smoggy, T.B. ridden city for their families. And possibly something more beautiful too. Or they were bored men needing new challenges, dragging their families along.

These settlers were not technologists informed about irrigation, nor historians knowledgeable of how the land happened to be available, whom they were replacing— Indigenous people there for over 10,000 years. They were innocents, come to a river still so clean that one said you could drink straight from it most of the year, and the most basic of systems: water wheels first, then pumped water or diversion dams.

Thirty-seven years later these mid-Columbia settlers were no longer important in the global picture…exiled, then forgotten. To be replaced by a new technological rage more fascinating for the country than dams, but also demanding a river with lots of water—atomic power. (A few thousand other humans slaughtered in the meantime.) Then, in only a few more decades, this biggest plutonium producer in the country was shut down, humans overwhelmed by what they had created. Not cost efficient either. As that dream closed, another burst forth, again in the form of hydropower, but by dams a hundred times more productive. It made possible a way of farming, that like the dams is hardly recognizable in its industrialized new clothes. By the late 1940s it was blossoming upriver, and twenty large dams were soon raised on the great Columbia-Snake system, hundreds of smaller ones. Big profits were now possible, but also big trouble for rivers, and river people, and especially the almost vanished wild salmon. Technology won again! (The bomb palace is still waiting to be torn down.)

Leon got up for coffee. This was certainly not the sort of letter you sent to a newspaper. A professional journal? Not hardly. He paced a bit, poured more coffee, checked the rain, no change, no temptation to even take a walk, and sat down to continue.

Now today, the 1990s and a new cause! Technology more and more dominates its human bosses, out of control, threatening Nature. And so, another anti-technology movement, a new generation of Luddites, bursts out, fanatical Nature lovers (Is it really fanatical, or informed?) Dams must be breached, the blossoming of the deserts reversed, the natural flora and fauna restored. The largest stretch of shrub-steppe left in the country, surrounding much of the Columbia River, must be saved. And along with that, the river's wild salmon. (A lot of people, again, couldn't be saved.) The great dams, only 50 years old or less, as they age, are not to be replaced. Back to sagebrush and bunch grass, and sage hens, and lizards! And wild salmon? Maybe even sturgeon? No more rivers turned into canals; any remaining nuclear plant must be closed; even fossil fuels must be left in the ground, along with them their smog, heat, and toxins; factory ships in the ocean must end their illegal dumping; agribusiness's toxic chemicals must be outlawed. Yes, say the new Luddites, we will fight all of this century's brew of evil. But wait! What to do with the radioactive wastes along the great Columbia? From all the war plutonium production, but from the new plant too! The biggest such dump in the country, over half of the total, just a few miles from the river, seeping toward it. Can we sell it? Can we give it away? Can we pay someone to take it? (Or do we need to make a new bomb?)

He stopped and looked at the last line. *(Whew! Thank you for your letter, sir, but I don't think we have space for this. Can we, uh, shorten it?)* Leon laughed at himself until he had tears and got up to pour himself a real drink. He needed to put aside rambling analyses and give Bruce-the-Action-Man another call. He was looking for some anti-nuke action group to get involved with, wasn't he? Leon hadn't heard back.

As the fall rains continued to batter Puget Sounders, Bruce's mood was worse than Leon's; he couldn't laugh at himself. He knew he couldn't force his outdoor survival students on too many more sodden marches through dripping forests. Stuck in a classroom, he had them practicing snakebite treatments, figuring caloric burn. Only Marta ignored the weather, burying herself in research and her small job grading papers for professors. One day Bruce found a notice of interest and after some protests from Marta, he got her to go with him to a meeting of the Lower Snake River Dam Breachers group. Unable to see a way to be useful to the Hanford Plant waste dilemma, he was game for any action, anything to help the Columbia, and the Snake River that fed into it, along with it the once great runs of sockeye salmon.

At the meeting at Walla Walla, they listened to the breachers strategizing, and admired their perseverance, but Marta wondered about their chances.

"They want to take out four dams? On that barge highway? That's really biting off a big chunk, fighting big ag and big government too."

"I know. But they've studied the problem and are wanting to do something that will count."

She sighed. Big chunks were what attracted him, but he was right.

⊶⊷⊷ ⊶⊷⊷

Suki arrived back in Seattle anxious to see Ike and be assured the magic was still there. Then he wasn't there to meet her, saying he couldn't make it until the next day. Why? Because a potato load he had been hired to haul wasn't ready. She was upset. *Potatoes over me? But is it any different than my sometimes saying I can't be with you because I'm finishing an assignment?* Then, finally, Ike was there with a big empty truck, and she climbed aboard, lunged into a long embrace, and forgave him. But she was now so far behind in completing her papers that she said she couldn't go with him for the weekend. She got out of the truck, but a moment later changed her mind, rushed for notebook, laptop, and change of clothes, and climbed back in.

At Wolf Rapids she found that all had gone well. The team of Harold, Orville, and Dorothy had interacted well with the students in her absence, talking with them about the orchardists' eviction. Esau compared it for them with their own people's numerous evictions: fish campsites, grazing grounds, a whole region. Suki had prepared a talk on Nagasaki for the students on the plane ride home, counting on Ike's daughters to ask questions as needed, and they did. And more of the students were now taking active part. They asked her questions about the Japanese view of the war now, and moved into questions like, "Why must countries have wars? Do they have good reasons?" They had already heard a lot of grumbling about the plan for a museum at Reactor B, and several had seen the sprawling buildings from hikes on the plateau across and above the river. Until now the sight had been, for them, a collection of empty, ugly, ghostly buildings.

As Alice had warned, Suki had to be ready for anything. The class contained much heavy information, perhaps too much for kids. But while she had been gone, the students had changed the class atmosphere. Ike had noticed that some had started getting a little restless. Through a hint from him they had come up with the idea of a skit. They were keeping the topic secret amid shouts of laughter. Suki wondered what could be funny about any topic she had raised with them, but they just laughed harder. Most of them were headed again with their families for days in the mountains to pick berries, the others down river for a special fall king fishery. They would pick up on the skit as soon as they got back.

As for her other question, Suki had hoped to come home to new ideas from Ike. They went on another of their riverbank walks, and she commented about the cottonwoods already changing to brilliant yellow. The shorebirds and ducks were gone. Soon she would have to be gone much more, and she waited for him to say something about their own future closing in. *I love him; I do want us to be together.* But he didn't bring it up, though she saw he was thinking hard about something. It was Suki he was thinking of, of course. Especially the times alone along the river, how full of beauty and spirit. A hand held, a smile, a comment. That water fight, where everything began. And then, lovemaking beyond belief. *How to hold onto all this.*

⊷▌◉ ◉▐⊷

A few days later, Suki ran into Marta on campus and went with her to have coffee with Bruce. She saw their abstracted looks.

"All is well with you guys?"

Marta nodded, stirred her coffee. "Me? Plowing along. But it's always interesting."

Bruce shook his head. "Suki, I'm stuck on the banks of the Columbia. I can't quit thinking about that radioactive mess. And I'm not a scientist, or an Indian, or a politician, or a professional environmentalist, or a rich sportsman—I'm nothing with any political influence. So, I'm thinking to join an anti-nuke group, a big one. And I've been talking to Leon; he has some interesting insights, not very encouraging, about how technology ends up controlling us, not the other way around. How we have to stop that somehow."

Suki sighed, "Right on the Columbia, great example. But stop it? How in the world do we do that? To start with I was just about to put up a message on a wall."

Marta said, "I guess that's why I seem to prefer the past."

Bruce grumbled, "One short chapter more and we'll be in the past."

Suki felt the vacuum of his missing energy. *The same Bruce that crept through the sagebrush; now he's down, down in the weeds. Marta's no help, consumed by her own project.*

"Well, then, I want to pass on to you guys something remarkable." And she shared with them the news about the Great Bear Lake people's apology about Port Radium and saw their amazed eyes. But then Bruce's expression slipped back to his dead-battery stare. She decided to share more.

"Here's more inspiration for you, about museums, what they can be, should be. There's already a museum about the bombing at Nagasaki—no surprise, eh? I went there this time with my mother. And the B Reactor committee needs to visit that one, and a few other people, believe me. It's photos mainly…well, what else could there be? And a plaque at the exit that says, *'Please learn the reality of what happened beneath that cloud. Please don't forget. Please tell others….*

"So I'm telling you! You don't walk away and forget that place! It made me think more about that reactor museum, what it must include, and not giving up on that."

Bruce looked her in the eye, "Well, I'm not surrendering either. There are many anti-nuke groups; I just need to decide which one is best for dealing with the Columbia's problem. But my goal is bigger than that."

Marta said, "I know. It's good you guys are obsessed like this. In today, I mean, not yesterdays. We have to be."

That made Suki think again about her own need to choose a dissertation topic. One from history or today? But it had to be a simple topic or how would she finish it soon? The next Friday she steeled herself to attend the meeting she and Ike had anticipated, as announced in the *Tri-City Herald:* an invitation to the public to an "envisioning" of a B Reactor museum. She caught a ride with him as he once more returned through Seattle with an empty truck, traded to his own at Ellensburg, and drove her on to the meeting at Richland. He saw her grim look as she emerged two hours later. She had spoken to the gathering of her recent experience at the Nagasaki museum. She told Ike that the members of the steering committee, all middle-aged white people, so far, were condescendingly polite as they told her the bombing would be covered, of course. After all, it had ended the war.

She assured Ike that she had argued in her best imitation of a polite college advisor voice, told them that the narrative could not simply highlight that the war had ended with a magnificent bomb because of plutonium produced at the Hanford Plant. What about the story of the survivors, information that for years had been censored—but now whole books had been written about their suffering? She told them, as an example, that of thirty staff at one elementary school twenty-six had been killed, and 1000 of their young students, to say nothing of the suffering of those that lived.

The committee chair protested. "Yes, we do know about such reports, but you don't understand. The Hanford museum is supposed to be a positive experience for visitors that they will pass on to others. We don't want something too gruesome to associate with their visit to the valley. People can read the books and visit the Nagasaki museum, too, if they wish."

There were weak understanding nods to her from two of those attending. Then, "Thank you very much, Miss Matsuda." Her time was over and they went on to others.

Ike felt angry over her disgusted report. "I'm sorry it turned out that way. But don't give up."

She didn't answer.

"Hey, it's like museum exhibits about Native Americans. The funders choose the romantic version, of course, and end up with cleaned-up displays for tourists, not a word about famine or slaughter. Hell no. Maybe one colorful battle? Maybe a mention about diseases brought in. I don't know that any displays anywhere go into the whole story, except reservation museums—maybe. Especially not today's problems."

He waited. At last she said, "Museums are not just for tourists. How many ordinary tourists want to see the remains of our internment camps? How many flock to the Holocaust concentration camps turned into museums? I mean, your heritage center isn't going to be just for tourists is it? But to make the Hanford museum more than a tourist draw—who am I? Nobody. This grand idea of putting that ugly B building on display, probably cheaper than tearing it down, and to be so proud of it! Well, I'm not returning to that group until I have one other person with me, a person from Nagasaki who was actually there and can talk about it."

"Of course! It's a great idea if you can do that. But no matter what, don't give up. Museum planning can go on like a long, mean winter, fifty ideas howling around. You could be in it for some time. But you can do it, Suki!"

"I'm going to do it. I'm just trying to figure out the best way."

She told Alice and Esau how she had been brushed off, and her solution.

"The trouble is, I don't personally know any people that were witnesses in Nagasaki or Hiroshima—people that are here now."

Alice thought a moment. She didn't know any either, but she had an idea.

"Suki, you have a perfect witness: your mother. Bring her over."

"But she wasn't there...."

"Oh...but she had relatives there, eh? Maybe one of them could come with her?"

Suki knew her mother was a thin possibility. *She's said she wants to forget it all.* Suki thought maybe she needed to as well—for a time. She was nervous that she hadn't met with her degree advisor.

Later, when they were alone, Ike was thinking again of his plan for moving, and said, "I wonder, what is your experience with prejudice? I'm thinking of my girls. It will be so different at a high school in a town."

Suki felt guilty, that she thought too much of her own problems.

"Prejudice? Well, it's there, of course.... Not so much people saying '*Why don't you go back to the rez?*'—though they may hear that—but more like, '*Why do Indians get 50% of the fish when they are a small group?*' I'm not sure what your girls will encounter. But in high school, they didn't say to me *'Why don't you go back to Japan?'* It wasn't like what the Hispanics get. It was more like using a fake Asian accent to talk in front of me. But it was usually even more like someone introducing you to a new person and they say, *'Oh, I just love Oriental food.'* To be always singled out."

He snorted, "Oh yeah, like *'Pleased to meet you. I just love Indian beadwork!'* But *'I am glad to meet a sober Indian, your people must be proud of you.'* That's not very subtle."

She sighed. "I had two sides pulling at me. My parents were telling me I had to be the best, always try to be the best. And from the other side, 'Why do Asians think they always have to be the best?' I felt like I could never try hard enough and at the same time that I was getting special breaks I didn't deserve, or that I ought to let someone else be the winner. But it's better in college. There are so many different groups that you can go with; you can just ignore the others if you want."

She watched him soaking this in. "Ike, they have to face it sooner or later, but junior high can be an especially hard place."

"But the binge drinking at college..."

"Oh, I probably gave you the wrong impression. There are plenty of students who don't ever do that. You just need to be open about everything and be there for your girls."

He was sure she didn't think it was that simple, "just be there", but decided to drop it for now. Suki looked at him and knew the topic wasn't finished, not when it concerned his girls, and that it would require another car ride.

She did keep her promise to Ike, going with him to a public session of the tribal/state consortium on salmon issues. She soon understood his frustration. The hall was half full of observers. The members were seated at tables with piles of reports in front of them, microphones at hand. As soon as they reviewed one problem, argued it, at times someone proposing an action they could all agree on, but more often finding objections or complications, then another problem took its place. And they never got simpler. To her, the participants, all of whom obviously wanted to save the salmon, were bogged down over strategies. Ike noted the commercial fishermen didn't even come to the meetings anymore, if they ever had.

"I don't know how to be useful here," she complained to him at a coffee break. And she was envious that he had easily kept his part of the bargain. Even though he had told her he felt foolish, he had gone to talk to her college class about the river from thousands of years' perspective. The students had listened raptly and inundated him with good questions. Unlike fisheries meetings, he had felt his time well spent and his duty to her accomplished.

Suki complained, "I don't feel I'm any use at all at a fishery meeting. I want to yell at you all to quit debating and agree on a project and do it. Salmon need you to act."

"Don't you see us trying to do that?"

"Well, hang in there!"

Then, one rare clear day in early October she was rushing through the campus to catch a ride to one more fishery meeting, she swore her last, and she found Jason waiting with Ike by the truck. She almost didn't recognize him. With his braids cut, he looked like all the other college boys who came to the UW from every part of the world. And he was taking part in the fishery meetings? *Hurray! Mom, a tangible outcome from the bullsnake's energy?* She congratulated him that he'd gone back to college, this time to the Pasco campus.

"Yeah, I did it. I just needed time to think."

Suki asked how Alice had managed to spring him from jail so fast. "Only a day, Jason?"

He looked away, shuffled his feet, embarrassed. "You guys probably won't like it, and I sure didn't, but...well, they never saw me at the island, so the only charge was for my speech at the radio station. Disturbing the peace."

"A crazy act." Ike shook his head.

"Yeah? But they dropped even that at court. You can thank Grandma Alice, Suki. She blamed my bad behavior on the college professors, ha-ha. She met with the Plant people and told them I'd gotten all upset over what was said in a social science class. That the government knew a long time ago the Hanford waste tanks were eroding and would be leaking soon. And she said my instructor claimed nothing was being done, which was criminal. She told them

I'd reacted impulsively 'like kids do for these respected educators'—he quoted Alice in a faked pleading voice—'*and the boy did something foolish. Those professors, you know, the kids look up to them.*' That's what she told them! Yuk! A professor had nothing to do with it, for me anyway. So I was humiliated, but I kept my mouth shut. You don't defy my grandma lightly, right, Ike? And they accepted it. *Those damn professors!* Case closed. They knew better of course, just wanted it closed."

Suki and Ike laughed so hard that people passing by turned to look at them.

Jason went on, "But I'm not going to let it be closed. I'm not going to do any lone warrior stuff, or latch onto whoever comes paddling down the river with wild ideas. It's going to be well thought out. But I'm not going to let the waste issue dry up, and I'm not going to just smile at their idea of a so-called museum honoring the bomb either. And don't get pissed now, Ike, but sure, I am doing this partly for Arni, and people like him that are a little different, that get offed, or discounted, or punished some way by the great global industrial complex."

Ike gave a surprised laugh. "Whuff! That's some classes you're taking!"

"Well, it's the truth isn't it? Are these new discoveries? I don't think so."

"Old truth, just bigger words."

Ike was relieved that his nephew was making a lot more sense than two months ago.

"What about the kayakers? Have you heard from them?"

"Yup, through the grapevine. Plotting something to do with the Hanford Plant again, I'm not sure what."

Suki gave him a raised eyebrow, "Be careful, hum? Do you know how they got off so easy—'misdemeanor trespassing'? How about her backpack with the so-called bomb?"

"Oh, she threw it out in the river as soon as she made it back to the island, just a minute before the security boat came roaring up. That must have got her pants wet!"

Suki smiled and glanced at Ike. She wasn't going to say anything about what actually set off the alarm unless Jason brought it up; he surely knew by now. Ike shrugged. *Up to you.*

She passed. That evening Ike treated them to buckets of clams at a waterfront restaurant as a break from salmon worries. But Suki's ears perked up when she heard that Jason was taking an elective class, "The History and Future of Energy".

Ike said, "That should be interesting and useful. Have you gotten to nuclear energy yet?"

"Oh yes, we actually started with Chernobyl, and then went back in time."

Ike frowned, "How about wind energy? Got lots of that over in our country."

"Yes, we talked about that. A very old idea and getting new attention."

Suki said, "But what's your conclusion about nuclear plants—so far?"

He grinned at her, "I haven't changed my mind, just my methods." After a moment he added, "I guess I have some apologizing to do, though. Especially to Bruce."

She gladly gave him Bruce's phone number, but she and Ike both wondered what new methods he had in mind.

⋅⇥▪▭ ▭▪⇤⋅

On Suki's next weekend trip to Wolf Rapids, Ike's younger daughter, Judy, couldn't keep the secret of the skit topic any longer. They were almost ready to perform their grand entrance into the dramatic world: "It's 'The Flight of the Dung Beetles' and the kids all danced around in glee. *What?* Suki was flummoxed. She had assumed that a serious play was in the works. How could an audience take a skit on bugs seriously? Why had Ike let them have free choice—just kids! But he had. And she found out that when Esau had seen the kids were restless, he had told them about the beetles, and of course made it a colorful story just waiting to be staged: the waste problem, a debate over fleeing the Plant area, the beetles' actual flight. An action play! Suki had to control herself. *My god, how can they allow kids to make a joke out of that monstrous place?*

"The story, the plot, was already there! And now we have the costumes and the speeches figured out," Starla explained. "We just need to practice a couple times."

"Wow! That's amazing, kids!" *And after all the time I've put in? What can be done?* She looked for Ike, but he'd slipped away, wanting no part in a conflict between his daughters and his sweetheart. She knew it was an honest mistake, but she excused herself, about to explode, and took Alice aside. *Help!* Alice wanted to burst out laughing but swallowed it fast when she saw Suki's look. Her solution was quick and simple.

"We'll tell them it's fine; they can put the play on right here. Everyone will get it—how it's funny, but really, it's serious. Suki, we have lots of stories like that, lots. Then, if they want to put on different play down at Richland, or anyplace, they need to come up with one just as good but more clearly serious. And then I think I can find a group that will host them."

Ike had slipped back to listen. "Thanks, Auntie, good solution."

Suki saw the kids already carrying over the costumes they'd worked on: black trash bags, sticks, egg cartons, and twine, all turned into bug bodies, legs, heads, and wings, with headbands and twigs for feelers, and donated make-up for faces. Two hours later the first dress rehearsal was hilarious, the kids very proud, and Alice had to remind Suki again that Wolf Rapids people would see the serious message with no problem. *But what about the kids? Do they see it?*

In the evening Suki and Ike went on their customary walk along the river. Again, the wind was hard to walk against, blowing sand in their faces, so they turned to walk the other way.

"Doesn't the wind ever quit here?"

"Once in a while. Why don't we have a wind energy project here, I wonder?"

"Hey, why not?" But her thoughts went back to the skit, the hilarity over it. Behind it lurked another question. Was anyone beside herself really serious about the toxic monstrosity so close-by? She knew Esau and Alice were, and Bruce of course. How much did the rest of Ike's people care? Or the settlers? Or the world? Just the Great Bear Lake folks? As soon as she'd returned from Nagasaki she'd done as she'd promised and called the Dene' man and found out she'd missed him. He was in Ottawa with another delegation, she was told, demanding government acknowledgement of the suppressed information, and admission of the physical damage and deaths caused among his people. Who else was admitting anything in Canada or the U.S.?

Now she asked Ike, "Has there been any other apology you know of besides Pt. Radium workers?"

He guessed the thought behind it. "You're maybe wondering about us, with it right in our backyard? I don't know. If the idea of an apology was ever brought up, I never heard. But you know, we never worked in the Plant. We didn't know what was going on there."

"Neither did the Great Bear Lake people. The uranium was just shipped out. I've read more about it; lots of information has been released."

"Suki, we never asked to have the plant built here."

"Neither did the Great Bear Lake, I'll bet. I just wonder how many people here, or that were here before they got evicted, would want to make an apology? Just wondering."

He pondered her point as they walked on. *But what good are apologies unless you work to make changes?*

"You know, I didn't even think about it enough until just lately, when so much started coming out in the news about the dangers here. Suki, we can't change what happened fifty years ago. Let's concentrate on what we can do now."

But he heard his words, and how they stretched to other debates, and Esau's view: how "now" couldn't escape the past.

She said, "And it's not too late, now, for the U.S. to apologize, too."

Ike closed his eyes. *Not another big project!*

Then they heard people coming. Two young dogs came racing up and jumped on them, Starla and Judy close behind.

Starla began, "Dad, what you said, I do need to go to a bigger school. Seriously."

Good! "Oh, really? So you can get more science and math?"

"Well, uh… more sports!"

Judy cried out, "And she wants to leave me here alone!"

Ike was totally off-guard: this from Starla, his prize student? Well, maybe it could be a deal: sports, but heavy on science and math too. And why not for Judy as well? Suki watched curiously. *So this is what it's like to be a parent now!* She didn't remember having that sort of conversation at that age. But she didn't have memories of many happy conversations at that age of any kind, not with her father so ill. How she loved these girls' bouncy energy, just like the pups they played with. The four strode along, the girls talking about "a real high school". When they arrived back at the house, Jason was there. He had hitchhiked up from Pasco, to get some real food, as he explained it, and was wolfing leftover salmon. He found out they were going to have one more short class that evening, asked if he could sit in to listen. Alice, knowing he was popular with the kids, said yes.

"As long as you sit in the back and don't say much unless they ask you."

Later, Suki thought that Jason, attending closely, had something operating beside simple curiosity. When she asked Ike about it, he shrugged and told her Jason's grades so far were okay.

"I think he's got more than grades in his head."

Later, when Ike asked him again about classes and activities, Jason simply smiled.

"Well, keep it legal, huh, Jason? If you want to see this heritage center win a grant."

"Hey, Ike, I'm not into throwing things at fences."

"Okay. But you're with students with all that energy and no experience. Think about it."

"I think about it all the time. How about you? I hear you are trying to pass off the fisheries duties."

"To you, maybe. If I do, it'll be to take on something else important."

"Suki?" A smirk.

"Are you jealous? It's okay. Yeah, Suki. But something else, too."

CHAPTER 29

WHO HAD IT WORSE?

THE NEXT FRIDAY Suki and Ike were at Esau's and Alice's for what they knew could be the last meeting with the kids for a while. The hay loads were finished; Ike had rustled one more load of potatoes to go across to a number of highway roadside stands. After this he had no more hauls for sure, while Suki had to apply herself to her two unwritten papers. The kids' class that evening was to be about the future of nuclear energy: the risks, the gains, what it meant for the generation growing up. She decided she would talk a little about what happened at Chernobyl, just enough for kids, so they would understand the danger was not only from bombs. She would explain that too many had denied the facts or refused to talk about this for too long.

Ike had already passed onto his daughters the story of the apology from Port Radium and saw how fascinated they were. They wanted to go see the great arctic lake and the town, "We can put on our skit for them!" They were disappointed to hear there was no way to drive there. Then they thought of Japan.

"Why haven't we made an apology?" Judy, said, "We can go do it ourselves!"

Esau, sitting off to the side and listening to this excitement, broke in to tell them they didn't have to travel so far.

"You girls, the Spokanes, our neighbors, discovered uranium on their reservation in the Fifties. And the price was good so they decided to develop a mine, and everyone was happy—big paychecks for years. You think the government warned them of the risks? It did not, even though it knew. And lots of places have these uranium mines. Anyway, the Spokanes told me they took the dust home on their clothes and their bodies. After a while the price dropped and the mine closed. I don't know when they noticed the big increase in cancers, but the guy said all four of his brothers developed it. So, you students, why didn't Indian Health Service or Public Health or someone educate those Spokanes? How could they know? When the mine reopened for a while in the 1980s everyone's wearing masks. Hanford isn't the only scandal, just the worst."

Judy said, "Why do we need to have uranium mines?"

Esau frowned, "You should remember! That's what our other neighbors made the plutonium from for the A-bomb!" And he waved down river.

Starla looked at her sister and made vomiting motions.

Esau said, "The Navajos found out the same about their uranium mines."

Starla said, "Did you talk to the Navajos, Grandpa?"

"No, I read, I read! That's the only good thing the BIA ever did for me—made me learn to read. You girls be sure to be good readers, not just good at lay-ups."

Starla rolled her eyes.

The class on Saturday went well, even though the topic was so grim, so many accidents at nuclear plants where there were no bombs produced, just power, and what must be done for people to be safe. The students decided they wanted to send letters and photos to Port Radium families.

After breakfast on Sunday the girls asked her to play card games with them, but she postponed that. She wanted to be out on the riverbank alone with Ike. He had told her he had indeed thought of a project for himself, not counting the fisheries meetings. He had said he couldn't tell what it was yet, but she would like it.

It was with windy again from the southwest as the two walked downriver and then up on a rise so they could see as far as possible. Each was waiting on the other to begin. As they stood hand-in-hand, gazing at the bluffs and river, Suki happened to peer downriver, then whispered, "Oh, damn, there it is again. I can't get away from it ever."

She pointed at a distant thread of steam rising until the wind dispersed it.

"Will it ever go away? It's horrible, what was cooked up there! You can't imagine it, Ike!"

He saw her sudden fury. He thought the trip to Nagasaki had stoked anger inside her, now to flare up.

"Maybe I can. It's not only your people that have been slaughtered. History is full of it." As soon as he said that he wished he hadn't.

"This is history, Ike! Two cities full of innocents, flattened! Hundreds of thousands of people, mostly civilians, families, roasted! Three generations now, living with the scars. No other people has suffered that."

"Suki." He put his arm around her. "It was horrible, yes. But do you know, more of my people were scarred, a lot more. All across America, and millions, not thousands. The difference is…just not in two days."

He wasn't looking at her, but she saw how his jaw clenched.

"What? How can you compare, it? The bombs were deliberate, carefully planned to slaughter thousands. What happened to your people, I know…but it's happened throughout history when one group invades another's territory. It's very ugly, but it's…"

"We don't know how many died here in America, never will." He wouldn't look at her.

"But it was mainly disease, wasn't it."

"Suki, swarms of hungry people, and greedy ones too, coming from Europe—they wanted the land and they were going to get it one way or another, weren't they? Disease just made it faster. Every treaty was broken whenever they wanted more land. Every treaty. So…to reservations. And you know what that's like, eh? Maybe worse than the internment camps, and the reservations kept shrinking. And you've heard about the Aleut people, also U.S. citizens, that got sent to camps?"

She tried to think how to answer. "Yes, I know." She took a long breath and thought he must have given this speech before. Her resentment flared. *He cares nothing for the Japanese people; why should he? He doesn't even know them.*

He touched her cheek but she shook it off. He burst out as if he'd heard her thoughts.

"I never really have known any Japanese people—or Japanese American, hardly any. But Japan started the war, remember. Took over a lot of Asia for itself didn't it? Did its own slaughtering? Treated its prisoners horrible? Am I making this up? And anyway, why didn't the emperor surrender after the first bomb? He knew they were losing. And my people never started the wars with the whites; they were fighting to hold onto their homes, their subsistence. And now the U.S. has rebuilt Japan to be a world power. Who rebuilt the Native American nations, huh? Reservations, yeah."

He stopped, chagrined at his own flare-up, and not even sure of his facts. What was the use of this? She didn't answer, wouldn't look at him. How could she answer about what the emperor chose to do, or why? Or how/why Japan was rebuilt to be a world power? She could only tell what happened to the common people like her own family.

But with her silence, he couldn't help going on, "And speaking of museums again, America has the heart to create a Holocaust Museum to remind people of that genocide, but we can't tell the truth about Native American genocide?"

Her voice shook in her answer, "So Ike, how is it 120,000 were in the internment camps here, but just for Japanese and Japanese Americans? This country never put any German American or Italian American U.S. citizens in camps. Well, now the government does admit it was racism. Nothing else!"

He stopped and stared at her angry face. Then his voice dropped low, his eyes soft. "Of course it was. Hey, what are we arguing about, Suki?"

"We're not arguing! We're discussing, trying to get at the truth." She walked away a few steps. He had earlier thought about how great it would be to find a grassy low spot and make love. *Forget that.*

She turned, swallowed her angry tone. "Ike...sorry, I get this way in U.S. history classes sometimes. I must stop this! What good does it do? I don't know. But I was at that museum at Nagasaki just a short time ago, and I haven't told you all of it. So...you're saying, that what happened here was worse than Nagasaki and Hiroshima?"

He knew he should just drop it. "My people didn't die in two cities by the hundreds of thousands, no. They were pushed and pushed away from their land, to land no one wanted...or not yet, but soon enough. Land for more Europeans. Moved on, and then moved again. One little town or village, one camp after another, year after year, people shot, bayoneted, raped, infected, starved, frozen. I'm sorry, but didn't Japanese soldiers...?" He stopped. He knew some tribes had also carried their own small massacres of settler groups. But nothing like what happened to his people.

"Oh, Suki, what's the difference? It's all…murder…yeah, isn't it? Now some people call it all war crimes. I do."

He has not seen the hideous scars that some of Nagasaki's old people are now finally showing in public, no longer so afraid of being rejected, even by their own people. After decades, no longer having to argue to get treatment for pain. I'll take him there, to a real museum.

But she couldn't answer him yet, and he removed his hand from her shoulder and strode away down the ridge, alarmed at all the emotion that had surged up. He took a few deep breaths. *It's insane, this argument—who got treated worse! Who's the worst murderers! My god.* But she followed him down and waited a moment while he kept his back turned.

Her voice was low now. "Ike, you're right. Our histories have more in common than anything so different. What's important to me now is to make sure this doesn't happen again, and the way to do that is to be sure people know. I want them to know, and feel, and not forget! Sorry I blew up…at you of all people. I'm sorry."

He turned around to see her wiping tears. "It's okay." *I wish I could cry.* He took her hand and gave it a warm reassuring squeeze. *I have to understand this. She's closer to the pain than I am. She goes to Nagasaki every year; she feels she owes that— and gets another dose. I know, I've seen the photos after the bombs. Here, I see wounded children everywhere, but the scars are mainly invisible till you get close, see inside. They're tangled, the lines pointing all directions now. In Japan, I don't know what it's like today. One big empire against another, or marching side by side? Where are the common people in that picture—I can guess, but I don't know. I only know what happened here. But now here, all the more pain for her. My parents died, but not like her father, not slowly in front of me. I understand; she's afraid of more loss.*

He got her to turn and look back upriver, away from the torturing smoke-like steam, and showed her how he took deep breaths when he felt the rage of demons inside. He felt her calming down as she held onto his arm.

I need to find out more. "You've lost a lot, I mean you, personally. Family?"

"Yes…but especially my dad, later. Like I told you."

He nudged her to start walking back up the river, turned away from the Plant, holding her hand, feeling she was keeping things back from him. He knew about these un-talked things that made trouble. Better to talk, and not just about the bomb.

After a few moments he made himself say, "I know that was tough for you, and how your father ended up drinking too much when he got so sick. So…is that another thing that worries you, people that drink too much? And could die? And like Indians drink too much, some of them?"

She took a deep breath. "My dad, yes…anyone drinking a lot, yes, sure it bothers me. All around me on the campus. I don't even know if you ever drink." *What do you do, besides drive, when you're not with me? I don't know!*

He thought about his plans for his girls on a campus. *No way are they going to do that!*

"Well, I did my share earlier. And one day I woke up and, oh-oh, I noticed I had two little daughters to raise. And I knew what booze does to families, so…everything in my life got changed, big time."

"You know I'm very happy for your girls. You've done so well. But as for boozing? Families that never went through such things as my family did? I don't understand it. People with simple, safe lives."

"Simple? I don't know. You could see for yourself what was causing your dad's crash. For many people it isn't so right in the face. Everyone has problems to deal with. Maybe listening to bad stuff from the past too much. Or maybe just burying it, and then it pops up. Or, Suki, maybe just not being able to find a good path for yourself, nothing that really grabs you."

"So what about you? What's grabbing you?"

He reached for her hand, pulled it toward his leg.

"I'm serious, Ike!"

"My kids grab me. Now you too! And I do have a new project in mind. That's plenty."

"Not fisheries?"

"No, well that, too, until I get someone to take my place."

"Oh, good. And I've been waiting to hear, what is your new project?"

"Hum, well, how about I sue the government for all the land and fishing rights taken away from the Washington and Oregon Indians? Maybe Idaho too."

"Come on, Ike, get serious! That's what I wonder about for us. It's not a joke; everyone has to have something to challenge them that they really care about. Whatever is right for them. Right now it seems like you're angry a lot about what's been assigned to you. That's why I say, it must be your own project!"

Oh, that's the way I seem? "Me, angry? Could be, Suki. I do notice a lot of anger around us. And people can't stay angry forever, or they do end up drinking. *Like Bruce, he'd better be careful.* Yeah, we must...to quote Aunt Alice, 'turn that around and replace it with positive action.' I hear that a lot; it's what she says to her clients." He paused, then laughed a bit. "Is this what you worry about for us, Suki, that we won't be active enough, that we won't hunt rabbits anymore, or swim in the river, or even go to meetings, and we'll just sit at home, bored angry drunks?"

She smiled, but hoped he was listening. He put his arm around her and steered her to keep walking back toward the house, to the waiting family. *I'm sure not going to tell her my own nightmares, not for a while anyway. Maybe lately it's been too much of "save the world" for her? I should take her set-netting. Real life.*

At the house, they found Esau holding the attention of Judy and Starla.

"Think of it, girls! Scooping up baby salmon, dumping them in a truck to go down to the ocean!" He gave them his quizzing look.

Sharla said, "Trucks? Why, Grandpa?"

Ike broke in, "The river is too low for them to swim." He and Suki found space to sit on the floor.

Esau frowned. "Hey, let the kids answer. Now hear a solution just as good. Get a whole army of trucks, fill 'em up with crushed ice at the fish plants down on the coast, drive them up the mountains and dump the ice in all the creeks. It melts and runs down and the rivers rise up. There go the little fish downstream, just like they should! What's wrong with that?"

For a minute no adult in the room could keep from giggling, but then Judy said, "But Grandpa, if the river is so low how can the fish plants pump enough water to make enough ice to truck up the mountains?"

"Smart girl."

Starla, not to be beaten, said, "And if the river is so low, how can the dam make enough electricity to sell, so they can make the ice? Or run the gas pumps so they can gas up those trucks?"

More laughter. Esau looked at Ike. "These girls should be the ones going to the meetings."

"I know. That's what I keep thinking." And he was also thinking, but didn't say, *Sure they're smart; their mother had more than powwow dancing in her brain.*

"So, Uncle, are you going to the next meeting with me?"

Esau shook his head. "We talked enough about it. No, I'm not. I'm going to work on the Heritage Center where I have more chance to be listened to. I'll tell your managers, and you pick one of these younger guys to go with you. They never saw Celilo Falls; they know it's an important story, but it's not a terrible pain to them."

He's right on that. He saw his uncle's mind was truly made up. "Okay, if that's what you want. Help me then, find someone to go with me and learn that frustrating job."

CHAPTER 30

STUDENTS STIR THINGS UP

Jason heard that a fellow student named Keene was looking for him. Jason had transferred to the Pasco campus so recently that he hardly knew anyone yet. Why would someone want to see him? The message bearer said, "Keene is the guy with the 'Make Love Not War' T-shirt. He must have a couple of them; that's all he ever wears. Maybe his shorts too."

Jason smirked. *Pretty good.* He guessed then it might be about his grand act at the radio station. He'd already gotten a few thumbs-up and head shakes for it. When he finally spotted the t-shirt, it turned out that Keene had joined in on a day of the settlers' reunion, partly for a paper he had to write for his Washington History class and partly for his own interest as a descendant of the early orchardists. But Leon's question that day: *"What was the worst thing for the settlers?"* had pointed to Keene's own special issue, one shared by several other campus students. How had Richland residents been so callous as to allow their kids (*the Richland Bombers*), and indeed some local businesses (*The Bomb Hatch*) to use their local popularity to brag about the destruction of cities full of civilians?

Yes, it was an effort to stop a terrible war, Keene believed, but when did moral communities brag about such an act? *Yeah, when did the U.S. ever brag— yeah, brag—about the fire-bombing of Dresden?* The comparison had come to him from his class in modern world history. Yet, he wondered, was bragging any worse than hiding the truth? And there was the more immediate issue. He had been seeking out Jason to ask him if he had been the person at the radio station?

Jason didn't hesitate, "Yeah, sure, that was me. What did you think? Did you approve?"

"I'm all for doing something about the radioactive waste, yes. And a few other things. But did you gain anything?"

"Well, I got charged with disturbing the peace, but only at the radio station, that's all. So, probably better ways to protest. And to involve more people would be good…intelligent people."

"I know some intelligent people you'd probably like."

"Good…what are you thinking of?"

That Saturday Roger was on his way to an auction, just for fun. Passing through the center of Pasco, he saw a small group of people standing with signs on the sidewalk outside a super market. "WE WANT OUR RIVER CLEAN", "TOXINS & SALMON DON'T MIX." "JUSTICE FOR THE DOWNWINDERS". Roger recognized them as probably college students. Then he saw Keene, and he parked to investigate.

'Hi, Roger, you're welcome to join us!"

Roger looked over the group and their signs. College kids involved in the issues on the river? *Great!* Keene waved him over; he knew Roger, knew he liked to see action for the environment.

"This is just a trial run. We'll be doing it again next Saturday at Richland at noon—more people, more signs. We welcome anyone that agrees with us. What do you think? Will you come? And pass it along?"

"Sure, I will." Roger watched for a while, then went to find a phone. He got what he hoped for: Bruce so desperate for action that he was cleaning out a closet.

"You bet I'll be there next Saturday if this car runs. Maybe even if I have to hitch-hike."

Roger was pleased with Bruce's response but not surprised. He went back to watch the students as they stood with their signs and talked to passers-by. The kids were being peaceful and engaging. Then a passing pickup familiar to him slowed. *Wouldn't you know it.* He watched Croaker park and stride over to him.

"What's going on, Roger?"

"Hello, Walt. College students doing their own protesting. And I see you had a little fun with the feds lately."

"Yup. Made the news. I'd like to join those kids but I better not—on probation."

Roger thought he didn't look too unhappy about it.

After a minute Croaker said, "I wonder if they would carry a couple signs for me?"

"Uhh, they might. Anything positive and relevant they said. And they say bigger, next Saturday at Richland."

"Well, you're my critic, Roger. You'll be there? Hum, relevant...how about 'Justice for Evicted Settlers'?"

"Sounds good. Walt, just don't get rowdy. Let the college kids do their thing."

"Who, me, rowdy? That's why I'll stay away. How about 'Small Farmers Count Too'?"

"Sounds all right. Who's going to fight that?"

"If you'll be going, can I drop any signs off to you? I'm low profile for a while."

Roger wondered if Croaker was sincere or already planning a disruption. It was high risk, for sure, but he decided to take a chance since Croaker already knew all he needed to if he decided to make a scene.

"Okay Walt, if I agree with what you put on the signs. You're not going to get me to confuse these kids' message with your rangeland battles. One thing at a time."

"Do you think it's going to stay "one thing" with a bunch of college kids? But...all right."

"So, if you can stay polite, drop the signs off. I may make one too. Maybe 'Pay Up the Downwinders'. "

"Roger, sometimes you and me see eye-to-eye."

That'll be the day.

In Seattle, Leon was busy revising his essay, trying to change it into a publishable letter that still had punch, when his phone rang. He heard the excitement in Bruce's voice, something missing for a while.

"Hi, Leon! Hey, you still want to go someplace with me?"

"Yes, I think so. What's up?"

"A little different than we talked about, though I'm still planning on that. This is another event over at Richland, next Saturday. But students from the Pasco campus are involved this time."

Bruce explained the demonstration, that it included the steaming issues around the Hanford Plant and their effect on the river.

Leon threw down his pen and almost spilled his vodka. "I'm glad you called!"

"Yeah? I just thought you might like to go. They say anyone is welcome to join them that agrees with their general concern, health of the river."

"Do you need my car?"

Bruce counted his potential troops. "Marta is too involved, she says, but she needs to go. I want you to talk her into it. Suki's always too busy, but I'll bet she'll go. I thought I'd make a couple signs to wave. Any ideas? And yes, might need your car. I've got Keene's number if we want to ask anything. But now I need to track down Suki. Call you back."

Leon grabbed pen and paper again. *Signs!* He'd turn his essay into slogans. "Waste not, want not. We don't want your toxic waste!" *This could be fun. Or maybe trouble, of course.*

Later Bruce drove to Leon's sporting a smile like none Leon could recall from him.

"All set! Got Harold going. But where's Suki? Where's Elena when we need her?"

Leon returned him a smile just as big, "Why, Elena's on her way, as soon as she finishes a blessing at the Klamath. She called me early this morning, *'Leon, what's going on up there?'* I said I'd heard nothing. She knew about the student protest before I did!"

"Weird."

"But real. I've seen it a few times. By the way, when is that big nuke meeting?"

"I'm looking for the right one, but soon."

Bruce, back home and happy with his efforts, looked over at Marta, lost in her research.

"Harold's going, and I'm sure Suki will if I find her. Are you sure you don't want to go?"

No answer. Many hours of the day she said nothing to him. He was used to this.

"I asked you, are you sure...?"

"Yes, I'm sure. I'm really into something on the co-op. Harold recalls lots more details not in the memoir." Then she thought more. *Hey, you're on probation!* "Bruce, demonstrations can get rowdy. You shouldn't be involved in anything like that."

"I'll take off if that starts."

I'd better go; he can't know what might start. "Bruce, if I can ride with Harold and pick his memory some more, I'd like to go."

"Great. You'll be happy you went."

She took a swallow of cold coffee and rubbed her neck. "As for Suki, you might try Esau's place."

Returning from another riverbank walk, Ike and Suki found Alice packing them a sack-supper for their drive back to Seattle. She stopped and with a wink invited Suki outside to see what remained of her vegetable garden. Suki had learned that in such a small house when one wanted to speak privately one found an excuse to step outside.

Alice gave Suki a thoughtful look. "In case we don't see you for a while, we understand Ike's hopes for his daughters. It's okay; he's been thinking this way for a while. In a couple years they would have to go somewhere for high school anyway. Don't worry, we don't blame it on you. It's his idea, a good one in the long run."

"Well, I'm relieved you think so, because he's determined."

"Just a couple important things you can help with, Suki. Help him get the girls back here every month for a visit? We want them to remember this is their real home, always. And the other thing is, don't let him drop his duty to the salmon fishery. We have to have someone there going into the future. Any improvements, if they come, can disappear overnight if there's no one there to remember."

Suki smiled at the requests. "Auntie, I completely agree with both things, even if you'd said nothing. I'll be sure. Not that he lets me tell him what to do."

They were going back inside when the call came in from Bruce. Ike shushed everyone down; it was not usual for Bruce to call, and his voice was that of a man on a mission.

"Ike, you may want to know about this. Is Suki there? Good. Listen: Roger was driving over to Pasco today and he sees a bunch of college students standing with signs. They say their name is 'Students for a Clean Columbia.' How about that! They are for getting the waste taken far away. They want more people to join them next Saturday at Richland; I thought you'd want to know. And Suki—is she there? Got two cars going from here!"

He quoted some of the signs' messages. Ike took in the news and swallowed.

"Bruce, does Roger know if Jason is there?"

"He says he only knows one of them, named Keene. He seems to be their spokesman. I've got his phone number. They invite anyone to join them and to bring signs, anything relevant. What do you think?"

Ike could tell from his voice that Bruce was totally recruited, but he saw it as possibly good, possibly a problem...*Jason involved? And like Bruce, on probation?*

"Has anyone complained?"

"Just one guy driving by, hollered, 'Why aren't you kiddies in school?' Only person from the plant so far is Chuck, you know—the community liaison. Roger says Chuck looked at their permit, just shook his head and told them keep it peaceful; no shouting, no chanting, no throwing stuff, no insulting people."

Ike was thinking fast. "I need to know, if you can call this guy Keene, ask if Jason's around, and to have him call me, and soon."

"Okay. So what do you think? It's good, eh? Youth in action?"

"Uh…you bet! *Just what I was saying.* But I need to talk to Jason."

Bruce was in glee when he hung up; one more carload possible.

At Wolf Rapids, people waited to hear more as the news spread through the households. How had all this started? Esau shrugged, "It's Jason." Then he began to chuckle. An hour later came another call, and Ike, waiting, grabbed the phone again.

"Hi, Ike, this was sort of a practice they say. The big one will be next week."

"Jason, you're on probation. What are you thinking of?"

"Hey, I have nothing to do with this. I was up the street, just watching."

"Yeah, sure. You stay way off target."

"Okay, okay, don't worry. And there's an old white guy here, Roger, who knows you. And that you should come and bring some youth."

"Tell Roger hi. But what do you think the point is?"

"To make a statement, to get public support, man, you know."

"Well, one step up from running around with fake bombs. Are the kayakers involved?"

"No. They're at another campus. Hey, how come you're so wary of college kids speaking up? I heard you telling Alice that youth will be the ones to solve the problems. Well…?"

"Remember our Heritage grant? From the feds, right? We hope? I'd like to know what the kids' official goals are, what we're getting into. Who's going to listen to a bunch of college kids anyway? Except maybe the feds that we need our funding from."

"Okay, I'll get back to you with the goals. But nobody's going to listen? You ever hear of Martin Luther King? I have to remember you never took any real history classes."

Smart ass. "Call us soon, little nephew." Ike hung up and walked outside to cool down.

Esau stood up. "Good for those students! I like it—someone showing some guts."

Alice shook her head, "Ike's worrying too much about everything lately, and it's freezing him up. No more kid left in him."

Esau's eyes sparkled. "Well there's still kid in me! I want to go down there, is it next Saturday? And maybe join them."

Alice's eyebrows raised; she was not totally surprised.

Suki, hearing the whole thing, had been wordless so far. Now she had to speak. "Don't you want to go, Auntie? I'd love to see a demonstration about that Hanford Plant, if that's part of it!"

Alice went outside, followed by Suki, to confront Ike. "Esau says he's going down, maybe, to join those students."

"Great." Ike didn't look up and pulled out the cigarette pack that still stayed with him for such moments.

"Why are you so hesitant, Ike?" asked Suki.

"Hey, these folks put so much into planning this Center. It needs to get that grant."

"More publicity could help," said Alice.

He frowned at her, "That kind?"

Esau joined them, his eyes full of energy. "Do you know, where is my war bonnet?"

"Ohmygod." Ike threw down his cigarette and stomped it. "A war bonnet? Really?"

"Well, we're still at war, aren't we? In the courts, all the time? Until we get our horse pasture back and a lot of other acres? We're still at war."

Suki stared at him, wondering if Esau was serious about the costuming.

Alice said, "I think you ought to drive him down, Ike. If you don't he'll just find someone else."

"Okay! Uncle, you want your picture in the paper, fine. I'll drive everyone we can cram in the truck if that's what you want. War bonnets for everyone. Drums! Spears!"

Suki had never heard him talk that way to his elders. She never had to her own elders.

The girls joined them and began yelling in chorus, "We want to go! Go! Go!"

Starla saw Ike's look and cried, "Dad, don't be so stodgy."

"Stodgy! Where did you get that word?"

She laughed, "From you! You called the fish managers that last night!"

Ike waved her off. He hadn't talked to anyone yet of his worry over the display of footprints at the reactor fence. He saw he needed to, and now. He took Alice aside and explained. She saw the potential problem, but not a good reason to run and hide.

"Wait." She went to Esau, "Should I tell him about our new plan?"

"Go ahead. Feed him some spirit."

Alice went to their steaming nephew and put a hand on his shoulder. "Stop worrying, Ike. There are other ways to raise the funds if we lose the grant. I'll tell you something if you'll keep it confidential for now? Okay? You know our people up at Priest Rapids have a grant from the PUD that they say is enough to go ahead with their own heritage center. They say if our federal grant doesn't get approved we can combine with them. We have lots of valuable things here they could include, and they'll guarantee us a paid position. They do have a better location, you know, more away from the Plant. So one way or another the Wolf Rapids Wanapum will have a place in a heritage center. So. Now you can stop worrying."

Ike was relieved. "Auntie, that's...brilliant. When did you work all this out?"

"Last week, your uncle and I were up there."

He shook his head. Again, while others debated, or retold history, Alice got things done. *I should have been following her around more.*

Esau recruited more bodies for the protest, and by evening three small truckloads were organizing. Ike said no more on the topic. For now, he had to drive Suki and that last load of potatoes to Seattle. He was tossing things in his truck when Jason called back to report what the group's goals were: To get the removal of the waste expedited, to support the downwinder's case, and to be sure the river was cleaned up for salmon spawners. They planned to keep the action going until the weather got too cold. Then to start up again in the spring if needed. Ike thought it was just as he had feared, plenty to upset the Plant authorities. He thanked Jason, told him to be damned careful, and hung up to see the girls dancing around.

Suki was beaming, "Finally something solid!" She told him that she could probably catch a ride over with Bruce and meet him and the others at Richland.

Alice said, "And Harold? He's one that should go."

Ike frowned, "He is going. But what if someone gets arrested? You know what happened last summer."

Suki turned to Esau to see how he felt about that.

He was on the phone and waved his arm, "So let 'em."

The girls insisted their group go and put on the skit. Alice thought fast. She didn't want to see them disappointed, but there were only so many trucks, and was the skit appropriate, for what the college students had going? Or for the permit?

"Girls, here's a better idea. Lots of white people won't understand the dung beetles—the serious message. It's better to have another one that's clearer to them."

She explained the need to take time with a new skit, maybe make it a set. If they got the new one ready they could tour around with them.

"I promise we can get the invitations. People love to see kids perform: churches, tribal councils, art councils. They'll love it, believe me. But you can make signs now. Just not beetles."

As Ike and Suki left the girls were already sketching out slogans with a duet of giggles. 'SALMON LIVES—OUR LIVES'. Alice nixed 'EVEN BUGS KNOW TO GET OUT.'

Alice was used to being a problem-solver, but life kept getting more complicated lately. After some pondering, she saw another opportunity and motioned Esau outside.

"I just had another idea about this demonstration. You want to hear? Well, those young men working on the buildings—they need to do more than carpentry work. Like Ike says, they are the leaders of tomorrow. So we should stay home to let them have the space in the trucks. Tell them it's their chance to show they can drum and sing for the public. We don't need that experience, and we can stick to what we have to do."

She said nothing about so many footprints at the plant fence, how it could work against them. Why make him feel more to blame for Bruce's arrest? Esau gave her a long, calculating look.

"Oh, that's good, let's do that, have them show what they can do! But they need to understand—no joking around. So…I think I better be with them."

He went to tell others of the change. And no war bonnets. He'd been kidding, and Ike should have known that.

⋆⊨⊙ ⊙⊨⋆

Three days later Elena was at the Eureka airport about to catch a small plane to Portland, then on to Seattle, then Richland. She, too, was excited, heading back to the Mid-Columbia and the challenging energies around it. She had felt some success in her attempts at spiritual healings this year, but now she believed she had left the Columbia too soon. She had worked with such a variety of people there, some she thought of as friends, some as obstacles. Now what could be better: the youth had taken on the battle! It was their show. *But I will be there for them with prayers and do more if they ask.*

CHAPTER 31

CONFESSIONS

ONCE OVER THE pass with the potatoes, Ike stopped the truck at one of their vantage spots, one where they could look down the dark fir slopes toward Puget Sound. He commented that involving more youth in everything was the right strategy, and he was sorry he had been so crabby. He had been worried at a lack of serious planning, but maybe he was wrong; Suki had seemed not bothered at all. While they ate their sack-supper, she laughed as she dug in her memory for songs from undergraduate days to sing next week at the demonstration—if the moment came. "Down by the Riverside", "This Land is Your Land", and her own version of the old spiritual: "Go tell it on the mountains, to let our river flow," and sang them out at high volume to the Cascades.

"Wow, Suki. This is a whole other side of you!"

"You know what? I'm going to make up a couple signs for that reactor museum. 'Reactor Bee: Go Sting Yourself.' 'Museums: Tell the Dam Truth.' So, your ideas?"

"Funny, but we should be a little less aggressive maybe? We don't know much about the museum plan."

"We do know. I saw them. You seem like a cautious person. Didn't we agree that museums have to tell the truth?"

She's really rolling. "Sure, absolutely. But what do you mean, I'm cautious? Like compared to Bruce...or Jason?"

"Ha-ha...well?"

"Bruce is a wounded vet. Jason is a kid. I was like him once; I'm trying to get some balance now. Maybe you think I've gone overboard on that?"

"I just see it in myself; I've been too cautious, too worried to make a mistake. And now I feel like breaking loose."

"And look what you got!" He pulled her to him, "And aren't you glad?"

She hugged him back. "But I know what you're thinking. You're afraid it could be the heritage center versus a day's action. And I agree, it can't be just one day, or it's not worth much. But maybe it won't be. It could grow and grow. Ike, I'm tired of being patient. I was patient for years before I went to White Bluffs. And now I've done too little. I've been at the museum meeting, and a little refresher at Nagasaki. And I hear, 'be patient' from you and others. I'm tired of that. I'm going to call my mother. I want for her to come in the spring, can't we? Why drag our feet, Ike?"

"Does it seem like I drag my feet? I'm running fast as I can to keep up!"

She laughed, then was quiet, and he thought he could almost see the wheels spinning in her head as they drove. But the students' demonstration was a week away, and he had his own question now.

"So, come on, Suki, talk about cautious! I've been waiting to hear from you!"

"I was waiting to hear from you, I thought."

"Okay. I know what you think, that I need to have a project of my own and keep out of your hair. Well, I told you, I do have a project, an idea for one anyway. I just have to check out a few things before I go public." He grinned at her. "You also think I need to stick with the salmon issues. Well, it's more complicated, that whole scene. While you were gone I went to another meeting, and there was new information I want to tell you about. But I still have to have a real job, not just challenges. Because if we are all together, someone's got to have a job, right? And I'm thinking long-range—I hope you are?"

"I am."

Well, looking ahead, when you have your degree, don't you, um, want to have children? *Hope I'm not going too fast.* I mean for us to have children? And babies would take your attention. So I for sure would need a steady job by then." He saw her face, not encouraging. "Well, maybe I'm jumping ahead a little?"

Babies? I've known you not even two months! "Uh…no, we don't really have to…have babies."

"Oh? But I thought you liked being around kids. You like the students."

"Oh, I do. I really love your girls especially."

"Well. I need a job, not begin six years of college."

She looked out at the wooded slopes and didn't answer for a while. He waited.

"Ike, I don't have to have babies. I haven't planned on it."

She could see that he was bewildered. *He thinks all women want to have babies.* She had to tell him; he was waiting. This wasn't going to be easy; her throat grew a huge lump she had to work down.

"Why no kids, Suki?" *Is this something about being from two different cultures? No, she's like me; she's already used to dealing with that.* He looked over at her, saw how upset she was.

"I haven't been completely open with you, Ike, I'm sorry. But now I have to be. I can't...have kids...well, maybe I can, but I shouldn't. Okay, a long story, but time you knew."

He was in shock. *Do I know this woman, really?* He heard her long troubled sigh.

"Well, truth is, I'm adopted. The woman I went to see is my adopted mother, and my father that died, he was my adopted father. My real mother was a little kid in Nagasaki at the time of the bomb. When she was about seven, her own mom died of radiation sickness. My mother was pretty close to the center of the explosion, I think, but she wasn't really given treatment for any problem. She became one of the many orphans studied by scientists as to the effects of radiation."

"Oh, Suki."

"Yes. The young people were warned of the risks of passed-on defects, but she grew up, got married anyway, many did, and had me in 1970. And then she died of cancer when I was about five, and my real father already had died of some kind of cancer. I lost both of them. And I became one of the second generation of orphans from the bomb effects. Ike, those serious defects could still show up."

Ike had known so many heartbreaking stories among his own people; why hadn't he guessed there was more to tell from Suki? He knew people who couldn't forget, yet couldn't talk about events that had shaped them. *When she exploded down at the river, when she would cry out at night and wake me?* He was shocked but glad she had opened up, and felt he should do more of that now.

"Suki, why didn't you tell…"

She was going on, "For some years Japanese Americans and others came across from the U.S. to find the orphaned kids and adopt them. So the woman I just went to see, my adopted mother, has been a real mother to me, and a wonderful one, Ike. And the one I know as my grandmother is her mother— another survivor, one who took care of many orphans. I told you that after I was in college, my mother went to Nagasaki to take care of her, old now, with plenty of her own physical damage to deal with. A brave, generous woman, my adopted grandmother."

Speechless, all Ike could do was stare at her, at her tears blinking. He had his own thoughts about orphanages and boarding schools, stories he'd heard plenty of times from his own people.

"And you were in an orphanage for a while. That was real hard."

She looked out into the forest, and it calmed her. "That place. All I remember is people going back and forth, and me—scared to do anything. I remember just sitting by the wall, or being herded around. Crying at night, traumatized is the word. Most of the kids probably the same."

"But you survived it."

"I did. I was so, so lucky, got adopted by an understanding family, my own family. It was probably only a year I had to wait. Then they home-schooled me a year here. And I gradually got over being so shy at school. I forced myself to, or maybe I wasn't naturally that shy to start with. It was all fine…until my dad got ill."

She was quiet for a while. *Have I told him enough about my childhood? Everyone has childhood pain of some kind.* "But, back to your question…so, my love, I could be like my real mom. I could be carrying those defects. I could come down with cancer or some terrible thing anytime. I don't want to have kids and have them become orphans like I was. And kids who might carry those defects from me? I couldn't stand that. I know, it's a slim chance, I know the risk is very low now, but they are still studying these things in Japan, and they have not reached a conclusion yet. I mean, as to how long those defects, like micro-cephaly, are passed on. Most people would probably put it aside. I know they do, but I can't, Ike. I've heard of cases…And I've gotten used to the decision."

Ike had to get out a smoke to help take all this in, then made a face and threw it away.

"So these damages still go on?"

"Yes, at a higher rate for the people whose parents, as kids, were close to the bomb, or inside the mother who was close. It's a choice people make, whether to have children."

She took a long shaky breath. He saw then how his girls were important to her. *It's not just me.* He reached over and wrapped his arms around her.

After a while she went on in a brighter voice, "Ike, I'll probably live to be ninety. And of course we can always adopt children, after I get through this college siege and have a good job. And you already have such terrific kids."

He took a deep breath. "Well, thank you for telling me. Suki, it's okay, it's okay. I'm sure glad I have these girls I can share with you." He hugged her more.

After a moment she said, "I suppose you've been wanting a son. Men do want one."

"No, no, that's not so true anymore. These girls of mine can do anything a guy can and probably more. That's what I see. No, I haven't been thinking that way."

She didn't completely believe that, but perhaps. They were both quiet for a few minutes, realizing they still had much to learn about each other.

Then she said, "So, you see, I am more than happy to help get your girls through college. As my adopted mother has helped me, and after my dad died, all on her own, Ike, at hard menial jobs. She still does."

I can't know her pain, really, her deciding no children. I never had to decide that; I never even decided to have children…I was handed gifts.

After another quiet time he asked, "Do you remember your real mother?"

She wiped her eyes. "A little. My best image is that we are at a beach, and we are playing in the water. But I can't picture her face."

More pain there. "Your life, lots of bravery there."

He kissed her hand. "Suki, I love you a whole lot, you know that, right? And, as for kids, believe me, I have enough kids. I'm very lucky to have them, and they are just right."

He reached to start the truck and after a nod from her, moved out onto the highway. She hoped he was telling the truth. *Anyway, I have no more secrets from him.* After a few miles she wanted to go on to another topic— how to finish her two still missing class assignments. If he would help again.

"Can I ask yet another favor of you, Ike?"

"Anything...almost."

"I have this other class where I have to do an interview and write it up. Can I do one of you? Because when do I have time lately to interview anyone else?"

Back to the papers! "Oh, Esau would be better."

"Well I have to do a short article too. I think I can make one up from everything he told me of the history around the river. But is the interview of you okay if I make it anonymous?"

"Well, if anonymous. I don't think the great leaders would appreciate me shooting off my mouth on how stupid fisheries management is."

She raised an eyebrow, "I could give you a fake name, like Jeremiah Angry Hawk."

He grinned. "Maybe not quite that attention grabbing? Like...John Hawk, maybe. Uhh, can I see it before you turn it in?"

"No time for that. I can just leave out the insults. But it won't be nearly as interesting."

"Well then, if you make me sound angry, say I'm a treaty tribe Indian, don't say Wanapum. They don't think us Wanapums are important. Good enough?"

"Okay. Thank you again, a whole lot. And I'm glad my own problem is out in the open now. So are you going to tell me what your idea for your project is? Because we're back to that other question. Like I told you, my life as a student is different from what you've seen with me so far. Where are you in this picture, my man so full of energy and intelligence? So I'm over in the corner buried in books, you come home, wolf down a dinner maybe you made, you fall asleep in front of TV, and I'm still scribbling away, facing a deadline. End of romance."

He shook his head. "My project? First I have to check out some information, I said. I know you'll like it."

"Come on, tell me."

He muttered something under his breath in his own language.

"What did you say? I'll bet you said bossy woman."

"You're right! You can read minds?"

"It's the common response—universal, I'm guessing. And while I'm being bossy, don't tell me again 'we will pass it on to the youth'. Ike, you are not seventy! Sure, the youth will inherit the problems, but they need decades more of your leadership."

He felt a little bullied. But then a snapshot of his children's mother burst out. The pow-wow dancer, so totally engaged she was in that life, and he didn't fit in, and let it show. He'd drifted, and she'd left him behind. *And Esau picked me up, gave me an assignment I don't like much. Why be mad at Suki for all this? Okay, I get it.*

"I'll tell you just as soon as I check some things out, see if it can work."

Suki, much relieved, was ready to talk about something less contentious: another paper on salmon. The professor had given the class an odd question, and she wanted somehow to tie it in with everything she'd been thinking about these recent weeks: rivers, radioactive waste, future of nuclear energy, human societies, salmon, and their management—how they all were related. And she believed Elena had seen this, how the river itself (and other rivers, too?) was what so many of the stories circled around. She got out her notebook and started diagramming the connections. Ike glanced over at her spider web drawing.

"What the heck is that?"

"It's the Chiawana. And these lines are the stories, so many stories, the connections to the Columbia. Lewis and Clark had another one—here." She drew it in.

Ike laughed, "Oh, those guys. We had to give them dog meat to eat, they were so sick from having nothing but dried salmon and not being used to it."

"They were used to dog meat?"

Good, you can joke again. "Maybe they just needed any change of diet."

"That's what we are—for each other?"

"Dog meat? Or change of diet? That's got to be it."

He reached over to give her knee a horse bite. She thought about all that had happened since she'd walked into that settlers' reunion and introduced herself to Bruce, and how her simple comment about the eviction had started a spin. Or was it Harold's memoir that started it all? She put the question to Ike.

"No, Suki, it was you started all this."

"Then you mean my mother. Wait a minute! I had nothing to do with the kayakers, or Jason's little gambit either. And I'd never met Elena, never even heard of her, never had met Bruce either, or Marta, or Leon, or Harold. I never decided to go on a trek down all the reactor fences. And I got drafted to teach some kids by what person? And who came up with the idea about going to the reactor museum committee? Who brought in the story of Port Radium? And by the way, who gives the cool little speech on the reunion bus, hummm?"

"Okay, okay. Well? Weren't they good ideas? But I said I would help you with any salmon paper. So don't I have to? What's the topic this time?"

She dug in her notes. "Here it is: '*Why should people who will never fish for salmon, who probably will never even eat one or see one, care about the way they are managed?*'"

"Wow! He's making you work this time. That's a different kind of question. This professor of yours is a thinker; he must be quite a guy. What's he look like?"

"Don't worry. He's old."

He snorted, then drove in silence, thinking about the question, looking out at the western forested foothills. He pictured the creeks flowing through them, and the tiny stump ranches scattered about those hills and streams. Those people probably ate salmon, even fished for them at times. But how about people much further removed? Why should they care? And for that matter, why should anyone who would never see the Chiawana care about it? They had their own rivers to worry about.

So why should everyone care about salmon? Everyone? He thought of the different committee meeting last week that he had attended, just to have a look at the bigger picture. The topic was problems of salmon in the ocean, something he had never given much attention to, but now he saw that out in the ocean was part of the answer to this professor's question. But nothing to raise his hopes for the salmon runs. The presenter had stated that ocean waters were noticeably warming along with the rest of the planet since the 1970s. Now several international meetings had been called, and a debate was heating up. Was the warming caused by humans or natural forces? But whichever, it affected the food chain. He informed them that the plankton were dropping to lower waters, to their preferred colder temperatures, and that the forage fish that fed on them, and then the salmon, too, would therefore seek colder waters. So it wasn't just the droughts affecting rivers that salmon now struggled with, it was the warming oceans where they spent most of their lives. Would they, and other important fish, like cod, move north to cooler waters? That was the presenter's question. And Ike had been thinking ever since what that meant for all of nature, including humans. He didn't even want to tell Esau what he'd learned. What in the world they could do about it?

So, the question: Why should those people care? "Suki, maybe salmon are messengers for all of us."

CHAPTER 32

SKIRMISHING

TWO CARLOADS WERE on their way to Richland early the next Saturday. Leon, driving one, shared his personal experiences with Indigenous cultures and their modern problems with Elena. Suki half listened, asking questions at times, while she drafted her article from Esau's history lessons. Leon was following Bruce, who had decided he wanted to see more of the Columbia, and took the freeway south to where it merged onto two highways that ran east along the river. To save time he chose the faster less scenic one that that ran east from Portland along the south shore. They had a close view of Bonneville Dam, and of the Columbia's role as an industrial canal, with its railroad tracks and long chains of waiting freight cars. Leon thought it another exploitation of nature, a wrong caused by too much technology, and Elena agreed. Suki stared out at the sluggish current moving through a scene—such a contrast to the Hanford Reach. The view brought her back to another time on the river, as a child with her mother, driving down to visit friends near the Columbia's mouth. The estuary had been stormy that day, gray, vast, and scary, nothing she wanted to get near. *This river takes so many forms, all of them powerful.*

Then they passed the Dalles Dam, once the location of Celilo Falls, now of the town with the museum photos of horse seines that Ike had described to her. She recalled Esau's vivid picture of the earlier camps of hundreds, fishing at the Falls. *No wonder Leon says it's wrong, Esau despairs, and Ike feels trapped. But how do you turn an industrialized river around?*

Suki's spirits had already dropped from the prior weekend. She had called her mother to ask if she would be willing to come back briefly, to attend a reactor museum planning meeting, and her mother had said no, that she would not leave her own elderly mother. "While she is alive I will be with her, Suki dear. You must understand." Suki did understand, but she wasn't going to face that group alone. That disappointment fed into her recent recognition that there was no way she could keep up all this new engagement she'd gotten drawn into, when facing her was the last stretch of her program. How did Marta do it? But she knew how Marta did it; that was what she had been trying to picture for Ike. The new quarter had already begun and she had to meet with her advisor and settle on a topic. Yet she had willingly joined this day of protest. *I'm so unrealistic, so...hooked!*

Riding with Bruce, Harold carried on non-stop conversation with Marta. He had seen this part of the river many times and didn't mind at all that she kept him engaged with more recalls of settler history, from his own and two earlier generations. Unwritten scenes kept leaping out, and he would exclaim,

"Oh shucks, I forgot that! I'm going to have to do so many revisions!"

To Marta, that was hilarious. *Join the club!*

Arriving at Richland in plenty of time, the two carloads parked at the supermarket lot where the manager had agreed to allow the demonstration. He was sympathetic to clean environment causes, and had allowed other picket lines before on such subjects. The demonstrators could stand with their signs as long as they stayed thirty feet away from all entrances and did not obstruct traffic or create a disturbance. Marta was happy to find the weather was now cool enough to make standing for hours possible. She spotted Jason across the lot and saw that he was more cautious than that other probationer, Bruce, and stayed away from them. What none of them knew yet was that the city fathers, anticipating sensitive subjects regarding the Hanford Plant, had contacted its management, which suggested limiting the protesters to ten only.

Roger and Thelma were waiting for the Seattle group, and were intrigued to see Elena again so soon. They all went to a coffee shop where a half-hour was spent with news and guesses over what the day would bring. At 9:30, Chuck, still working for the Plant despite his vows, pulled into the store parking lot. He had his usual mixed feelings about his duties today. He was from a family of medium-sized wheat ranchers on the Slope, not evicted orchardists, and he personally thought the government had done the 1907 and later settlers a favor by evicting them from places that would make very few a real living. But he understood the nostalgia for old times that dominated the reunions. This new project by college students was a different story, however, and worrisome after the odd happenings recently.

Chuck had reported the students' small demonstration last week to his boss and was instructed to be watchful today. A limit of ten should be enough for the rights of citizens to assemble, small enough to keep from drawing too much public interest. But Chuck knew that ten was ample to create a disturbance if certain groups showed up—such as the Sagebrush Rebellion. He was thinking about what might be required of him when he noticed a police car pulling in a short distance away. Then more cars arrived, and he recognized the six college youth from last week. *Oh shit!* That meant only four more allowed. He forced himself to go over to tell the new rule on their permit. They were upset, and, without yelling, stated their minds.

Keene, in his usual t-shirt despite cooler weather, decided to confront the policeman.

"That's not fair. That's not constitutional to limit a peaceful protest to such a small number."

The cop shrugged and glanced over at Chuck. Keene saw the message: *the Plant.* Okay, he knew he'd make things worse for his group by arguing. He backed off but wouldn't drop it.

Chuck also had news through his teen son and the high-school grapevine that he didn't like. Irate members of the high school sports teams and their coaches would very likely show up. They had already confronted the protesting college students last week, stating that they were proud of their team name, "The Bombers". Some of them were not sure which bomb, or which war was referred to, but everyone knew we had won. *What's wrong with being proud of that?*

Chuck himself had always thought the team's name was insensitive. He wondered why after almost fifty years no one had complained enough. Now he was uneasy about the more belligerent of the high school sportsmen, especially if they mixed it up with any Sagebrush Rebel types who might have gotten got wind of the demonstration. The Rebels loved a ruckus if it spoke somehow to their issues and made headlines. To them the whole Hanford Plant complex was one more illegal government take-over of public and private land, as opposed to other locals who saw the Plant as their only claim to fame and a statement of national patriotism. Chuck looked at the milling crowd and once more swore that he wasn't paid enough for the heartburn this year.

At 9 a.m., Roger spotted Orville driving into the lot and went to tell them the bad news. They were puzzled as to what to do next: by now there were well over ten people waiting. Worse, when they saw three men climbing out of a car halfway down the lot, Roger recognized one as a man he had seen at times with Walt Croaker. Nor had Walt dropped off any signs to Roger. *Oh, drat it; I let Walt rope me in.* At the same time both the policeman and Chuck recognized the new group. Chuck cursed and walked over to them with the best he could do for a smile, followed by the cop. He saw that the men, all three in brimmed hats over tanned and wrinkled faces, were wearing loose barn jackets that could be covering pistols. Showing his I.D., he began,

"Hello, gentlemen, I guess you know I'm community liaison for the Hanford Plant, and I hear there might be a demonstration today. You folks hear anything like that?"

One man gave him a look-over and pointed at the college group nearby. "Ask those kiddies."

Chuck saw more students with signs getting out of a car. "Yes, I see them…. So, umm, are you folks from the Sagebrush Rebellion by any chance?" He looked at one of their signs: "Save Small Farmers, not Birds and Bugs."

"None of your business if we are, but no, we are from the Farmers for Freedom Alliance, and in case you don't know, it is our constitutional right to join any demonstration we please. Freedom of assembly, right?" He showed his fist.

Chuck frowned at the fist, "Any peaceful assembly, right."

"You bet." The man looked over toward other people waiting and called, "Long time no see, Orville, Roger. How come you're never with us?"

Roger was too annoyed to answer. Orville gave the man a scornful look and called back, "When you get serious, Virgil, maybe I will be. Something useful."

The man smirked, glanced around, waving his hand, "Isn't this something useful?"

Chuck studied the three. He knew he should say nothing to incite the so-called "Farmers", but he couldn't resist one innocent question.

"Where's Walt Croaker these days?"

"Never heard of him."

"Well, we have a problem here in that the city issued a permit for only ten people."

"Why the hell did they do that? It's a fucking violation of our rights again! Again!"

The policeman, listening, said, "Okay, take it easy, sirs. We need to talk to the college students."

But as the two walked toward the frowning students, they saw high school football team members getting out of two more cars. They looked fresh and muscular in their usual tight jeans and sleeveless sweatshirts, their faces grim. No signs.

Chuck was disgusted. *That's it! I'm quitting this job.*

Bruce's group had come into the parking lot by now and were waiting a hundred feet off without visible signs. It was 10 a.m. and there were now at least eighteen potential protesters, and the Wanapum group they expected hadn't arrived yet. Jason was watching from afar. Roger looked at the eager faces of the Farmers and saw what was probably emerging. He went to the policeman, and Bruce moved to just behind him.

Roger said, "Officer, there are three more truckloads that we know of coming to do a peaceful demonstration already approved. They don't know it's been limited to ten persons and some have come a ways."

The cop shrugged. "You are who?"

"Roger Brownley. And a few of us old settlers from this area, not an organization. But we want to peacefully support these college students."

"You look familiar to me."

"Sure, you've seen me at public gatherings of 4-H and FFA."

Orville now joined him, and Roger held his breath, but Orville kept quiet.

"And who are you?" The cop pointed at the high-school sportsmen hovering.

"Students."

Keene came over and said in a clear voice, "Hey! We are students from the Pasco Campus, and we are the ones who got the permit in the first place! "Students Against Pollution of Nature".

A swell of cheers went up. Then a swell of young male voices, "Bo-o-o-o!"

The policeman looked at his notes. *Wrong name.* Now he turned to the local school sports heroes. "Why are you kids here?"

"We don't like what's going on. These are unpatriotic anti-sports shit-heads that want to close down the local sports teams!"

Bruce broke in before Roger could, "That is absolutely, totally untrue. We just want you to change your name to something that respects other human beings' lives."

"What about us? We're human beings too!"

Bruce, unable to hold his rage, blared his answer. "Named Bombers! You don't have any idea what you're talking about with those bombs! Go home and read your history books for a change!"

A great melee of shouts broke out on all sides.

"Shut up! Shut up! All of you! And who the devil are you?" The officer pointed to Bruce.

Bruce took a deep breath. "Officer, I'm Bruce Wilder, grandson of settlers near here and a vet, wounded and honorably discharged."

That quieted the officer and crowd for a second, and Bruce quickly went on, "I want to see this defunct nuclear mess at Hanford cleaned up, removed, and the land and grazing rights given back to the farmers and ranchers and Indians." He waved his arm at the growing crowd.

A man from "Farmers" shouted, "The vet's right! Damn right, this Hanford Plant and now a Hanford Reach land grab—it needs to be given back to real Americans!"

Bruce waved his hand, "Let me finish! And by the way, I'm the only one here, maybe, who knows firsthand what bombs do to people, except that retired Marine right here." And he pointed to Harold by his side. "He saw Nagasaki! Saw it three days after the bomb dropped on them. Did anyone else here see that, anything like that? Do you Bombers here," he pointed at the team, "even know where Nagasaki is, for godssake? Huh?"

A second of silence. Then Suki stepped up and answered, "Well, I do."

Everyone turned to stare at her. Bruce gave her a strong nod. The parking lot by now had begun to fill up with shoppers, and Suki spotted Ike's green truck driving in at last.

"Yes," she said, "I do, and I'll be right back if anyone wants to talk about Nagasaki!" And she sprinted off to warn Ike and his crowd to hold back. But they were already out of the trucks, and were pulling out their drums. "Hey, look!" pointed a student. One of the Farmers seized the moment he'd been waiting for and punched a football player twice his size in the stomach, who in a flash socked him back in the stomach and knocked him to his hands and knees. Fists immediately were flying amid a chorus of roars: "dumb rednecks!", "bunch of druggies", "commies", "faggots", "retards", "Mama's-tit suckers!" The only slam not heard was "Jap lovers", as Walt Croaker muttered from behind a tree a hundred feet off.

Bruce saw the Farmers' purpose was to make their scene, and that it could close down the whole protest. He lunged over ready to grab the noisiest one by the collar to drag him off and scare him, pummel him as needed, when he remembered the cop. *It's his call. And I'm on probation.* He wheeled to Harold and muttered, "We're losing this. It's turning into a stupid show." And he and a disgusted Marta moved off a safe distance to her relief. *He stopped himself!*

The policeman, one hand on his holster, the other pointed at a wordless Keene, yelled,

"Mister Love-Not-War, I give you three minutes to pick your ten people and tell the rest to leave, or I'm closing this down. I'll close it anyway if you all don't quiet down!"

Most of the crowd stepped back a few feet to see who would be picked—except the "Farmers", who continued to shake their fists and grumble taunts, "Come on, sissy girls!"

Keene, sweaty-faced, found his tongue. "I'm sorry, folks, but this is our party. So, you six," he pointed to the ones who had arrived with him, "and I pick...you", he pointed to Orville, "and you," he pointed to Bruce, "and where is the Japanese woman? Over there? Are those Indians part of this too? Okay, tell her she's picked, and to bring one of them. And, I'm sorry, but that's ten. Okay, Officer, I've done it, and yes, we will be peaceful."

He turned to Chuck with a glare, "We are complying, but we are not quitting. You tell your boss we have a right to assemble, and not limited to ten next time. "

"So do we!" cried a Farmer, the biggest one, who rushed to slug a sportsman, sending him to the ground. Roger reached to help the boy, then caught on that his fall was faked, and yelled at them,

"You kids stop this now if you don't want to be suspended!"

"Who the fuck are you, grandpa?"

"I'm on your school board, that's who." It was a lie, he was on the Prosser school board, but it made the boys look at each other and back away; there was a limit to what their school administration would tolerate.

"Chickens!" called the three Farmers. "Fascist!" a Farmer snorted, and spat on the ground by the officer as he walked off.

The melee seemed to be over. The policeman, who'd steamed to arrest someone, caught his breath. The *Tri-City Herald* hadn't even had time to get there. Suki came back alone; none of the young Wanapums wished to join the madness. Keene could hardly blame them. He chose Thelma for the last of the ten and she hesitated, then agreed. Roger turned to Leo and Elena, who hadn't said a word the whole time.

"What do you think? Maybe the rest of us should forget it for now?"

Leon frowned, shook his head, "Not yet..."

The cop broke in, "Okay, you others move off, and you people with the signs, go do your thing quietly...now!"

Keene nodded, "Okay, bring your signs and let's meet down near the storefront."

Chuck moved off a few feet, and radioed his boss, whose answer was cautious.

"Chuck, just keep your eye on that sagebrush gang. Tell the cop to let the ten do their thing peacefully. It will be worse if he closes them down. Hurray for democracy."

The chosen people collected their signs and headed for their space several feet from the store entrance, some grumbling, some laughing, some like Bruce, downright angry. Bruce saw Esau and his group still standing by their trucks, and he and Marta went to thank them for coming and to ask if they would still perform. Esau assured him they would if it looked safe, and gave him raised eyebrows. Right now, they would go find something to eat. Bruce, calmed down, thought Esau was amused, Ike exasperated, but they were sticking to the plan. The people who were not chosen moved off to whatever they needed to do, more angry than amused. Bruce watched Marta go off with Roger, Dorothy, and Harold. *At least she'll get something out of this trip.* Moving into the line by Suki, he turned to grumble, "It just makes me all the more determined."

Suki decided to tell him an update on her own project, that she, too, was determined...to make the reactor museum an honest one, but that her mother could not come. Perhaps instead he could go to a meeting with her? And he agreed to; again, how could he say no? But later said,

"You know the better person to go with you would be Harold. I've seen enough bombed-out villages, but he's seen the actual place."

Suki waved her sign at passers. She protested that she didn't know Harold, had just met him.

"Well, today is your chance. We three can talk later."

Over by the singers, Jason had joined Ike.

"Well, what you think, college student?"

"Huh! It's not a new discovery, but I think white people are crazy savages to watch out for. Probably drunk and on drugs too."

Ike shook his head, "I wish only drugs and whiskey makes them act that way."

Then, about to walk off, they saw Leon and Elena hurrying across the lot, waving at them, and heard Leon calling, "Wait, people, it's not over yet!"

He reached them to explain that there was another act that could use the singers' help.

"Elena's all set to do a ceremony! Esau, what do you think? This is what we'll be passing out."

PLEASE JOIN US today at the Riverside Park at the bank of the Columbia at 3pm for a blessing of this River of Peace and Fertility. The Columbia for eons has blessed humankind with its bounty. Today you are invited to thank the Columbia (known to the Indians as the Chiawana), and pray for its healing and its restoration as our provider of peace and good living. 3PM TODAY here in the park. RIVERS OF PEACE AND FERTILITY ASSEMBLY

Representative: Elena

Dressed to perform, but now with a Yurok beaded buckskin jacket added, Elena gave them her uplifting smile. "We can still make this gathering work. I want the drummers to start it, if you will? Yes?"

Esau read over the flyer, chuckled, and nodded.

CHAPTER 33

A RIVER OF VOICES

OVER ON THE picket line the protesters were passing Elena's flyer along, looks of surprise turning to chortles. From then on, their faces showed more sparkle as shoppers came over, some to talk to them, some to stare at their signs, a few to scowl. Many knew Orville or Thelma, and several knew Keene, who handled the critics calmly. The policeman read a comic in his car, with a glance around every five minutes. Chuck studied the flyer and took a walk down by the river, hoping the Farmers would not return. He had decided not to call his boss. This new thing could be seen as just another church meeting, couldn't it? They were common in the park, no permit trouble, and just maybe no trouble for him.

Suki, standing by Bruce, looked at the flyer and at the line of cheerful sign-wavers. It could still all turn out fine. But later, after standing two hours, she felt clouds of questions moving in. Would they, or even Elena, be able to change anything significantly? Bruce felt her worry and gave her back her own earlier encouragement to him.

"Suki, it's a first step. We're going to get the people that live around here to realize that the government shouldn't be able do any damn thing it wants with this river and to act on it."

Suki frowned, nodded, and raised her sign, "Don't Destroy This Great River!" A fresh smile spread on her face. Bruce understood her brief funk and was glad he'd helped.

Down the line, Keene stood with his sign, "This River Needs Love, Not Poison". He turned to Orville standing next to him. "So, you're Orville! I hear you have a group that's meeting about the problems around here."

"That's right. And I hope you students will keep going."

"Oh, we're already planning our next event. We thought of including someone from the downwinders, but they are already doing their thing in court, so it might work against them. But how about your group? And how about Riverkeepers?"

"My group's just getting started. I'll give you my phone number. As for Riverkeepers, you must know Thelma, ask her." He pointed across the lot, "And those Indians over there, you could ask them what they want to do."

Keene nodded and went on planning, as he smiled to passing shoppers. He wondered, should the students go broad or stay focused? There was the breacher group, the people that wanted many dams removed. That would be one huge fight! And that new group, very broad, touring the country with a huge sculptured fish: "Save Our Salmon".

Orville pointed down the line at Bruce, "That one—he wants to do something, a lot of something, on nuclear. And that other old guy, that's Harold, his uncle. He really was with the Marines that landed in Nagasaki. And Suki? She's determined to make the Reactor B museum, if it comes to pass, to tell the damn truth."

Keene's head was full. This was a complicated project he had taken on. To say nothing of opposition: the Farmers—how to manage them? Or the Bombers?

By 2:40 many cars and trucks were already parked near the river and about forty people gathered, with more coming. Some already knew Elena; most didn't and were curious. There were two new signs in evidence: "A Clean River is a Healthy River", and "This River is a Gift to Us: Care for It." Most of the other signs were gone. Four young Wanapum drummers and singers, sitting on the groomed grass, had an overture ready. They had no costumes, just simple headbands. Suki and Ike sat to the side at a picnic table with Esau and another elder.

When the drummers began, Suki forgot her disgust over the earlier fracas. She had heard the young men practicing on the weekends; now she was overwhelmed by the result, the true power in their singing as it flowed with the drum beats. The crowd stopped gabbing and moved closer. Many had heard Wanapum singers before, but this was a new, younger group, and the event was more intimate.

After the song ended, one of the young drummers spoke up just enough to be heard, "This next song tells of the love and respect we have for this river and its salmon."

Then the two elders got up and walked to the drummers to stand behind them. They sang out in their strong voices of many years' training, and the drums sent out the message clear across the park to a growing crowd. Suki's heart thumped along with them and her eyes flooded.

"Can you sing like that Ike?"

He smiled, "I have a ways to go."

As the song was ending, Elena emerged from Leon's car and walked slowly toward the riverbank. The drummers stopped as she turned to the crowd and it closed around her. A gentle breeze blew.

"Hello friends," she gave a broad sweeping smile, "I am Elena, and I am very happy to be back with you. Last summer we did blessings on this great river, and today is good time to continue. Stay with us. We must continue to pray, and also to demonstrate, as some of us did this morning, until this river is clean from poisons and returns to natural life. People of this valley and other river valleys will thank you."

She motioned with one hand and a drummer gave four slow, resonating beats that pulled in more curious people. Some were muttering to each other, what is she? *Some kind of medicine man...but a woman!* Another commented that she sure didn't look like any Wanapums he knew. And another laughed, "You haven't been to any powwows? You'll see costumes just as fancy."

Then Elena raised her arms and gave a short prayer in her Indigenous tongue. The audience waited. When she ended, a nearby college student with an Asian-appearing look, spoke out to her in the same language. Elena, surprised and delighted, beckoned her over. The young woman explained that she was an exchange student from Yakutia, in Northern Russia. Elena, with a huge smile, took her hand, said a few words, and went on in English.

"You see, all over the world we face this problem of toxins. The toxins from my country and hers may blow over to you here. The ones from Japan and Korea may drift to this coast. And from this river toxins sweep all along your coasts in great currents circling the Pacific. We must stop this. It is God's answer to us that this young person from such a distant place came to this gathering, unknown to me. And speaks to me in my own language! So we are surely in touch with healing spirits. I will pray now."

She raised up one arm and offered another short prayer, with a closing in English. "River, we honor you. You are our source of life and health. You are our gift from the Great Creator. We wish to care for you more, to help you regain your natural health and beauty." A murmur rose from the crowd, and a few cries: "Yes!" and "Amen!"

The exchange student spoke again to Elena, who went on, "She tells me that near the small settlement of her ancestors there is such plant as we have here at Hanford. It, too, is now closed down but not cleaned. And like us, they also have plant near there that is operating. So you see, the problem is not just Hanford," she waved her arms across the horizon, "it is all our problem, our children's problem, I am sad to say. And we have not only radioactive problem. I am returned this week from California rivers full of mud from logging, and toxins, but not from plutonium. Instead, there we have poisons from pesticides, and from algae that grow in rivers that are too warm now. And these algaes drift to oceans where they create huge dead areas where no creature can live. Yes, it is true! Another human problem all across our ocean."

She waved an arm and spread a wide smile across the crowd. "Friends, you can read about it on Internet. Now I want to pray more for this river, for its cleansing. You can join me, any language, if you wish."

She turned around to gaze at the river and they waited. Even those who were skeptical of such ceremonies were quiet. How could they not be? They all loved this river in their own ways, and worried—some a little, some a lot—over its future. Most of them knew something about the problem of leaking waste, or knew downwinders. The Columbia was beautiful today, but how much longer? Elena turned back and signaled to the drummers, they gave four beats of powerful sound, and she began again in her own language, but in a while switched to English.

Suki said to Ike, "I have to join them!"

"Do it!"

She strode over by the two, and prayed quietly in Japanese, while around her she heard both Spanish and English. Elena finished and motioned toward Suki,

"Now look! We are joined by person from Nagasaki! She is not born yet when it was bombed, of course, but radioactive poison does not just disappear but carry through generations. Do you know what this means? She knows. You need to know."

How does Elena know this about me?

Chuck, standing off a little to the side, grimaced; he should have known it was going to get political. Too late now; the best thing to do at this point, was nothing, and say nothing later. Nothing ever came of these events, did it?

Elena went on, "She is here today for same reason we all are, dear people—to bless this river, to make it clean again. This is not by magic; it takes human effort. Help now!" And she motioned to the drummer again and began in a stronger voice,

"Oh, great river Columbia, oh, great Chiawana, you wonderful river that brings good lives to so many, many peoples, and still, sadly, is also misused by other people to hurt others, we come here today to ask your forgiveness for abusing your gifts—your salmon, your pure waters...."

More calls broke out: "Praise the Lord!", "Amen!", and Leon heard behind him someone mutter, "This is of the devil." But it was drowned out by the most cries of all: "Yes!"

Marta turned to Roger and muttered, "My god she's powerful!" Roger didn't answer, but totally agreed and was grateful. He had been humiliated that Walt Croaker had outfoxed him again, and now could put it aside. Leon, standing by them, smiled as if he'd seen a rebirth. Like Bruce and Marta, it was his first time to see Elena perform a ceremony. Esau, and Ike, too, were moved, Esau regretting that Alice hadn't come; she had given up space in the truck to one of the young drummers. Off to the side Ike heard some negative rumbling, but the few people it came from left without a commotion. The great majority were standing transfixed.

Elena, silent, looked around, smiled, and motioned to the drummers, calling out, "Would one of you young men please come here?"

Esau poked one of the drummers. He hesitated, got another poke, and stood up to walk slowly over. Elena put her hand on his shoulder.

"Here we have another youth." She motioned back to the Asian girl, "These two represent our human future. They come here today for us—and his people, after all, have been here for many thousands of years. We must do better for these youth, and for all of us. And to all youth here today, we are proud of you. Do not be discouraged by...opposition. There will be always misguided people who try to introduce chaos. So always you must have fall-back plan. And remember that those people also suffer."

Looking around in her most commanding way, she said, "Now I will make short closing prayer in my language, and you can in yours."

She raised her arms and began, *Chiawana*...and a murmur around her also began, this time in concert. It was call and response, Leon recognized. She ended amid more spirited cries from the crowd, and waited until they quieted, then said,

"Let us just be quiet for moment and feel spirit of this river. Let it speak to us."

She motioned for people to come close and turned to walk through the crowd to the riverbank. Everyone seemed to understand, standing quietly as the Columbia flowed past. Leon thought it was a perfect ending, this space of silence for the spirit to flow into all of them. Was the transported feeling within him from his own bottled up feelings, stored from years ago, was it from Elena and her own powers, or was it from the river itself? All three, he guessed as he watched her stare out into the current. Elena gave a slight motion again to the young drummers and they filled the park with one more song. Then they put away their drums and moved off, and others followed.

It was over. Bruce's crowd converged with wide grins around. Harold turned to Leon,

"That was really something! How did it all happen?"

Leon wanted to be silent, but found words to explain how Elena had planned it.

Harold shook his head, "Never saw anything like it for a long time. Sort of a revival?"

"A revival of spirit, yes."

"Not exactly Christian, but I don't think it matters. What's the word?"

"Ecumenical, maybe?"

"Yes. For everyone."

Those remaining near them were quiet as they looked over at Elena by the river.

Roger at last said, "So, Leon, you and Elena were prepared for all this. Genius planning."

"Marvelous wasn't it? I hope the college students thought so."

The students, except for Keene, were leaving. Roger pulled him over and introduced him.

"What do you think, Keene?"

The young man grinned hugely and thrust out his hands, "I loved it! Saved the day. I wasn't ready for all that business earlier. I have to thank Elena—how did she know? Or did she just invent it all on the spot?"

People looked at Leon, who shrugged.

"Well, people will remember it for sure." Keene looked around at the non-students who had joined in—Roger's friends, he guessed. *This is what can happen!* "And we'll do our thing again, soon, but with a better permit—we'll demand it. And all of you please come next time."

Suki hesitated, then said, "Keene, next time could we include Nagasaki on a sign?"

He hesitated. "That's my goal. But we have to do some education on that. Fifty years of...I guess you could kindly call it misinformation. Well, it's hard to admit a mistake that huge."

So you face what I do. "Thank you for sticking with this, Keene. Thanks to all of you."

She said goodbye to everyone, seeing that Ike was waiting at his truck, gave Bruce and Marta a quick hug. She explained that she must visit with Alice and the girls, knowing it could be the last time for a while. Talking to Harold would have to wait too. She absolutely had to settle down to her other obligations.

CHAPTER 34

MORE MESSAGES

CHUCK CHECKED TO see that the college students had picked up all the discarded flyers, then walked slowly to his truck. He decided he would definitely consider Elena's event as another church meeting on the green and nothing special he needed to report. She had gone off with that anthropologist; let him write it up. The policeman was long gone, and the Farmers had disappeared—as usual more smoke than anything. But he realized he needed to talk to his son more about which kids he hung out with at high school. The Plant didn't need their help.

The Indian singing had touched him; actually, all of it had, even though he was skeptical about what could fix the river, or how badly it needed fixing, as yet. He couldn't imagine what would come of the day's performances—or what was in the college protesters' heads, or how much influence in the region Esau had. He was familiar enough with the Farmer/Rebels; he'd have to keep his nose to the wind.

Bruce put an arm around his uncle Harold, then looked around and reached for Marta, put the other around her.

"This could be the spark, what do you think, Uncle?"

"I don't know...but I think the best thing I did was stay away from the reunion this year and make you go!"

Marta murmured, "Thanks, Bruce, for insisting I be here." Privately she was trying to define just what had happened in cultural terms: a religious revival, a paradigm shift, mass hypnosis, magician's manipulations, spiritual awakening...She'd read about it, now she'd seen it, whatever it was, and it was powerful. She wanted Leon's impression, Suki's for sure, and certainly Esau's.

Roger said, "Thanks to all of you for coming. I didn't know what I'd get from that phone call, well, I knew I'd capture Bruce. And I'm proud of all you students, Keene."

Thelma said, "But I'd like to know how the Sagebrush Rebellion knew to show up."

Roger looked at the ground and sighed.

Bruce shook his fist. "I saw Croaker over there watching, and I wanted so bad to go punch him out."

Orville said, "Just a bunch of horseflies, those guys! What bothers me is that sports team—the 'Bombers'? Young bungholes."

Thelma shook her head, "These high school kids? I don't know what kind of education they get nowadays. They've got no idea what those bombs did to kids like them."

Bruce said, "Well, I was a kid like them once. Thelma, you wouldn't want them to go through what I did to get educated. There's still hope for them. But, hey, it all turned out!"

The late afternoon wind was gentle enough that they decided to get carryout food and eat in the park where they could all be together at two picnic tables pulled together. Once their burgers and tacos were half-eaten, Bruce glanced around, and decided it was time to show more leadership.

"Well, we all agree it was great, but now what do we do next? We can't just go home and turn on the TV, can we? I'm going to an anti-nuke meeting in Stockholm and Leon's going with me. How about you, Uncle Harold?"

Harold looked off across the river. "I've been thinking I'd like to work on getting a museum for the whole valley, not Reactor B, for lord's sake."

"Great! But we do need to have our voice on that reactor museum too, if they're really going ahead with it. Maybe your input there too, Uncle?"

Harold frowned. "You really think they'd want it?"

Roger smiled at Bruce from the can of beer he'd snuck into the park along with his fries.

"For now, I think Thelma and I will carry on with stream-clearing. We found out it's gotten to be quite a movement of volunteers along different coastal streams. They're trying to revive their salmon runs just like we are. And it's working a few places—salmon coming back!"

Thelma added, "And of course Harold's right. we do all need to push for a real museum for the region. We all have stuff that should go there." She marveled at how their lives had started to change from the time Bruce first sat down at their table. What had over the years become unchanging routines could easily turn to lively days. She looked over at her friends.

Orville responded, "You already know what me and Dorothy will be doing. Be there! Will you be at our next meeting, Keene?"

"Absolutely, and I'll try to bring someone."

Marta said, "Invite Jason! Oh, wait, he's on probation, no protest groups for him."

By then the evening wind was rising, and they hurried to finish their food and be on their various ways, all of them feeling energy mixed with wonder and questions.

Walt Croaker drove home at high speed, annoyed that he had been forced to stay in the background of the day's drama. His buddies had gone overboard harassing the kids, he thought, but that could be salvaged. His next move: to find out what the college kids planned for the future, if anything, and how to turn it from what was a hopeless issue to a living one for the whole region— the return of all the region's federal lands to public use. Meanwhile, he would take a pleasure trip down into eastern Oregon where real men put on real range battles, not sissy demonstrations, and he wasn't going to ask his probation officer's permission.

Esau rode home with surges of pride for the young singers and drummers. He'd had no idea how they would do and they'd been so great. He and Alice and the rest would keep right on with heritage center developments, and he was now sure that they could provide traditional music as well. But more immediately, due to Alice's ingenuity the first performance of "Dung Beetles Speak" was already scheduled for the weekend after next, with the kids' planning for the next "serious" skit already. And somehow they would keep Suki and Ike involved.

Leon, meanwhile, had finished his lunch and gone to stand at the river a little distance from Elena. He felt happy though exhausted and was pleased to watch the ripples passing and the canvasback duck still paddling in the eddy, still with nine ducklings. Elena at last walked over, her face expectant.

"I thought it was marvelous," he said, as he stared at her and once more felt fatigue swept away. "How was it for you?"

Her answering smile was victorious, he thought, but not arrogant. "Very, very good. And the drumming and singing add so much. I'm so glad. And, Leon, youth was part of it this time—so important, with troubling news almost every day."

"So, shall we have coffee before you leave?"

"Oh yes." They walked off across the park, and she went on. "You know, I am already traveling again. They wait for me at another part of Klamath River—terrible drought. Would you like to come down and meet them? And study how they use indigenous plants?"

"Could I be helpful?"

"Yes, you could. If a tribe invites me, they organize it all, but if it is mixed group, like this one, it needs help to be best. You understand."

Leon's heart leaped. He had a son in Sacramento he didn't visit often enough, and he could even make a plant research trip out of it. As for blessings, he knew about the California rivers. What could be worse for them than drought, the normal snowfall in the mountains gone missing? She told him more, about the Yurok Indians' demand that old dams on the Klamath be taken out to help salmon run rebuilding. Another interesting battle going well. But he soon realized he had a conflict and had to explain that the blessing she was inviting him to would coincide with the meeting Bruce had already made their plane reservations for.

Elena said, "Ah, he needs you, yes. It is fine. I can find local people to help. But you must come with me on next one, Leon. Soon."

"Wonderful. Just give me time to arrange it at my job."

He was relieved; his invitation was still open. Even though he didn't have faith in blessings, alone, being able to stop the destruction of the world he'd known, or thought he knew, he was the happiest he'd been in years at the blessing today. Why? He tried to sort it out. He knew it wasn't only Elena herself, or simply group hypnosis; it was also the people he'd come with, and more, it was the drummers and singers, how they had sent the feeling of the event back to his memories of a world that, even though he never understood it entirely, he'd missed so much. His vision for his own future now certainly had more brightness than he'd expected.

"Stockholm, Leon! Maybe Sami people I know there. I was at conference in western Russia last year and meet them. Brave people you will like...say hello for me. Tell them about this river and people."

He nodded. *Of course, Sami, another fascinating group.* He stopped and looked back once more at the Columbia. *I should just retire and be a full-time anti-toxins, anti-nuke activist! Can I do that at my age?*

They walked to find an uncrowded café. A while later they were sitting in the airport, Elena waiting for a flight to Portland, and they talked about how the radioactive waste moving toward the Columbia was a message for the entire world.

Elena said, "If they do not do something here very soon, people may require evicting again! That is why I must keep going. Leon, send me your message when you are home from Stockholm, ready to come to me. And I will call you."

He wanted to know her movements better. "How long will you stay in the U.S.?"

"Oh, I am resident alien. I do not need to go back and forth on visa."

He was not going to ask her how that came about, but she volunteered.

"My husband, American doctor. I meet him when he comes across in 1992, when border is more open. He wants to study our health system, our health problems. Very intelligent man, very good man, Leon. Also already ill, but never listen to me—on smoking, foods. I cannot cure cancer always. I only have him four years. But I stay here. Many shamans in northern Russia to help there. My call is here."

Leon drove the rest of the way home alone, as Marta and Harold had each wanted to ride with Bruce, to feel him out more on his next move. And so did Leon, since they were together headed for Europe. *All of a sudden my plate is full. And I'm glad.*

⋙◎ ◎⋘

Driving with Ike again toward Wolf Rapids, Suki was still in awe of the whole day, especially of Elena's performance. As for the Wanapum drummers and singers, she had always liked the traditional Japanese performances her mother had taken her to, and these young men had reached the spirit even more powerfully. For the first time since the snake's sacrifice she felt a strong surge of hope. But then would come that swirl of doubt that kept intruding. They passed the operating nuclear plant off in the distance, reminding her how huge the problem was. It was not just the Columbia, not just the United States government; it was the world's problem. Elena—how much could healers like her do? How many were there? How many nuke plants? Hundreds. She wanted to be useful, but she couldn't, like Bruce, just hop on a plane. For miles she and Ike were silent, but then at last he shook himself from his own pondering.

"Well, what do you think?"

"I think it was perfect how it all came out. Beautiful. And your young guys really got into it, so powerful! And Esau, how he can sing—gave me thrills."

"That's right, you never heard him before. Yeah, I was real proud of them. And Elena was amazing how she turned it all around. She seemed to just create her message as she went, and she knows how to pull others in. What I've wanted to do at fishery meetings."

Suki thought about that. *You can too!* "It was so great, but will it make a difference a month from now? Or just a feel-good time? I have no experience with this kind of thing, if it can really waken people, really change things."

"I don't expect she can turn poisoned ground or rivers into healthy ones, but I think she can wake people up, you bet."

"But how about turning that to action? Can she, can people like her, do that?"

"Some can. We get all kinds of prophets coming by, not at Wolf Rapids, but at the rez—New Agers, Jesus people, sobriety leaders, shamans, missionaries, herbal salesmen, government self-helpers, private ones—you name it. Some folks get pretty nutty, but some do start living better."

"Did this ever happen to you?"

"To me? You happened to me! You! Anyway, yes, people like Elena can do that, but it has to tie into their real lives. The Ghost Dance was great for a while, some say, but it didn't work in the end."

The Ghost Dance? Esau never mentioned that yet. "But today, things could go either way, couldn't they, Ike? Feel good or actually do good. She said we have to act."

He waited, knowing by now she would have more.

"And what about your theory, 'the youth must solve these problems'. Seems like there were different versions of youth in action today."

He laughed. "I know. Keene is the kind of youth I meant."

Ike agreed that it had been a great event, but couldn't help thinking it was indeed like religious revivals he had gone to twice and then quit. Everyone got high on the spirit of the moment, then went home and what next? *Did they act? Yes, some did. Alice did, Esau was already plenty full of spirit, came to it on his own! But yeah, what next now?* He drove on, deciding to keep his skeptical mouth shut for a while. Suki had been uplifted from her worries for a time at least. But a museum committee meeting was no revival meeting. And her mother wasn't coming.

They could stop for only an hour at Wolf Rapids. Suki praised the girls for their signs they'd sent, and told Alice she wished she had been there.

"It was marvelous! Great signs you sent! We can't stay, but Esau can tell you all about it."

Alice turned to Ike, eyebrows raised.

"Yeah, Auntie, different from what we expected, but even better. You know? I think the feds will award your grant if they see energy like what we saw today."

Alice was pleased at this coming from him. "The people of this region will see that a center gets finished."

She turned to Esau, "So how did our young singers do?"

He gave her a big smile. "They did great. And I maybe did my best singing. Well, it was all powerful, Russian shaman and all."

Suki nodded, "You guys sure helped make it, Uncle."

"We did, so you tell those boys so."

Later Esau did describe to Alice the whole beautiful scene at the river park. Would it make a difference for the Chiawana a month from now? He couldn't say. But he knew it gave new life and confidence to the young performers.

"How about Jason?"

"Well, he was there, trying not to be noticed. We'll hear more. But Ike—his wind is blowing every way lately. Is it the woman?"

"Hummm, yes, but even before her. It's his girls, worrying about their future, and Suki adds to it."

"We need to be easy on him."

"I think so. I want them to be together, she's good for him. But they do need a place of their own—to relax a little."

"Is that what you call it now?"

⋅⊷⊜ ⊜⊶⋅

Bruce's attention as he drove home was already on his next moves. In addition to the nuclear disarmament meeting—he and Leon were leaving in three days—he had told Keene to call him anytime. Even better, a veteran had stopped to talk to him as he stood with his sign, "No Nuclear Waste into Our River", and he had found out there was a "Vets for Nuclear Disarmament" group in Kennewick. He thought there surely could be some teamwork with them. Marta was relieved that all had turned out well, giving Bruce enthusiasm for his trip, and peace at home for her work.

Harold was still trying to absorb the events of the day. He saw that he would have to write an addendum for his memoir, just as Suki had predicted. But Bruce was demanding an opinion from him about where everything stood, as he prepared for his contribution to the big meeting.

After mulling it over, Harold said, "It's possible, all the new public attention to the waste and the river could produce some real action from the government. And that could influence other countries, considering we do have the biggest waste problem."

Then he reached his hand to Bruce's shoulder. "You know, I never told you all I felt, every reunion, when I took that bus ride out to the old place and walked around. Seeing that—that war zone! Lately, I just decided I needed to stop going out there. It makes me too angry. Truthfully, that's why I asked you to go to the reunion without me. I just couldn't stand seeing the ghost of White Bluffs one more time if I didn't hear some positive news. Once I was at the reunion, I knew I'd end up climbing on that bus anyway, and it's just too painful. Today was different. Some hope."

"So you got me to go out there and passed your pain onto me! And Suki, her being along at the old place, made it all the more painful. A meeting sure meant to be, eh? But it's okay. I needed to see the place and feel it. But today was something I needed too."

"Everyone from here does."

"Say, Uncle, you need to have some time with Suki." Then he told Harold about Suki's time with the Reactor B committee and her determination to go again, but not alone.

"She needs a Nagasaki eye-witness, like you."

Harold was caught by surprise and didn't answer for a while, then gave a troubled sigh.

"Ahhh, it depends on who's on that committee. If it's what I'm guessing— one old settler family, no Indians, the rest Chamber of Commerce types…oh, and a couple people that worked at the Plant? Bruce, if I told them about Nagasaki and they started to argue, I'm afraid I'd just walk out. And if they did let me talk about what I saw, you think it would stay on that? Oh, no. Next thing, they'd be asking, *Who's to blame? Not us!* And then, *Why didn't the Japanese surrender when they had the chance?* Then, on to talking about the Japanese taking over Asia, and then my point would be lost. They are locked in their myth of how they won the war and saved our country. You know, Bruce, it's a difficult thing, what Suki wants. Why would the government want that story told?"

Bruce. "You need to be on the damn committee, Uncle."

Marta broke in, "Harold, he's right, you know!"

Harold didn't answer that. After another minute of scenery gazing, he said,

"Bruce, I thought everything was beautiful today, but I have to say I think that most of all we have to fix the problem with that Plant waste, and not a generation from now. But no country that we'd want to sell it to, or give it to, is going to accept it, unless they're flat broke. Maybe resell it for a profit? Or, god forbid, might want to make it into a nuclear weapon? And the black market in nuclear junk, think about it! So we just go right on building those replacement containers? And the same in other countries."

"I know, I know. That's what Orville's speech was about. It's why I'm going to the anti-nuke meeting. Find people that have some answers."

"Answers, I hope so! Well, good luck, seriously. I am happy I took part today, but I don't have a lot of hope unless…. Bruce, we have to make such a huge noise, or we're handing it all to my grandkids—and your kids someday. And grandkids." *Whuff!*

Bruce wondered why his great-uncle had never shared these thoughts with him before. *Was it really just too painful for him? Or was there something in me that stopped him?*

Marta said, "I was reading that they have the same problem at Chernobyl. And all they could think of to do was to put a huge metal casing around that destroyed plant, knowing that it will only last so long."

Harold said, "I know, I've read that too. I read whatever I can find about these plants and their waste, a huge international mess. And still more being built. Though not many here at least; we've pretty much quit. But not the others. They have to quit too!"

Bruce smacked his fist on the car door. *Wow, Uncle!* "Well, it's too huge. Maybe I should just give it up, do something realistic."

"No, no. I don't mean give up. I went to the demonstration with you, didn't I?"

Bruce could see his elder had more steaming in him and waited.

"I've had a lot of time to think about this. I know I should have talked more to you. Fifty years, and then new containers! We have to use those fifty years to get it right. You think I ever forget what I saw in Nagasaki? No, don't give up. Keep building on what you all did today. But you know that saying, "Choose your fights!" I have to think hard about that museum committee. But I'll help if I can."

He'll help if he can. It was the third such offer that Bruce had received this week, not counting Suki's own plans.

"Uncle, I think you're saying the only real answer is worldwide nuclear disarmament, and then go further and close down all the plants, world-wide, clean up the waste—pay whatever it takes, go for some other form of energy. And so I'm going over there to hear what others are thinking."

"That's a good start."

They stopped then. What more was there to say? Marta thought, *Elena has turned us loose to use our own heads. That's what she does.*

⊶⊷ ⊶⊷

Ike and Suki once more crossed the desert toward the pass, both of them silent for miles. She had decided she was not going to ask him again about his personal project. It was up to him. Then he recalled some news he'd put aside in the drama of the day.

"Oh, by the way, I got a call from Louise that a bus tour she'd said I might do for the museum planners? Well, it's postponed. She's heard that the Hanford Plant will become part of a national monument for the whole Manhattan Project."

Suki was stunned, then a sick urge swept her, as from a hideous smell. *Part of a national monument? Then those buildings are never going away. Never."*

Ike saw her expression and regretted his bad timing, just when he'd felt she was happy.

"I know, I know, but it might be better this way."

"Ike, if it was made of wood I'd personally burn the damn place down."

"Hey," He reached over to her. "I know, Esau and Alice both told you they wanted the whole complex hauled away, everything cleaned up and returned to nature. But I'm not so sure. Then it would be easier for people to forget what it did. One more piece of evil history buried. Better, maybe, to have it standing there. An ugly lesson for humanity."

She hadn't thought of that. *Ugly. Monstrous. But a lesson.*

He went on, "Suki, being there at meetings will still be important, even if the Park Service is doing the story. They could leave things out, and the feds can take years to do anything, that's our experience."

She tried to picture such a monstrosity standing there forever. Other images flooded her, the worst from the Nagasaki museum. *Oh, great snake, can you help us again, turn this into something good?"* Then she told him of Bruce's idea to draft Harold to go with her, and how that couldn't replace a resident of Nagasaki, but would be next best. If Harold wouldn't go, maybe he, Ike, would? He didn't answer as they drove on up into the pine foothills, and she worried that she'd again gone too far demanding decisions from him. *I wouldn't like that myself. We can just keep driving a cross-state highway...forever.* She laughed at the image.

But Ike was not feeling pushed; he wanted to help her but was picturing Harold going with her to try to influence the museum committee. As Ike knew him, Harold was a storyteller, not a fighter. From what he had heard driving the tour bus, Harold's old neighbors had general agreement on only three things: that White Bluffs had been mainly wonderful, that they had been robbed by the federal government, and that U.S. history had forgotten them. Of course no one wanted radioactive waste in the river or anywhere near it. But none of them had serious ideas about what could be done about it, and that conversation would trickle off. Some of the former settlers, like Roger and Harold read the newspaper every day and knew what was going on at Hanford. Others probably never read the paper, knew only hearsay. Or didn't want to think about a scary problem they believed they couldn't do a damn thing about. If the settlers and their descendants got onto the topic of what took place in Japan, Ike could guess the disputes.

Suki had bitten off a huge chunk to think that Reactor B lovers were ever going to let the display tell the whole story. *And I was the one who gave her that idea—that she could make it happen. Why?* He looked over at her and suddenly saw the comparison between what he faced at fisheries meetings and what she would face. He sat in meetings with people who at least did all agree the salmon runs should somehow get rebuilt. That could be all they agreed on, but it was ground to stand on. And the Reactor B group? Ike bet Harold would give them one chance to hear his story, and if they gave him the stink eye, he would quit. *I put her up to it, and it'll be another heartache for her.*

But Suki's thoughts had already slipped back to her more personal problems. She wanted to be together with Ike as much as he wanted it. She was just as tired as he was of love-life-in-a-truck. But she saw how her days kept getting filled, how she had to stop these political adventures she'd taken on. Not drop them, but postpone them. She had to be able to tell her mother and grandmother she'd gotten that PhD. And to take years at it? She couldn't, especially for her grand-mother. She might lose Ike as well. Did anyone ever write a dissertation in one year? *Well, I have to. I gave Ike a big chore, and now I'm backing off my side of it.* But she felt she was committed to one more class with the kids, anyway, after everything the others had put into it! Then that must to be all, for this coming year anyway.

⊷⊷◉ ◉⊷⊷

Bruce called Orville just before he and Leon were about to depart for Stockholm. He wanted to know how Orville's letter-writing project had turned out, to have something positive to report if local reports were part of the big meeting, or if not, just for his own girding.

"Well, Dot and I got over forty signatures and sent it off. Waiting now to hear."

"That's great!"

Orville said, "Well, it's not great, but it's okay. So now what? I can't look at the river—I see it every day you know—and not think about it. For years. Anyway, have a big time in Stockholm, do good work, and big thanks for your support."

Bruce wondered if Orville would hear anything back beyond a govern-ment form letter, but they'd acted, and that was a start. Settlers that had acted. He then called Roger, thanked him again for everything, marveling again at what his own little agreement with Harold had led to, and went back to pack-ing, so grateful that Leon was going with him.

⊷⊷◉ ◉⊷⊷

A week later Marta met Bruce and Leon on their return home. They were both a bit woozy climbing off at the plane at Sea-Tac, having made the long, long flight from Stockholm more endurable through alcohol. As they waited for their baggage to come down, Marta wanted to hear all about the place, the people, and the conference. "Very interesting" was all she got from Leon, who'd had little sleep, and said he tell her more later. Bruce was in better shape, but she saw no gleam of victory.

"Well, how did it go?"

"Great town, great people. But..."

"But...?"

"I need to collect my thoughts, as they say. What have you been up to?" *As if I don't know.*

"Hum, looking at why empires fall."

Bruce looked at her, "Huh?"

"Oh, I needed a break from settler survival struggles, and I picked up this book from the library discard pile: *"Why Empires Fall"*.

"And so...why?"

"Nothing new there, really...droughts, plagues, or wallowing in decadence by the rich, overthrow by the hungry ones, and back to subsistence level."

"Well, at least we have a chance to help write a new chapter now."

"My love, I'm glad that you come back with a joke, such as it is."

Leon broke in, "And here I am, about to go to a blessing on a river, and to overcome drought. Cycling back!"

Marta grinned, "Leon, just remember you're supposed to have a little fun when you retire."

Bruce smiled, "We had fun! You should've seen him doing the schottische on that so-called sprained ankle."

Then Bruce quit stalling and commented that the main interest of the delegates, which he said shouldn't have surprised him, had been defense issues, like expanding the ban on intercontinental ballistic missiles.

"Everyone was against nuclear war threats, of course, anything like that. But it was frustrating when we tried to get people to look at our issue—do we really want all these plants when we haven't solved the waste issue and the threat of accidents like Chernobyl and Three-Mile Island? Do we really want to see more new plants when we haven't got a handle on the long-term problems? They wouldn't give it the same energy."

"Not the dramatic interest of bombs?"

"Partly that I think, and partly they don't know what the hell to do."

Leon added, "Some of the European countries are reprocessing and reusing the waste, even selling it, and that way they can reduce their own storage problem."

Marta shook her head. "But then it's still there, just smaller, or moved down the road."

Bruce nodded, "They know. What worries people so much about the Hanford Plant is a worry all over the world. We tried to get them to stay on that topic, but didn't make any real progress."

Leon pointed, "It wasn't all so discouraging. Just no sudden epiphanies. What did we expect? So, lots of work to do. But here's our stuff. People, let's get out of here, I need some sleep."

Later, in the car, Marta driving, Leon gave more detail. "The Swedes are smart; they stay out of wars lately. The Scandinavians, in general. But they don't have the population explosion problem. They don't have to believe their only means for raising the standard of living for millions in a poverty-stricken population is nuclear energy. It's countries like Pakistan who say they've gone as far as they can with hydroelectric and seem to believe that they must keep building nuke plants, that there's no better way to produce the energy they need. And some like being able to build bombs too."

"And the waste?" said Bruce, *"Oh, shit. Deal with that in the future—sometime."*

Marta said, "Did you tell them about the situation at Hanford?"

Leon shrugged. "They all know about it. I suppose they assume that if wealthy countries like the U.S. can't solve the waste problem, why should they think they can?"

"Was Russia there?"

"Oh yes. They have more understanding, after Chernobyl, about accidents. But Russia's like the rest; they're more worried about war threats, or the mistaken punching of a button. No one was ready to talk about actually closing down their operating plants soon."

Leon said, "Of course there were scientists who are plenty concerned about the waste, and the problems with more plants being planned. But they're not the most powerful voice."

No one could think of anything more helpful on the topic.

At last Marta, said, "So what's next on your list, Bruce?"

"There's a meeting in about two weeks; and will you please go with me? Leon's too busy…ah, doing blessings. Travel's easy this time, right at Portland, and I'll bet they pay more attention to us with the Columbia flowing past Hanford right down into their backyards."

"Hah! If they don't get it, who will?"

Leon gave her a pat on the shoulder. "Go with him." Privately, he was relieved that he was going to deal with farming toxins, droughts, warming water, and dead salmon for a while and get some distance on the frustrating anti-nuke meeting. Not that a warming planet was any easier to solve. *Elena, call me tonight.*

⤳▬◉ ◉▬⬸

Suki squeezed in one more meeting with the kids and explained to them why she would not be able to come back for a time. Returning to Seattle with Ike once more, she decided she had to tell him grim facts before she lost her nerve. She could no longer use waiting on his "project" information to delay her answer. That scared her; was he going to keep on being so understanding? For a while she watched him drive in silence. *I don't want to do this.* Then she began her speech.

"Ike, I've decided I have to be realistic. You know, I have to get this dissertation process over with—I've explained all that—and I have to do it as fast as possible. But here's the problem, I see now I can do it only if I'm by myself. Look at me! This is not getting my assignments in, even with all your help! Much as I want to, no way can I live with you and your girls until I'm all finished. That sounds exaggerated, I know, but just look how I've procrastinated all month. It's not your fault, I've been having a great time with you and your kids, and your family—everything. But I have to get back to what I've already spent so much time on. Finish and move on! You understand, don't you?" *But he doesn't understand, doesn't want to.* "So, I'm going to stay living by myself, and I'm going to choose a simple, straightforward dissertation topic, something I don't have to lie awake nights over, not something philosophical like 'why must everyone care about salmon'. And I'm going to get it done in record time, I promise. But I'm sure I'll be able to see you on most weekends, maybe every one, unless you're gone yourself. Ike, sweetheart, you know I'll want to be with you!"

He was wordless. He'd thought she was with him on the plan; she hadn't said anything like this. Did she just want to be free of him after all, and this was a kind way—to blame herself? He could understand that. But, all of a sudden? He had been planning to drive down to Puyallup and look at housing there. He had been trying to figure out where to ask for a small short-term loan for a rental deposit. And he'd figured out his special project to stay out of her hair. He was going to tell her all about it tonight. *Now what?* He couldn't look at her and drive. They were coming up on a highway fast-food place, and he needed to park, calm down, and talk. He turned in, telling her he needed a break, and she followed him into a noisy crowd of truck drivers. He nodded to a couple of them and took a table far back.

They sat in silence over their coffee, Suki sick over her pitiful decision, but sure that it was the reality they faced, and Ike casting about for a possible compromise. She had said they could be together on some weekends. *So, weekends, that's it?* After toying with his coffee for a time, he told her he just remembered he needed to call Doreen and see if she was home this evening, as he had dry fish for her. Before Suki could say anything, he got up to ask the café manager if he could make a phone call to Seattle. She looked him over.

"That's long distance, you know."

Ike laid a $20 on the counter. "It's not a social call, it's urgent business. I won't be more than five minutes, probably not even that."

He got another look, then a nod; the $20 went into a pocket. Luckily, he caught Doreen just as she was going out the door. She sat down, listened to the story, the parts she didn't know, of Suki and her over-commitments. She wasn't surprised; the problem they faced was too familiar to her.

"Ike, she's telling you the truth; Suki is no liar. And she does love you, I can tell by the way she looks at you, talks to you, does the classes. Now listen to me, dear cuz, she does want to be with you, but she has made promises; you can understand that. And she knows what this coming year is going to be like, and she's right, believe me! I know! She'll get it all done much faster if you trust this plan of hers."

Ike said nothing.

Doreen went on, "I can tell you I never would have finished my program if I'd been involved like you two have been…with everything. I'd still be waiting tables today. And I didn't even have to write a dissertation. And as for your girls, just leave them where they are for a year; it won't hurt them a bit."

"So that's what you think."

"That's what I know! And she really must forget the nuclear waste and the museum, and even the kids' classes for the year. And you just stay busy with your truck-driving, your fisheries, your girls, and catch Suki on the weekends when she says she's able. Real world, Ike."

He was wordless again. His practical cousin. No wonder she was such a success as a nurse.

"You still there, Ike?"

"Yes, and thanks. You make it all simple. Too simple."

"No, not simple, but possible. You can do it."

Then he asked her something he knew she'd probably say yes to.

"So then, can I borrow your couch until I have enough saved up to rent a place near her?"

She laughed. "You can't afford any place near the campus. Maybe out the south end, or up in the hills. But yes, borrow the couch as long as you need to. Just know my hours are long and crazy, so I sleep when I can, and don't say anything about who or what I bring home once in a while. And don't eat up all the dry fish sent me."

"We won't touch it. Almost. Thank you very much. And you can bring home a wolf if you want to."

"Settled then. Oh, and can you tell me what project you came up with, aside from salmon rebuilding, to keep you from bugging Suki, or getting bored?"

"I need to tell Suki first, tonight, and then I'll tell you."

"Okay. You can do this, Ike. Hey, you can use my place if you want. I was about to leave for a three-day camping trip—some friends—when you called. I'll put the key in the usual place."

"Oh, thanks, thanks! And cuz, let me know anytime you need some good advice. I love you."

Back with Suki, Ike gave her the smile she'd been hoping for.

"Everything's okay. We'll work it out, Sookalook. Just don't call me and invite me to go with you to some anti-nuke meeting, or it's all off."

She gave him a little punch and breathed in relief. "I'm not going to any meetings of any kind for a year. Not even your fishery meetings."

"I don't blame you. Wish I had your excuse. But no, I'm going into the next meeting with a different strategy. We always talk strategies there; well, I'll have new one. And for now, we have three nights to ourselves at Doreen's. The days are yours; don't say no."

She said yes.

CHAPTER 35

LOVE, PROMISES, SMOG

IKE AND SUKI drove off, Suki wondering how Doreen had apparently solved something for him. She wasn't going to ask, not now. She stared off into the passing evergreens and waited for him to fill her in. But before long Ike said, "All right, let's go back to that last salmon paper, so you can get it turned in and forget it. Tell me the question again?"

By then they were already over the pass, and they agreed to use this driving time for her papers. She was grateful that they still had the deal.

"Here it is: *Why should people care about salmon who never will catch one, never eat one, never even see one?*"

"Oh yes, and I did think about it. That question isn't really about salmon, it's about people. I can't give you any better answers than you already have."

She sighed, and got out her notebook. "But they're a jumble. I want to tie the salmon question into everything about the river, with salmon as the way to understand it, so that people won't just say, *Huh???* Today, Elena's prayer—I don't think she mentioned salmon, but I think she knows…. Oh, wait!" She pointed. "There's that pullout, the one I wanted to stop at…here it is!"

He saw it just in time, pumped the brakes. Suki peered into the evergreens and brush.

"Yes, this is it. Can we stop here a bit?"

He turned in and parked. She had told him about this place where her parents used to bring her to pick huckleberries, like his own folks. He looked at the horizon to the west; the sun would still be up for a short time. Her paper again put aside, *for a little while,* she climbed out, happy to find the temperature just right and the seasonal gnats gone. She looked around in the mix of salal and other brush and grabbed sandwich bags.

"There should be some over there," she pointed. Ike walked off into the waist-high berry brush a slightly different direction. A few yards in he found black dead-ripe clusters of huckleberries. He reached for mouthfuls, gulped them down, reached for more—*Ah, that special flavor...and I've wanted to take her and the girls picking. Why didn't we ever find the time?* He saw her busy picking fast, and glancing around, pushed on a little farther. He was not accustomed to foraging in tall trees and dense brush. Normally he would be watching out for rattlers, not bears. But the berries were at their very best, and he put caution aside, soon lost in the pleasure of fast picking and eating, wishing he had a bucket, and lots of time.

Then he saw of flash of something, something large and tan, just glimpses through the thick brush. He froze. A tan bear? No, too low. A deer? A tan wolf? No. But an animal. He held his breath as the shape moved a little, and he saw the broken outline of a cat-like form, and he knew it was indeed a big cat—had to be a cougar. Adrenalin rushed through him. Still motionless, he worked to be calm, took deep quiet breaths, and finally saw the face come into view, peering at him. He had never seen a cougar before; his legs wanted to run, NOW! But inside his head, a voice: *You know what to do. Stay, calm, calm. Don't run from predators. Esau talking to us all, "Face them, stand your ground. You are in their territory, but talk to them, show you are not afraid. Respectful. Calm."* But Ike's heart raced, and his stomach cramped in a knot. He forced himself to take another deep quiet breath. He had only a jackknife in his pants pocket, hard to open, useless. *Just be calm.*

The brush shook, the cougar moving a little toward him. *Talk to it....* He tried in a quiet voice,

"Hello, big cat. Uh, how are you doing today?" His legs still felt like running, but he would not; they were now so weak, his voice shaky. *Breathe deep.* The cougar stopped moving and stared at him. *It's just a big cat. I know how cats fight, fight it if I have to. But face it, never run.*

"Hello again, big cat. You are real powerful looking. I'm glad to see you up close. *Breathe deep.* I don't want to fight though. Just you go your way, I'll go mine."

The cougar moved a little and was now harder to see. It was better to see it; he wanted to run again. *They rarely attack adults.* "You are so beautiful, you...you just go away now, and I will too." The tan form disappeared without a sound, just a shaking in the brush, and he heard movement in the brush behind him. *How could it get there so fast?*

But then came a call: "Ike, that you?" *Oh no!* "Hi...Suki, uh, just stay there, stay there...I'm coming back now. Coming in a sec."

Then he saw brush moving farther away. They strode to the truck, Ike working to get over his shaking as he told her about the encounter. She was envious. "Oh, a cougar! I wish I'd...were you scared?"

"Nawww, they're just big cats. Only dangerous if you run from them. Uhh, well, actually, part of me was scared shitless. I really had to talk to myself. How do people live in deep woods like this? You can't see what's coming! I walked right into it!"

She looked at his face, his expression one she hadn't seen there before. *Scared...just a little?* She'd never felt that way in the woods, but her family had no experiences with cougars, or even bears.

Back in the truck, he was silent as he waited to feel like driving. Sitting there, it came to him that the cougar had been a message for him. *Esau always says to be open for them.*

She said, "Are you thinking about the cougar?"

"Yes...and you know, I feel like it gave me a message."

"I hope it agrees with me."

"Well, it was *'Don't run away'.*"

"A good message...good for me too."

"Yup.... So I was going to tell you, I decided—we decided—I do have to stay on with the salmon management. Thanks for helping me work that out in my head. *Thanks, big cat, you too.*"

"And you feel okay with that?"

"Yes. I need to make some changes, but I can. And my new project that's not too much to do with salmon. But in the end, it'll help salmon too." He took her hand. "You'll hear about it later."

She smiled. "Later. And what else is on for later?"

"Well… we have Doreen's whole place to ourselves for three days and nights."

"Hum, I should be able to finish the incompletes!"

"Yeah. Incompletes. That's us…for a while."

She reached up to stroke his chopped-off hair. "Grow it out again, okay?"

As they drove on, Ike realized how low-down he had been before he met Suki, just going from day to day except for times he enjoyed with his girls. Suki hadn't seen him that way—blue, abstracted, and worse at the meetings. Right now, he was often frustrated, but he wasn't unhappy. They could make it work. She had to concentrate and he had to have some vital project. Well, he had one, one that would be good for him, his people, and the whole valley. He went over the arguments he'd have to make to win a demonstration project.

We have to get off our dependency on salmon-killing dams, and nuclear energy too. Wind power is the answer! All the wind we'll ever need is right there! This huge region, lots of it still sagebrush and river and wind. Other parts of the country are already switching over— why not us? We'll get that going, and poor people will have their power bills cut way down, not just the big outfits. And no endless arguing over what causes what…Fight over wind? He laughed. But it wouldn't happen overnight, he knew. Oregon was moving on it, but Washington had yet to really get behind it. He admitted it could mean another long fight to get funding, just like fisheries. Why wouldn't it?

Well, in that case, what would be the difference, one fight or another? But he knew the answer. The difference was it would be a new fight for him, a new challenge. He could quit arguing with Esau and plunge back in where he was needed. *Don't turn your back. Face what's laid out for you! Let Esau work on what he feels right about, the Heritage Center, and I'll do whatever it takes on the fisheries. But I don't need to go to college for that, I just need to be better at what I am. I'm not an eloquent elder, but I know I can speak up stronger for myself. For what's right. And when the salmon battles get me down, I'll put on my wind energy hat. And she'll calm down when she drops all of her projects for a while, and knows it's okay. We'll be together when it works for her schedule, no more crazy rushing back and forth. The girls will be fine. I'll see them as often as they want to see me.*

He helped himself to more berries that Suki held out, so glad they had stopped for them, for the message. First he needed to talk more to his own people—go see them, get more of their information and viewpoints on both topics: salmon, wind. And do more reading so he could talk the scientists' jargon. He had read fishery reports for years; he just needed to be able to dish it back to them, in their style, their language, so they'd pay attention. *No more of their ho-hum, Indian rambling again. I'll plan it out and say what I need to say.*

Suki felt his new energy and said, "I have another favor to ask...will you go with me to the museum committee next time, then, if Harold says no?"

What?? "Hey, wait a minute! I thought you were giving all that up for a year? You're giving me and everything else up for your degree, right?"

"Oh...thanks for reminding me. Uh, sorry. I guess I'll need some more reminding, so you tell me when I start getting off track."

"Sure. Happy to."

"Ike, the year will go by so fast! And I really thank you for being so understanding. It was hard to admit to myself that I wasn't going to make it the way I was going." She put her head on his shoulder. "I was kidding myself—and you. I'm sorry!"

"It'll be okay. Now can we go back to that salmon paper? Your last chance! So, your idea?"

She sighed and reached for her notebook. "Like I said, I want to tie some things together, because I believe they are related. To start with, I thought about how Esau would answer that question—*why should people care about salmon?* I can hear him say that if the salmon are going to survive—if we are going to survive, any of us humans—we have to go back to where we were in our beliefs, about the river, the salmon, about ourselves.... Back to the Celilo Falls he remembers. That's the way he might put it."

"Yeah, he would."

"Back when people understood how salmon are important, for the spiritual center of life as it should be—I've heard him say that. You have too. But that's an ideal, not possible. And the question is about all people."

"He knows that's an ideal; he knows that we're not going to go blow up the dam, and make camps again at Celilo Falls. The picture of the Falls is... it's a...there's a word for that."

"Hum...a metaphor?"

"Yes, that's it. I have to fight to hold onto high-school English. My daughters…." He stopped. He saw how he talked too much about his daughters and how they were going to do everything he should be doing.

She thought a moment and wrote: *Salmon could be a metaphor for all of us.* "That's what I think the instructor is getting at, is that there's a problem everywhere with people's attitude about nature, believing that we can be in charge of it. That salmon, and the river, and nature in general are… commodities. So, Ike, it's not just about salmon. But the connection I want to make—nuclear energy is also treated like a commodity. Is that too big a leap?"

"Not for me. You can say the ways we relate to salmon stands for all of our attitude about nature. So that includes the rivers, and hydropower, and nuclear energy too. But they're not just something to sell, or something to have fun with, or control things with."

She wrote fast. *"Salmon…their life cycle is so complicated; there are so many ways we can completely upset it. And we humans aren't exactly simple. And nuclear energy is so complicated, so many ways to get in trouble, and now we are so involved with it."* She stopped writing. "And industry is so dependent on dams, on river power, and those plants, and not on salmon, that it won't back down. And the government supports that. So the salmon runs suffer, but now the rivers too; the rivers near nuclear plants are threatened."

"That's so. So can the health of the Columbia be another metaphor?"

"Oh, I really like that, yes. And not just the Columbia, rivers in general— all human society threatened. Yes, that's it."

It was a strong insight Ike thought, a true one. Probably not the first time someone had thought of it; yet she had put it together. *That prof will like it, I hope.* But now what he'd heard at that marine fisheries committee meeting, *oh boy.* The alarming fact of the warming of the oceans and the probable causes. Not just talking in metaphors. Worldwide. It could have more impact than anything humans ever did to salmon, to rivers, even worse than the radioactive waste. So how did that change her insight? Did it undermine it, or expand it big time—humans' impact, technology's impact, now on oceans—on all of nature? *Well, no way am I going to bring that up! This paper has to get finished, this week, and turned in. And she'd better not choose something like that for her dissertation or I might as well join a monastery.*

Suki had stopped writing. She studied her notes, underlined some, then put them away.

"Thanks! That's how I need to tie it all in, how I can say that people that never have seen a salmon should still care about them. That it's a way of looking at the big picture of human society, the way it's moving...Hey, you really got my brain moving."

"As if it ever needed help." He reached her hand; she pressed her face to his. "More later...hm?"

But after several more miles of scenery gazing, Suki had more to bounce off him.

"Ike, I'm not going to get more involved, I promise, but I do want to try to call the guy at Port Radium again, tell him thanks. I need to thank a lot of people. And...when I go to Nagasaki next, when this degree business is all over, if you're not busy, would you go with me?"

He had to laugh. "Okay, but only after you have your PhD, then I'll go to Nagasaki with you, if you pay my fare! I'm kidding, yes, I'll go. But, seriously, back to all you're taking on yourself for next year, but also after you are Dr. Matsuda. And you start thinking about Reactor B again. You know you're going to have your hands full, dear Doctor. And not just of me. Our little tribe's been fighting for our river for generations. You can't fix any of this in one season! Even dung beetles have figured that out, that there's no easy fixes. Please remember that; even the little projects are huge."

"But the beetles were leaving."

"Esau says they will be back—they have their own job to do."

They were now were winding down through the foothills toward Puget Sound. Rounding a curve, their eyes were seized by a sudden, brilliant display: oranges, reds, and violets streaking across the waters of Puget Sound. And they saw it was no message from nature; it was from the smog of Seattle—or was it Beijing, or Tokyo? Or from wildfires on drought-ridden Kamchatka? They watched the colors grow until the whole stretch of western horizon was afire. They saw its beauty, yes, and the warning. There was never a simple message, if there ever had been.

AFTERWORD

In October, 2018, Dr. Suki Matsuda, Professor in Ecological Studies at Central Washington University, finished her prep for her next morning's class, "Climate Change: Influence of Government, Industry and Citizens", turned on the heat under a pot of venison stew, and moved to the couch. She picked up an old, mislaid page of the *Wenatchee Desert Notes* and gave a cry of surprise. She had spotted a shortened story from one originally in the *Seattle Times*.

"Hey, listen to this!"

"Wait just a bit," Starla answered. She had dropped in on them and was handing Ike a copy of a report she was to present at the next morning's meeting of the Fish and Wildlife Board. As one of its salmon scientists, everyone would be listening closely to her, and she hovered over her father, waiting for his comments. Ike liked having a first look at her presentations. Although he had passed his seat on the consortium some time ago to a young man with new energy, for Starla's work he would break off from whatever he was doing.

Suki cried again, "Hey, you two, this is about Reactor B!"

They came quickly then. Only Starla's ten-year-old son stayed oblivious in the corner, welded to his electronic game set. They were shocked as they read.

A-BOMB SURVIVOR VISITS THE HANFORD REACTOR MUSEUM

The Reactor B exhibits still do not contain a whole picture of what the A-bomb did to Nagasaki, according to a bombing survivor in his eighties. Probably the first visitor to the Hanford site from among the survivors, he had come with a delegation of Japanese citizens to see the historic plant. Speaking through a translator, Husaka Yushido shook his head at the coverage of the bomb's effects on Nagasaki families. He asked, "When are the displays going to go beyond expressions of pride to consider the future of human society with such instruments of destruction?" He was also disturbed by what he saw on a Richland High School mural, showing mushroom bomb shapes, and in the sport teams' name: "The Bombers". "Where is the humanity here in these?" He went on to tell how so many of his family died of cancer, and that some of their children were born deformed. He said that Nagasaki families may still inherit health problems from the fifty-three-year-old radioactive releases, that the final word on this is not out.

Suki said, "Someone finally came."

Ike looked her thoughtfully. Did this mean she was going to jump into that hopeless task again: a museum display that told the whole story? Some time ago they had agreed, looking into the future, that getting the active plants closed down and the radioactive waste taken care of were more important. But the man's visit had been a great opportunity for publicity, and somehow they'd missed it?

"We should call Judy...and your mother. They'll want to know, if they don't."

Judy, a certified Indigenous healer, had taken time off from her job to go to Nagasaki to visit relatives with Suki's mother, and had taken along her video camera. It was a hobby that, she hoped, was about to turn semiprofessional. Her plan was to make videos on topical issues, and aside from meeting extended family there, she wanted to do a follow-up on the Fukushima nuclear plant disaster. Then she would relate it to the issue of the Hanford radioactive waste, still without a home. Congress still hadn't awarded adequate funding to carry out permanent storage on site, nor found a safe location elsewhere. Other plants with the problem were also waiting.

Ike reached for Starla's paper but said, "And we need to tell Bruce and Marta. He's still in Berlin, Leon too. Leon says it's his last trip, but what a tough old guy, he's sure stuck with it."

Suki said, "I'm going to call Marta. She'll want to get more details for her book. The *Times* is sure to have more."

Even though Marta was teaching only half-time at the Astoria campus, she was busier yet, now the mother of a toddler and expecting another soon.

To provide the rest of the family income Bruce had increased his own number of outdoor survival classes through different campuses and other groups, but still kept up as many anti-nuke activities as they could afford, all with Leon's help. Suki and Ike chipped in to the costs too. She saw Ike's expression and smiled,

"Don't worry, my dear, I'm not going to start bugging the museum committee again. I couldn't change them, Harold couldn't, and I doubt this guy Yushido can."

Ike nodded. "I'll hold you to that!" He slid over to his computer to send Bruce the news. He had always stayed in touch with Bruce and Leon by email, but especially this time, as Germany was far ahead of other industrial nations in moving away from nuclear energy. It had closed down half of its nuclear stations already, and stated that the other half would be closed within four years. Ike, whose regular job was public education and finding project support for community wind generators, had been intrigued to learn that Germany was switching rapidly to wind and other alternative energy. The U.S., in contrast, still had active commercial nuclear plants in 39 states. Yet, to Ike and Suki it was progress, if slow, as the government was considering applications for only a handful of new plants, while twenty-five were already retired, and twelve more scheduled for it. But the reason for so few new plants in the U.S. was apparently not a safety or moral issue, but a business matter: nuclear plants couldn't compete with the lower operating costs of natural gas and wind power. Bruce, on this trip, hoped to find out if that was the main consideration, rather than public health or ethics, when other countries closed down plants.

Suki, brought back to the nuclear energy issues by the news story, was glad that she had not framed her whole future on them. She had a job she loved, the man she loved, and conversion to wind energy, Ike's major work, was moving rapidly along with the wind blowing strong, indeed ever stronger with climate change. In their free time they enjoyed their family, travel, and their subsistence life. They liked being part of stream restorations with local volunteers, which, on Roger's suggestion, Suki had taken on as her dissertation topic. The two had decided that the work was good for their mental health as well as essential for the in-the-field part of her PhD.

Their whole family's interest in the Columbia's salmon runs would never be forgotten with Starla right there at the conference table. Restoring those runs shouldn't have been so difficult, Ike was sure, but it wasn't getting easier. Yet rebuilding Columbia's runs would cost a fraction of sending just one nuclear plant's waste to a safe rest, and would not gamble with the life and death of populations of people. He was holding Starla's paper lost in thought.

Yes, gamble only with a culture, but what are people without a culture? The basic technology to rebuild spawning grounds was known and no state had refused to do it. And few large dams without ladders were being built anymore. But still, a big dam, government or privately owned, would be closed down only when the costs of conversion to some other energy technology was cheaper than maintaining the old dam. The government was shorting the funding there, too, just as it was with the nuclear waste problem.

As Suki had written so many years before, the issues around rivers were all tied together. But on a brighter side, with wind generation taking off in Washington, Ike had more requests than he could handle for introductory workshops and eventually installations.

Ike saw Starla was waiting. He looked at the title of her paper, and frowned.

"Who chose this topic? 'Ocean Acidification's Potential Effects on the Columbia's Salmon Stocks'?"

"Not me! It was assigned to me."

He was annoyed. Why couldn't she have stayed in an area where she could see some progress? Were they just getting her off their backs? Too much attention on restoring the river?

"Dad, it's okay. You know everyone finally agreed ten years ago to make restoring the spawning areas top priority, and it hasn't worked for the kings. The biggest problem now is out in the ocean. So please, will you read it?"

Suki had the stew heated up and told them they should eat first. Ike shook his head to wait a bit, and read the report. Starla had done a fine job, as usual, but there was no suggestion of realistic remedies for the warming waters of the Pacific. What could there be, short of major societal change? He handed it back to her with compliments, minor suggestions, and was glad that, just as Esau had predicted long ago, the loss of the great runs wasn't so painful for her. She had never seen Celilo Falls.

Over dinner they continued to comment about the reactor museum, which had been a focus of Suki's energy for years until she gave up. The Hanford Plant had lately been in the news even more than usual, but they had said little about it, simply shook their heads in disgust. The federal government had again cut the budget for dealing with nuclear waste. The production and transfer of permanent storage containers would take billions at Hanford alone. Though recognition of the dangers in nuclear energy had been much revived after the accident at the Fukushima Plant, the new bill in Congress to cover federal funding for decommissioning of private plants was stalled.

Some of the social projects in the valley had seen more satisfactory outcomes in twenty years. The Wanapum Heritage Center and the Hanford Reach Interpretive Center both told their stories well and were complimented by visitors and locals alike. Ike and Suki were glad that Esau, Alice, Roger, Orville, Dorothy, and Harold had been among the elders able to be part of the grand openings and were recognized and honored before they died, while Thelma, always the healthiest, was still working part-time at the Reach Center.

Jason had wanted to stay involved with salmon, and tried a few seasons as crew on a struggling gillnetter, but had soon seen there was no future in it with the growing political pressure to close gillnetters down in favor of sport fishing. He was a junior high social studies teacher, but for the summers he liked the outdoors and worked with Ike on small wind generator projects. Climbing those towers, as long as he felt up to it, would add enough outdoor challenge for him. He was thinking about training with Elena as a retirement plan, another way to be outdoors.

How much good did the blessings do? Jason knew the test was, of course, how much local people were willing and able to take up the fight for river protection. For everyone along the west coast that also meant salmon protection. And in the long run, Elena kept assuring her crowds, it was all linked to human survival. But now in 2020, the progress in restoring the Columbia's salmon runs was as much in limbo as that of radioactive waste disposal. A few returns of spawners to a restored stream was all there was to show for success with Chinook.

After dinner Ike mused over how little progress had been made on all they'd cared about and had worked on. And of course they weren't alone. What was missing? Marta, he knew from past conversations, would just shrug. *That's human society.* He looked forward to talking with Bruce and Leon when they returned, hoping for answers from somewhere.

Starla's son, back at his games, broke away to say, "Next time Judy goes to Nagasaki or somewhere, I want to go too! How come we always just stay home?"

And his grandfather's reply, "If you don't put that game away and do your homework, you'll never leave home. You won't get any scholarships, and you'll be working two jobs just to pay your rent. You won't have a car, you'll be riding an old bike."

Then he looked at Suki and had to choke back his laughter, hearing the echo in his words. *I miss you, Uncle!* The boy was grinning at him. These grown-ups couldn't ever solve their problems. They were already experimenting with electronics to drive the sea lions away from the base of Bonneville, so why couldn't someone invent an electronic device that, spread across the ocean, would deflect all the warm current south again, and another that would direct the salmon into the river mouths? Problems are there to keep our brains active, the boy thought, no different from these games. Ike smiled back at his grandson and thought that next time there was an interesting stream restoration project available, he needed to sign up not just Suki and himself, but his daughter and his grandson, too. Then, knowing how Suki liked to be up to date with her class materials, he passed Starla's report onto her. "You'd better have a look at this."

Suki looked at the title. "Oh, yes! Believe me, it is not bombs my students want to talk about, it's the Blob. Climate change is now their top issue." She smiled at Starla, "I think we know what Esau would say." Ike nodded, but he was aware of how fast things moved lately. Just that week he had read in a regional on-line news source that the Washington Physicians for Social Responsibility believed that the biggest issue looming was not salmon losses or contaminated rivers or climate change or nuclear waste, but a new nuclear arms race. And he recalled Bruce's remark, *Well, I know what Uncle Harold would say, 'Follow the money!'* And Leon's response: *That would certainly be a good start.*

APPENDIX

Partial list of news stories regarding safety concerns and "clean-up" events at Hanford Nuclear Plant, and other related issues,1998-2019

1998. 53 million gallons of radioactive waste are stored in steel tanks on site. (The Hanford Nuclear Plant had stopped manufacturing plutonium in 1989.) Some tanks are observed as badly corroded and soon will be leaking into the ground, or already are, and to the river, less than ten miles away. No site has agreed to take the tanks for permanent storage.

2005. Northwest Territorial Government, Canada, says there is no link between the Pt. Radium mine and cancer cases among workers.

2007. Clean-up begins at Port Radium mine, NW Territory.

2008 The B Reactor at the Hanford Plant becomes a National Historic Landmark.

2009. B Reactor tours begin. (Universal access, all ages, etc. begins 2011.)

2010. *Crosscut* (on-line periodical, Seattle) The Dept. of Energy, EPA, and the WA Dept of Ecology have entered into an agreement to build a vitrification plant that will enclose all Hanford radioactive waste in glass tubes. All tanks to be emptied by 2040, all waste stored in glass tubes by 2047, then to be shipped to a permanent underground storage, yet to be located.

2011. Japan's Fukushima nuclear plant accident causes 1600 deaths during the evacuation, with more probably to come due to radiation exposure.

2012. June 19, *Crosscut*. Yucca Flats declines to accept glass containers of radioactive material from the Hanford Plant after Nevada residents and politicians protest.

2012. Clean-up begins at the uranium mine on the Spokane Reservation.

2013, May 19. *Scientific American,* Valerie Brown, "Hanford Nuclear Waste Cleanup Plant May Be Too Expensive."

2014. The Hanford Plant's B Reactor becomes part of the Manhattan Project National Historic Park.

2016. Demolition of more buildings begins at the Hanford Plant.

2016. President Obama reduces funding for radioactive waste using glass containers.

2016, March 1. NWnewsnetwork.com. "Expanded investigation in safety culture at Columbia Generating System (CGS) in Hanford Reach. (The largest of two domestic nuclear energy producers in the state, opened in 1984.)

2016, Dec.? Tri-City Herald. com. "Hanford Vit. Plant cost estimate jumps to 4.5 b."

2017. Demolition at the Hanford Plant is halted when over 40 workers are radiated. Tunnels holding cars full of solid waste collapse.

2017. State of Idaho blocks further shipments of drums of lower-level radioactive waste "from a site in Washington" to Idaho Falls where it is temporarily stored until a permanent storage can be identified. (DOE had already paid $3.5 million in fines for not moving faster on these drums; a few that had arrived at Idaho Falls were already leaking and others soon would be.)

2017, Oct. 17. Union of Concerned Scientists protests when the Nuclear Regulatory Commission proposes to change the Columbia Generating System in the Hanford Reach area to a regular self-assessment of safety, saying that the NRC has been too liberal and has continually fallen short in its own assessments.

2018, March 9. " SeattleTimes.com., Hal Bernton. "What went wrong at Hanford cleanup where radioactive contamination spread?"

2018. Mar. 24, *Tri-City Herald.* The old Hanford Plant containers have been replaced with temporary ones of double-walled steel. Many of the old ones had already leaked, and sixty-one square miles of ground around the old Hanford/White Bluffs sites are identified as contaminated. However, the official word is that this waste is diluted enough that once it enters the river it will not to be a hazard to humans. Protests immediately arise.

2018. March 11. (summary of several newsstories.) A survivor of the A-bombing of Nagasaki, Mitsugi Moriguchi, comes as part of a Japanese delegation to tour the Reactor B museum, sponsored by the Council Concerned with Nuclear Energy Dangers. He expresses disappointment that the displays have little coverage of the effects of the bombing on Nagasaki residents, and is shocked at insensitivities in local business and public-school exhibits referring to the bomb.

2018. There are 444 nuclear reactors presently operating in the world, 54 more are under construction, and 111 planned.

2018, Nov. 83 Downwinder claims against the Hanford Plant have been entered; 28 allowed, 6 denied, and 49 pending.

2018, Dec.? *Seattle Times.* The U.S. Justice Dept is suing Washington State over its law passed requiring compensation for sick Hanford workers, claiming it discriminates against other workers. (10,000 workers have been involved in the clean-up at some point.)

2018. The GAO now estimates the cost of cleanup at Hanford to be 100 billion. Just this year, 2.4 billion. 20 billion gals. of ground water have been treated but never will be clean enough to drink. 56 million gals. of high-level waste sit in 177 underground tanks. Of the 149 older tanks, 67 have leaked. Only one of the 28 new double-shelled tanks has leaked.

2018. President Trump reduces funding for nuclear waste processing.

2019. Germany has half its nuclear plants closed down, with the rest scheduled to be closed in four more years. It also plans to close all its coal-fired plants. Alternative energy is taking over.

2019. April 18. SeattleTimes.com, Hal Bernton. "Hanford waste-processing plant closer to start-up but questions remain about clean-up". By 2022 glass logs will ready to cover the waste. Other sources say the total project will take until 2040.

2019. Negotiations still go on with Nevada over possible use of Yucca Mt. for waste storage.

2019. State of Idaho, in addition to State of Washington, sues the federal government over nuclear waste not removed as per agreement.

2019. The infamous Three Mile Island plant joins the list of plants scheduled to close.

ACKNOWLEDGEMENTS

I am much indebted to my great-grandparents, grandparents, and their children—my mother, aunts, and uncles—and their neighbors on the mid-Columbia for their letters, other writings, and many hours of interviews regarding life at White Bluffs, 1907-1943. I was also fortunate to be able to attend an entire White Bluffs-Hanford Pioneer Association reunion in 1999 and to spend real time with my uncle at the historic White Bluffs site and at my family's orchard site. My thanks to Annette Heriford and all those who made those annual reunions possible.

Special thanks to Lesley G. Thomas for her excellent on-going editorial support, and for information on the area's flora and fauna. Special thanks also to the late Dr. William Keep for sharing his experiences fishing and exploring at the Hanford Reach, and his always right-on-target editorial suggestions. Huge thanks to Dennis Brown for his special understanding of the place, the characters, and their issues, and his thoughts on how to let those all emerge in a complex story. And for my husband Perry, great thanks and gratitude for his unending patience and support during my mental absences from the home scene and normal conversations in order to get this story told.

Of great help was the research and commentary in these books and collections regarding the social history of the Hanford-White Bluffs area: Martha Parker's "Tales of Richland, White Bluffs, and Hanford, 1805-1943"; unpublished documents from settler families that contained recollections they shared during the years of the reunions; the recent "Nowhere to Remember" edited by Robert Bauman and Robert Franklin, (interviews and republications from residents of the Hanford area); recent fiction about the Hanford Project by Sharma Shields, "The Cassandra"; Michele Parker's book "On the Homefront: The Cold War Legacy of the Hanford Nuclear Site"; Susan Southard's

"Nagasaki: Life After Nuclear War"; and my own "Orchards of Eden: White Bluffs on the Columbia, 1907-1943". Thanks also to the HanfordHistory Project.com of Wash. State University Tri-City Campus; OurHanfordHistory. org; and information from The Atomic Heritage Foundation.

Thanks also for the many relevant articles that have been in periodicals or their on-line versions including *Washington Post*, May 11, 2017 for its articles regarding the Hanford cleanup issues; Sarah Zhang's articles in the on-line *Atlantic*, April 26, 2017, "Nevada Fights the Latest Attempt to Give it the Nation's Nuclear Waste", and her May 10, 2017, "What to Make of the Tunnel Collapse at Nuclear Cleanup Site"; Hal Bernton's article in the on-line *Seattle Times*, August 3, 2017, "Will Nagasaki's story be told at Washington state's new national park?" and many others by Hal Bernton on the Hanford Plant issues; *Tri-City Herald* for important articles by Annette Cary on the Hanford problems and by John Trumbo on salmon issues; *Crosscut* for its coverage of the Hanford Plant's nuclear waste problems and other matters of social concern; and *Yakima Herald* for its coverage over the years of radioactivity problems and other articles on the ecology and culture of the area.

Regarding Pacific salmon and their management many thanks to: George Aguilar, Sr., for his one-of-a-kind "When the River Ran Wild: Indian Traditions on the Mid-Columbia"; Roberta Ulrich's "Empty Nets: Indians, Dams, and the Columbia River"; James Lichatowich's "Salmon Without Rivers: A History of the Pacific Salmon Crisis", also his "Salmon, People, and Place: A Biologist's Search for Salmon Recovery"; Freeman House's "Totem Salmon: Life Lessons from Another Species"; David R. Montgomery's "King of Fish: The Thousand-Year Run of Salmon"; Kevin Bailey's "Fishing Lessons: Artisanal Fisheries and the Future of Our Oceans"; and my own "Rough Waters: Our North Pacific Small Fishermen's Battle," and grateful thanks for interviews with George Morford, skipper, F.V.s *Rocket*, *Helen McCall*, and *Sidney*.

Regarding the efforts of the Wanapum Indians to create their Heritage Center, much thanks to the Wanapum Heritage Center Museum; to history link.com; to Wikipedia for "Wanapum Tribe of Native Americans"; and to the

Tri-City Herald and Rex Buck Jr. for the article on October 14, 2015, describing how the Wanapum Heritage Center came to be.

I am grateful to all others who provided information about the Hanford Reach and the ecology and culture of the area including the Hanford Reach National Monument and Interpretive Center; US. Fish and Wildlife Service; Washington State University Library; and thanks to Vincent Mendenhall and to an anonymous traveler across the area for their information on dung beetles.

My thanks also for information regarding Port Radium people and their case: Peter van Wyck's book "The Highway of the Atom"; The Canadian Encyclopedia.com's information about Great Bear Lake and the Port Radium mine; to The Dominion.com, for an article by Kim Petersen "Canada, Racism, Genocide, and the Bomb"; to www.ccnr.org for the March 14, 1998 story by Andrew Nikiforuk, "Echoes of the Atomic Age"; and to concordia.ca, cbc.ca, and Japantimes.com for recent articles on the effects of exposure for the Sahtugotine people as uranium mine workers at Port Radium, also for an article telling of the Pt. Radium delegation's travel to Japan in 1998 to apologize for their role in producing the bomb dropped on Nagasaki. Finally, the health risks of work in the uranium mine on the Spokane Reservation were described in articles in the Seattletimes.com, Feb. 24, 2008, and in the Spokesman.com, June 5, 2011; thanks again.

For any group, story, or individual that provided information used in this novel which I neglected to acknowledge here, I apologize.

ABOUT THE AUTHOR

Nancy Danielson Mendenhall's spirit is rich with the Columbia River's stories. As a child she spent summers at her grandparents' farm on the riverbank until 1943, when everyone was evicted from the area for the manufacture of plutonium at the Hanford atomic project. Among the evicted neighbors was a group of Wanapum Indians whose fall camp was upstream a quarter mile from their orchard. Grown, with her own children, Mendenhall chased Columbia salmon, commercially and for subsistence, on the Washington and Alaska coasts. With family, she still fishes at a subsistence camp on the beach near Nome, Alaska, where she's lived since the 1970s.

In 1999 she was able to attend a pioneers' reunion at Richland, downstream from the defunct Hanford Plant, and listen to stories from the days before their eviction. With an uncle she walked through the remains of the old White Bluffs site and the Wanapum fall camp, and saw steam rising from the dismantling of a reactor upriver. Her sense of loss was a mere fraction of what the ex-residents still feel. She gained another perspective on the river's history from a relative who was among the first American troops in Nagasaki in WWII who saw firsthand the effects of the bomb that used Hanford plutonium. From all these stories, interviews, and collected letters, Mendenhall began to write about the mid-Columbia River, its history and its people. This is her first novel.

Her other works are *Beachlines: A Pocket History of Nome;*
Orchards of Eden: White Bluffs on the Columbia, 1907-1943;
Rough Waters: Our North Pacific Small Fishermen's Battle--A Fishing Family's Perspective; and miscellaneous poetry.

Visit her website: **www.nancydanielsonmendenhall.strikingly.com**

www.ingramcontent.com/pod-product-compliance
Lightning Source LLC
Chambersburg PA
CBHW020502260626
47156CB00006B/1829